THE ASSIGNMENT

Books by Mark Andrew Olsen

The Assignment

*Hadassah**

*with Tommy Tenney

MARK ANDREW OLSEN

THE ASSIGNMENT

BETHANYHOUSE
MINNEAPOLIS, MINNESOTA

Cover design by the Lookout Design Group, Inc.

This is a work of fiction. Names, characters, places, and incidents either are the product of the author's imagination or are used fictitiously, and any resemblance to actual persons, living or dead, business establishments, events, or locales is entirely coincidental.

Published by Bethany House Publishers
11400 Hampshire Avenue South
Bloomington, Minnesota 55438
www.bethanyhouse.com

Bethany House Publishers is a Division of
Baker Book House Company, Grand Rapids, Michigan.

Printed in the United States of America

Library of Congress Cataloging-in-Publication Data

Olsen, Mark Andrew.
The assignment / by Mark Andrew Olsen.
p. cm.
ISBN 0-7642-2817-X (pbk.)
1. Immortalism—Fiction. 2. Good and evil—Fiction. I. Title.

PS3615.L73A94 2004
813'.6—dc22 2004002025

To Connie,
My wife and best friend,
Who has walked every step of this road beside me . . .
Thank you.

And I, the last, go forth companionless,
And the days darken round me, and the years,
Among new men, strange faces, other minds.

ALFRED, LORD TENNYSON,
Idylls of the King, "The Passing of Arthur"

And would you want to see
if seeing meant that you would have to believe?

JOAN OSBORNE, "One Of Us"

PROLOGUE

REELING IN THAT SLOW-MOTION moment before the soldiers reached her, she blinked away blood, sweat, and dust, and glanced wildly about the scene. Her retinas jammed into her brain images of Arabs in long robes, reporters in khaki, soldiers aiming guns, dignitaries in western suits—all running through clouds of dust and puddles of blood amidst a deafening clamor of screams and shouted orders.

Then it struck her. She had blanked out for a minute and was unable to recall what in the world had brought her—an antisocial, twenty-something American graduate student—to the heart of this scene in global history being broadcast live to over half the human race. She could almost hear the commentators now, their heads shaking at the unlikeness of it all.

Nora McPheran, unwitting star of one of the most dramatic events the world has ever seen, and still one of the most cryptic.

What about her years alone, navigating the quiet corridors of Harvard, had qualified her to play such a role, at such a heart-stopping, perilous time?

One man's love for her had just saved the world from a brush with war. She knew that much. She knew it in her marrow more than her mind. The strong residue of his ferocity still remained with her like a scent, as heavy as the weight of his lifeless body in her arms. She began to sway as the surrealism of all around her threatened to drown her senses.

At the instant she fell backward and felt the arms of the young

IDF infantrymen catch her, she thought she glimpsed her mother. Mommy was still alive, as was her father, holding her tightly as a little girl. Their faces appeared relaxed, their smiles as free and open as she had rarely remembered them.

They seemed at peace, as if relieved of a lifelong burden. A centuries-old burden, even. And that was when Nora remembered why she was here, in Jerusalem. Why in fact she had every reason to be here in the spotlight of the century's most bizarre and precarious incident.

And why the story had been strange and unbelievable long before she'd become a knowing participant.

POLAND

1

Brzezinka, Poland—Present Day

SILENTLY, CEASELESSLY, seven priests shoveled beside the death-camp fence line. Their cassocks smudged the mist with spectral black silhouettes, dark shapes swaying in the gray twilight like a gathering of crows.

Finally the oldest of them lifted his gaze from the pit and turned to face the veil of descended cloud. "Father Stephen, do hurry," he called in a quavering voice, thick with the accent of his native Brittany. "Time is short."

The young man glanced up from the shadows. "Yes, Father Thierry. I will ignore my fatigue."

Father Thierry closed his eyes as if gathering patience. "Think of *him*," he said in the singsong rhythm he usually reserved for his Latin masses, "waiting all this time. How fatigued *he* must feel."

"Yes, Father."

Stephen bent back down and with a shake of the head heaved his shovel into crumbling clay. How many times had he heard the litany? And he was only the Order's newest member. He glanced at his colleagues and wondered how they had endured it all these years. *Time is short*. It had become a quiet, apologetic joke among the younger men that, even after fifty years, time was still as short as ever. Father Thierry continually insisted they were just minutes away from the object of their quest as if the very next thrust into hard earth would end the search.

In his disappointment, Stephen could barely remember how the Order of St. Lazare had once seemed to him, before his invitation.

STEPHEN HAD FIRST HEARD rumors of the Order during his first year of seminary: a secret order shrouded in legend and arcane folds of history, its very existence debated by overexcited students and denied with rolls of the eyes by members of the faculty. Records would only concede that something resembling the Order of St. Lazare had existed in centuries past, but they implied that it had faded into oblivion early in the twentieth. Nevertheless, students had perennially ascribed a hundred swashbuckling mandates to the Order's members, from guarding the Grail to perpetuating the Templar knighthood to the stewardship of Rome's dirty secrets, even the hit squad assassinations of satanic proselytizers. There were other hypotheses more incredible still, too fantastic for serious contemplation. Upperclassmen took elaborate pleasure in initiating newcomers into knowledge of the Order, punctuating their speech with raised eyebrows, furtive glances, and conspiratorial hesitations.

A former student at Stephen's seminary was rumored to have joined the Order's globe-trotting escapades twenty years before, although a church history professor had told Stephen with a paternal smile that the young man had merely perished in an auto accident. Whatever the Order of St. Lazare truly was, its secret had officially died along with the Order itself years ago, gone the way of all quixotic follies.

Then one evening during the final chaotic week before graduation, Stephen had returned to his room late and flicked on his light to the sight of a stranger sitting calmly, legs crossed, in his bedside chair. A man with thinning gray hair, wearing a black cassock of a design Stephen had never seen before. The elder priest had hardly blinked at the sudden brightness but gazed inscrutably and greeted him with a vague smile. He had gestured toward the bedspread and beckoned for Stephen to sit as though the room were his own.

"Stephen," he said warmly in a faint southern drawl, "I am Father Dennis. Forgive my intrusion, but I wish to speak to you privately. I must confess, I have not been back here since my student days twenty-two years ago."

"That's a long time," Stephen said.

"Yes. The ensuing years have been very busy and have taken me very far." His brow furrowed as he continued, "I remember my days here. So much anxiety, so much anticipation. Looking ahead to the coming years, asking myself whether a lifetime in God's service would be interesting enough, challenging enough to engage such a teeming brain, such an overheated imagination." The man looked at his folded hands and grinned. "You know, a Protestant writer once remarked, 'How little they know who think holiness is dull.' He didn't know the half of it."

"Neither do I," added Stephen.

"Ah, but you will. I believe you will. By the way, congratulations on completing your studies with such distinction. Your work here has been exceptional."

"Excuse me?"

"Oh, yes. I have acquainted myself with your papers on church history for almost a year now. The one on 'History's Roving Holocaust'—well, I must admit I learned something. And I have been most struck by your grasp of current technology. You possess a first-rate mind, Stephen. As a matter of fact, that is why I have come. You meet every single criterion we have. High grades, impeccable moral stature, physical fitness, intellectual curiosity. You see, the Order to which I belong has sent me to offer you an invitation."

"Thank you, but I am about to accept a parish in Minneapolis."

Father Dennis waved his hand dismissively. "You are free to decline the invitation and return to your first choice at any time. However, if I may be frank, I think you would be wasted on such a post. I am here to invite you on a mission older than the Church. A mystery deeper than any you have ever read of." He paused and allowed the level calm of his gaze to convince Stephen that his assertion was no exaggeration. "But if you would like to hear more, you must first promise me never to reveal the remainder of this conversation."

"I promise," Stephen said.

"On your soul."

"On my soul."

"Good. Now, Stephen, do you know the meaning of the term *catacon*?"

"It's spoken of in Second Thessalonians. The Greek word for the Restrainer, the one who holds back the secret powers of lawlessness. The one who will be taken away just before the end of time."

"Very good. Tell me, who do you think that Restrainer is?"

"I believe traditional interpretation holds that it is the Holy Spirit."

"Yes. And though I would never seek to impugn the work of the Spirit, I know that interpretation to be incomplete. The catacon has a human component, as well. The Restrainer is also a person, a man who's been given a mandate by our Lord to co-labor with his Spirit in doing battle with the archdemon destroyer, architect of death and war. A man who has worked in secret for many years to help hold the world back from the brink of chaos. My Order was consecrated in 1282 by Pope John the Twenty-second. Our numbers are small; we are six priests—seven when we are complete—all of us sworn to the service and protection of this one man."

"I don't understand. Is this human catacon a single person, or an office?"

"I cannot tell you everything at once," said Father Dennis.

"I have never heard of such an order. What is its name?"

"The Brothers of St. Lazare."

A long moment passed. Eventually Stephen became aware that his mouth was open, that he needed to swallow.

"I see the students here have not forgotten about us."

"No, we have not. I thought—"

"Don't tell me. Certain faculty members are still telling students I was killed in a car wreck."

"Yes."

"Listen closely, Stephen. This man, the catacon, has been lost to our world for many years and his influence has gone with him. I cannot tell you the facts of his disappearance tonight, but I can tell you that the course of history depends on his being restored to his holy mission. My Order's present task in the service of the catacon, its only mission for the past five decades, has been to find him."

THREE WEEKS LATER, Stephen's father stood on his well-tended Kentucky lawn and held in trembling hands an unsigned letter from Rome. The onionskin paper bore a laser-printed message stating that his twenty-three-year-old son had accepted a missionary assignment of a highly sensitive nature and he would be beyond the reach of normal communication for several years.

That same day, four thousand miles away, Stephen stood before an altar high atop the island perch of Mont St. Michel, shivering in the chill of a storm that pounded the Brittany coast, and accepted Father Thierry's consecration. And it was only then, standing in the gloom of St. Michel's Abbey, that Thierry had ceremoniously clasped him about the shoulders, leaned in and whispered into his ear the words that had buckled the younger man's knees, torn a gasp of shock from his lungs, and caused the five surrounding priests to lower their eyes with faint, knowing smiles.

NOW AS HE STOOD in the mud, swaddled in Polish fog, none of it mattered to Father Stephen anymore. This wasn't romantic, and it certainly wasn't adventuresome. Poland, Czechoslovakia, Germany, Argentina, Paraguay—he'd had a hand in despoiling the cemeteries and trash heaps of two hemispheres, and he was tired of it. He felt more like a ditchdigger than a priest. Some days he even allowed himself to entertain doubts about the one whom they were sworn to protect. The word of Father Thierry had once been enough to buttress his belief in this person's existence. But today, in the face of such unrelenting futility, the certainty had all but faded. To swing a shovel and take part in hard labor for years, with no hint of an outcome, on days like this the once fantastic mission seemed like nothing more than the indulgence of senile fantasies.

It was torture enough just having to be in this place. *Birkenau.* Raw and untended, unlike its infamous twin, Auschwitz 1, just three miles away. On the first day Stephen had worked for hours before once looking over his shoulder, though his peripheral vision had told him all he needed to know. The fence line's barbed wire still stretched taut, still bent cruelly inward at the top; the brick barracks and crumbling chimney shafts still presided over cement slabs and pits overgrown with weeds. Crematoria and peeling guard towers. The Death Gate and the railroad tracks converging underneath, their graceful curves leading to an entrance Jews had come to call The Hole in the World.

And floating above it all, the perpetual stench of evil. He could almost smell it.

Silence weighed upon this place like a reproach—as though nature lay hushed before its horror. His mind recoiled at the thought. *How could God,* he wondered, *have allowed such a spot to remain on the earth?* Stephen could hardly wait for Thierry to receive another one of his obscure clues and yank them to a far-flung piece of the continent to resume their futility elsewhere. Another cathedral garden, forest glade, green Bavarian pasture. Anywhere but here.

Stephen's blade struck something hard. An echoing clang touched his ears just as a sharp pain wrenched his shoulders. Father Thierry wheeled around with the agility of a young man while the other five diggers bolted upright from their stations.

"Quick!" Thierry shouted. "Everyone over here!" The younger priests' skepticism could never quench Thierry's ageless enthusiasm at such moments, despite the unbroken string of disappointments—the junk piles and rusted automobiles and rotted wood caches that stretched back to the early postwar years, a time when Thierry was rumored to have been a young man already on this mission. Already tormented and obsessed.

Within a few minutes they uncovered a stenciled swastika, its once bright-red arms dulled to ochre by years of interment. Then a cracked concrete wall emerged from the earth. The word *Achtung!* appeared inch by inch, with the digging now grown slow and careful. When the moon finally vanished four hours later, one side of the structure stood uncovered. A concrete vault fourteen feet by five by eight, its thick walls scrawled over with German warnings and Nazi insignia.

Father Thierry stood in the darkness with his hands on his hips and muttered, "*Mon dieu.*"

Stephen's mind raced back to the day before, when they'd sat in the chapel of Birkenau for a briefing by the parish priest. Local peasants harbored strange rumors of these structures buried along this side of the camp, objects the Nazis had called *Judensargen*. They spoke of vaults used to bury victims alive during the early experimental days of Auschwitz-Birkenau, before the use of sealed vans and gas chambers. Conscious prisoners sealed under the earth. A living death. Father Theodore's seismograph readings had shown promising signs, and so they'd undertaken the excavation immediately.

They dug all night, until the dim light of morning rang with the striking of pickaxes on old concrete. It happened fast now—the brittle surfaces shattering easily beneath determined blows. The first glow of dawn found a spider web of cracks spread out across the vault's uppermost wall.

Father Olkeswisz's pickax broke through, and the momentum of his swing almost stripped the instrument from his hands. With shouts and warnings, the others converged on his spot. The priests hammered at the fissure until a black hole lay open to the sky. Father Thierry waved the others away with wild swings of the arms and shouted, "Back! Back!"

Olkeswisz scrutinized the surface, wound up and swung. His point struck hard, and he leaped back just as the entire top of the vault caved in with the sound of a small rockslide. A cloud of dust rose and quickly wafted away in the breeze.

Then gasps filled the morning air.

The man inside opens his eyes and the light sears his vision.

The rush of cold air causes him to think for one hopeful moment that he is once again back at that morning when it all began, when the tomb flooded with the warm glow of dawn and the shadow of that face stood just outside, the face of his best friend.

Slowly his eyes sharpen into focus. Blurry pools of blackness above him resolve into moving figures—pinched, frightened faces and soiled robes, all testaments to their humanity. The illusion shatters, and he realizes his long journey has not ended after all.

2

Oswiecim, Poland

BETSY ARENS RECEIVED the call midway through a breakfast of cold coffee and care-package bagels. The phone erupted with that peculiar European ring she could never grow accustomed to. It was her boss, his thick English accent made even less intelligible by the fact that he was panting.

"Betsy, you must come now! To Birkenau. The police say there's been some kind of discovery. And desecration. Please come at once. Eastern fence." He hung up without waiting for her acknowledgment. Another peculiarity she was certain she would never grow familiar with.

The oddity of Polish customs had faded from her mind by the time she threw her tool bag into her Volkswagen and pulled away from her apartment overlooking Oswiecim's bustling central square. Speeding toward the Sola River, which separated the city from the camps, she thought of how some days she actually managed to forget about its past. In any other academic science it was considered desirable to develop emotional distance from the more disturbing aspects of one's work. Not so in Holocaust research. Most of her peers regarded smoldering rage a prerequisite to excelling in the field. To be Jewish and to study the genocide of your people—how could one go about such a business without being consumed with an unscientific fire?

Therefore it troubled her to admit how often Oswiecim managed to seem like any other Eastern European city of cramped old streets moldering under rows of public-housing towers. At times these modern behemoths of water-stained concrete depressed her so keenly that she felt compelled to look away from their dreary gray slabs, brightened only by the collage of laundry-strewn balconies.

She consoled herself, almost perversely, by reminding herself that, even after a year, she hadn't yet grown comfortable with living and working here. If only her grandmother, a Treblinka survivor, could see her today, or the relatives whose murders had hung so morosely over her childhood like a shroud. If only they could see her now, as she drove freely through the city where so many had perished. Would they applaud her work or shun her? she wondered. What would they think of Betsy Arens choosing to inhabit such a place—daughter of Kenneth and Connie Arens of Haifa—formerly of Queens, New York—archaeologist-in-residence at the National Museum of Auschwitz-Birkenau, on loan from Israel's Yad Vashem? She who was a rising star in her field, a force to be reckoned with?

Nearly every day on her travels through town an elderly woman or two would quietly turn away from her. Not out of hate, it seemed, but shame. Betsy thought she saw tears sometimes, gleaming on wizened cheeks.

She tightened her grip on the steering wheel and accelerated across the bridge, picturing herself as a woman with a mission. A mission that might well be served by the summons at hand. She was, after all, being called just now to Birkenau, and promoting Birkenau—over the sanitized, ethnically nonspecific tourist park Auschwitz 1 had become—was one of her missions, her *raison d'être* in this place. Maybe the discovery awaiting her would give Jewry the occasion they needed to press harder for a museum at Birkenau, still the neglected of the two sites.

And, far from incidentally, the one where most of the Jews had perished.

FOR THE SECOND TIME in a month, searchers traversed the meadow between the Birkenau chapel and the camp fence line. All but a few wore drab green uniforms. Each bent toward the ground, stooping periodically to pick up a small stone or paper scrap. The Oswiecim police station had produced a contingent of three detectives and five uniformed men—not an inconsiderable response, for desecration of a Holocaust site was a crime of international consequence.

Inspector Leonor Belka turned at the rumble of a racing Volkswagen and swore softly. The woman was late. Of the countless bureaucratic stupidities of modern life, few rankled him more than the fact that he and his men couldn't step foot near the camps without having to placate some representative of the Jewish people. A dozen men had been forced to wait for the proper amenities to be observed. Inevitably, this had resulted in yet another imposition on his duty: the presence of a woman who would surely declare every convention of investigative police work a deliberate affront to Judaism.

Belka was far from an anti-Semite, he often reminded himself—unlike his father who had helped to build several of the camps. And certainly not like his ancestors, who had considered hatred of Jews an intrinsic part of being a patriotic Pole. Instead, just like most of the local residents, he had a close understanding of the atrocities committed in his hometown and considered them revolting. But like any good Pole, he resented having the actions of a murderous invader considered a blemish on his country's national psyche, let alone a reason to be bossed around by foreigners.

The policemen stood idly above the pit while Betsy approached and briskly apologized for the delay. She turned abruptly and began descending into the pit's cement jumble, grumbling about the site having been left exposed to the elements. She first peered at, then fingered, the Nazi markings on the structure's outer walls. Looking up at Belka, she shouted, "It's authentic!"

With that, Belka turned and started assigning his men to the work of a crime detail: analyzing the tire tracks in the mud, questioning the priests of the nearby chapel, searching the tall grasses for clues.

Betsy fell silent, however, when she stepped inside the exposed vault. The first thing she noticed was the smell. It was not the odor of a decaying corpse—far from it. Instead, its pungency brought her back home to crowded Jerusalem buses on holy days, crushed against the outstretched arms and sweaty torsos of poor Arabs and bleary-eyed yeshiva students. The instant her brain processed the odor's origin, she shook her head with a start. How could a tomb have become saturated, *this* saturated, with human sweat? Obviously it could have been left by the site's desecrators. But she was standing in a puddle of standing rainwater. No brief occupancy could have left a stain strong enough to withstand last night's brief yet intense cloudburst.

She fetched her bag and took out a flashlight. Its beam skirted across the crypt's far wall, a cracked surface sheltered under a surviving portion of ceiling slab. What appeared in her light was a mass of random scratches. She shuddered. But there was something else, a pattern, a coherence to the marks. She squinted, stepped forward, stared harder at the scribblings. She felt the blood leave her face. *Aramaic*. Carved into the curving, overlapping pattern of someone writing with no light to guide him, were most certainly letters in the language of ancient Hebrew.

She crouched down and, for the next twenty minutes, ignored repeated inquiries from the anxious police officers above, waving them off with backhanded gestures.

Belka finally descended awkwardly into the hole. Betsy regarded him with a brief scowl and returned to her study of the walls. "You see these markings?" she said, pointing.

"What are they?" he asked.

"They're written in ancient Hebrew. In the old-style hand. I interned years ago at the Shrine of the Book, and this is the manner in which the Dead Sea Scrolls were written. This kind of Hebrew died out in Europe centuries ago. Even assuming some strange devotee of dead language was put in here, this makes no sense at all."

"Why not?"

"Well, there are only two options. Either the markings were made before the lid was sealed or afterwards. The Nazis would not have permitted this sort of inscription. But if they buried someone alive, once the lid was moved into place whoever inscribed it would probably have less than thirty minutes of oxygen left. How could they have had the time to write all this before dying?"

3

Rome, Borgo Nuovo District—Dawn

WRENCHED FROM A DEEP sleep, Bishop Johan Eccles bolted upright in his bed. His breath shuddered in short, panting rasps. He felt on the edge of panic yet had no idea why. In his gut gnawed a sense of alarm, as if somewhere a nuclear blast had just detonated. He glanced about his bedroom and saw only the bleak dawn light filtering through brocade onto oak wall panels and the gilded spines of his Freud first editions. He heard pigeons cooing above the streets of Rome and knew immediately it was no dream. No nightmare could shake him so profoundly. Something had happened. The dark being that had occupied him for years was stirred. The voice that was not a voice began to urge him out. Out of the building, out of Rome, out of Italy.

Return to Oswiecim House.

Three hours later he received a call from the House itself. It was the supervising priest, Father Marco. "Something has happened, Bishop Eccles. Right before dawn, the holding rooms erupted. The patients are in a frenzy. We do not know what to do. Please come at once."

As he always did on such clandestine occasions, he avoided Vatican travel arrangements and drove his own aging Mercedes sedan instead. From Rome the trip took two days, first through northern Italy and Austria, then eastward through the Czech Republic and into Poland. He stopped neither to sleep nor eat. It would not allow him—the longing that beckoned him northward drew him with an urgency he'd never felt before.

At the German-Polish border, the presence felt like a hot breath curling along his spine, a ravenous whisper. It grew stronger, closer by the kilometer, more intense the farther north Bishop Eccles drove.

Then, only miles away from his destination, he intentionally drove past the main exit leading to the center of Oswiecim. At the next turnoff he slowed and turned left onto a road used mostly by tourists. He had to see the place once again; it was a diversion he made on nearly every trip. A mile later the fields gave way to a forest of large overhanging elms and then a clearing filled with buses—streamlined monsters adorned with garish stripes and Scandinavian names. He looked farther across the parking lot and saw the crowds before spotting the gate itself. Bishop Eccles thought them to be without question the most forlorn-looking tourists anywhere in the world. A cluster of middle-agers walked slowly, almost reluctantly, light jackets folded neatly across their forearms, yarmulkes covering the back of their heads. He smiled coldly at the thought of Jews streaming in of their own accord. Two-dozen high schoolers wearing identical navy blue cardigans lurched through the gate. Their pink faces tilted sheepishly up at the steel arch and its stark, world-renowned lettering: *Arbeit Macht Frei*. Work makes you free.

As he watched the procession, the thing he had dreaded for nine hundred miles finally happened. The presence inside him surged hungrily and engulfed him whole. All went black; he felt as if his heart were being ripped away from its cavity. Then a wrestling, a momentary struggle for control. He felt his consciousness tossed aside like a tattered garment, then a powerful hand take the reins of his senses.

The spirit's control complete, Eccles stopped the Mercedes, lowered the window and leaned his face outside for a long, blissful breath of air. *Aahhh.* If only he could have been there, he now told himself, to see the black trains chugging down the tracks, smell the smoke of genocide, witness the bustle of a proud people at work radically reshaping their world.

He peered into the shade beyond the gate, along the tree-lined lane which flanked the rows of brown brick buildings. The museum shop disgorged a matronly woman busy stuffing her purchases into a shoulder bag. Two elderly men walked out from another door, both sipping coffee from paper cups, talking intently. He wondered if the cups bore a logo; perhaps some rendering of smokestacks over artfully curled barbed wire. He sneered. *The cowards are so terrified of the place's meaning, they dress it up as some sort of an amusement park. Death-lite. Ethnic cleansing, Disney style.*

At the moment Eccles preferred the past. What a time it must have been. Unpleasant business at its core, to be sure, yet that was the whole point. He couldn't help but admire the sheer will required to carry out such a bloody task, to pursue power so fiercely that one was willing to exterminate an entire race in the pursuit of it. When had humanity ever risen to such heights of self-assertion? If the craven old dinosaurs back in Rome possessed one ounce of such determination, they might be worth saving. Yes, but wouldn't he love to build an Auschwitz of his very own right on the stones of St. Peter's Square. He pictured it, and his mouth quivered with a low chuckle. To frog-march the dogma-encrusted fossils down their own selection lines . . . *You, pope, off to the gas chamber, along with your pathetic pieties and the shriveling superstitions you and your predecessors gave birth to. Let us transform your bodies into a pillar of smoke rising in homage to the lord of the air.*

Deep inside the bishop cowered a soul who found such thoughts repugnant. Yet that soul was no longer in command.

He returned to the highway and drove into Oswiecim. The

House lay only a few miles ahead. He maneuvered his car toward it, through the city of sixty thousand Auschwitz had become in modern times. After circling the town square, he veered onto a side street and parked. Beyond a high brick wall sat an unremarkable three-story building with mud-colored walls and windows obscured by thick maroon curtains. He killed the car's engine and stepped out. The pull was so strong within him now that he didn't even bother to look up at the House, didn't bother to scan the street as he usually did to note the townspeople scurrying about their business, to congratulate himself on his secret knowledge that right here on an ordinary street in the center of Europe sat the Vatican's secret center for the study of demonic possession.

Twenty years ago local priests had submitted a report to the Vatican stating that Oswiecim seemed cursed with the world's highest rates of madness and suicide and, most of all, demonic possession. It was a well-known fact that pregnant women left the city to give birth. Officially it was said that no one wanted their offspring to bear the stigma of having been born near Auschwitz. However, most of Oswiecim's residents suspected something more sinister. Babies born in the city were prone to a grotesque array of mental and physical aberrations: animal-like facial features, retardation, psychotic fits. The spiritually aware found it hardly difficult ascribing a cause to this phenomenon; in fact, given the location of the death camps, it seemed appropriate.

So, wishing to avoid attention regarding the controversial and sensationalized subject of demonic possession, Church authorities had quietly purchased the large home through intermediaries. Soon the House had begun accepting patients on condition of complete confidentiality, for observation, medical and spiritual care. Over the years the House had blossomed into a hive of secret activity as clerics from around the world came to learn exorcism, to pray and map out the unseen geographies of spiritual darkness.

Eccles could barely remember the days before his first visit here a decade ago on one of those very missions. A bold, ambitious young bishop newly assigned to Rome from his native Spain, drunk with his own intellectual fervor and the power of a newly acquired Ph.D., he had looked up at the nondescript building and thought its choice brilliant. No signs or markings of any kind, on orders of the cardinal. He'd been told that the locals, noticing mainly the comings and goings of priests and nuns, believed it to be a Catholic retreat.

It was here, in the House's miasmic chambers, less than a week after first arriving, that Eccles's soul had first been invaded. Until then he'd never known that the soul could experience such horror. That it could scream for release with all the torment of a claustrophobe clamped tight inside an inner dungeon, unable to move, unable to breathe.

Before his being invaded, he hadn't pondered very deeply the mechanics of the soul. He had been a believer, or at least he told himself so in those moments his tormentor allowed such recollection. Still, his belief had meant far less to him than his career and the mastery of the psychological sciences, his easy recall of Jung and Freud and the intricacies of reconciling modern theory to Church doctrine. As for spiritual matters, he'd found them elusive and therefore less interesting. His faith had been cerebral, grounded in the intellect, and proved no match for his invader. Eccles understood that now.

He knocked on the heavy door like an ordinary caller, waited for the eyehole to fill with the magnified gape of a nun's pupil. When it opened he strode inside without so much as a pause to mouth a greeting or attempt any of the childish amenities he always felt constrained to observe. He walked ahead as though drawn by a rope—through an antechamber painted light green, with its statues of the Virgin and fading prints of Jesus and the saints, through the hallway door and then the basement door, down the worn concrete steps and into the passageways ordinary citizens would never see. Long ago he had shed the despair he first felt in these long, clean halls whose white painted doors absorbed the sounds of people barking, snarling, even whimpering in terror.

Today, had it not been for his jadedness, he might have blanched at the cacophony all around him. The vast basement echoed as never before with the howls, shrieks, and simian mutterings of the damned. He stood and listened, not a single muscle moving.

A young priest hurried up to him, his face slack with fear. "Bishop Eccles! We're so glad to see you. Father Marco is beside himself."

"Be quiet." The priest recoiled in surprise at the command. Eccles closed his eyes and allowed the clamor to wash over him, trying to discern a pattern, a message. He turned swiftly toward the young man, eyes ablaze. "Tell me, is there one patient who is silent?"

The priest thought for a moment, then nodded for him to follow. They walked past eight doors to a spot near the end of the main hall where the younger man stopped. He turned to a wood door with a painted numeral 7 on its surface. The priest leaned in carefully and held his ear against the door. Then he nodded, pulled out a keychain from his vestments, and unlocked the door. Eccles waved the priest away as he turned the knob, stepped inside, and closed the door behind him.

In the corner of a stark white room stood a middle-aged woman with shoulder-length brown hair matted into greasy, jutting clumps. Her eyes trained ferociously on Eccles. She grinned at his entrance and held out two trembling arms.

Eccles took one step forward and lunged. His lanky frame landed on her and the woman emitted a shriek of delight, even as his weight drove her down to her knees. He clasped her head in his hands and bent down, his face approaching hers, and then engulfed her mouth with his own. A second shriek drowned in the cavity of bishop's mouth.

Still locked on to the madwoman's mouth, Eccles began to shake with a violent motion which overtook his spine and shook the two of them together. Their chilling kiss never broke.

Eccles felt a new presence fill his being and chase out the weaker inhabitant, a roaring yet inaudible voice more horrible than any he'd ever heard, a blend of growling dog and rushing wind, shouting for all to be gone to make way for a strongman.

He saw the images he had always coveted.

Smokestacks poured forth gray columns. A proud SS officer with patrician features walking between the longhouses turned to salute him. "Guten tag, Colonel Gebhardt."

A voice in response came from himself. "Heil Hitler, Colonel Mengele."

Then came the stark interior of a laboratory, its cement walls lined with attentive guards holding machine guns, inmates cowering in their striped uniforms. In the center of the room stood an operating table, and upon it something his mind's eye could not quite focus on, something even he could not face. Suddenly all went blank.

Then came the voice, speaking to him.

"Here in this very place, a mortal enemy of our dark lord has just been freed after decades of captivity. You will stop him, or you will be consumed in the foulest way under hell."

WITHIN HOURS, news of the discovery attracted most of the Auschwitz archaeological contingent. Soon a tarp and later a canvas tent went up on the meadow between the Birkenau chapel and the camp fence line. Betsy Arens, who assumed de facto authority over the site, spent the next four days crouched in dirt, analyzing soil samples, ash residues, hair, bones and bits of cloth. Rumors of the so-called *Judensargen* had always been dismissed by the higher echelon of Holocaust research circles; now she would be credited with a pioneer discovery.

Betsy began by examining one of the site's most tantalizing features: the Aramaic writing on the crypt's preserved wall. Her first observation about the script proved to be the most puzzling. The writing had actually been carved into the concrete, presumably by a bent nail she'd found nearby. The first piece of writing occupied the far end of the wall, beneath the hole left by a corner of slab that had crumbled into dust. It consisted of three lines which appeared to form some sort of list. The second, in the wall's preserved center, was simply a mass of jumbled sentences. Transcribing it proved painstaking work. After finding the start of a sentence she was forced to follow its progress across overlapping lines, feeling the shape of the letters with her fingertips. She faxed the transcript to a linguistic expert in Jerusalem and waited.

On the afternoon of the fourth day, Betsy stood in the lab tent watching a Polish colleague as he leaned over the microscope observing samples of the black residue coating much of the site's interior. He looked up at her with a mystified expression. "These samples," he said, "they do not make any sense."

"How's that?"

"It resembles combustion ash of some type. Not the human ash we find at Auschwitz, but from some sort of explosive detonation."

"Is that so strange?"

"No. Except for the fact that the residue is so thin I can hardly measure it. It's only a few microns thick."

"So the blast must have been very brief."

"Probably a bright flash of light rather than a chemical or concussive force. Like somebody turned on a million-watt lamp in there. For a thousandth of a second."

Betsy shook her head. Nothing about the site had so far made any sense.

"The very strange thing is this," he said in a low, subdued voice. "Do you know the only place I have heard of such a residue before?"

"No."

"The Shroud of Turin."

"Oh, please. I wouldn't trust that kind of science. Besides, it's been proven the Shroud is barely a thousand years old."

"That's not true, Betsy. That study was performed by a biased bunch of modernists, and their methodology has since been roundly condemned by even their ideological allies. Other studies using the same techniques have yielded far older dates. But no matter what you believe about the Shroud, it's been proven that its image was formed by a photo-reactive flash."

The fax machine started to hum beside Betsy. Ready for a break, she walked over and scanned the page that rolled out. The message was preceded by a note from the Israeli linguist. *Betsy, good news and bad news. Good news: the first sample was what you thought it might be—a family tree of some kind. The second sample is like a strange religious soliloquy. Whatever it is you've found, it smells fishy. Sincerely, Dov.*

Betsy turned to the second page and the translation.

Henry McPheran, born 1901
Joseph McPheran, born 1922

Below this, the longer piece of text:

December 19, 1942
Dear God,

Please take me. Remove me from this place the world has become.

Oswiecim, Poland

THE SQUAD ROOM billowed with clouds of cheap Bulgarian cigarette smoke and echoed with angry mutterings. Security Minister Jacek Balcerowicz, who had taken the first train in from Warsaw, edged his vast behind over the corner of Inspector Belka's desk and stared into the vapors with the weary sigh of a martyr.

"This is undoubtedly a Nazi artifact," Belka muttered. "My protocol says to inform Mossad."

"You will not," grunted Balcerowicz. "Not until we find out who broke into the vault. Too many unanswered questions. Anyway, the Birkenau priest is involved somehow, and I will not have those Jews attacking another Catholic site."

The senior-level officers nodded somberly. Several years before, Jewish protesters, angry over the presence of a Catholic convent near Auschwitz, had rioted, provoking an international incident. No one wanted another fracas like that. In the eyes of local authorities, Oswiecim had enough on their hands with Jewish tourists streaming through the sites without angry hordes of them returning to make trouble.

"If they find out we've covered up the desecration of a Holocaust site, we'll have Jewish attacks right here," Belka said, gesturing around his office.

"I will take that risk. Clearly, the Church is involved somehow. The getaway vehicle was parked behind the chapel for five days. And I'm not putting myself between those two factions."

"Then where do we go to find out what was inside that thing?" asked Belka. "Put a squeeze on the Birkenau priest?"

"He has revealed nothing," Koskiesky, the head of detectives, said. "He's not going to, either. Besides, my men are reluctant to use stronger methods on a Father in their parish."

"No Nazi artifact is worth going to hell over," Belka said, chuckling ruefully.

"Do we talk to the Vatican envoy?" asked Koskiesky.

"No," replied Balcerowicz. "I want neither side contacted. The Jews or the Mother Church."

"Interpol?"

"No. That would be like posting it on a billboard. Everybody in the world would know within a day."

Belka sighed heavily and rolled his eyes at the minister's coyness. "Sir, would you tell us what you want done, then?"

"First, contact all your sources on the black market. See if some Holocaust trinket surfaces in the next week or so. I'll bring in stronger allies to protect us." The minister heaved himself from the desk's edge. "I have a friend at the CIA."

Langley, Virginia

"WHY IN THE WORLD is Balcerowicz calling *us*?"

Mike Stayton glanced down at his papers and tried to suppress a chuckle. His boss, James Schorie, enjoyed kick-starting meetings with these surly outbursts. Stayton figured it saved the Deputy Director for European Intelligence from having to employ the inevitable clichés of their trade. *So, what have we got here? What does this mean?*

Despite a shared knowledge of Schorie's management style, a nervous pause took hold around the conference table. However familiar everyone was with his tactics, none of his agents was ever quite sure when the mock gruffness would subside.

Stayton went first. After all, the call had come in to him. His old Warsaw drinking buddy, Balcerowicz, had initiated the contact. "Because the Israelis are going to go ballistic when they find out—especially when they learn that Catholic priests were doing the digging. This story is spreading fast, and it's about three days away from turning into a catfight between two of the world's biggest religions. So the Polish need a referee. Us."

"It's not just religious, sir," said Stayton's office mate, Dan Wallis, an expert on Balkan blood feuds. "It's U.S.-Israel relations, Vatican-Israel, Poland with all of the above. Last time the Jews and Catholics mixed it up at Auschwitz, there was a riot and the pope ended up having to ride herd. Didn't make His Holiness very happy, from what we were told."

"And the rabbi who started the riot came from New York," Stayton added.

"I knew we'd get in there somewhere," Schorie said. "So, do we have any idea what was in that thing? What all this handwringing is actually about?"

"No," said Stayton. "Rumor is, there was someone alive in there."

"What?" Schorie exclaimed. "Didn't you say that this crypt was sealed for fifty years?"

"Affirmative."

"I'm listening."

"We don't know," Stayton continued. "It's far-out stuff, sir.

The priests are part of some renegade group that hasn't set foot in Rome for years. Some kind of mystic sect with a whole mess of rumors and theories swirling around it. I've been checking our Vatican sources, and they tell me this Order of Lazare gets tagged with all kinds of hypothetical missions. Undercover archaeology. Something called 'spiritual warfare.' 'Protecting saints.'"

Schorie stared out the window toward the green canopy of flowering elms that encircled CIA headquarters. "Okay, back to reality. Bottom line." One of his favorite meeting-enders.

"This Order seems to have stolen something out of that thing. But no one knows for sure what."

"Do we know what the scribbling says?"

Wendy Butcher, their language expert, started with her customary smoker's cough. "Balcerowicz faxed us some photos," she said. "Our translators say it's Aramaic, the ancient form of Hebrew. Hasn't been used in common parlance in almost two thousand years. Doesn't reveal anything we can use. Some plea to God or something."

"But no body?"

"Sorry, sir. I'm not making this stuff up," said Stayton.

"Well, this is the strangest thing I ever heard of." Schorie tapped his pen on the table. "I'm not sure we should even touch it. Even if we were entitled, which I doubt we are."

"Why is that, sir?"

"Because this is one of the worst kinds of scrapes you can possibly get mixed up in. Did any of you jokers read last year's Global Threat Assessment?"

"Of course, sir," Stayton replied. "What part?"

"The part that talks about how Eurasian sectarian conflicts have higher odds of escalating into global warfare than any other category."

Schorie let that sink in.

"Tell you what," he finally said. "First, we find out what was in that crypt. Then I'll make the call. Bring in a field agent from Berlin or someplace and have him snag those priests before Mossad finds out."

5

Tyniec Abbey, Outside Kracow

HIGH ON A LIMESTONE cliff above the waters of the Vistula River, the stone battlements of Tyniec Abbey glowed white in the morning sun. For nearly a thousand years the ramparts and their twin spires impaling a green oak canopy had dominated the horizon, testifying to the Church's enduring power in a chaotic corner of the world. Although the centuries had seldom been kind to the Benedictine monastery, here it stood at the dawn of the twenty-first century: a curiosity lately engulfed by urban sprawl from greater Kracow. And yet it still resembled a medieval fortress more than a haven of worship and contemplation.

Had this day fallen in summer rather than the month of October, the abbey's typical visitors would have consisted of a hundred tourists quenching their thirst for monastic ambiance with a stroll around the chapel's Baroque interiors or an evening concert featuring its famous pipe organ. Many would have arrived on sightseeing boats, sailing down the Vistula straight from Old Town Kracow to Tyniec's riverside landing.

On this day, however, its only guests were a group of eight men who had emerged from a van and quickly disappeared into the abbey's depths unseen by any others, insulated from the now-deserted public rooms by several bolted doors, secluded passageways, and politely worded signs.

Deep inside the Tyniec visitors' quarters, Father Stephen

stood guard, staring down a hallway shrouded in gray reflections of old stone. Around his left cheek curved the thin microphone of a headpiece he had not worn since his initial training. His ear crackled with the voices of colleagues scattered across the abbey grounds, each priest muttering half-remembered instructions and code words they hadn't repeated in years. He looked down at the floor stones, worn smooth by a millennium of soft footsteps, and strained to keep his mind on his own instructions. "*Guard our chamber during the initial debriefing. Deflect any intruder, any distraction during the next two hours. Use physical force if necessary. Walk the perimeter, and pray as though your life depended on it.*"

Useless gibberish, he had told himself, until today. How many times had he seen his brothers' eyes narrow in silent exasperation at Father Thierry's endless action plans and contingencies. He had long ago ceased to repeat and remember them, despite his vow before Father Thierry on that cold Consecration Day at St. Michel.

Now the terseness of the electronic exchanges in his ear bore witness to the shock and amazement which hung about each of them. "Pax nocturna, Catacon One. Catacon One to Catacon Father, confirm Pax nocturna. . . ." Yet Stephen knew that beneath the chatter they were thinking exactly what he was: *Could I have dreamed it? Did my eyes really see it? It is too much. It is too unbelievable.*

He tried to concentrate, but the morning's events would not stop reeling through his mind. The sequence had now acquired the languid pace of slow motion. Concrete caving in, dust blowing away, and there amidst the rubble, too astonishing to be true yet seared forever on the record of his retina—a human form. A man lying in the ruined chamber, a seemingly middle-aged man, nearly naked, the dust around his slack limbs giving him the appearance of a corpse sprinkled with lime. Who then blinked.

Yes, blinked. As in *alive*.

Stephen shook his head even now, remembering it again.

Next a low moan rose from the living cadaver's parchment-like lips. He moved. His arms bent behind him, his hands pushed at the ground, his biceps flexed. He began to stand. Gray dust cascaded down lean limbs and floated to the ground. He stood naked except for the clinging tatters of a thin, striped cloth. Behind his back, a thick mat rose with him that the priests soon discerned as hair, half a century's worth of growth woven into a chaotic nest.

The man stood to his full height with a contented narrowing of his eyelids, then performed a motion that was undeniably human. His fists curled upward, his arms moved back and stretched behind him, then his back bowed deeply. His mouth opened into a yawn.

He looked ahead and seemed to absorb his surroundings for the first time. His gaze, now fierce and self-possessed, fell on Thierry's awestruck face. The man winced slightly, as if hit with a bittersweet memory. Father Thierry fell to his knees with a torrent of French prayers pouring from his lips. The others followed suit, crossing themselves, and filled the chasm with echoes of astonished voices.

Father Stephen felt his hand rise to cover his mouth and mask a look of astonishment that now felt faithless, even blasphemous. In his mind echoed that first sentence Thierry had whispered to him in the abbey, perhaps the most difficult to believe. "*The man we serve has died once already and been restored to life by our Lord. Stephen, he is immortal.*" Stephen now realized he had believed it only in the shallowest of ways. He had believed it as myth, as abstraction.

Now he'd seen that abstraction stand before him, move his limbs slowly and blink in the morning light.

Then Father Thierry's thin, sharp voice had wailed orders, and priests scurried about their tasks. A blanket was brought from somewhere and wrapped around the human form while the van lurched toward them through the grass. He could not remember climbing in, yet they were all inside the vehicle, the fields and forests of Upper Silesia flowing past the windows. Father Thierry kneeled in the narrow space between the two front seats and faced the stranger. What should have been a corpse now sat silently, breathing, glancing out at the trees and the recently overcast sky, with a sadness about him that kept them all hushed like children, staring.

The man's head turned slowly toward Thierry and his features tensed with a glimmer of recognition. His lips opened as if to form a word, but then closed again. His eyes grew shiny and released two tears which trailed down his dusty cheeks. The man shook his head slowly as if to say that, no, he couldn't speak after all.

Father Thierry's voice filled the van, frail once more. "Please, my friend. Forgive me for taking so long. I never stopped looking, not one day, never gave up hope." The stranger's hand reached out from beneath the shroud, took the old priest's hand and clasped it, gripped it tightly. Father Thierry bowed and began to weep—long, gasping sobs that made the other priests look away.

They had driven on in unbearable silence until the sight of Tyniec's stone battlements filled the windshield. The wrought-iron gate stood open, and the driver entered the courtyard without slowing, circled and came to a stop with a light chirp of the brakes. No one waited to greet them. Father Thierry yanked the door open and stepped down with the stranger's hand still in his, heading off toward large wooden doors.

Thierry's muffled voice pulled Stephen away from the memory and back to the present. Beyond the thick oak door at his back, the debriefing was under way. What he wouldn't give to be in that room just now, listening to the conversation. Yet Father Thierry's last order still rang in his ears. "*Brother Stephen, guard this door while I debrief our friend. Do not interrupt us for any reason.*"

Stephen could recall the heat of the old man's breath across his cheek at Mont St. Michel two and a half years before. "*For two thousand years,*" Thierry had whispered, "*the catacon has survived and carried out his appointed mission through human history. In the furtherance of his mission he has lived under a hundred names. Rabbi Mordecai Schlom, Robert of Saxony, Bishop William of Chartres, Count of Saint Germain, Ambassador to the Court of the Tsars, and so many more. But I will tell you now. His true name is far older still.*"

Father Thierry then drew a wavering breath and muttered in Stephen's ear a name that was beyond belief, its very utterance in a modern context outrageous.

THE MAN HAD NOT yet spoken, but he could feel the capacity for speech gathering within him, like a spring filling one droplet at a time.

The intensity of it all began to overwhelm him, until he remembered that this was merely the sensation of a body aflutter with the rhythms of life. The twitch of muscles flushed with blood as vital and alive as springtime rain. The throb of a single touch leaping from fingertip into nerve ending and across synapses to a waiting brain. Irises retracting before the onslaught of daylight like bellows before an oven blast, then etching an intricate palette and whisking it to his overheated senses . . .

Dust motes adrift in a blazing, sunlit column. A rusted bar cleaving a medieval window slit.

He blinked to dispel the illusion of a prison cell. The room was ancient, ageless. What was this, the Middle Ages? The Renaissance? He could not settle on the present, could not discern the era, to say nothing of the year. Behind his eyelids the years spun by like digits on an old cash register.

His mind plunged into a free fall, and it felt as if he were drowning in time. Images swirled through his head: faces, costumes, conveyances from mules and crude carts to ornate carriages, then even sleeker carriages without horses, puffs of dark smoke trailing behind them.

His head swam with dizziness and a tinge of nausea. He couldn't get enough air. His breath squeezed shut in a claustrophobic spasm. The world lurched—the careening images gathered speed.

To orient himself, he rose up, leaned against the stone wall and focused his gaze on the man sitting on the cot beside him, surrounded by documents and a copious pile of hair clippings. He squinted at the ancient priest and tried to place him.

The priest smiled at him and said, "Hello, my friend."

That voice. Last seen and heard on that terrible day when the children had been taken away by the SS.

Ah, yes. The twentieth century. Airplanes. Automobiles. Telephones.

The Third Reich.

Father Thierry, he remembered. The faintest hint of a smile began to play upon his lips. It felt so good to recall the priest's name. Though withered with age, his face remained familiar: dominated by the bold hawklike nose, the burning blue eyes, the thin mouth quivering with too much to say. Even now, the old Breton clutched a stack of documents as if this last captivity had only been a momentary interruption in some earth-shattering business meeting. Thierry handed him the papers.

"You are André Lassalle," the old one said, "born 1964 in St. Germain-des-Prés. The farmhouse was razed twenty years ago to make way for a highway. Other than that, all the houses are safe. Your affairs are in order. At last report, the accounts held four hundred and eighty million dollars. Non-liquid assets are in the billion and a half range. You are the third wealthiest Frenchman alive."

He wanted to grab the old man and squeeze him in a bear hug. But clearly, Thierry was in the mood for business. The twitch in those wrinkled eyelids and the brusqueness in the old limbs' motions made it seem their owner had delayed this briefing as long as he could stand to.

Even so, he raised his hand dismissively. Money and logistics were the last things on his mind. And then it struck him. Thierry's obsession with business reflected the man's insecurity, his determination to prove he hadn't been idle all these years. Yet, if the signs were true, the priest's nervous energy indicated he'd been working feverishly, had never allowed himself a moment's pause.

He wanted to speak now.

His first words came out barely audible, halting and trembling as though unaccustomed to speech.

"I am so grateful to see you again." A pause hung between them. He spoke again, his voice low. "Thank you."

Thierry's face fell and tears traced down his gullied cheeks. "There is nothing to thank me for. I am ashamed for taking so long. I should have dug up every inch around Auschwitz and Birkenau from the very beginning. Only there was much scrutiny here, the politics—"

"No apology needed, my friend. I'm sure you've worked harder on my behalf than any other Elder Brother in history."

"I tried. . . ."

"Tell me."

"Yes?"

"Everything. Tell me everything." He closed his eyes wearily, and for a moment he almost wished to return to his buried vault. "First, how long was I in there?"

"Over sixty years."

He gasped at this and, after a pause, breathed the words, "The Allies won then, I take it."

"Yes. The Germans were defeated, praise God. Such bloodshed. After your capture they shipped the entire Order to the camps. Frederick, Phillipe, Stephen—they were all murdered."

His eyes half shut, he smiled at the priest. "Your escape was one of the most thrilling moments of my life. You were so brave. I owe you so much."

The man reached down, affectionately cupped Thierry behind the neck, and, closing his eyes, remembered . . .

A door smashes under the blow of a shining boot and gives way to flashes of dark green uniforms, glints of machine guns, echoes of barked German commands.

In a single wave of terror a hundred children sweep away from the door with shrill screams, and through the chaos he notices their hands reach reflexively to obscure the yellow stars sewn on their coats, their earlocks and dark thick hair.

Gunstocks and kicks drive the children into the shocking light of day, a sight they have not seen in weeks. Noonday sun hides behind the steeple of the cathedral whose crypts have sheltered them until now. Snarling dogs and men herd the children onto army trucks with engines running, and above their bobbing heads he sees the figures of his dear priests, his accomplices in mercy, being led through the cathedral doors. He locks onto their faces, their resigned expressions. Fathers Marquand, Connelly, Dolgin, Patrizzio, grizzled old Father Lewis stumbling, then finally his rebellious friend, Father Thierry, who meets his stare and whose eyes, in that one moment, brim over with a mad resolve.

The young priest rears up, throws off his SS armlock and breaks into a sprint. The square rings out with the cocking of guns and cries of "Halt!" Machine-gun fire shatters the air. Priests, children, and gawking citizens drop as one to the pavement beneath bullets that explode around the escaping priest and trace his jagged path toward facades of stores and cafés, along a stone wall to a gate through which he disappears into the maze of the city's medieval heart.

A scream rings out, and he recognizes the voice as his own: "Run! Run and avenge your brothers, Thierry!" A gunstock rears in his eyes and all goes black, the beginning of the last and far worst of all the nightmares. . . .

"Oh, and I must tell you," Thierry resumed. "The most wondrous event. Three years after you disappeared, after the war was over, Israel was reborn."

His listener stared, uncomprehending. "You mean . . ."

"I mean a Jewish state in Palestine. The retaking of Jerusalem. A Zionist homeland."

He looked awestruck. His eyes stood wide open, unblinking. "The Temple?"

Thierry's face changed. "The Muslims still hold the Mount. Jerusalem is a divided city. There is so much for you to learn."

"What about the line of the firstborn?"

"Joseph was killed in the war, but he left a two-year-old son. That son, Walter, disappeared in 1990. Presumably taken by your enemy; I was not able to investigate."

"Children?"

"One daughter. She would be twenty-five now, living somewhere in America. I haven't had the time to follow her closely. Unless she has had a child, the line ends with her." Thierry stopped suddenly. "My friend, the world has changed so much. There are many things to prepare you for."

"I have learned before. I will learn again."

"Yes, I know. But the world now changes much faster than ever before. Mankind has walked on the moon. Literally launched himself in a giant rocket and spent days wandering the moon's surface. So much. I myself do not recognize the world I lived in only twenty years ago. And I have been here to watch it happen."

Turning away from the old priest, he addressed his question to the ground. "Thierry, how many of my people did the Germans kill?"

Thierry stared grimly into the shaft of sunlight and watched dust float in silver light. Finally he answered, his gaze still cast downward. "Six million."

The man uttered a sound as if someone had kicked him across the midsection. His whole body stiffened in silent rage. He raised a shaking fist, kicked the nearby cot, and turned toward the wall. He slowly leaned into the cold stone, pressed his palms into its unyielding surface and tapped his forehead against it with a soft moan.

He shoved back against the stone and launched himself backward. His face was flushed red.

"You murderer!" he shouted. "How much blood, how much death will it take to avenge your vanity?"

6

Tyniec Abbey slept in the stillness of midnight. Shadows which earlier had repelled the light of day now flooded the rooms with utter blackness. Silences deep enough to swallow whole the chatter of tourists now reigned ponderously over the halls. The monastery seemed to hold its own weather, its own frozen sense of time.

Incapable of sleep, he sat on one end of a long peasant bench, hunched over draped pages mounted with old newspaper articles.

He turned a page and visibly shuddered, his eyes almost closing involuntarily. Yet he forced himself to part his eyelids and look.

The page bore a legend: *Birkenau, 1945*. Below it, a photo.

Before a brick wall bulged a pile of naked, emaciated bodies. Withered arms and legs dropping out of the heap like errant stalks of grain. A man in a Nazi uniform standing before it, holding a pitchfork—as if the corpses were nothing more than hay.

He growled and threw the pages to the floor. He reared his head back and thought of Birkenau, only miles away. He could hardly bear the thought. And it was only the culmination; hardly the beginning. He tried to prevent the dizzying recollection, but it was too late. His mind reeled before all the pogroms that lined his memory with dead bodies in an endless grisly procession. The suffering of his people was something he could hardly stand to contemplate. The sadness of their dispersion, the senselessness of their enemies. The sweetness of their longing for home.

Thierry's news of a Jewish state struck him with emotion beyond words. He felt bliss mingled with pride, yet also melancholy for all the generations that had spent themselves in exile, himself among them. "*Next year in Jerusalem.*" How many times had he heard the Passover lament, uttered in ghettoes from Cairo to Kiev, Paris, Prague, and Warsaw?

He picked up the pages again and turned to a picture of British troops marching into Jerusalem. The year 1937. An elderly Bedouin leaned in the foreground, eyeing the incoming soldiers with eyes barely parted.

The scene launched him back to the Jews of Europe and other worlds which no longer existed. He pictured each one filled with ordinary human beings trying to survive, navigating their way through cultures now mere annotations in texts of ancient history. Their homes and streets just dirt beneath the crust of a modern world. Their vibrancy extinguished and forgotten. A drop in the sea. All of those he'd loved now reduced to memory and dust, gone so many years ago that even their headstones had crumbled and blown away.

He shook his head, turned back to his reading. Next came pictures of wars and massacres. Chosin Reservoir, Dien Bien Phu, Khe Sanh, Pol Pot's killing fields, gassed Kurds in Iraq, beheaded Tutsis in Rwanda. It brought him back to all the faces of the dying he'd held; bodies dispatched in battles and assassinations, from the countless ingenuities humanity had devised to murder its own. But also all those lost to plagues and illnesses, even the ones who had drifted away of old age, some cursing their lot, others radiant with heavenly light.

He bent down and retrieved the pages of clippings, replaced them on the bench.

The next page read, *Jerusalem, 1948*. A photo of teenagers in front of the Western Wall wearing yarmulkes, grasping machine guns half their size. Behind them, a waving flag he hadn't seen in a very long time. A white field with a large Star of David at its center.

His memories of Israel—the ones he'd worked so hard to leave behind—suddenly came rushing back to him. He winced against the image of a man drenched in blood who stared at him for just a second. In that one second the man's eyes brimmed over with sadness, abandonment, betrayal.

Yet another memory flashed: the gruesome contraption built of timbers, silhouetted against a dark Judean sky. The same man's shoulders, rising more and more infrequently.

No, he could bear this no longer. He forced his thoughts back to the present. But that direction gave him no solace. He turned the page, and there was a mushroom cloud boiling over an expanse of New Mexico desert. The climax of humanity's bloodlust.

Then came the skyscraping grace of the World Trade Center twin towers against a piercing blue sky. Their walls punctured, giant flames shooting out, black shafts of smoke. Beside the intact portions of wall fell dark tiny shapes. He focused. *They were people. Jumping.*

He was sick of it. The anger that had simmered in his veins now boiled into rage. Centuries of accumulated grief and frustration ignited all at once in a blast of volcanic fury that seemed to set his limbs on fire. He swerved abruptly and gave a swift kick to a chair, sending it tumbling loudly into a corner.

"God," he shouted, "what do you want?"

He threw his hands and his gaze upward. He wanted answers, and he wanted them *now*.

"Have you turned away?" he screamed. "Do you not care? How can you watch your creation murder each other year after year after bloody year? Watch your Chosen People get slaughtered by the millions? Watch terrorists murder women and children?"

The thought wrenched him again, and he kicked the long dining table. It overturned and struck the floor with a great, echoing thud.

"Death factories? Weapons of mass destruction? Suicide attacks? *Sick!*" For a moment his revulsion became too deep for words, and he let out a series of guttural grunts. A moment later, speech found him again. "What is the point of prolonging all this? End it! Put us all out of our torment!"

He peeled off his shirt and began to yell directly at the ceiling, his arms raised wide.

"Am I being disrespectful? Blasphemous? Fine! Then take me, God! Because I quit! Do you hear me? I quit!"

He rushed over to the chair lying on its side and lifted it.

"Did I fail at my mission? That's fine too, because I'm finished!"

He struck the chair full over the table's edge, smashing it in half.

"I've poured my heart and soul into your sorry creation, and now I'm through!"

He became still and then pushed his voice to a near roar.

"What Satan and his demons don't accomplish, humans finish themselves! Their bloodlust won't be quenched, no matter what I do! It's an impossible job, do you hear me? *I quit!*"

The scream strangled into a wounded cry, and he slumped down against the wall, tears already flowing down his face.

"I quit. . . ." His now plaintive cry trailed off against the stones.

HIS CANDLE HAD BURNED to darkness by the time light returned with the encroaching dawn. The light found him still leaning spent against the stone wall with destroyed furniture lying on either side of him.

He woke adrift in a hazy mixture of exhaustion and despair. The evening's emotional firestorm fueled by the relief of liberation and soured by the news of what had occurred during his captivity, now left him drained of hope and joy.

He raised his hand to his forehead and winced. What had he said to God, anyway? He thought back over the things he'd shouted at the ceiling. From time to time he and God had these sorts of arguments, as old friends are known to do. Yet like any wise man he feared his Creator, as well. *Please*, he thought, *let me not have gone too far.*

He offered up a short prayer of apology, then almost in a reflex rekindled an old habit to probe whether he may have actually offended the Spirit. He closed his eyes, diffused his concentration, and nudged his spiritual senses into the space around him. He leaned his head back, pictured his mind melting and floating outward like an invisible cloud. A sensor net for the unseen world.

Mortals might not have understood the ability, but to him it was simply a sniff of the ethereal breeze. A hound pricking his ears to hear things human beings could not. He'd learned long ago that traces and smudges of the spiritual realm could be detected everywhere—if one possessed the humility and sensitivity to discern them. Because the Spirit's presence was a constant, like the hum of the electromagnetic spectrum, the old "music of the spheres," he could sense changes in its warmth and timbre intuitively.

No changes. He smiled. God understood his frustration. Perhaps even shared it.

Then an alarm.

A mere shadow passing. A wing's flutter. A flicker of spiritual darkness on the fringes of his consciousness.

He rose to his feet, opened his eyes just enough to discern his surroundings. It wasn't coming from indoors. He left the refectory and walked into a side hallway. Something ineffable beckoned him toward a round window in the wall. The sense of unease was emanating from outside its ancient glass. He pried the old steel frame open and cautiously peered out.

Outside lay a damp, cold dawn, gray and bleary. The village street was quiet and deserted except for a shiny new minivan edging slowly around the corner. He narrowed his eyelids and tried to read the scene before him. Trails of wispy darkness revealed the presence of residual demons. Nothing unusual; the earth's atmosphere was practically crammed with the beasts. But he felt none of the gnawing dread or tug at the pit of his stomach that usually signaled entities of unusual size or authority.

No, this threat was not threatening in nature. Simply the local wolf pack sniffing at an intruder.

Government, then, he concluded, as the van doors opened silently and well-coiffed men stepped out.

Police.

They were coming for him, he was sure of it. Or at least coming for answers to the questions he had provoked.

They were headed for the side street entrance. Thinking fast, he raced down a nearby set of stairs. His feet flew over the gnarled stones, racing only half as fast as his thoughts.

How can I thwart their purpose? he wondered.

He reached bottom, the answer in his mind. He turned, moving on instinct, and saw the front door already shaking under heavy blows. He swung back around and ran to a smaller wooden door.

He burst into the room where Thierry was sleeping on a rickety cot, rushed over and began shaking him. "Thierry! Thierry!" he said in a furious whisper.

The old man was instantly awake and alert, his eyes wide.

"Police are here! To question us, I think. Gather all the men in the hallway outside, right away. And act submissive to me. Understand?"

Without waiting for a reply, Thierry rose and strode out of the room.

Straightening his collar, he walked confidently toward the entrance while rehearsing his part.

The door flew open just as Belka's fist pulled back for another blow. It opened to reveal a clearly un-priestlike face that Belka could not place. The man inside frowned conspiratorially at the sight of them and spoke in an oddly accented Polish.

"Please, no need to break the place down. You're the *go* team, right?"

"Uh, yeah."

"I'm from Internal Security. A little bird in Warsaw spilled the news, and we were doing preliminary surveillance. We weren't going to move in, but I think our targets got word of your little . . . raid, and were about to flee, so we pulled the trigger."

"You've got them?"

"Special group of out-of-town priests, unknown, uninvited. They're in the hall behind me, ready for a little trip to the station."

"No bother. We can interrogate them here."

"Impossible. Seal their chambers off for a search if you like, but I'm not turning this monastery into a crime scene. Orders from the top. I'll take them in to the station myself, and you can follow me and interrogate them there. All you want. All right? All right."

Before Belka could even think to give his assent, the newcomer had turned and was walking off down the hallway. The men behind him then began to crowd in, asking questions. *What in the world was going on?*

He turned, shrugged, and grasped for words. "Some do-gooder

from national police. He thought they were going to bolt so he got them first. We'll have to talk to them at the local station."

"Coming through!" shouted the interloper. Indeed he was already on his way, behind the downcast faces of half a dozen priests shouldering the newcomers aside.

The police shook their heads at each other and obediently turned sideways at the briskly moving group. "They were sleeping in guest quarters in this wing," the uninvited cop said. "Secure that if you want, along with the refectory. They ate there last night. By the time you're through, I'll have them booked in and ready for you at the station."

Just like that, he was out. Belka watched him shepherd the group to a waiting van, motion them roughly inside, then take off quickly.

He looked down and shook his head. Why would Warsaw have sent surveillance without telling him? And why did the guy say he was from "Internal Security"? That was the name from the old days, the Communist secret force.

"Hey, Jace," he called out to his federal liaison. "You ever see that man before?"

By the time Jace could answer no, the van and its occupants had disappeared down the street.

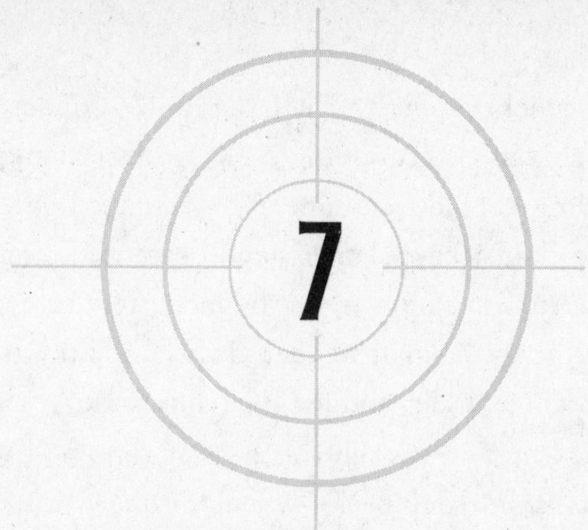

THE VAN WAS REPAINTED, refitted with French license plates, and driven into Germany and eastern France. It skirted Paris and continued on into Normandy, heading unerringly toward the English Channel.

At the coast's edge the priests drove through a gauntlet of darkened tourist hotels and onto a road leading to one of the most recognizable and venerated silhouettes in all of Europe: the nearly triangular rock of Mont-Tombe, the Tomb on the Hill.

Bathed even at this hour by a sea of spotlights, the small triangle of an island jutted upward from the tidal sands below to pierce the gloom with its high monastic spire, crown of the abbey, which gave the sight its name—the most familiar name—of Mont St. Michel.

For over a thousand years this silhouette had ranked among the most famous and inspirational in all of Catholic Europe. The golden statue of St. Michael atop its abbey spire had spurred on a medieval movement, which had once rivaled the Crusades in its numbers and influence. Hundreds of thousands had trudged across the continent to express their fervor for the saint. Today their journeys were all but forgotten, even by the most learned scholars. Yet the statue remained, and the abbey's dank chambers had scarcely changed for centuries.

After the quarter-mile drive to the island's ramparts, the men climbed out quickly, quietly. The group walked under the medieval entry arch, with its surviving trellis gate, and up St. Michel's single, winding cobblestone lane. They climbed away from the small village that occupied the island's base and climbed to the street's end. At the summit stood the monastery gate. One of the men turned to face a small wooden door beside the ticket stand, produced an ancient key, and led them all inside.

He looked up and thought of the first time he had gazed on this summit—from horseback—when the place was little more than a walled abbey crowning a giant finger of rock. He'd been coming to this place since the birth of the Order itself. The cult of St. Michael had been one of the most potent revivals in all of Europe, back at the dawn of the thirteenth century. And its spiritual heart lay right here, where old Father Aubert had seen his vision of Michael and birthed the movement that would eventually bring hordes of pilgrims to this shore for centuries to come.

He had seen the island become a seaward fortress, attacked by ship more times than he could count. The fact that Mont St. Michel had never been conquered, even after whole armadas launched against it during the Hundred Years' War, had become a major source of pride to the French. After the Revolution it had been converted into a prison and had continued as one until just a century ago. Throughout this time the Order had managed to ensconce itself in the abbey's most hidden chambers, sometimes even disguising themselves as soldiers to avoid detection. But the Lazares' use of St. Michel had never faltered.

He shook his head at the satellite dishes discreetly nestled among the medieval rooftops, overlooking the brightly colored tourist buses parked far below. He had finally, after all this time, lived too long.

A lone, middle-aged woman wearing a purple running suit sat on a low wall reading a book and looked up periodically, in apparent anticipation of sunrise. She watched the men disappear with an inquisitive look.

Strange, she thought. But the strangers had entered the sprawling tower with such ease and confidence. They did not wear the Benedictine robes of the monks who officially inhabited the abbey, yet they looked like they belonged.

HE AWOKE AN ETERNITY later from an exhausted traveler's slumber. Beyond the thick wool blanket over him, his face and neck told him this place was chilly. Damp, too. On the other side of the small room, a narrow window issued a pale white light through leaded glass. A candle sat adding its glow on a crude bench beside him, burned to a nub. For all the furnishings around him, he could well have been in . . .

What time, what year, is this?

Again his head swam. He tumbled through time, stumbled to his feet.

He stood and found warm clothes folded neatly at the footboard of his bed. After pulling them on, he opened the room's ancient oak door and glanced down both ends of a long passageway. His eye fell on the nearby sleeping form of a man in monk's robes. A lookout, he supposed, and derelict in his duty, by the looks of it. He tiptoed past the sleeper and on down the hall. The sensation of being lost in time persisted, so strong now that he extended his arm to steady himself against the wall.

He walked along aimlessly for several minutes through a maze of stone passages that turned and twisted until he could not have retraced his steps to save his life. He climbed a stairway for what seemed like an hour, then emerged at last into a column-flanked hallway. He looked between the pillars and saw, far down below him, the intricate stone walls and floor of the abbey's nave. Above him curved the ceiling's soaring medieval arches.

He reached the end of the hallway, spotted a door and opened it. What came next dazzled and delighted him—first, the blinding glare of daylight and, next, the refreshing breeze that engulfed his face and hair. Beyond, perched seemingly in the sky itself, stretched a narrow stone walkway that stretched across the spine of a flying buttress.

He remembered. *The Lace Stairs.*

The relentless wind reminded him that he'd been entombed for over half a century. He stepped out onto the walkway and strode forward. He looked down at the plunge below and squinted. All that stood between him and the bottom several hundred feet down was a profusion of old stone ramparts and the green canopy of trees. On the other side of a stone wall he saw a vast landscape of sand bulging with inter-stitched currents of seawater. Next to the wall, a parking area. Something about the scene struck a familiar chord in him. The area was filled with moving objects.

Motorized vehicles. He remembered. He recalled arriving here the night before in a similar contraption.

He felt freedom as though for the very first time and opened his arms wide, even parting his fingers to catch the most of the seaborne wind. At the wing's apex he stopped, exhilaration coursing through every inch of him, closed his eyes and turned his face toward the sun.

And remembered.

He stands right here, on this very spot, an eternity ago. Two of the Order stand next to him in a bitter winter chill. Far below, a burlap brown, blue, and crimson chain of pilgrims snakes off onto the shore and a far, green horizon. Families with children on their backs and farm animals in tow. Widows and young men, their tattered garments bearing witness to dire poverty and low estate. But also, far off at the end of discernible vision, he makes out a noble party approaching in a flash of gilded coach and shining armor escorts.

"Sire," says the youngest of the two beside him. "Look at them. The Miquelots seem as constant as the waters of the river. Ten thousand yesterday. A total of forty thousand last week. Is it not amazing, this cult of St. Michael?"

"Yes, lad. It surely is."

"All these people dedicating themselves to fighting evil and establishing the good. It seems the darkness of our day may birth a new dawn. The tides turn at last."

He feels himself pull away from the younger man's naïve enthusiasm. "It is a great thing, but I would not go that far. History follows its own way, usually one of endless circles. Follies repeated over and over again. All we can do is to try and live each day for the glory of God. But in tides of righteousness sweeping across mankind, I have little faith."

The other priest guffaws. "Speaking of tides, witness what is about to befall them."

All three peer, and that is when he sees it: a surge of water churning rapidly toward the line of pilgrims. He gasps at the sight: a blue mass reaches inexorably across the sands, and finally, when it seems the tide is upon them, the tracery of human cargo bends desperately away from its onslaught. Screams reach their height. Once-standing people are tossed into bobbing lumps, pitched and carried away. The younger priest clasps a hand over his mouth. The older one, whose observation had presaged this spectacle, shakes his head somberly.

The line of pilgrims has now severed. The nearest half has disintegrated into antlike figures sprinting toward the ramparts for their lives.

An unsteady hand landed softly on his shoulder. A shaky voice spoke.

"Well, my friend. Are you glad to be home?"

He turned to the tanned, shoe-leather road map that was the face of Father Thierry, cleaved just then by the crevice of a smile.

"Thierry, you shouldn't be out here."

"Oh, I've been in far more perilous spots in pursuit of you."

"I never thought of it that way. Yet this does feel like home."

He scrambles over a troublesome knot of stones. A friend walks beside him, breathing heavily. Ahead of them a chapel looms poised atop an outcropping of rock like the promontory at St. Ferret. A square bit of human intention perched upon land's end.

His companion calls out, "They finished building it just last month. It is called the Chapel of Saint Aubert."

He nods absently, for the chapel is indeed beautiful, on the island's tip like this.

But his gaze searches elsewhere. Out toward the misting ocean wind, and the Channel. The thought of what lies—or what used to lie—across that water pierces him again as though the agony had just freshly descended. He can hardly bear to think of Britain, that lovely green archipelago, and all he lost there so very long ago.

He turns back to his friend.

"Yes, Brother Eric. I will come here and pray often."

"It's as much of a home as you've ever had," Thierry continued, dissipating the memory. "And still the Order's home base, you know. I've managed to hang on to that, despite your disappearance. The Vatican has tried four times to disband us, and every time we've survived. Barely."

"I have made it so difficult for you."

"Nonsense. Hardly worse than what you endured."

They paused as the wind hurled a wet gust into their faces.

The old priest smiled. "Anyway, St. Michel has always been a wonderful home base for your mission."

He turned to Thierry with a cold, impassive expression and spat out the words, "My mission? What mission?" He turned back to face the sea and set his lips in a grim line.

"Please. Don't say that," said Thierry.

"Why not? I fight and I fight and for what? For humanity to invent some new form of genocide? Some new weapon of mass murder? Two thousand years and I haven't accomplished a thing. Things are getting worse. I'm the longest running failure in human history."

"But that's not true!" Thierry replied, his voice rising. "Every minute of the last two millennia the destroyer has plotted to kill off humanity in some giant bloodbath or other. You've kept him from succeeding."

"How can you say that? The blood has flowed in rivers the whole time! Maybe my enemy never did want a final massacre. Maybe he was just content with consuming a few million a year. Apocalypse in increments."

"Yet you have succeeded so powerfully, so many times over. And today we need you more than ever!"

"No." He clenched his jaw and shook his head against the sea wind. "The world has left me behind. I know nothing of your . . . technology. There are too many new ways for people to annihilate each other. Too many fronts. Once history could only sustain a few tyrants at a time. The spotting was easy. Today . . . where would I start?"

"You let our helpers inform you; they've always known how to spot your enemy's whereabouts."

"It's so futile. I can't cover up my failure any longer."

"I must tell you, my friend, I do not understand this thinking. It makes me wonder. It makes me question if . . ."

"What, Thierry?"

"This is a question which has pursued me and my predecessors for centuries. No one has had the courage to ask you."

"Please, ask me now."

Thierry began to scrutinize the tops of his feet. His voice, for the first time, took on the nervous tremble of a first-time Lazarian.

He drew a deep breath and began, "All right. So many times you appear to be tortured, pursued by something. Some inner affliction beyond what we would consider the burden of immortality. It seems out of place to us—for someone who has seen heaven, who knew our Lord, to be so deeply tormented."

He winced at Thierry's description. Apparently the old priestly line had been more discerning than he'd thought.

"I want to ask you, my friend," Thierry continued. "What is it? If I am right, if we have all been right, what is it that besets you so?"

He sighed. He'd never expected to face this question.

"Is this improper of me, to ask this? Please tell me, because I do not want to offend you. I only wonder if this is also why you are disillusioned with your mission."

"No, it is not improper," he replied. "Only difficult. I don't know if I am prepared to answer."

"I feel somehow you would be even more suited to the catacon if you *could* answer. And then put it behind you."

"You are very astute, my friend. But the unhappiness you talk about has its roots in failures too old and too deep to change."

"Any wound can be healed. It is the central message of our faith."

"Yes, but . . ." His words trailed off as his limbs constricted suddenly. His eyelids then fluttered as if struck by a foul, cold wind. The image at the core of Thierry's words now flung itself upon him once again.

Blood soaks the man's hair so thickly that it mats into clots. It trickles down past the woven thorns to already sweat-lined features. The man walks slowly, bent low by the weight of his burden; the square wooden beam compresses his cheek flat against its splintered surface. He does not try to duck or avert his face from the rain of rotted fruit and rocks and animal dung that fills the air around him. Nor does he wince at the roar of curses and derisive laughter which fill the lane on either side.

Each new cobblestone jars the load's dragging end; each bump seems to shred another drop of life from his eyes. But he continues walking. To the hill.

Then something catches his attention and he turns slowly to his right, into the crowd. There, behind three shouting teenagers and a man handing stones to a toddler beside him, stands a figure against a stone wall. A man whose eyes gleam with tears.

The two men make eye contact. The condemned man barely registers emotion yet raises his head slightly in recognition. Then his gaze resumes its stare of grim perseverance.

The man at the wall resumes his weeping, and when his sobs cause the spectators before to turn curiously, he steps forward and darts away into a shadowed alley.

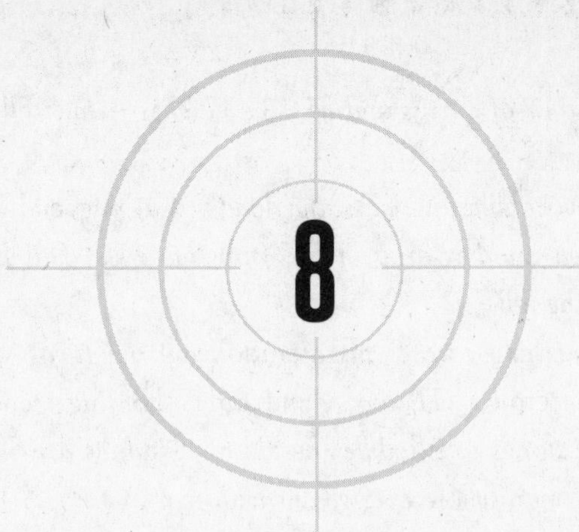

8

HE SHOOK OFF the memory with a vigorous wave of his head. Thierry hadn't noticed the absence, engrossed as he was in his own decisions.

"You will not tell me, then, what it is that makes you so unhappy?" Thierry said. "What happened to make you so reluctant and disheartened?"

"I'm sorry. I see little use in it."

There was a long pause. It seemed to take Thierry some time to absorb the fact that, after broaching a sore subject eight centuries old, he would not be rewarded with an admission. "All right," he said finally. "I suppose the only thing I can do is to show you these, and prove to you how often and how well you have restrained the plots of our enemy. Stay here a moment." The old man rose slowly and shuffled away into the battlements. His shout could be heard before the thick door had even closed behind him. "Stephen! The journal!"

Waiting, he closed his eyes and let the moist wind buffet his hair. He immediately regretted having aired his disillusion to the old priest. Thierry had certainly worked hard enough to find him, and he deserved a little satisfaction for his effort. If only he could have kept his mouth shut. Yet the state of their world had been so shocking, so gut-wrenching. All reserve had fled him immediately.

He opened his eyes to a rustling beside him. Thierry was back, the young priest Stephen behind him, his arms filled with four enormous leather books. The elder gave Stephen a stern look which caused him to dispose of his load with a loud thud.

Thierry turned around and winced at the awkwardness, but then his composure quickly returned. He straightened his neck and shoulders, tapped on the top book with a bony index finger, and said, "These, my friend, are the collected volumes of your journal, written over two thousand plus years. Or at least two of twenty-three volumes we've collected, copied, and translated from Hebrew, Latin, and Old English."

The man stared at the book.

"Here," said Thierry, struggling to lift the book toward him. "Read it. You'll see what a failure you've been."

So he took the book from the old man's trembling grasp, flipped it around and opened to the middle, then began to read.

Paris, Isle de St. Louis—1942

It is two in the morning. As I cannot sleep, I might as well write and make a record of this awful day.

A late night thunderstorm has blown in from the north, not only bringing moisture but a balm of sorts to my thoughts. I hear the patter of raindrops and remind myself that these same clouds, this same weather, stood only hours ago above England and freedom. A damp breeze billows the curtains and fills the room with a cool intrusion I find soothing. The drumming against my old tiled roof calms me. The slurping of water in the drain gutters takes me back to Ireland, to happier, more serene times—spring nights when the rains never seemed to end and life's sheer abundance warmed my chest like the glow from an old wine. Tonight, distant lightning flashes against the apartment walls, silhouettes the old menorah above my mantelpiece and the hulking armoire I rescued from the siege of Orleans. The sudden light of it brings back the recent nights of shelling, back when France was free. I choose to think of another memory, though. The spotlights from those old sightseeing boats that used to sail by in better days, loaded with people soaking in the ambiance of nighttime Paris.

Once I cherished the peace and quiet of Isle St. Louis, isolated on its small island by the timeless lapping of the Seine. But I realize now that the serenity only meant something next to the liveliness of the Left Bank, indeed of Paris herself. Today all the music and dancing and boisterous café life has been swallowed up by the echoes of jackboots and perfect German columns, by the emphatic warnings of curfew posters, everything stamped with that horrible slanted cross of theirs.

I cannot believe what I learned today. Even now, buried in my blankets, hours removed from the hearing of it, I can do little more than shudder my thoughts loose from the knowledge. The image. I fail, of course, and my stomach heaves at the very words used to name such a thing. I first heard of it this morning, from the gasping breath of Yves Debuirre, a young resistance courier fresh from the pursuit of a group of plain-clothed Gestapo through the alleys of the Latin Quarter. His ordeal had made him over an hour late for our rendezvous; Brother Michael and I had walked seventy-two rounds around the church in itchy, ill-fitting civilian clothes, trying to conceal our dread by keeping our eyes fixed on the cobblestones ahead and the tattered shoes of our fellow Parisians.

Then a clatter of footsteps erupted behind us. Brother Michael was about to wheel around, but I, the more experienced prey, restrained him. The source of the commotion passed us, and we barely recognized him from the faded identity card handed me by his captain just two nights before in a Montmartre bar. In an instant, I recognized his bulging ears and prominent nose, and his knapsack, its free strap tied with five centimeters of red string.

Spinning around, he almost fell backward at the sound of our voices. Then, amused by his own awkwardness, he broke into a broad grin and steadied himself upon a stone wall.

We ushered him inside to the church's deepest chamber. It was there, after taking receipt of the forged identity papers, coded safe-house maps and intelligence memos, that he told us. Once beyond the physical comedy of our meeting, he had reverted to a haunted, maddened young man. His eyes unblinking, lips perpetually twitching this or that half-formed word, he seemed fixed on a place faraway. It became clear he was terrified by something far more horrible than his own recent brush with death.

He threw down his last gulp of ersatz coffee, then began to stare wildly at the black shape of the escape passage in the chamber's far corner, barely in reach of the waning candlelight. He would not look us in the eye. For a moment the only motion his body made was the bobbing of his Adam's apple.

Finally he took three photographs from his front coat pocket. "It's true," he said bitterly. "There have been rumors of them for months. But it's true."

The first photograph showed a large brick edifice, its central wall plastered with a large Nazi flag. Behind it towered a high smokestack spewing a thick brown cloud. In the foreground snaked a railroad line and a procession of old cattle cars. People were issuing from their black doors, pooling into a vast crowd surrounding them. German soldiers with dogs stood in a row before the crowd, frozen in poses of imperious command.

The second showed a squat brick building with a smokestack rising up from its rear roofline, the same chimney from the previous shot.

And the third, dear Lord, showed a huge pit filled with naked, emaciated bodies. At the forefront a miserable-looking prisoner stared at the camera, his arms holding up a wagon loaded with corpses. It hit me then.

The wagon was headed for the building with the smokestack.

It is not a concentration camp, as most of the world supposes, but a death camp. The very term chills me. An entire complex dedicated to the speedy and orderly eradication of human beings.

Brother Michael and I forgot to breathe for nearly a full minute. When I thought to return to myself, I felt rooted in place by a lead ball in the pit of my stomach, a dread as heavy as the earth itself. I looked over to Michael and his eyes were shut, his mouth shuddering open, tears streaming down his cheeks.

I remember being struck by a single terrifying thought. He has succeeded at last. Destroyer has sought without success all these eons for the perfect, efficient means to slake his appetite for death. Now he has brought it to reality. His new, foul masterpiece, centuries in the preparation. Even the flimsy pretext for making the Chosen People his first victims betrays his handiwork. The enemy of humanity has reached his zenith.

I know this is a challenge I must meet. Still, I wish to be taken from it. I do not wish to live in a world where such things can go on. Even my own mental picture of hell itself, nurtured over centuries of thought, cannot match the horror of those pictures. Those cattle cars, the corpse-filled pit.

These days, to be human is nothing. I am ashamed of my own species.

His first words after looking up were filled with dread and a palpable sense of loathing.

"I remember now. I did go to Berlin. There was a greater concentration of demonic forces surrounding that man than I had ever seen in my life. Destroyer was alerted to my presence before I came within a mile of Hitler."

"You were almost captured by the Waffen SS."

He nodded.

"But instead you returned to Paris," continued Thierry, "and redirected your efforts toward resistance. Especially after you learned what they were doing in the camps."

He began thumbing frantically through the volume, finally settling on a page. "Here. Here is the entry for the day, years earlier, when I first realized what a threat Hitler would be."

Paris, Les Deux Magots—April 22, 1932

It is raining this afternoon, and glorious. Paris is never more herself than on days like this one, her leaden sky perfectly matched to her soot-stained buildings, clouds drizzling a fine mist which fogs the café windows and, when I venture out hours from now, will have caused the sidewalks to glisten and the cobblestones of Boulevard St. Germain to shine like Dutch clogs at a high polish.

Never do I feel more anonymous and assimilated into the ordinary stream of human life than on languorous Parisian afternoons like these. This city causes me to feel that time does not actually race forward at a gallop but inches forward instead through a mire of history and emotion.

Which is not to say I have not seen the city change enormously. Only that in the midst of her reinventions, she has never stopped seeming eternal. I look out across Rue Bonaparte at the weathered stones of the chapel and a knot of melancholy forms in my chest. Modern life vanishes from my sight; the beeping motor scooters and Citroëns and diesel vans disappear, along with the whole background roar of modern Paris.

Then memory's eye returns an image almost a thousand years old: the view from St. Germain's yet unfinished bell tower on a windy, blue morning. Beside me stands a thin young novice as nervous of my exotic reputation among the clergy as of the risk he has taken to afford me this clandestine view. The humid breeze, fresh from a dawn rainstorm, has pushed away the residual stench of Paris's open sewers, and I remember taking an exuberant lungful of air and throwing out my arms at the sight.

A quarter of a mile away, beyond the dirty ramparts of the Phillippe-Auguste Wall, the largest city in Europe lies before me in a jumble of brown roofs and upthrust chapel spires. To the side I can make out the path of the Seine and its clear waters dotted with a dozen or so hardy swimmers' heads. On our own Left Bank, the steeples of two old churches, St. Severin and St. Sulpice, tower over a burgeoning student district where hotheads like Abelard have begun sowing seeds of intellectual discord.

To their left, even grander sights dwarf them: the twin bridges Pont Neuf and Petit Pont, their spans lined with the high roofs of houses in whose shadows thrive the land's busiest markets. And behind them, the most stunning sight of all: Notre Dame, her piercing heights a century old yet still girded with the ladders and scaffolding of unending modifications. Closer still on the Ile-de-la-Cité, the slate-roofed towers of the king's palace shine brightly in the sun. I look down, beyond the abbey's gardens and their stagnant moat, and watch a cordon of ox-mongers and farmers deliver poultry and livestock for the Petit Pont's variety of food vendors, and I think, this is life. No matter its miseries, human existence can have its exquisite moments.

I have never stopped needing Paris's agelessness. I hunger for that sense of permanence, of the past not only surviving but defining the present. Today makes me feel that I could sit forever with the old wall at my back and let the reek of Gauloise cigarettes and the bliss of good wine drift me through until evening. And were I fortunate enough to fall asleep for a decade, I would wake up and find the world little changed.

Yesterday, the seat I sit in now was occupied for nearly three hours by a popular American writer by the name of Ernest Hemingway. I remember his name mostly because no one could forget him; his booming voice and outsized bearlike manner filled the room to bursting. I imagine he would have been kicked out in minutes had it not been for his literary celebrity and the excellent polish of his French, two things which count for a great deal in today's Paris. The comedy of it is that he sat huddled with a darkly beautiful native girl and tried to seduce her with every physical tic in the male arsenal and every bit of slang in his impressive yet far-from-native patois *vocabulary. Every few minutes the girl would reach back in her long black hair to flip it backward and with a rapid glance assess the extent of her betrayal in the eyes of her surrounding countrymen.*

Addled by his romantic failure and the multiplying shots of Pernod, this Hemingway character grew red in the face and increasingly intense in his demeanor. By the time he offered to write her into his upcoming novel, a proposal greeted with an almost communal guffaw by the assembled patronage, the girl was rolling her eyes and actively sweeping off her coat in anticipation of departure. And finally she did leave, with nothing more than a patronizing kiss in the beard and pat on the thigh to the American. Hemingway sat and stewed for another half hour, comforted by four more shots, before stumbling out the door and into the waiting outflung doors of a taxicab.

That is Paris life, and it seems it will always be so. But for one major exception. In the pages of Le Monde *newspaper, I just read where my age-old enemy will strike next. An hour ago this very newspaper informed me of the end of all that lies about me. It seems the destroyer has found a predictably mad human host from which to resume his murderous work against the human race. Once again he has selected a pawn from within the coterie of madmen who continuously jostle for power behind the surface hum of everyday life. Part of me wants to yawn at the predictability of it, except for the innocent women and children whose bodies, I know, will soon line the roads of central Europe like cordwood.*

The newest human carrier of the destroyer and his henchmen is a megalomaniac named Adolf Hitler. He has marched across the Germanic stage for years. But today's picture in the newspaper shows the man leaning from a podium before a crowd of Nazis that seems to stretch to eternity with such an expression in his eyes that I can practically see the destroyer's spirit clinging to the man.

I looked up from this photograph and saw a figure I had not seen before, sitting at a small table like my own, not five meters away. A handsome young man who stared intently into my eyes.

I could see the booth behind him through his transparent chest cavity.

He nodded and looked down at my paper. I looked down instinctively, then up again, and he was gone.

It is my signal. My alarm was confirmed; in fact, it was most likely planted there by the spiritual helpers who serve as my advance scouts and vanguards.

I will go right away, tomorrow even, to Berlin and find a way to approach this beast and the archdemon inhabiting him. With the help of others, I hope to get close enough to say my exorcist's prayer.

Truth be known, I find the tyrants of today somewhat of a bore. One-dimensional thugs compared to the fascinating lunatics of yesteryear. Frederick the Great, now that was a conqueror worth watching for an evening's entertainment. I came within twenty yards of the man once, in his stateroom, before the destroyer spotted me and leaped from the man with a supernatural shriek.

I've been spoiled these last fifteen years, huddled in the cozy hum of Paris life awaiting the destroyer's next move, lulled into passivity by the end of the "War to End All Wars," the comforts of my great wealth, and my crushing fatigue with battles and tyrants and the relentless nature of evil.

Tomorrow I will contact the Order and begin a plan to get close to this madman, make yet another attempt to dispatch this demon to hell forever. It will be my first encounter with Hitler, but with the infernal beast manipulating him, I cannot count all the battles.

Sometimes I ask, dear Lord, what is the point? In all these years, have I accomplished a thing with all the scheming, the endless cycles of pursuit and escape? Prevented one death which would not have someday occurred through pestilence or accident, or even old age? Are the poor souls dispatched in the century's wars any worse off, truly, than the living dead who trudge through the muddy roads of rural Europe?

I know I would join the dead in a heartbeat, if I could.

It will happen soon, I can feel it. The titans will jostle each other vigorously enough to set off some sort of conflagration for their own amusement. And millions will die.

For the moment, I think I'll have another glass of pastis.

And in the morning, it's off to Berlin.

9

After finishing, his eyes scanned the ground and his head shook, whether as a gesture of negation or some residual palsy the old priest could not discern.

"I do remember. The war. The Nazis. The resistance. The camps . . ."

They fell silent as a young tourist passed just behind them, gazing upward at the spire of St. Michel. Soon they were out of earshot again.

"Why don't you spend several days with four or five of the volumes. We will try not to disturb you until you return to us. Until you want company."

A fine mist drifted among the towers of St. Michel. Had anyone stood on the abbey's terrace and looked out toward England, they would have only seen tiny droplets hurled against their face, and an implacable darkness. At this late hour all tourists had deserted the island and slept in shoreline hotels miles away. Most of the Mont's inhabitants were asleep, too. It was not a night for walking the walls or climbing the steps of the Grande Rue.

Yet had anyone navigated the claustrophobic darkness and descended to places which the thickest St. Michel guidebooks labeled with such vague phrases as "Romanesque substructures" or "Chapel basements," they would have been astonished. Even the monks who had occupied St. Michel for decades did not know what lay behind some of its moldering, hopelessly locked doors. The place was so full of old, abandoned passageways and unsafe halls that even they did not attempt to explore or catalog all of them.

Furthermore, the secret denizens of these forgotten places had not returned to their haunts in many years themselves. In years past, they had mingled with the regular monks as though merely day-tripping clerics. They'd proven so unobtrusive and fleeting that no alarm had ever been raised to their presence.

There had been rumors—back when France's secular revolution had turned the Mont into a prison—that mysterious, reclusive figures of priests haunted its lower floors. The religious inmates had satisfied themselves with the explanation that these sightings consisted of the souls of recently martyred priests.

Only thousands of miles away in Rome, written in the Vatican's most obscure documents, was Mont St. Michel registered as home base to the Order of St. Lazare.

Deep inside their hidden quarters, so deep he actually occupied a hollowed-out spot in the Mont's stone foundation, he sat huddled in robes on a pine bench, reading yet another of Thierry's enormous volumes.

Reading about his life. Reliving what he had tried so often to forget.

New York Harbor—May 2, 1889

I must be the last passenger occupying a deck chair on the Finlandia. *Every other soul aboard this ship has taken a place at the foredeck rail to watch the magnificent sight of New York City inch toward us. Brits and Poles and Irish and Italians line the rails before me with their derbies in their fists and their jaws slack in awe. I would be with them if not for my need to recline while writing this entry, and for the fact that I can see the most astounding part of the panorama above the watchers' heads.*

It would seem most logical to write that a cacophony of exclamations and shouts of wonder has filled the decks, but the opposite is true. Rather a hush has fallen over the spectators ever since the Statue of Liberty glided into sight, and it has persisted since. All I hear now is the wind, the cry of seagulls, and the slapping of waves against the ship's hull.

How can I describe what I feel upon seeing such a sight as the skyline before us? In all my years I have never seen such a monument to human strength of will. It seems as though a mountain range of steel and glass suddenly thrust itself skyward from the depths of the sea. Along with this, although I cannot see them just yet, a race of scurrying, industrious, indomitable caretakers called Americans.

I cannot believe I waited so long to visit this land. Well, actually, I can. In the early years, while reports of its size and majesty stole one's breath away, the place was also described as alternately disease-ridden, uninhabitable, blood-soaked, choked with murderous savages, and wracked with innumerable wars of conquest. I could see its attraction for poor class-locked Europeans looking for a place of new beginning, or refugees of the horrid Potato Famine. Yet I craved no such excitement myself.

By the time its proverbial smoke cleared, more sober reporters nevertheless failed to paint an appreciably prettier picture. While various persecuted groups made haste to voyage here and set up housekeeping, the New World remained a harsh, unkempt cauldron of lawlessness and death. I had far too much preoccupying me in Europe, what with the task of thwarting the destroyer at every turn in every royal court in the continent. For every prolific bucket of blood shed in

America, it seemed a river of the same flowed in Europe.

This new nation, the United States of America, I admit I never thought would last. My first reports of its Constitution made it seem too drenched in the gauzy sentiment of Rousseau and his fellow French moon-gazers to appear workable. Finally, twenty-some odd years after its adoption, I chanced across a copy of its words in a London bookshop, and found it eminently cunning and practical.

I think more than anything, I underestimated the pent-up desire and energy of the European underclass, trodden upon and held down for millennia, for a piece of their own land. Not that I doubted such a sentiment existed; rather I failed to grasp its potency. Watching this continent rise from the sea, I realize now the power unleashed by the discovery of hope, of the sentiments etched into the base of that marvelous statue still in my view.

I have seen that strength shining in the eyes of my shipmates, for I have enjoyed a few serviceable conversations with some of them on this voyage. One was a beautiful young couple from Portugal, Daniel and Rosa DeSilva. Rosa possesses the clearest, almost turquoise eyes. They marveled at my command of their language, which I tried to explain away with some mumbled excuse. He is a metalworker who hopes to find work in the construction industry of New York. From the looks of it he will find plenty. She is six months with child, their first. I cannot tell if the terror brimming from those eyes results from their uncertain relocation, or impending motherhood, or both.

Altogether, though, I find ships to be one of the loneliest ways for me to travel. Something about it makes folks inquisitive and gregarious; they feel unusually free to inquire into the respective stories of everyone they meet. After all, on a trans-continental steamer, everyone is a story. But the practice forces me to become reticent, even dishonest at times, a tendency I detest.

Through the railing I can see the quays themselves. What a mass of humanity! The number of souls crowded into this one large city, let alone the continent beyond it, boggles the mind. All I can see is a quivering ocean of gray suits, waving arms, and pale, upturned faces. The scale of this place makes me want to huddle in my flannels with eyes wide as saucers.

How could a place this enormous have remained unknown for so many years? It is unbelievable. I think of all the generations past who lived ignorant of this landmass larger than Europe and Africa combined.

And by the looks of these things called skyscrapers, the balance of power and influence has shifted. The familiar haunts of Europe no longer house the seat of control. This country and these unstoppable people will fashion a new world and a powerful economy for its inhabitants—I am sure of it. Europe will seem dusty and tired after this. No matter her virtues, her beauty and charm, she will always seem like a faded garment lying folded in an old trunk beneath a crumbling mothball. There is a vitality attached to this land that no empire or kingdom could possibly match.

And that is why I am here. For where there is ascendant power, my enemy will be there also. Every spiritual sinew within me screams out that the archdemon I have pursued for centuries has taken up residence in this upstart nation and plans to exploit it for his evil purposes.

I am here to find him, to ferret him out from this massive society and catch him unawares. I know he considers me an effete Continental and so will not expect me, especially having tarried from coming here for so long.

Another fact also draws me to this place. Since the awful famine of 1848, most of my surviving descendants have moved to these United States.

I have flesh and blood in this land.

FATHER THIERRY LED his friend down a winding staircase and into the abbey's interior, their movements illuminated by candles guttering from wall sconces.

They reached the refectory, where the old man stepped aside to let the other enter first. At first the man hardly recognized the room. It now glowed with candlelight flickering orange against a barrel-vaulted ceiling. Along one of the dining hall's long tables, the other six members of the Order of St. Lazare sat before bottles of wine, hot French bread and steaming plates of food. The men rose as he entered. When he smiled in surprise, they broke into a light applause which echoed eerily through the chamber. He covered his eyes with a look of faint embarrassment and turned to Father Thierry. "Of course. I had forgotten," he said.

"I never did," Thierry answered. "I have looked forward to this night for many years."

The old priest pulled out a chair at the head of the table and motioned for him to sit. After he had done so, Thierry stepped forward and grasped a corner to steady himself.

Sitting among the other priests, Stephen thought Father Thierry had never looked so frail. It seemed the culmination of his quest had quenched that energy which had always animated his ninety-five-year-old body. He'd first noticed the change in Thierry three hours earlier, when the old priest had gathered the others in his chamber and addressed them while resting on a cot. "*Of course you know,*" he had said in a low voice, "*that this is the fifth time the Order has rescued him from such a horrible confinement. You would think the enemy would get the message, but then again, the dungeon is his only recourse against an adversary he cannot kill.*" Thierry had drawn a deep, wavering breath. "*Our Order has a tradition of sharing a meal to celebrate his rescue. He does not need nourishment, of course, but the taste of good food and the warmth of human companionship help him readjust to this world. It is a chance for each of you to commune with him, to befriend him for yourselves. So prepare a hearty meal, Brothers. You deserve it.*" Then Thierry had shut his eyes and, before the priests could rise and leave the room, fallen fast asleep.

The men had thrown themselves into the task of preparing a feast. Stephen and several of the younger priests staged a covert raid on the abbey's larder only to find a meager store of vegetables and a few chickens. So the men shed their cassocks and walked incognito to the village store and had returned with special foods that for years they'd dreamed of enjoying.

Now, with the dinner before him, Stephen eased himself into the chair across from the man they had rescued. *Lassalle*, he reminded himself. *André Lassalle.*

Stephen thought their guest seemed far more ordinary now than when they had first seen him—a wild man standing in the rubble of a ruined grave. His hair was cut neatly short, his body clothed in a gray wool sweater and corduroy pants.

"Thank you," he said in a voice so low some of the men had to lean forward to hear. "Thank you for believing. No generation of the Order has ever persevered so long with so little direct knowledge of my existence. You honor me."

After Father Theodore uttered the shortest prayer of thanks in ecclesiastical history, the feasting began. Many people outside the Order wouldn't have considered it a sumptuous meal, but to priests who were used to years of monastic fare, it seemed beyond description.

The wine was poured, and platters of coq au vin, rotisserie chicken, steamed asparagus, and Camembert cheese with baguettes began crisscrossing the table. The conversation started out slowly. Father Moll asked for the butter in a halting voice, glancing awkwardly about him with his gaze roaming everywhere except to the head of the table. Stephen eyed the full glasses of Merlot with a sly grin and asked, "Who here will be the designated driver?" But only a few tentative laughs resulted.

Finally their guest spoke. "Please, men, celebrate. I am so happy just to be here. There's no need to be timid." The men exchanged glances and soon a spirited debate ensued concerning the relative beauty of the world's cathedrals. For priests deprived of newspapers or television, it was as controversial a topic as they could imagine. Each one asserted the superiority of his native land's churches, with Stephen finally pointing out the splendor of the National Cathedral to a chorus of snickers and good-natured gibes about America's lack of culture.

At one point in the dinner, Stephen glanced over to the head of the table. Lassalle's eyes were closed and his head reclined as if he were inhaling deeply. Soon the food started to run out. One by one, the priests began to rise and walk over to meet their guest. The first was Father Justin, who embraced the smaller man in a bear hug. A tall, muscular forty-year-old from a long line of Welsh miners, Justin pulled back and spoke in a voice husky with emotion, "We have so longed to see you." He engulfed the man in another hug to hide his sobs. Over his shoulder the men saw Lassalle's eyes also fill with tears.

They hadn't dried by the time Father Carl, the German language scholar, crouched meekly before him and, in a shaky voice, said, "I cannot imagine what it would feel like . . . to live so long. Or if I could even bear it."

Their guest shook his head. He paused for a long while before replying, "At times it is a blessing." He looked away and brushed at his eyes. "But now so many people and families I loved are gone. . . ." His voice drifted off. "I have you men. You are my family now. I have no one else left."

Carl looked into the man's eyes, smiled and said, "Of course. And we will always be there for you."

Stephen went to meet him last. When he sat beside the man, he looked away, unable to meet his gaze. "I must ask your forgiveness," Stephen said abjectly. He felt a hand touch his shoulder and knew that his friend was smiling at him.

"I know what you're going to say. You're the youngest, aren't you?"

"Yes."

"As the youngest you are also the farthest removed from the last time I walked the earth. And so you have harbored doubts as to my existence. You have struggled."

Hearing it spoken out loud, and by this man, was nearly too much for Stephen. He clenched his jaw, blinked rapidly and willed himself to breathe. "Yes . . . and I had no cause to disbelieve, except that the work was hard. But that is no excuse."

"I understand. Let me tell you something, Stephen. If I were your age and knew what you knew, I might have walked away from the Order altogether."

Stephen nodded gratefully as the man leaned in with a grin. "Besides. You remind me of Thierry when he was younger."

Thierry erupted into a spasm of protestations at the remark, and the Brothers of St. Lazare indulged themselves in a long communal laugh.

EXCEPT FOR THE WHITE WOODEN cross towering from its rooftop and the tall visitor in bishop's robes knocking at its door, it would have resembled another of the dark-bricked Nazi ruins. Yet, for the last ten years, the former *SS Kommandatur* building along Birkenau's far northwest corner had served as a Catholic retreat center, a place for spiritual contemplation in this bleak remnant of evil.

The building's heavy doors swung slowly open and plunged a wedge of autumn light into the darkened vestibule, as well as the soft features of the parish priest, Father Tsackiewski. The priest's expectant smile, an expression he reserved for important guests, faded instantly at the sight of the figure before him. His visitor seemed etched in gray from a halo of light; all the priest could make out was a slate outline. Tsackiewski took a step closer and saw through the shadow a pair of eyes whose cold fire reminded him of the starving pack of dogs he had run from as a boy. He suppressed a shudder and revived his faint smile for the guest. "Bishop Eccles?"

"Yes."

"Please, enter."

"Thank you."

They walked inside, crossed the vestibule into the chapel. Tsackiewski was accustomed to wide, assessing glances which new visitors aimed across the chapel's understated furnishings. Eccles, however, kept his gaze glued to his host.

"Father Tsackiewski," Eccles began in a low voice, "it must be quite remarkable, ministering in such a place."

"Yes, it is."

"So much evil. So many . . . enduring scars."

The younger priest shook off his malaise. He nodded, his usual manner of launching into the familiar speech. "I have learned to think of this chapel as an outpost, Father. A beachhead if you will, here on the edge of a spiritual void. Like Saint Patrick before the boundary of a wild, pagan land."

The bishop turned and fixed a half-lidded sneer upon the young man. "I can see you think highly of your station in this place."

"No, you misunderstand me, Father. I . . ." Tsackiewski swallowed before engaging his defense. He had not intended to appear self-important. "Before coming here I read the stories of the survivors, as a form of penance almost, and I came to account after account of highly religious Jews screaming in the gas chambers, 'God, where are you? Why have you deserted us?' After reading such horrifying tales, I reached the conclusion that the Nazis had actually managed to carve out a spiritually blighted corner of the world. A place where God did not show himself."

"So you think this is a place unlike any other?"

"I do. Nowhere else have such monstrosities been allowed to take place."

"But surely you do not believe this place to be free of all spiritual activity?"

He hesitated. "No, I suppose not. But so much of the activity has been purely, utterly evil."

"Ah, so you have heard of Oswiecim House, then."

Tsackiewski blanched and sputtered, "You mean the, uh, research center?"

Eccles smiled benignly. Knowledge of the House's existence was an official secret, yet hardly unknown to most within the local diocese. "Of course. I am its Vatican liaison."

A chill ran down the priest's spine and caused him to shiver so suddenly that he worried the bishop might notice.

"And as such," Eccles continued, "I would disagree with your theory. This area experiences huge amounts of supernatural phenomena. I would call it anything but a spiritual vacuum. Quite the contrary. It's as if the Nazi misbehavior created a fertile breeding ground for forces—spiritual armies. Only of another sort. A most useful dynamic, from a research point of view."

The younger man felt the last of his patience evaporate. Bishop or not, the visitor was proving maddeningly combative.

"You draw a fine distinction, sir. Overall, though, I find my contemplation time better spent elsewhere than upon the subject of the demonic."

Eccles smiled again at the gentle rebuke. "That's most regrettable," he said. "I was going to invite you to come visit us sometime."

A long silence passed between them. Tsackiewski would not offend his guest with an outright refusal, but the thought of entering the House filled him with a dread even greater than the one he felt in this man's presence.

"Father Tsackiewski, I will come to the point. Have there been any unusual goings-on in the last several days?"

"I don't know what you mean."

"Have you had any visitors?"

The young priest opened his mouth to speak, then suddenly felt an inner urge not to answer, not to tell this man what he'd seen over the past ten days. Still, the voice of obedience ordered him to reply. The man was, after all, a bishop. He felt the words leave his lips. "Yes, of course. The diggers."

"The what?"

"The priests who came to excavate. They spent six days in the meadow just outside. They would not say what they were searching for. And one day, they left with no warning."

"Who were they?"

"Priests, that's all I know. They were very secretive. I did not recognize anything about their cassocks. Their leader was a very old priest, introduced himself in the name of the Holy Father."

The bishop's expression turned angry. "What exactly were these men looking for?" he asked.

"I'm not sure. But they asked a lot of questions about the Birkenau boundaries and the existence of any buried structures in the meadow between us."

"What did you tell them?"

"I told them why the plot just east of here has never been farmed. Local peasants say the Nazis buried cement vaults containing live prisoners between this spot and the camp gates. They swear the ground is cursed. Few even walk on it. If not for our chapel, the surrounding area would be deserted."

"What did these priests do then?"

"They brought out underground scanning equipment and spent the next few days digging the pit you see outside."

Eccles planted his fists on his hips. "You did not bother ascertaining these men's identities before allowing them to dig up such a revered site?"

"With all due respect, Bishop, I know a brother in the cloth when I meet him."

"Oh, really! And all your heavenly discernment never led you to notice that the clergy is riddled with half-baked fanatics, seniles, and outright lunatics?"

"Well, I know great differences exist. . . ."

Eccles stepped forward, only inches now from the younger priest's chest. "You fool! You've signed the death warrant of this chapel and your own career. You allowed the most delusional sect in all of Christendom to desecrate a Jewish site. By week's end this place will be crawling with protesters. The only way to placate the Zionists will be to close this place down."

Eccles turned on his heels and strode out the front door. When the doors groaned again and then shut, Tsackiewski breathed normally again. As menacing as Eccles's words had been, he could only think of one thing. How relieved he felt at the man's departure.

Walking back to the Mercedes, Eccles reached inside his cassock and, with an impulsive jerk of the wrist, flipped open a cellular phone.

"Tiller, it's the Lazarians. Start a full-scale campaign. Today."

Mont St. Michel—Two Days Later

"WELL, MY FRIEND, have you reached a decision?"

"What decision?"

"Are you a failure? Will you abandon the mission God entrusted to you?"

He smiled at Thierry's inflammatory phrasing—although none of it was inaccurate. He stepped around a throng of Japanese tourists milling their way through the Knight's Room's broad esplanade and smiled at his aging protector.

"I've read many of the diaries, and I am still reading them. The translation is well done. I suppose my contribution has had some impact. It's not for me to say. As for a decision, I have only decided one thing. My hatred for the destroyer and all of Satan's works outweighs my disgust for their human lackeys."

"So you will continue?"

He chuckled at the priest's persistence. "Yes. I will make one last attempt at finding my enemy and dispatching him."

"The Order is at your disposal. Never forget that."

He turned to face Thierry, clasped him about the man's bony

shoulders, and said with a smile, "I know. But this I must do alone. My enemy has always started our engagements by picking on a member of the Firstborn. I'll start there."

"I understand. If you get into trouble, please call on us."

"I will. I will call you on my new . . ." He reached into his pocket and retrieved a phone. "What is it you call this device?"

"A satellite phone."

"That's right. You and Father Stephen have taught me so much these past days."

"Be sure to check your e-mail, too. Again, if you need assistance, call us."

"Thank you. I will."

He stepped out of a tourist's snapshot frame and disappeared.

THREE DAYS LATER, he went missing. The priests of the Order searched the abbey from top to bottom, but he was nowhere to be found. Stranger still, his clothes had remained in his armoire. Thierry spent an hour in the refectory, moaning in his native Breton that the *least* he expected was prior notice of the man's departure. Bad enough the man had abandoned the Order on some of his most sensitive missions. But not to tell Thierry, to let him fear the worst . . .

He immediately sent the Brothers to investigate the areas beyond the abbey, to search for any sign of his having been abducted.

That's when Father Stephen found him, out on the bay's sand flats. He had in the end not proven hard to find, for he'd erected an ungainly pile of sand, one nearly as tall as himself.

When Stephen reached him, he was perched on one foot. He whirled around and delivered a brutal punch that struck the sand with a flat *thud* and almost sent the pile toppling.

He paused at the sight of the young priest and began to wipe sand from his hands.

"*Kan shu,*" he said, turning back to the sandpile.

"What?" asked the priest with more than a trace of irritation.

"*Kan shu.* The penetration hand. An old Chinese method for building up a fighter's hand endurance. You're supposed to start by hitting powder and work your way up to pebbles, but I only have sand."

"You practice martial arts?" Stephen said, sounding surprised.

"Out of sight from the Order, whenever possible. Thierry and his predecessors have known I had made several trips to the Orient. I think they pretend not to know that I studied."

He turned back to the sandpile. In a split second his body became a whirling pivot, his arms and hands delivering whiplike blows that slapped loudly and left deep indentations in the sand. He paused and spoke without turning away from the structure.

"*Kwonbop.* Another unarmed Chinese form that spread to Korea in the Middle Ages. I also studied with a Muslim teacher in Sinkiang who taught me *Cha chuan*, a northern Chinese form of *kung fu*.

"You don't actually believe their creeds, do you?" Stephen said.

"You mean, do I embrace eastern spirituality? Don't worry. I am a follower of Christ. I simply recognize the knowledge that others have acquired. And in winning the fight in front of me, I have to prepare, take any advantage I can."

Without taking his eyes off of Stephen, he launched himself against the shape and slammed his hands together. Had the spot been a human neck, it would have been pulverized.

"What do you practice?" Stephen wanted to know.

"A little of everything. I've traveled widely. That last move was from *Liu Gar*, a *kung fu* derivative which I learned in southern China. It is designed especially for close-range fighting. I threw in a little *Kogusoku*, probably the oldest of all the Japanese martial arts, especially in the unarmed category." He looked sharply back at Stephen. "You know I'm going to America, to challenge my enemy. I have no doubt their operatives will be armed with the latest weapons. I don't intend to kill any of them. I've always found a way around that."

He pushed the remaining sandpile backward. "*Ch'ueh Yuan*. Ancestor to karate. This is my way."

Rome—Two Days Later

ECCLES'S FIRST STEP into the room still hung midair when the fist struck the back of his head. His body careened into the wall as the Persian rug slid out from under his feet. His right ear smashed into wood. Suddenly his vision filled with a gun muzzle and a face with young features.

"Hello, my friend."

Hands patted his sides, searched his robes and pockets, then gripped his arms and pulled him up. His attacker now grinned at him like a collegial acquaintance as he brought the weapon around to his shoulder.

"Bishop Eccles, I am so glad you returned from your trip. I myself have come a long way to find you."

Eccles reached up to feel blood trickling from the side of his head. "Who are you?"

The man grabbed the skin around his own neck and pulled. A thin mask peeled off his head with a rubber squeak, revealing a dark complexion and black mustache. The smile never faded.

Eccles recognized the face from the cover of a dozen newsmagazines and television reports over the last fifteen years. Jamail, the Palestinian terrorist. Responsible for the massacre of fourteen Israeli tourists at a refueling stop in Athens. Architect of countless Hamas bombing campaigns. Reputed al-Qaeda liaison. Ideologically indifferent, simply committed to slaughtering Westerners, and feared across four continents.

Jamail spoke again, only this time his voice was deeper, otherworldly. "I am your servant. I have waited my whole life for this moment." Suddenly he knelt on the bunched-up rug, took Eccles's hand and kissed it reverently. The brown face looked up, saw Eccles furrow his brow, and snarled, "No, not you. Him. Destroyer."

At once, Eccles's consciousness was not his own as the monstrous voice spoke through his lips, "My human enemy is loose. I want him and his work finished once and for all. And then I want everyone who knows of his existence killed."

Jamail stood and said, "Yes, my lord. A worthy task. Who do I kill first?"

BOSTON

11

Cambridge, Massachusetts, Harvard Yard—One Week Later

THE SIGN OUTSIDE THAYER HALL read, *Ancient Athens: History's First Dysfunctional Family*. Inside, an oak-paneled auditorium contained a scattering of graduate students wearing jaded faces and blearily awaiting the mandatory lecture. The time came. The promised visiting professor of psychology, bearded and rumpled in the requisite corduroy attire, stood at a Harvard University podium and began to speak.

Five minutes later, the stranger walked in and slumped in the back row, dressed in jeans and a denim jacket. At first glance, his blasé expression and cynical body language might have made him out to be a slumming faculty member. But under lowered eyelids, his glance moved at lightning speed, inventorying the audience.

There she is. The beautiful dark-haired young woman sitting alone, feigning interest, dressed in the worn-out jeans and oversized sweater of someone who did not depend on fashion sense for her attractiveness. She was writing something in a notebook, and he would have bet anything it wasn't lecture notes. He had scrutinized her picture for longer than he'd admit even to himself, on the flight over from Paris.

She is the only one. The only one left.

A minute later he spotted a possible enemy faction—a cluster of Arabs who looked out of place. They sat in a group of five, wearing starched button-down shirts, preppy slacks, and penny loafers. One of them sported a thick sweater tied around his neck. He'd only been at Harvard for a few hours, but he already knew this was not the uniform. The oldest one had draped his arm ostentatiously around a seat back and was pretending not to look around the room.

He leaned his head back, breathed deeply and brought his eyelids almost shut. Then he looked at them again.

This time their figures appeared smeared and distorted through the semi-opaque swirls and deformities of demonic beings. He squinted harder. The one clamped onto the oldest man's head was enormous and, going by the size and repulsiveness of its head, probably a midlevel general. The tilt of its eyes and leering length of its mouth identified it as one of the old ones. He would have been an archangel once, thousands of years ago.

He rekindled a familiar thought: *If only they could see themselves*. What they've come to. These once brilliant, beautiful beings, reduced to such loathsomeness. Their rebellion was already the ultimate failure, and the war wasn't even finished yet.

It would take the creature only a few seconds to spot him, what with the usual contingent of angels who accompanied him. Not to mention his own peculiar spiritual footprint.

A shiver of bravado ran through his limbs. He would throw down the gauntlet first. Identify himself brashly to these demoniacs and make it clear he was issuing a challenge.

His opportunity came right away. He tuned in briefly to the speaker and heard him say in passing, ". . . and of course our archqueens Plato and Aristotle, two of history's most flamboyant homosexual men . . ."

Then a smatter of knowing laughter rang through the crowd.

He heard his voice ring out across the void, terse and biting. "You're wrong."

The speaker recoiled visibly and squinted in his direction. "I'm sorry?"

He stood so the professor could hear him. His voice was on the verge of a shout now. "About Plato and Aristotle. They made it clear in their writings that, not only were they not homosexual, they were adamantly opposed to the practice."

"Oh, is that so," said the speaker with a broad smile. "Well, I'm the new acting chair of the American Society of Classical Studies, and I'm unaware of any such writings. Perhaps you ran across these revolutionary gems on the Internet, or the back of a cereal box? Please share with us the origins of such an astonishing discovery."

The same laughter now sounded again, doubled in strength. The professor drew strength from the sound and waved jovially. "I mean it. Let's hear what you have."

In his seat, the challenger wavered. He had only intended to make his presence known, not engage a debate. But this man's attack was beginning to wear thin his reserve.

The professor wouldn't let it go. "Come on. We'll start with Socrates. Chronological order."

"All right. You no doubt base your opinion on Lysis saying Socrates had made a man of him. No one remembers Diogenes' rephrasing of that statement. Lysis said Socrates' *exhortations* had made a man of him. In fact, anyone who knows the Socratic method can see that the philosopher was using that passage to expose the insincerity of an older pedophile in the room. He was actually working against the practice."

"Diogenes, huh? I'll have to look that up."

"You do that. As for Plato, he was actually raped by the King of Sicily, and hated homosexuality with a passion. He wrote that the practice was below the level of the beast. Have you read *Laws*, sir?"

"Certainly. Not the most thrilling of all his works, to be sure."

"Probably why you've overlooked whole portions of it. Such as where he says, 'The intercourse of men with men, or of women with women, is contrary to nature.' Or where he accuses the Cretans of inventing the Ganymede myth in order to justify, quote, 'unnatural pleasures.'"

The professor nodded downward with a deepening scowl. The graduate students turned around with necks craned, sensing a serious challenge.

He continued, "Or where Plato writes, 'How can we take precautions against unnatural loves of either sex, from which innumerable evils have come upon individuals and cities?' Or where he states that the, quote, 'unwritten law has condemned these practices from our youth'?"

The professor took a deep breath, smiled, and said, "Impressive recitation. You have an active imagination. Aided, I'm sure, by the convenient fact that I haven't a copy of *Laws* here with me in which to verify these obscure sources."

"Paragraphs 636C, 637, 836 and 838, respectively. Not to mention that in 838 he also says, 'Censor those who believe in and practice the vices associated with the abuse and misuse of eros. Declare that they are unholy, hated of God, and most infamous.' Oh, and the *Phaedrus* was paragraphs 244 through 277."

The students were beginning to scribble down the reference numbers. The speaker's face had turned a luminous red.

He held up a conciliatory hand. He hadn't meant to humiliate the man, but he'd been stung by his sarcasm. "I'm sorry. I've interrupted you enough. I know it was a minor point to you. I'll sit down now."

The speaker did not respond, his features locked in a sullen stare. He absently nodded his assent, then shuffled his papers and regained his composure. "Well, now that we've had our homophobia break . . ."

The laughter did not come this time.

The stranger walked out, satisfied. The Arabs were now conferring furiously among themselves. Even the girl had looked his way a few times during the exchange. He was now known to her, however minutely. He had accomplished his goal. He'd been spotted and had made his identity quite clear to those looking for him.

The game was on.

Cambridge, Outside Harvard Yard

THE BLOW STRUCK HER straight from the darkness of night. Her world shattered into a nightmare of pain, spilled textbooks, and streetlights glinting off car fenders. Coming to rest in the center of the street, she glimpsed the bright slash of Massachusetts Avenue only thirty yards away. Beyond it the wall of Harvard Yard mocked her terror in stately silence.

And in a burst of odd clarity, Nora thought, *So it's my turn now. This is where it happens, while walking to my beat-up* Corolla *with four bucks in my pocket, late on rent, worn out from the last boring lecture of my academic life. This is how it ends. . . .*

A knee drove into her back. A leather-gloved hand clamped over her mouth and dug hard into the skin beneath her cheekbones. A male voice behind her growled in a language she couldn't understand. She smelled cheap cologne. The voice continued to speak, some Middle Eastern tongue. *Arabic*, she thought through her fear.

Hands yanked her to her feet and to the sight of three men, their faces bearing identical cartoon expressions. Four, including the one holding her from behind. For a fraction of a second their masks made her convulse in an attempt at laughter. *The former president.* She was being attacked by four caricatures of William Jefferson Clinton—cheap plastic renditions of close-cropped gray hair, leering mouth, and bulbous nose. Maybe, she thought in a flash of optimism, this was nothing more than a twisted prank. Maybe the College Republicans were making a point, or the

Hasty Pudding boys had drunk themselves into oblivion again. But then she remembered the foreign speech, and realized that there was nothing amateur about the men's efficient, lightning-fierce movements. Two of them reached for her and began to drag her along the sidewalk. Through the pain of their pincer holds on her arms she looked around for help, but the street was deserted. It occurred to her that the proctors' warnings against walking the streets alone at night had been valid after all.

They veered abruptly from the street, and Nora realized the lights were out over the Holyoke Center parking lot. The space was shrouded in a darkness made even deeper by high walls overhead and the clouded winter night. A crinkle of broken glass underfoot told her why. *They planned it this way. They put out the lights themselves.*

She began to scream, but just as the sound left her throat a gloved hand covered tight her mouth. Arms jerked savagely on the neck of her cable-knit sweater. They reached the parking lot, and as they walked through its shadow the men glanced around with what seemed like eagerness. The eyes behind the masks scanned every inch of their surroundings. Something had changed, Nora sensed. They were no longer so confident. The muscles of arms and necks flexed in anticipation of something, of someone.

One man barked a phrase in Arabic, and they began pulling her faster toward a white Mercedes sedan parked alone at the end of the lot's first row. The voice behind her shouted another command. The men twisted around, pulled machine guns from straps around their backs, and cocked them with a ringing ratchet sound. She realized they were frightened. Now the silence was broken only by the footfalls of their loafered feet and Nora's muffled groans. As the man behind her strengthened his grip, they spread out across the pavement and aimed their guns straight ahead.

Nora heard an aborted yell and a light rustle of clothing, then the farthest man simply disappeared from view, swallowed into the dark.

The others opened fire: a deafening wall of flame ignited the gloom into an inferno. They began inching Nora again toward the Mercedes. One of the men angrily yanked off his mask. The others instantly followed suit and revealed dark faces taut with concentration. The first one to unmask, remarkably handsome, began to shout challenges into the gloom as if defying their attacker. He moved forward, ripped the shadows with a single machine-gun blast, then stalked between two cars.

Then came the soft gurgle of a clamped airway and a shuffling of feet. Nora heard a thud, followed by the clatter of running footsteps. The other two called out, "Rachan!"

There was no answer.

HE FELT ALIVE. Wildly, terribly alive. Yes, this was a horrific moment for Nora to be sure, yet he could not deny the thrill racing through his veins, the adrenaline surging across his nervous system, the cold air searing his lungs in a way he hadn't felt in years.

At one with the night, he moved through the dark like a specter. His hands tingled with the sensation of the attacker's head in his hands, the wrenching of the man's neck as he twisted it in his tensed fingers.

He followed it with a quick, soundless shift to the left on the balls of his feet, a vicious lunge forward and a sudden *Kuan tao* punch to the windpipe—a move he'd acquired in the Philippines. The man went limp, and he caught the body on its way to the ground.

Another one down.

12

FINALLY THE BLOOD POUNDING in Nora's head subsided and she began to make sense of what was happening. Only two gunmen now remained: the one holding her, giving the orders, and the youngest standing alone. This one waved his weapon about with the impetuous movements of an overexcited teenager. His lean face snarled. He stepped forward in the direction of their unseen foe. The one behind her shouted out warnings, but the young man in front ignored him, suddenly frozen in concentration. He had spotted something, someone in the darkness. Then he darted forward, and as he did the one holding her yanked her back, his grip more vicious than ever.

The shadows swallowed up the pursuer, issuing back only the sounds of rapid footsteps, the heavy metallic impact of something coming down on a car hood and the groan of a person exhaling forcibly.

Afterward, silence.

The last attacker dragged her to the Mercedes, around to the other side for their protection. She recognized his shouts as desperate cries to the men he'd just lost. "Abdullah! Rachan! Fashir!"

The cold ring of the gun barrel suddenly drove into her right temple. She could feel the man's arms flex and contract in fear. Her ears rang from his constant yelling, his challenging some invisible enemy to show himself.

A white-hot knowledge sizzled through her veins. The man was about to kill her.

"Noooooo!"

Her cry startled her kidnapper, and that was when she saw the man in the shadows. From the building twenty yards to their right came the blurred figure running so hard toward them that he seemed to hurtle like a projectile, his arms pumping, his head held low yet with his eyes locked on the man who held her.

The gunman flung her down and leveled his machine gun at the onrushing man. Again with a roar the darkness flickered brightly, only this time the bullets found their mark. The stranger's headlong run ended in mid-lunge with a spray of blood, and his body collapsed. His head struck the pavement with a loud crunch.

Ignoring her, the gunman ran over to the prone figure and nudged its face upward with his leather loafer. Then, with a wary expression, he set aside his gun, reached down with both hands, and pulled the body up by the shoulders.

In a split second something amazing happened. The prone man's left arm snapped forward, and his hand grabbed the killer's neck in a vice grip. An animal growl escaped from the terrorist's throat. Nora saw both men's knuckles turn white. Slowly the man on the ground pulled the other downward and through clenched teeth said something in a language Nora couldn't understand.

It sounded like Latin.

The words had a corrosive effect on the Arab-looking man, as if acid had been thrown in his face. He recoiled so violently that his neck wrenched free of the choking grasp. The man on the ground continued to speak the strange words.

Nora then recognized him. He was the one from the lecture who had stood and challenged the speaker, the man with the obscure knowledge of Greek philosophers.

A wail of sirens reached her ears. She turned to the sound and saw a campus police car pull up with a screech of brakes, its roof lights swirling, a side-mounted spotlight carving the blackness.

Her attacker spat out a curse, turned, and ran away. In a second the night had erased all sight of him.

Then came footsteps, swift and loud. Two uniformed officers approached her with revolvers drawn. One of the officers, a young man, stopped in front of her and said, "Don't worry, miss. It's all over." With a long sigh she lay back against the pavement and shut her eyes tight against the world.

The second set of sirens had wailed for some time at the far recesses of her consciousness, but when they burst into the parking lot she bolted upright with no idea of how much time had passed. She felt arms gently help her up. Her eyes opened to flashing red lights and looping strands of yellow police tape surrounding her. Her breath came in heaving, unsteady gasps. She tried to speak but all that came out were keening cries and unconnected syllables.

"Don't try to speak, ma'am," a male voice beside her said.

She was led to a warm, bright place where she sat down on a soft surface. The world jerked forward with the rumble of an engine, and then sirens sounded again, louder than before. She focused her gaze and saw that she was in the back of an ambulance. A white-uniformed man worked feverishly to thread an IV needle into a body on the gurney and shouted at the man behind the wheel.

"He's not breathing. Code three! I'm gonna tube him now!"

He pried the patient's mouth open, then with the other hand held up a plastic tube, tore off its paper wrap, and began pushing it down the victim's throat. Next he grabbed a large plastic bag, attached it to the tube and started squeezing the bag methodically. He turned and picked up a handset, and she saw the face of the man who had saved her—the strong profile of a man in his mid-thirties. Peaceful features, seemingly unconcerned with the blood pulsing from a dark hole in his chest. The paramedic shouted into the radio, "Incoming male with GSW to the thorax, seizing, massive blood loss, BP critical!" He paused and glanced at her. "Female with head and facial contusions."

He hung up the handheld and turned back to the gurney.

"Come on, man. Hold on till we get there."

He hears a soft pop, like the snapping of a flower stem.

His pain now lies somewhere far below him, replaced by a thick silence like that of being underwater. His world falls away—the emergency lights race along a boulevard receding into a filigree of city lights, until soon the metropolis itself shrinks to little more than a bright dot against the curvature of an earth silhouetted against the glare of the sun. . . .

And music. Multi-layered strains of violins and disembodied choruses of female voices weave melodies out of minor chords so rich that their notes seem infinite in number.

Leaving earth behind, he finds himself engulfed in a cloud of swirling lights, a hurricane moving rapidly toward a blinding core.

At the core's center glows a light so vast it seems he'll never glimpse all of its wonder, a beacon which entices him and fills him with a sense of beauty like nothing he's ever felt on earth. Its warmth approaches him, engulfs his horizon. His inward being softens and spreads into what feels like an embrace of this great light and the fierce current flowing all about him. He realizes that some deep part of himself, his spirit, is laughing.

The uncontrollable giggle of a child.

The ambulance approached midway across the Charles River on the Main Street bridge, only three blocks from Massachusetts General, when the stranger began to cry out. At first his words sounded unintelligible, but suddenly his pitch rose into a scream and the words took on meaning. At the sound of his voice the paramedic reared back in amazement.

"I want to go! Please let me come home! Please!"

With a jolt the ambulance stopped at the Massachusetts General emergency entrance. The ambulance doors swung open to a half-dozen people standing outside in medical uniforms. The paramedic crouched at one end of the gurney, lifted and pushed it out, then hopped down as it was wheeled away.

A nurse helped Nora down, and they walked slowly through the emergency room doors. The gurney before them cut a swath through a milling crowd.

"Let's clear a path, people!" a doctor ordered as he walked beside the gurney listening to the paramedic assess the situation. "Large caliber GSW over center thorax, last BP 40 over 30, pulse below 10, pulse ox 80, weak breath sounds both sides, seizing and in V-fib. GCS 2-3-1, although he had a brief episode of lucidity two minutes ago; 3 units epi running wide open. Black tag if I ever saw one."

"Yeah, well, you let *me* call it, okay?" The doctor turned away. "T-2 stat!"

A swarm of hospital personnel converged on the victim, transferred him to a hospital gurney, and whisked him away.

The light grows more enormous before him. He is floating with all the freedom and lightness he dreamed of as a boy when he would watch hawks soar over the Judean hills. He feels himself rising higher and flying through space with a sense of speed no living being has ever known. He looks around him and sees other forms traveling alongside, their shapes indiscernible and yet, like his own, swathed in a pale golden nimbus.

The white-hot core becomes even larger now, finally so huge that he can no longer take in its vastness.

He lets himself meet up to the light and, without fear, enters it.

If he were standing on earth he would believe himself to be in a windstorm, his hair and clothes rippling in a stiff gale coming off the sea. Only here the force pulsating around him seems composed of emotion somehow, of love that pours forth in an intensity that would shatter his mind were he back in the place he's just come from, a lesser dimension he's already beginning to forget.

Inside the light he realizes he himself has become light. The core converts everything that enters it into pure luminescence, and as this happens he senses his body shedding what feels like an irritating scab, which then shrivels up and blows away in the swift current.

Inside Trauma Room 2, the senior physician spun around to the nurses and barked, "Okay, I want a CBC, lytes, coag panel, six units O-negative and X-ray, now! And where's my monitor?"

As if on cue the EKG screen blipped on, and with it the somber tone of a flat line. Everyone looked up and paused for a long moment.

The senior physician broke the silence. "Let's give this guy a chance, okay? I want an IV bolus 500 milligrams of beryllium. Let's get the paddles ready! Make it 200."

While a nurse squeezed gel onto the paddles and rubbed them hurriedly together, the doctor reached both hands upward and brought his fist down hard against the center of the victim's chest. The precordial thump, or "love tap" as residents were inclined to call it, still occasionally struck him as a rather brutal method. He quickly reminded himself that it was still the best way to help provoke heart activity. The doctor looked back at the monitors, saw no improvement, and seized the paddles from the nurse. Staring at the man's chest, he waited for the battery's whine to end before yelling "Clear!" Everyone jumped back, hands held high. The electric thump jarred the victim's chest upward in a mighty heave.

The light flutters and dims into a beam of earthly sunshine flooding inward from behind a stone aperture. The entrance to a tomb, dusty and cold, carved from solid rock.

Along with the sight comes the feeling of containment in a physical body, the downward pull of gravity—all the limitations of earth.

Then, haloed by this sunlight, he sees the face of a man who stands just outside. A dark-haired, bearded man in his early thirties, wearing a robe. A man he knows and loves.

Weeping.

The victim's chest dropped away from the paddles and back down to the bed.

"Nothing. We're losing him. Okay, 360!"

It all started over again: the gel on the paddles, the whine of the charger. Once more all was ready, and gelatinous metal was thrust on the man's skin.

THUMP!

The bearded man, the one shrouded in light, has stopped weeping.

He now stands still and silent. Slowly, as though turning into stone, his expression alters, and sorrow turns into an air of authority. He reaches out a hand and the light now does not seem to come from behind him but from the hand itself. The bearded man speaks. His voice sounds like a thunderclap, the words as unintelligible as the rushing of wind.

The sound of those words fills the tomb and washes over him. He screams—a scream of agony. The scream of a man brought back from the brink of paradise.

13

THE FLAT LINE HAD droned for fifteen minutes now.

"Can we go after the bullet?" an assistant asked.

"No," the lead surgeon replied. "There's no time for that."

"Then call it," someone said.

He nodded angrily. Despite his years of experience, it never got any easier to glance up at the OR microphone and flatly pronounce a person dead. Especially someone who would still be on track for a long life if he hadn't wandered into the business end of a five-ounce bullet or an upthrust knife blade.

"Time of death, 2:54." He yanked off his latex gloves and turned wearily to the door. "Scott, finish up for me, will ya? And somebody turn down the heat in here."

He glanced at the operating nurse standing beside the table, and his eyes narrowed. Sweat poured from her forehead. She reached up and wiped her brow with a quick swipe of the forearm. He turned to his attending physician and saw that the man's green head wrap was soaked through with sweat. "What in the world's going on?"

The nurse turned to him, her eyes wide. "The heat—it's coming from the body, Doctor."

"What?"

He turned back to the body and realized not only was it very hot, but that the temperature was rising at an alarming rate. The surgical staff backed away from the table. The flat-line tone had stopped, though no one had touched the monitor to turn it off. Its screen showed a kaleidoscope of errant patterns. The room began to blur.

"Doctor?"

The nurse's frightened voice jarred him back to the body before him. At first he felt his head shaking slightly, trying to deny what he was witnessing.

The body was glowing. There was no other way to describe it, for the body appeared as if a white fire had ignited somewhere inside its internal cavities, an incandescence which grew brighter by the second.

"Everybody away from here," the doctor ordered. His voice hadn't sounded so weak, so devoid of authority, since his very first surgery seventeen years before. Just as he wondered if the heat was actually going to scorch him, a sharp percussion shattered the air. Patients and staff throughout the hospital would later testify that a gun had been fired in the emergency wing; others would describe the sound inside the operating room as a crack of lightning. Those personnel inside the ER later said a thin veil of light shot across the ward as the noise sounded.

The seven people standing in Trauma 2, however, would hardly remember the sound because of what happened next. The heat instantly subsided, the flat-line machine stuttered to life, and soon there was normal sinus rhythm.

The doctor felt his blood turn cold. The staff stood frozen in place. For a second it seemed the only one in the room who was breathing was the DOA lying on the table.

The patient's eyelids twitched. They blinked twice, three times, then opened wide.

A square bank of lights assaults his eyes. Masked people in green uniforms frown and stare at him, surrounded by shining metal shapes and walls of maroon tile.

The sharp pain behind his eyes, the remnant ache of a concussion, and the smell of blood all tell him something terrible has happened. But he cannot remember what.

The patient blinked in the glare of the lamps, then his eyes settled on the ring of doctors standing as wide-eyed and motionless as a wax-museum display. He stared at the lead surgeon. Finally he reached up, pulled the tube from his throat, and yanked the wired suction cups from his chest.

A nurse fell backward against an instrument tray and, amid a loud clatter, caught herself just before striking the tile floor.

The patient never looked away from the lead physician. His face radiated a fierce, almost hypnotic, intensity. He swung his feet off the gurney and stepped off. He kept his eye on the doctor and walked across the room. He turned to the door, punched it with his fist, and walked through.

For the first time in all his years of leading trauma teams, berating them for their mistakes, cajoling them through grief, congratulating them for superior work, the doctor stood silent.

The patient strode out of the emergency room without anyone speaking a word.

NORA MCPHERAN SAT ON the edge of an exam table while an obese medical assistant swabbed the scrape on her cheek. The curtain parted and two men stepped in. Both looked to be in their early forties, both wearing wrinkled sport coats and the kind of slacks advertised as never needing to be ironed. The one closest to her reached into his jacket and pulled out a badge wallet. He flipped it open before her.

"Cambridge Police Department," he said. "I'm Detective Barber and this is Detective Goldfarb. We'd like to ask you a few questions about your attack, if you feel up to it."

She nodded, then looked Barber in the eye and asked, "Who were they? What did they want?"

The detective answered with the painless empathy of a veteran. "We don't know, miss. That's what we're trying to find out."

The other man, a fleshier, gray-haired version of the first, blinked wearily. "What do you do, Miss McPheran?" he asked.

"Nora. I'm a grad student at Harvard."

"What do you study?"

"Psychology. I'm three months away from finishing classes for my Ph.D."

"Nora," Barber said, "where are you from, originally?"

"All over. California, Iowa, Montana, upstate New York. My family moved a lot. My dad taught."

"What did he teach?"

"English. Creative writing mostly."

"Do you work too? Do you have a job, I mean."

"No, Officer. I live off a trust fund set up for me by my industrialist parents." She smiled and shook her head. Many such people existed at the university, and she resented their ease of life as much as most Cambridge locals did. "Just kidding. I figured it's what you expected." The jab earned her an emphatic chuckle from the two men. "I wait tables at the House of Schnitzel. Six nights a week. Plus I do some graduate teaching. Freshman Psych."

"And where do you live, Nora?"

"I have an apartment on May Street."

"So, did you recognize any of the men?"

"No," she answered, suddenly feeling very tired.

"Have you had any dealings with members of the, uh, Arab-American *community*?" Goldfarb had leaned on the last word as if to underscore his disdain for the politically correct verbiage his job required of him.

"No, never."

"What was your relationship with the man who was shot?"

"I didn't know him at all. I think he attended a lecture I just came from. He sorta made a scene. Challenged the speaker, accused him of being wrong about his assumptions."

"Really? What was the lecture about?"

"Dysfunction in ancient Greek society. This guy had some beef about Plato and Aristotle being gay. He started quoting all this chapter and verse about how everyone's been wrong about that all these years."

"Some kind of right-winger?"

"No. More like an eccentric scholar with dubious social skills."

"Did you speak to him? Make eye contact?"

"No."

The men looked at her silently, like she had finally said something hard to believe. "So you're saying," Barber began, his eyebrows furrowed, "that you were getting beat up by these thugs and some guy you never met ran out to save you, took a bullet for somebody he didn't know?"

"That's the thing—I have no idea, no clue what this is about. Why don't you ask the man who saved me?"

"We can't right now," Goldfarb replied, his face a mask. "Tell us about the one who got away."

"I never saw him. He was behind me the whole time. I can tell you he shouted in Arabic, and he seemed to be in charge of the whole thing."

"Did they take anything from you?"

"No, and the weird part is, from the minute they grabbed me they seemed to be expecting someone else to come after them."

"For the guy who *did* come after them, maybe."

"Maybe. But like I said, I don't know why. I've never seen him before, either."

"Do you have any enemies, Miss McPheran?" Barber asked. "Anybody you've gotten on the outs with lately?"

"No. I broke up with my boyfriend six months ago, but we've been friendly enough. No hard feelings. Other than that, nothing."

"What about your family?"

"My dad was kidnapped in midtown Manhattan thirteen years ago." Something about tonight's events made the old lump—the one she hadn't felt in five years or more—harden in her throat. The hated images returned: she and her mother walking out of Macy's into neon light and his familiar figure, gone.

Worst of all had been the police officer's downcast eyes, his trembling voice minutes later when he said, *"He's gone, ma'am."*

Goldfarb leaned forward with an intense gaze. "Kidnapped by whom?"

"I don't know, Detective. He was never found."

"Never?"

"No, and there wasn't any description of the men who took him, just that it involved a late-model Cadillac. But no note, no ransom demand, and no sign of him. Ever again."

"What was his name?"

"Joseph. Joseph McPheran. Thirteen years ago, in a few days."

She saw the men glance upward to do the math, scribble down the information. Calls would be made to the NYPD, she figured. She turned glumly to the tile wall. Their inquiries would certainly produce the same type of negative responses she'd heard all of her adult life.

Goldfarb wiped his brow, his face suddenly shiny with sweat. Nora glanced from his to the face of Barber, equally flushed, and it dawned on her that the heat was climbing rapidly in here. Just then a loud report rang in their ears. Both men jumped and the medical assistant jerked back, slinging amber solution all over her uniform. The detectives' hands reached into the jackets and pulled out guns. Barber stuck an arm through the curtain opening and both men darted out.

Ten seconds later they came back, shaking their heads incredulously. "That was weird," Barber muttered.

"What was it?"

"Strangest thing," Goldfarb said. "Wasn't a gunshot, but there's some kind of commotion in Trauma 2. Your, uh, secret admirer seems to be getting a lot of attention."

Barber winced at his partner's lack of tact and shot the man an angry look. "Look," he said to Nora, "we're going to have to be in touch over the next few days. On account of the fact that these guys were, well, they present an unusual profile. You may even hear from federal law enforcement."

"Then you do know something about the guys who attacked me?" Nora said.

Barber shook his head. "Nothing for sure. Their car was full of exotic firepower, and their IDs look cooked." Goldfarb gave him a surly look thus causing his partner to pull up short. "That's all I'm gonna say for now," he finished.

"Well, I'd appreciate being kept informed," she said, hearing her voice turn sour and insistent. "I take it from your questions that you don't think this was a random act."

"No, ma'am," Barber responded, his voice thick with sarcasm. "Any idea why these guys would be carrying copies of your driver's license in their pockets?"

She didn't like the scrutinizing look in their eyes, the abrupt rise in their intensity toward her. "Are you trying to suggest something?"

"Not if you truly didn't know them," Barber answered.

"I told you the truth the first time, Detective. And I'll tell you what—I'm tired. Why don't we continue this another time, if you don't mind?"

"We'll keep you informed," Goldfarb said.

"Yeah, don't go anywhere," said Barber, handing her his card. "This case has got juice."

The men left. Nora leaned back against the bed, closed her eyes, and tried to wish the whole night away, to return to what her life had been only two hours before. The racing of her heart and the spinning of her head told her it would be impossible.

14

TWO HOURS LATER, her face heavily bandaged and her remaining strength drained by the interview, Nora walked into Trauma Room 2. It stood empty except for a young orderly mopping the floor.

"I'm sorry," Nora said, "but the patient who was in here a couple of hours ago. . . . Did he . . . you know?"

The orderly shook her head. "I'm sorry, you'd have to ask—" A door opened behind Nora, and a thin woman stepped through, smiling warmly. *Charge Nurse*, her ID card read.

"Can I help you?" she asked Nora.

"Yes. I was wondering what happened to the man who was brought in here. He had a gunshot wound."

The nurse's demeanor changed. The smile became a suspicious scowl, the eyes narrowed in barely disguised fear. "We cannot release patient information without written consent from family or next of kin," she stated flatly.

"But we came in together. He . . . saved me."

"And what is your relation?"

"None."

"How do you know each other?"

"Uh, we don't. He just came out of nowhere."

"I see. Well, in order to be allowed access to that patient's information, you'll need to submit a written consent form, and it must be signed by the patient himself. Or talk to the officers—it's a police matter now."

"But I don't know if he's even *alive*!"

"If he's dead, you'll have to show me permission from his survivors."

Nora stormed through the hospital entrance doors into the muggy gloom of early morning, swearing to herself that next time she would rather bleed to death than allow herself into another hospital.

Boston, Massachusetts General Hospital

FRESH FROM THE HARVARD command center, Stayton and Wallis of the CIA swept into a Massachusetts General conference room and nearly fell into their seats. Five members of the hospital staff sat calmly around the table, their gazes elsewhere.

"I have a flight back to Langley in thirty minutes," said Stayton with a glance at his watch. He had far too much on his mind: keeping local police away from the site of the shooting, not to mention keeping news of a terrorist attack on American soil from the public eye. On top of that, the bizarre desecration of an Auschwitz site he'd been handling only hours before. "So, when can we interview the victim?"

"You can't," replied an older man at the head of the table.

"Excuse me?"

The older man's nostrils flared. "I am Lloyd Garing, chief of emergency services. With me are Daron Blaschke, senior emergency physician, and Lydia Holt, laboratory manager."

"Please explain," Stayton said, the blood still full in his face.

"First," said Garing, "you might explain why the CIA is involved in this."

Stayton breathed in the precise manner his anger-management course had instructed him, then said, "Because as your staff reported to police, the man you treated last night held a French passport. We're from the Central European desk. Enough said."

"Who were these attackers?"

"I'm sorry. I'm not at liberty to disclose that. However, I would like to know why we cannot see the victim."

"I'll make this brief," Blaschke said. "He came in practically DOA. Gunshot wound to the chest, seizures, not breathing, massive blood loss. It was a lost cause, flat line from the moment we hooked him up. We defibbed him, but it was no use. I called time of death fifteen minutes after he'd arrived."

"He died?" Stayton exclaimed, his voice nearly a shout. "Why was no one informed?"

"Then he revived," Garing countered. "He stood up, walked out on his own power. Never said a word."

Wallis spoke beside Stayton, his voice low and incredulous. "He just walked out?"

"That's right," Blaschke said. "Just before that, the body started giving out heat. An incredible amount, too. I'd guess it reached a hundred and twenty-five degrees in the room. And then, right at the moment he revived, there was a sound like a gunshot. It was the most unbelievable thing I've seen in all my years as an emergency room doctor. Plus, there's the blood workup. The CBC, for instance."

"I was managing the lab," said Holt, a petite woman with red hair. "Where do I start on this man's blood. Complete blood count came back, well, unreadable."

"What do you mean?" Stayton asked.

"The man did not have human blood in his veins."

"Actually," Blaschke said, "it wasn't blood by any definition we know of. We've called in federal health authorities to come look at the samples because we can't make heads or tails of it."

Holt continued, "All we know is that he has no identifying

structures we normally would associate with human blood. No red or white blood cells, plasma, hemoglobin. Anything. If I could compare it to anything I've seen before, it's those pictures of fuel rods in nuclear power plants. Glowing, pulsating. I know this sounds ridiculous, but it looks like this man had pure, unrefined energy running through his veins."

"We left a small sample in a petri dish overnight," Garing said. "This morning it was overflowing. There was a puddle on the floor. As if it just started growing out of control."

Stayton raised his fingers to his temples. *Great,* he thought. *It isn't enough having a Hamas operation in the middle of Harvard. Now the target has to be some freak of nature.* He tried to imagine the bureaucratic hodgepodge that was sure to get dragged into this thing, and shook his head at the thought. "So where is he?"

"We told you," Garing said. "The man revived, stood up, and walked out. He was clinically dead, and the next second he was off the gurney and walking out. Of the hospital."

"You people just let him leave?"

"We were all so dumbfounded," Blaschke replied, "we thought we were seeing a ghost or something. Nobody moved. Nobody dared."

"The National Science people asked us to inform you that, based on our preliminary reports, this man should be sought with the highest level of urgency, more than the most-wanted federal fugitive." Holt looked straight at the far wall as though unwilling to face the feds with the grandiose statement she felt compelled to make. "His mutation could prove the most explosive scientific find in human history."

"Bottom line is," Garing said, "we desperately need to find him."

Stayton fixed the doctor with a vacant stare. "Join the club, Doctor."

Boston, Two Blocks From Massachusetts General Hospital

AS IF TO MIMIC THE SHIPS sailing through nearby Boston Harbor, the early morning pedestrian traffic in front of the old church suddenly developed a bow wave. A virtual parting of the seas seemed to divide the current of commuters as they veered abruptly away from the solitary figure of a half-naked, bloody man.

He was aware of his surroundings, but he did not care. He wanted nothing more than to run. Sprint fast enough to shed his earthly body like an unwieldy chrysalis and let it blow away in the morning breeze. It was almost unbearable, as it always was, to feel himself leaded down once more by the ponderous, decaying mass of a human body. He wanted out. Out of it, out of here.

Closing his eyes against the stares of the people, he let the testimony of his bare footsteps lead the way. Just a few minutes. A little more time and he would adjust, as he always had. The wondrous sensation of a heavenly body would fade before the overwhelming reality of this world, and he would be right again. Later, at some point in the next few days, his spiritual sight would reawaken.

Finally. He could feel the memory leaving him. Feeling its remnants fade from his mind, he tilted his head upward as if to drink in rain, held out his red-splattered arms and stood frozen in a pose most observers would have mistaken for ecstasy.

He knew he looked like a drunk. An injured one who had lost half his clothes to a vicious fight. But he had to live through the next half hour or so of tolerating a human body again. That task was foremost.

A cruiser crawled past and the thought hit him. He desperately needed to find a more isolated neighborhood. To hide. He was no longer in any condition to engage his enemies, and there was no telling who might be after him.

Turning onto a shaded side street, he began to jog. He remembered that he had a car hidden back at Harvard. It contained the bulk of his cash and forged papers. By now, though, it wouldn't be safe to return there. He had carried the satellite phone and wallet with cash and credit cards on his person, but they had been stripped from him at the hospital. He felt his pockets and pulled out a five-dollar bill and three ones.

He washed the blood off in a small park fountain. Five minutes after that, he saw a bum emerge from a large, cavernous building. The man was feeling his thick wool coat in the manner of someone feeling a new garment. *Goodwill*, the sign read. *Thrift Shop.*

He wandered in and, with the eight dollars from his pocket, availed himself of an avocado green shirt and a weathered tan windbreaker. He walked out a perfectly respectable street person.

Within five minutes he had blended into the throngs of onlookers along Beacon Street.

That's when the memory hit him.

The darkly painted side of a locomotive lumbers into sight. Its stack belches puffs of smoke in the same friendly manner as might an excursion train heading into a popular tourist destination. It passes under an arched gate, beside the rows of German shepherds straining at their leashes. Behind them, soldiers with their backs held ramrod straight. An officer looks around from within a cordon of other men, his look of indolence a clear sign of greater authority.

Mengele, *the mind's eye reports.*

A lesser cadre of soldiers rushes forward with loud canine-like shouts and thrusts itself into the cattle-car doors. Gangplanks are shuffled up and latches thrown down. First one door groans open and then a second. Pale faces begin to appear in the sunlight and peer sharply to either side. Somehow the newcomers seem aware of the sight straight ahead of them, and avoid looking at it directly. The dogs surge forward as the crowds begin to spill out. Older people fall; some of them are pulled up again. One does not rise; one of the soldiers steps up with a pistol in his fist, and a sharp report splits the air.

A scream seems to wash through the crowd but only for a few seconds. The prisoners continue to pour down from the railcars.

The soldiers' barking reaches a crescendo. The crowd is being contained.

And then Mengele steps forward, one hand gripping a riding crop, the other crisply behind his back.

In the background, between two low-lying barracks, comes the brief sight of a wagon being pushed by a man in prison garb. On the wagon, a sight the brain resists processing: a fleeting image of long, white and pink shapes—ones with hands and feet—being shaken over the side by the lurching of the wheels.

A scream. A single cry.

Massachusetts General Hospital, ICU Wing

THE NEW DOCTOR, a fiftyish man with a hint of gray at his temples, paused before the police officer guarding the door of one of the three hospitalized Hamas terrorists.

The doctor didn't speak to the posted guard; he merely nodded toward the door with a world-weary roll of his eyes, one which suggested a routine check.

With a blank expression, the cop nodded his assent. The man entered, and the officer resumed his half-conscious examination of the opposing wall's tiles.

Inside the hospital room, the patient awoke just enough to glance sluggishly at the handcuff binding his wrist to the bed rail, and then at his visitor. On seeing the newcomer's face, his features twisted in a mixture of grimace and smile. Most people did the same when they glimpsed the cold fire in the eyes of Bishop Johan Eccles.

The bishop walked to the edge of the bed and laid his hand gently on the patient's forehead. "Don't worry," he said. "He is a slippery prey. He has done this to better men than you."

"I will catch him, master."

"Will you? Can you stand up right now?"

"Oh no. My head won't stop swimming. I am dizzy all the time from when he struck my head on the hood."

"Ah, yes."

The dark shape of the pistol seemed to materialize from Eccles's outthrust left hand. His eyes remained steady, impassive.

"No, please! Give me an hour," the patient begged.

Eccles suddenly smiled—a smile of inner, cruel mirth. "You're right. I won't do it this way." He slipped the pistol back into the lab coat pocket and reached forward. In a flash his hands were around the throat of the man in the bed, squeezing so tightly that Eccles's knuckles turned instantly white. The man's eyes bulged, whether from pressure or mute shock was impossible to tell. The killer leaned forward and his face flushed, his eyes ablaze with a razor-sharp ecstasy. "I'll do it this way!" he hissed.

From his post outside, the rustling of bed sheets no doubt barely registered in the cop's conscious mind. By the time he roused himself enough to realize the nature of the sound, the door had opened again and a gun barrel had pressed hard into his side.

His world exploded into darkness.

The doctor vanished into a stairwell and was striding across the fourth floor of the hospital parking garage when a nurse noticed blood dripping from the police officer she at first had assumed to be asleep. She screamed.

The man walked up to a sedan containing three cowering Arab men and climbed in. The engine started and the car screeched off, moving twice as fast as any other vehicle driving away from the hospital.

The Vatican bishop and his remaining squad of Hamas terrorists had a man to catch.

"HEY!"

A man's shout, deafening.

"You awake, buddy?"

A hard, blunt object poked him in the chest. A scream died out, and he realized it was ending in his own throat.

His eyes flew open. Large and looming above him was a lean male face beneath a dark cap. Frowning.

Police.

He was completely present now. He reeled backward against the low retaining wall of a residential yard. A black-and-white cruiser sat parked at the curb with its lights ablaze, its doors gaping open.

"Hey, where'd you get all that blood on ya?"

He looked down. The gore from his injury and operation already covered his new shirt in a thick, rusty cake. He looked like a walking crime scene.

Think fast. . . . "I just had an accident. It's nothing."

"What kind of accident?" asked a second police officer who stood just behind the first.

He glanced down again as if to assess what kind of story would satisfy them. Yet he immediately knew the police had read the look, too. They weren't going to buy it. He ventured a try anyway.

"I fell. On a sidewalk, I think."

"Are you under the influence of drugs or alcohol, buddy?"

"Absolutely not."

"What's your name?"

He felt his eyes open further. He'd forgotten the name Thierry had given him! Oh, yes, André Lassalle. But could he use it? Was it wise? He decided against it.

"You have nothing on you? No wallet? No ID?"

"No. They took it away."

"Who's *they*?"

What was he saying? How stupid of him. "I didn't mean that. It slipped out when I fell."

The two men exchanged dubious glances, and it seemed a boundary had been crossed. They stepped forward and grabbed him by the armpits, lifted him, and then half-dragged him to the cruiser. A hand pushed his head down as he was unceremoniously wedged into the back seat.

The driver eased forward into traffic while his partner spoke quietly into the radio receiver.

"Either way, buddy," the driver said, looking into his rearview mirror, "you bear a little watching. If that blood didn't come from nobody else, then it came from you, and we may have to make sure you're not doing harm to yourself."

THE STRANGE MAN picked up near Beacon Street soon began to trace a slippery and largely unobtrusive path through assorted branches of Boston's municipal bureaucracy. First, the officers determined by radio, even before reaching their precinct, that no homicides had occurred within the last few hours nor in the immediate vicinity of the man's location. It was decided that the blood on his clothes was likely to be his own. A sample was drawn for a comparison and sent to downtown Forensics, but the ampule became lost in a daylong backlog of testing requests, then pushed even further back by the appearance of a fatal ingredient in south Boston's heroin supply.

So the blood was his own. Unfortunately, his persistent claims of amnesia continued to arouse suspicion.

The man waited patiently in the squad room—not under arrest, not charged with anything. Two hours later a social worker walked sheepishly into the room and, just minutes later, drove him to the city's hulking Human Services building.

Once he was in the more humane quarters of Boston's civil service, another decision was made. In order to check the veracity of his amnesia claim, he would undergo hypnosis at the hands of a graduate student and neophyte hypnotist. It probably wouldn't lead to anything, but at least it could be said they'd exhausted the possibilities.

Neither his name nor his description ever appeared on a police arrest report, contact sheet, or other public record. The unheralded nature of his apprehension left him undetectable to the nearly dozen different law enforcement agencies and independent groups deployed across the city to find him.

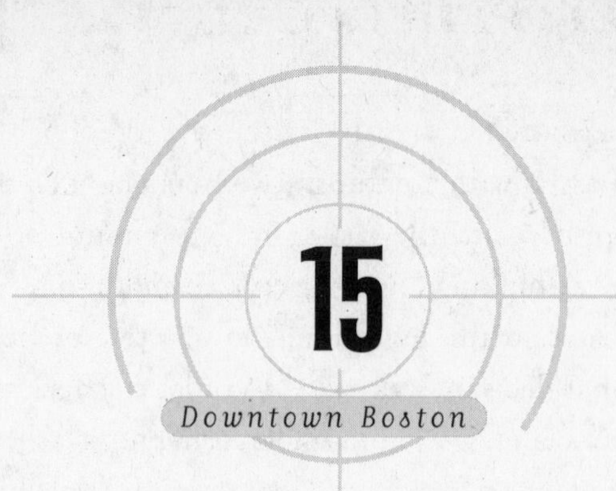

MOTORISTS SLOWED AND GAWKED at the sight—on the corner of Cambridge and Grove Streets, with the imposing backdrop of Massachusetts General now obscured by torrential rain, seven men stood outside in the downpour. Their heads bowed in prayer, gleaming with rainwater, they formed a perfect circle. The group would have been deemed inconspicuous on the streets of Boston if not for the complete sameness of their attire—all in identical gray flannel coats that flowed nearly to the tops of their black shoes—and also their inattention to the inclement weather. The oldest of them, a man whom the surrounding pedestrians would have estimated to be easily eighty-five years old, and who was actually quite older than that, spoke in a voice only his six companions could hear.

All at once he finished speaking and their heads tilted upward. Without a word, the men turned around to face equidistant directions and walked swiftly away into the storm.

Department of Social Services, Boston

"NOW, MR. DOE, we're going to move back just a bit. It's now yesterday. Tell me what you see." Lauren, a young Harvard graduate student, glanced behind herself. She leaned back and switched off the lights.

"I see a light."

"What kind of light? A streetlamp? A chandelier?"

"No. A great light, filling the sky. Filling the universe, actually. It's God, of course, although most of the people around me don't know that yet."

"Describe the people next to you."

"Well, they're not really persons. They're spirits. This is the afterlife."

"Oh." She paused. Nothing in her training or the literature had prepared her for this. Yet the subject seemed genuinely engaged. He had moved into hypnosis quite easily and convincingly, falling under in rapid time. "Of course," she said. "Tell you what, John. Let's move back a little further—a week, say. Seven days ago today. Look around you and tell me what you see."

"A living room. Richly decorated. Velvet on the walls. Rows and rows of books in bookcases. Old, leather-bound books."

"Does this place look familiar?"

"Yes. I think I used to live here."

"Where is this living room? What city?"

"Hold on. I'm moving to the window. There's a river far below, lined with people holding cameras. Big, gray buildings everywhere. On the horizon there's a pointed tower made of steel beams. It sits on four metal arms."

"Paris?"

"Yes. It is Paris."

"Who lives in this home?"

"I do. I have for years."

She shook her head in quiet surprise. A street person with an apartment in downtown Paris? Yet the man's facial cues betrayed no guile, no dishonesty. "This surprises me. You don't speak with a French accent."

"I'm not French."

"Oh. What then?"

A pause. "I don't know."

She made a snap decision, something to ascertain whether or not this man was a fit subject. "Okay. Let's move back to thirty-five years ago. You're a child. Tell me what you see."

The man before her recoiled as though struck by a branding iron in the chest. Loud, heaving groans tore from his twisting mouth. "Ahhh! No! The darkness, it's unbearable! I'm trapped! No light! No space! No air!" He began to gasp uncontrollably.

She quickly tried to regroup. "Okay, okay . . . now let's move ahead five years."

"No! Please! Take me out of here!"

Unable to make sense of his reaction, she let out a frustrated sigh. She decided on an absurdity test, the fail-safe method for exposing hypnotic falsity. "Let's go a long ways back. It's now 1915—describe what you see around you."

The gasping ceased immediately. The man's body instantly released itself from its agonized coil. He smiled faintly and cocked his head backward. "It's a sunny day," he said, "and very cold. I'm walking through a crowd outside the Winter Palace at Saint Petersburg."

"I see. Describe the crowd to me." Attempts at detail usually exposed the lie.

"Everyone's wearing coats, on account of the chill. I see a man leading six children and his wife toward a street vendor who's selling cotton candy. They're all wearing the same white fur hats. There's a circle of soldiers laughing and plowing through the sightseers. They are dressed in the customary excursion garb, long olive coats instead of the shorter black ones, so everyone knows they're not on patrol or anything. It's fairly safe. Lately there have been skirmishes and protests outside the Palace, and quite often the soldiers are on alert and quite trigger-happy. But not today."

"What about you?"

"I have just come from the Palace itself, and I'm quite troubled."

"Why?"

"Because Tsar Nicholas is away on one of his required military inspections, and this Rasputin character is having his way, literally and figuratively, with much of Court. I've been trying to counter his influence with Alexandra."

"You know the Tsarina of Russia?" Lauren's voice was now flat and openly skeptical.

"As well as a foreigner could, I suppose. She and I have become friends."

"How did that happen?"

"Well, she is enamored with my knowledge of Jewish history."

"Why would you have great knowledge of Jewish history?"

"Because I am Jewish. A follower of Jesus, but also a man of Jewish blood and deep love for the Judaic faith."

"And that makes you a scholar on their history?"

"No, merely one who remembers."

"What do you mean, *remembers*?"

"I mean I remember living it."

"Oh." She breathed deeply. This conversation was definitely consignable to la-la land—except for the very convincing way in which the man expressed himself.

She decided to hang on for the entire ride. "John, let's move back even further. Three hundred years. The year 1700. Springtime. Tell me what you see."

He closed his eyes, grimaced and said, "Crystal chandeliers, reflecting the morning sun. It's the prince's waiting room. I'm sitting on a silver-lined settee beside a portly old gentleman whom I recognize as a leader in Warsaw's tavern guild, and before us is a crowd of powdered, coiffed and pompously attired men I do not recognize. Like me, they are here to see the prince at his summer quarters, as the king is not here. We've been waiting patiently, none of us saying a word, for three hours. The prince is indisposed, they say. But from the voices filtering through the door, I would say he is having lady troubles. We say nothing, for this audience could either make our fortunes or land us in prison."

"Why are you here?"

"To beg the prince's mercy and offer, I guess, a bribe. I have heard it on good authority that local Jew-haters are plotting another pogrom for next week. I have come to offer the Crown twenty pounds of gold to reconsider."

"A pogrom. You mean, an anti-Semitic attack."

"More like a satanic murder spree."

"And you have this twenty pounds in your pocket?"

"Don't be silly. It's waiting in my coach outside."

"You seem to be a wealthy man."

"At the moment, I am the wealthiest commoner alive."

"Really."

"It is of little consequence, except to do good works like these. And it will change. A war will arise and half my holdings will disappear. The Lord provides over time."

Lauren had an idea. "By the way, John, how old are you right now?"

His eyebrows rose. She saw his tongue dart around his mouth in a silent counting of numbers. "Seventeen hundred and thirty-four years."

"And what is your name?"

"My current alias? My Roman name? Or my Jewish name?"

"I don't know. You choose."

"My name today is the Comte Simon de Saint Germain of Austria, Tuscany, and the Western Hinterlands."

"But this name's an alias?"

"My work demands it."

She decided to challenge him. "Your age tells me that you were born just before the dawn of what we call the Common Era, better known as the birth of Christ. That's quite a coincidence, don't you think?"

"It's no coincidence at all. Jesus of Nazareth is the reason I am here."

"Oh. So you're originally from . . ."

"Yes. From Israel."

"When were you born?"

"I was born in the Jewish year 3760, in Bethany."

"Okay," she interjected quickly. "The year 400, same time, day, month. What do you see?"

He reclined and stared up as if the answer were written on the ceiling. Suddenly he jerked his head around to face her and said, "I see trees. All the world is oak trees. Under their canopies I see a shining blue body of water. I am running toward the water, dragging my toes through nettle brush and vines. I jump in." He shook with a contented smile on his face. "Oh, it's cold. But I need the bath, and so do my companions."

"Who are they?"

"Priests. I am a priest myself."

"What are you doing here?"

"I am accompanying them on a scouting mission which will soon become an actual missionary expedition, leading to the legendary wild islands of the north. We've been hiking through forest for nine days, trying to reach a river that will take us there. This is the first large body of water we've encountered."

Lauren barely prevented herself from uttering a curse. This was becoming too confusing. She decided to try to stump him. "Tell me, what nation do you occupy, and who is its ruler?"

He looked at her with a bemused, condescending expression. "Nowhere. This is wild land. Someday it will be claimed by the Frankish king of Lutece, then later ceded to the Norsemen and called Normandy. But this is a time of chaos in this part of the world. The Roman Empire would like to claim this land, only it's too much embroiled in internal fighting and too busy defending itself against the Huns."

She sighed. "Has your swim ended yet?"

"Oh yes. The sun has come out, and the priests and I are now resting on the beach at the lake's edge, flat on our backs."

Her shoulders slumped. This was ridiculous. "All right, John. We're through. I'm going to count to ten. When I reach ten, you'll be fully awake, fully relaxed, and remember nothing about our conversation. Okay?"

"Okay."

Within ten minutes of his regaining consciousness, the stranger was released from custody, no questions asked.

He was taken back outside, to the streets from whence he came. His gamble had paid off. Agreeing to the hypnosis session had secured his eventual release, yet its results had been deemed too bizarre to seriously entertain. He doubted that Lauren would even file a report, so deep had been her confusion when he'd awakened. The system had spit him out with little more than a scratching of its communal head.

Within just minutes of his return, he began to find himself spiritually aware for the first time since his resuscitation. He looked down a broad downtown avenue and saw that the street was filled above the treetops with a constantly churning mass of demonic beings. He tried to control his breath and calm his driving legs. Where were his helpers? He looked around to the back of the street's alley and discerned, opaquely filtering the brick walls and piles of garbage, the shape of four tall warriors, smiling at him with utter confidence.

That's it, he told himself. *They're keeping themselves hidden for now. Engagement would only alert the beasts to my presence.*

He turned with feigned calm and began to walk away. What is it about this street, this place?

Working hard to keep his eyes averted, he pressed forward. He saw a church up ahead and whispered a breathy "Thank you." His step quickened.

He bounded up the steps, pulled open the large door, and then took three steps back. This house of God was as crammed with the beasts as the street. He grimaced, ran from the church building and was twenty yards away before he heard the heavy oak door slam shut.

Where can I go? he asked himself. Then he wondered, *Am I really asking God?*

Of course. It was a place he loved to go, a place occupied with angels from floor to ceiling. And no one in the spirit world asked any questions because this was their most natural and beautiful function of all.

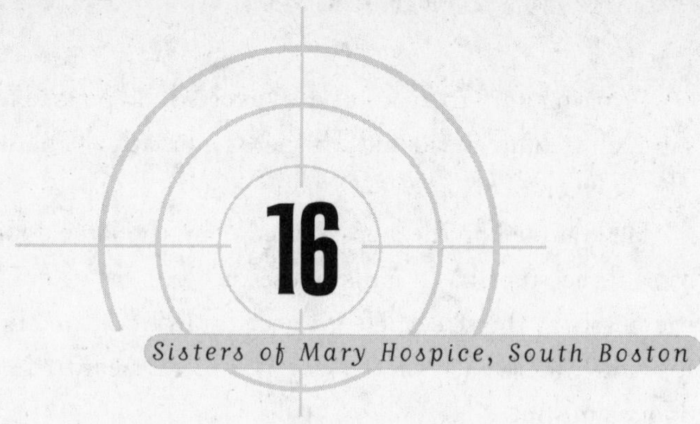

16

Sisters of Mary Hospice, South Boston

LIKE ANY DECENT HOSPICE, the Sisters of Mary had strict rules about who could walk onto the floor and volunteer to pray with their patients. A person had to undergo a perfunctory background check, twelve hours of training, and be invited back by one of the staff members.

But this man was different.

It could be that he happened to catch Sister Maggie on an especially emotional day. One of her favorites had just passed on the night before, and the woman had died all alone. Her children's schedules had simply proven too intractable for a last-minute gathering within a half-hour's notice. The soft-spoken sixty-year-old had slipped into a coma and passed away unnoticed, unmourned.

Except by Sister Maggie.

Maggie had the old lady's serene death mask on her mind when the man had showed up at the front desk, and it struck her immediately that his face possessed the same quality. He told her in a soft voice that he'd recently undergone a near-death experience and that he was a longstanding Catholic—a fact she knew instinctively, for who else could possess such a purity of gaze? And more than anything else, he wanted to spend a little time with someone who was passing on alone.

Sister Maggie decided then and there to break the rules. She knew just who to introduce him to. With a reverential hush she walked him into Room 23. The young woman in 23 was a special case. She was dying of AIDS, and though her records showed substantial family in the reasonable vicinity, there seemed to be a great deal of alienation between them.

Room 23 was dying alone.

He approached the bed and turned to Maggie with a look that said, It's all right, thank you, but I can take it from here. Ordinarily she would have insisted on making a proper introduction, but again there was something about this man's presence that set her at ease, that gave her, if she dared admit it, a greater sense of comfort and peace than she'd felt since joining the Sisters.

He knew that, having recently returned from heaven, his spiritual sense would be heightened. And he was right. The carrier angels were there when he entered. Two of them stood on either side of the bed, their outlines shimmering in the dim light. Their statuesque stillness made them look more like guards at the moment, which was customary while they awaited their turn. When the time came, they would usher this suffering one into a place she could hardly imagine.

Their presence obviously marked the young woman as one who walked with their Master. *Good thing*, he thought. He would scarcely have been able to comfort someone who did not.

When they saw him they nodded slowly, whether to him or the warrior angels trailing him, he could not say. Moisture came to his eyes, the same unexplainable tears that always arrived when he witnessed these beings faithfully performing their task.

He looked to the bed. Next to the head of a once-beautiful young woman, a minister angel knelt with its palm to the patient's forehead and the other grasped her withered left hand—directly over the place where an IV tube disappeared behind a bandage. He could almost sense the peace flowing from the angelic hand into the woman's being, and wondered for a moment whether he was even needed.

The angel turned at his entrance and smiled warmly. This time he knew the greeting was directed at him alone, and the knowledge filled him with a sweet, warm glow. After endless years of hiding and anonymity, it was so gratifying to be greeted by someone who knew who and what he was. It was not a case of needing approbation or recognition, just a sense of relief. Angels had been the ones to inform him of his unique calling. They simply knew, and their respect for him was always evident in their eyes. He felt almost as if he'd entered a kind of roving family reunion.

He stepped forward on the other side of the bed. All other sounds fell away as a great hush seemed to settle over the room.

The young woman's eyes opened blearily when he approached her. She registered no alarm or curiosity at his lack of uniform or unfamiliarity, only a smile which danced fleetingly across her lips. He knelt and placed a hand tenderly on her shoulder where it protruded from the blanket. He leaned forward.

"I came to tell you about what a wonderful place you'll soon be entering," he whispered. "You see, I've just come from there."

Stephen found him there an hour later, after following a strange inner urge that the man they sought would not be among the churches of the city but in a place of service. He'd investigated three soup kitchens before thinking of this hospice. He merely described the man he was looking for and was immediately ushered to Room 23.

The door closed behind him. The man he was looking for turned with a solemn yet joyful expression—the look of someone attending to a task of the highest importance. Stephen was immediately overwhelmed with a sense that he'd arrived in the middle of a moment of incredible gravity. He sensed he was intruding, although the man did not seem displeased at his being here—merely turned back to the sick woman and continued to whisper in her ear with a smile that caused Stephen's sense of the world to become undone. He could hardly stand to look at him, or at the tableau which he and the woman formed.

He looked down, and another feeling began to creep over him. The room seemed to have grown thick with a *presence*. There were others in this room, which of course was impossible because there was nobody else in the room. He felt his lungs begin to constrict, his knees to weaken. He found himself fighting a compulsion to kneel.

Was there in fact a glow, somehow an invisible, gentle radiance playing about the patient's face? Or across the countenance of the man kneeling beside her, who now appeared as unfamiliar as a complete stranger?

Suddenly the young woman's eyes fluttered open, and the man beside her recoiled slightly. He drew backward with a deep intake of breath. His own eyes closed in counterpoint.

Something had happened, Stephen knew in the deepest part of him. Something great was transpiring. He just wasn't sure *what*.

There was then a disturbance that seemed to flow through the presence in the room. Something was moving; he felt confused and agitated. What was happening, and why was he so ignorant of it? The thought of being excluded from something this wonderful and magnificent began to grate at his mood. Wasn't he a man of God? Why couldn't he grasp what was taking place right in front of him?

The kneeling man caressed her forehead, bent forward and gave it a soft kiss. He turned to Stephen with an expression the young priest would spend years trying to describe—an ineffable mixture of sadness, joy, resignation, and a dozen other variations of each.

"Hello, young Stephen," he said.

"Hello, Brother," he responded. "We have been looking for you."

"I'm sure you have." He pushed the Nurse Call button beside the bed and stepped forward, indicating with a jerk of his chin that they should leave. Sister Maggie was rushing over from a nurses' station when they emerged into the hallway and turned toward the exit. The nun caught the man's eye on the way out.

"Thank you," she said.

The pair departed in silence. It was not until the elevator door slid shut and they were hurtling back to the ground that Stephen spoke.

"What happened in there?" he asked haltingly.

"A woman died."

"Well, I know that. But somehow it seemed like more than that. I felt things."

"Congratulations."

Stephen glanced over for a sign of sarcasm in the comment, but there was none.

"No, I mean it," the man continued. "It's a compliment to your sensitivity that you could tell. Many well-meaning, spiritually gifted people would never have sensed a thing."

"So what happened?"

"A very simple event, one that's repeated a hundred thousand times a day across the planet. When a saved soul passes on, a number of angels are present to usher her soul through its transition. Usually a pair of carrier angels whose job it is to escort souls to paradise. The dying one may have no idea they are even there. But they accompany the spirit. In addition, depending on the suffering involved, there's at least one ministering angel. They are present solely to give peace and comfort and hope. These are the ones who most often came to me the times I've been imprisoned."

"When your hand jerked back a little . . . was that the moment? The moment of death, I mean."

His answer was a slow nod of the head. "You sensed motion?"

"I did."

"You were not mistaken. The ministering angel stood and moved aside for the carrier angels to move in and touch the soul as it left."

"I wish I could have seen it."

"You'll have more chances."

The elevator door opened to the rest of the world, and they proceeded forward. Stephen remembered that he had failed to inform his Brothers of his discovery. He reluctantly pulled out a cell phone while they exited the building and dialed Thierry.

"I found him, Brother Thierry . . . Yes . . . A hospice. Of course . . . We'll be there in ten minutes."

He hung up and walked a little farther before working up the nerve to speak again.

"Are you surrounded by these angels, then?" As soon as he asked it Stephen felt faithless, as though he should have known this all along. And yet it was so fantastic to contemplate.

"Yes, I am. So are you," he said with a paternal grin.

Stephen laughed. The concept was mind-blowing. Even though he believed in God and all the tenets of Christianity, to know for certain was intoxicating.

Another emotion began to push through the exhilaration: a sense of responsibility, of burden. For if all of this was true, what room remained for any doubt? He stared at the sidewalk for a while before speaking.

"You know, Brother, I think I've figured out why you make so many people uncomfortable."

"I've always wondered if it was some social lack on my part."

"Oh no. It isn't that at all. You see, most people, religious or not, live in a lifelong haze of unresolved belief. We believe, though much of the time not completely. Never quite a hundred percent. We can't—we don't have the final proof. Which is why faith is required. Yet most of us don't resent the need for faith near as we much as we say we do. Privately we cherish it for allowing us to hang back and reserve our ultimate commitment."

They came to his rental car and climbed in.

"And even the strongest of believers can grow quite comfortable with that last ten percent area of doubt. That vague fog. We grow accustomed to being ninety percent and letting that final ten percent float around unchallenged in our minds. It's what prevents us from having to respond radically to the reality of God. We end up, whether we know it or not, clinging desperately to our ambivalence. Without it, we might all find ourselves behaving recklessly, doing selfless acts like becoming missionaries or martyrs or something. So we cherish that ten percent of doubt. We come to rely on it."

"I understand," came the response. The man's gaze remained fixed on a place not of this earth.

"Then you come along," Stephen continued, "and you shatter that ten percent into a thousand pieces. I mean, your very identity is undeniable proof of the whole shooting match. An in-your-face challenge. It's a good thing you've stayed hidden and obscure all this time. There may be legends and rumors about you walking the earth, but as long as you don't surface too forcefully, we can all stay comfortable with our ten percent. Come to the forefront, and you'll make a whole lot of people very uneasy."

"I get the sense that is happening already, don't you, Father Stephen?"

"It's just beginning," he replied. "But yes, it definitely is."

17

Cambridge—Four Days Later

THE KNOCK ON HER DOOR came on the worst day of the year.

That year and any other, the tenth of May was Nora's most dreaded day. Even the hopefulness of spring's arrival, the end of classes and the beginning of the Red Sox season could not keep her from descending into a weeklong slump in the very anticipation of the day's arrival. Her few casual friends and acquaintances noticed little, especially given their own frenzy of finals studies and moving-out plans.

Nora would disappear from her usual haunts. She would take time off from her job at the German restaurant in Harvard Square. Bosses reluctant to grant her the leave would check her schedule and realize she'd been hoarding days off, planning for this week far in advance.

This year she'd even arranged for her classes not to have exams. Her papers were fully researched, spell-checked, and perfect-bound a full two weeks in advance. Typical, high achieving Nora, her professors assumed. Her professor of childhood development had asked her if she wanted to take the extra time to recheck her work or make any revisions. Nora had said no. She would be busy.

This year she hadn't tried to staunch the despair. Four days before, she began to sleep in late. To linger in her one-bedroom apartment above the garage of a Victorian home, foregoing her usual three-mile runs along its shaded residential street to the Charles River and the Band Shell. Two days beforehand she failed to open the blinds of her lone window and let in spring's brilliant sunshine, or the window's distant, partial view of Fenway's neon CITGO sign. On so many summer afternoons she might be found sitting alone behind the first-base dugout playing hooky from class, drinking too much cheap beer and cheering loudly for her hapless Sox. It was her only indulgence, but even that one she abandoned this week.

This year she moved from her bed to her couch and curled under a blanket to watch her favorite westerns: *High Noon*, *Rio Bravo*, and *Shane*. She ate nothing but party pizzas, instant meals, microwave oatmeal.

On the day the knock came, Nora was in the middle of the ritual's grand finale: watching old family eight-millimeter movies she had recently transferred to video.

On the screen her mother was young, her face as yet unmarked by the ravages of her husband's vagabond career as failed author and itinerant teacher of creative writing. Her hair was still a shiny brown, cascading onto bare, tanned shoulders in well-kempt waves. She smiled nervously into the camera, bending over to serve cake to a four-year-old Nora.

Her mother giggled at the camera, which struck her as all the more tragic. To realize her mother had once been so innocent as to consider a few moments before a borrowed Super 8 to be worth her making herself up as if it were a screen test for Paramount. Her mother had always been so gullible, so sweetly naïve.

Nora bent down, took a drink of the guava tequila she'd bought for that evening and squinted at her mother's face. At Nora's baby antics, her mother's laugh had turned from strained to genuine. Goldie McPheran had always delighted in her only child. Her smooth, unlined features suddenly contorted with unheard laughter.

Nora tried to fix that face in her mind. It was the face she needed to remember. Maybe she could have an artist draw or paint it for her, she thought, once she saved a little extra money. She could hang it up as a cherished icon. Anything to replace the lifeless version of the face Nora had pulled from the oven on this day eight years ago, the head which had lolled backward against her forearm, eyes staring wide open, tongue protruding thickly from cracked lips.

Nora took another drink of the tequila, her longest yet, desperately wishing to wash the image from her mind.

Another family episode lurched onto the video, this time a summer visit to her uncle Jimmy's backyard pool in Phoenix. The light was blindingly bright. Her father caroused with her in the pool's shallow end, throwing her up into the air with his knees against the pool bottom. His most recent layoff from a university faculty appeared forgotten in the glow of family togetherness.

It was *his* anniversary, too. A double whammy. Her mother had committed suicide on the fifth anniversary of her dear husband's kidnapping. New York City's only unsolved, still-open, unmotivated kidnapping case of the year. Her father there one moment, waiting on the sidewalk for his family to join him, and the next moment shoved into a waiting car by what eyewitnesses described as a pair of darkly dressed thugs. No link to organized crime had ever been found among her father's effects. No outstanding debts. No informer contacts to the FBI or any law enforcement agency.

Simply and completely unexplained.

Someday Nora would explain it. Perhaps not the actual reasons for her father's abduction, but she would at least find an explanation for the sorrow that had hovered over them for years before the twin disasters. Her family's pale demeanor, their cloistered paranoia and fear of the world. His disappearance had been a pain so wrenching that her mother had put Nora through the ordeal of finding her corpse simply to escape its agony. "A *moment's peace*," her mother had once pleaded to her. "*All I want is a moment's peace*." She'd groaned the words one year after her husband's disappearance, before the police had stopped calling.

Someday Nora McPheran, Ph.D. in abnormal psychology, would understand it all. And the understanding would help to salve the pain; she was sure of it. She had already analyzed herself sufficiently to realize the source of her own aloofness, the reason why she routinely sabotaged friendships before they could grow too intimate. Why she moved through the world as a loner, a black-haired, blue-jeaned enigma. The reason she'd jettisoned every romance that had shown signs of promise. She didn't want to leave a spouse or child the way she herself had been left. To make anyone else feel as bereft and betrayed as she did. That much her studies in psychology had helped her to understand.

But she still didn't know the cause—the source of the family curse. Someday she would, however, and then the healing process would begin. Only not quite yet. Not tonight.

She was yanked back from her dozing by the knocking. It sounded stronger and louder to her than necessary.

No one but her ex-boyfriend or department pals had ever knocked on her door. She turned off the VCR and TV, made a mental note of where she'd left the tire iron in a far corner, and walked up to the peephole. The head of a well-groomed man in a suit filled the view.

"Miss McPheran, may I come in? It's the police."

She cracked the door for only the few inches the latched chain would allow and peered anxiously out. She saw a young man not that many years older than herself, and handsome. A business card was thrust through the gap.

She took the card and read it. *Michael R. Stayton, Deputy Analyst, Central Intelligence Agency.*

"You're not an ordinary cop, are you?"

He smiled widely. "Truth is, Miss McPheran, I'm not technically a law enforcement officer. I just know that in certain neighborhoods, people need a quick assessment of their visitors. In a general sense, if you know what I mean. Especially if they're alone."

"You knew that?"

"The detectives' report said you were single. I presumed . . ."

She sighed good-naturedly. "You presumed right, unfortunately. So what do you want, Agent Stayton?"

"Follow-up on the assault against you, Miss McPheran."

"Oh. What does the CIA want with that?"

"If you'd let me in, I'd be glad to tell you."

She stepped back from the door to think. Then returned to the crack.

"May I see your driver's license and a few credit cards?"

"Excuse me?"

"Look, sir. I'm a woman alone, at night, and as you may know I have good reason to feel a little paranoid. I need a little confirmation."

A rustling, and three laminated cards appeared. She took them. Maryland driver's license, the same boyish face above the collar of a green polo shirt, a Visa bearing a small photo, and a CIA lapel pass.

She supposed he had to be legitimate. There was a long pause. Nora winced inwardly, thinking of the blanket lying on the couch, the tequila bottle, the video case.

"Give me just a minute."

She stepped back into the room, nearly closed the door behind her and began frantically picking up the scattered debris of her day. Finished, she returned to the door and swung it fully open.

"Sit wherever," she said with a weary tone. "Can I get you something?"

"No, thanks. Actually I'd just rather ask a couple of questions and be on my way, if you don't mind."

"Go ahead."

He sat on the edge of her couch, uncomfortably, and unbuckled an attaché case on his knees from which he produced a small tape recorder. "Nora, in your best recollection, how much contact have you had with anyone from overseas? I mean high-school pen pals. Exchange students. Distant relatives."

"Well, half of my classmates are from other countries."

"Are you close to any of them who are from, say, Lebanon, Syria, anywhere in the Middle East?"

"I can't recall."

"Think about it," he said flatly.

"No, none that I can remember."

"Okay. Now, where did you meet the man who rescued you?"

"It's like I told the detectives, I never met the man before."

Stayton looked down at his knee with a youthful grin. "Yeah, but that's one part we're all having a hard time believing. Considering what he did for you and all. I mean, they say chivalry isn't dead, but that's taking it a bit far, if you know what I mean."

"You mean you wouldn't die for me, Agent Stayton?"

"Not unless it showed up on my job description," he replied with a sharp, nervous laugh. Clearing his throat, he said, "Okay. Now I'm going to ask you some questions about your personal opinions. I know they're uncomfortable, but it'll be far less uncomfortable than doing so under subpoena. Trust me, this is important."

She nodded.

"Nora, do you hold Zionist views?"

"What?"

"Do you actively support Israel and believe that an Arab presence in the occupied areas is some sort of abomination to God's Holy Land?"

"God? I hadn't thought about it that much. I'm not a very religious person. I definitely think Israel is the Jewish homeland. But it seems like they could share it with their neighbors. So I guess the answer's no."

"Have you ever written a letter to the editor? Especially one on a controversial topic like feminism or religion or abortion?"

"I thanked the student body for their attendance at my sorority's service day once."

"Do you hold the Islamic faith in any particular disapproval or contempt, and if so, have you ever voiced those views to anyone?"

"I've said a few curse words about Saddam Hussein and Osama bin Laden. That's about it."

"Have you ever read or espoused the works of Salman Rushdie?"

She chuckled at that one. "Look, I didn't provoke this. I promise you. I'm the most quiet, unassuming, apolitical, uncontroversial graduate student you'd ever want to meet. So stop trying to make it look like the attack on me was my fault."

He took a deep breath, then exhaled pointedly and looked at her. "Miss, I don't have to tell you anything about this investigation. But if you'd like any chance of seeing your attackers brought to justice, I'd strongly urge you to cooperate with us."

Us, she noted. *So it's* us *now. By this use of the plural, he must mean the "company."*

With that thought, the defiance began to leak from her like air from a punctured balloon. But then another thought struck her, and the balloon quickly inflated all over again. *This is my living room, my town, and my country! Why am I being made to feel like a criminal because I was the victim of a senseless assault?*

Her blood surged. She began to feel the veins in her neck, that familiar tension in her jaw.

"I've got some questions for *you*, Agent Stayton. And if you want any help from me, you'd better answer them. Like who in the world's trying to kill me? What is the name of the man who saved me—I'm sure you know that by now. And forgive me, but isn't the CIA's mandate strictly on non-domestic matters? So why are you investigating a Boston homicide attempt?"

"I'm sorry. I'm just not at liberty to discuss these things with you."

"Then forget my cooperation. And forget my being discreet about this case, for that matter."

"You'd only be putting your own safety at risk, Miss McPheran."

"Yeah, and why is that? Because this is about me! My life. My safety. So why are you treating me as though I'm ancillary to the case?"

His eyelids fluttered, and he looked from side to side, making it clear he was only tolerating her tirade until it was over.

"Tell me!" she persisted.

Not a word issued from his mouth. He took another, even more resigned, deep breath. He eyed her ceiling, her carpet, her old poster of Middle-Earth in the corner where she'd dropped it after losing the nerve to nail through the wallboard.

Finally he looked at her and spoke in a lowered voice. "Because you're the only American in history known to have been the specific target of a long-range, multi-continental attack by the terrorist group Hamas on United States soil."

Nora's torso bent, suddenly feeling like that of an old woman. She felt suddenly cold. Her breathing stuttered and fell into a ragged gasping.

"Nora, would you happen to know where your driver's license is?"

"I lost it a few weeks ago."

"Where?"

"I'm not sure. I thought maybe at an evening lecture, but that's just a guess."

Stayton reached into his attaché and pulled out a small plastic bag. Inside, she recognized the small square and unflattering photo of her Massachusetts driver's license.

"It was found in your attackers' car, and they had photocopies in their pockets. They planned their moves carefully. This is the anniversary of your parents' death, isn't it, Nora?"

His knowing this, coupled with the smugness of his tone, made her turn ice-cold inside. "Get out of my face, Agent Stayton," she said.

"I'm sorry, Nora. It wouldn't ordinarily be any of my business. But you have to understand—it didn't take me long to learn of your annual routine, and I'm certain the terrorists knew it also. They knew that if they took you that night, it would be a week before anyone reported you missing."

So *he* was the man she'd heard had been asking about her, plying her friends and professors with casual-yet-persistent questions concerning her habits. She'd received puzzled calls from several of them. One had just assumed he was a guy interested in her. "*Kinda cute*," she had said. Although Nora figured them to be associated with the police investigation, the reports had only deepened her paranoia.

Then she realized what Stayton was saying, and the chill passed through every inch of her body.

"Why? Why me?"

"That's what we're trying to find out."

"Yeah, but don't you have all but one of them in custody? In the hospital?"

Stayton's face fell and grew red. "There was a security breach at the ward. Two men entered, freed the two who were ambulatory, and shot dead the one who was still unconscious. Then escaped clean. Some pretty sick men."

She was hardly listening now, yet she remained intent on regaining control of her breathing before he noticed that she was in the full throes of an anxiety attack.

"As for your rescuer, as you already know, he survived and then disappeared into thin air. His wallet, however, revealed many interesting facts. No clear information, but hints of a fascinating cover-up." Stayton rolled his eyes to the ceiling, recollecting. "His wallet ID identified him as André Lassalle. French citizen. Credit reports show great wealth—hundreds of millions—but no address. No employment or educational history. No family. And French authorities have found links to other identities. Whoever he is, the man has hidden behind so many layers of money and secrecy, we're not sure they'll ever find him."

He stood, gathering his papers into the attaché. Then he impulsively turned and grabbed hold of her hand. His demeanor became suddenly tense and alarmed.

"Nora, I consider your life to be in danger. If they are Hamas and they're not dead, they'll keep coming at you. They'll wait patiently, months even, until I and my caseload have moved on. Unfortunately, that's just my expert opinion. My superiors have other thoughts; they believe there's not enough official cause to justify full-time protection. We're asking the FBI to pitch in, but what with the turf wars involved, you never know if they'll do anything at all. Please remember that no one told you this. Still, you need to take a trip. A very discreet one. Just take off to someplace only you know about for a couple weeks. I assure you, the faculty administration will be well briefed on the reasons for your absence."

Her head felt light. "Okay, I will," she heard herself saying, then realized with a twinge of surprise that she had meant it.

"Leave your car behind. Rent one of those beat-up used jobs. Use only cash. Don't go anywhere predictable, like family."

She let out a small laugh. "That'll be easy. I have none."

"That's right. Sorry. Call me using the number on my card in a week or so. Would you like me to stay until you're ready to leave?"

The old self-reliant streak reared in her thoughts, and she instinctively nodded no, but with a grateful smile on her face. "Thanks, Agent Stayton. But I'll be out of here within ten minutes."

He nodded and made for the door. Before turning the knob, he wheeled around and held up a small metal object. A strange shape on a cheap golden chain. It was a pewter amulet, a tiny hollow arch flanked by a solid circle—an open door. He held it closer to his face and said, "Miss McPheran, have you ever seen this artifact before?"

She stared at it a second and was instantly transported. She was a little girl again, six or seven, rocking on her father's knee. The feeling was both specific and sensory: an amalgam of his after-shave's smell, the slant of light in the upstairs study, the solidity of his leg beneath her like a great soft rocking horse, and the magnolia tree waving in the window. All was safe, all was provided. And the world consisted of brief interludes between times like this, alone with her father.

"Miss McPheran? Are you okay?"

"Ah, yes."

"Have you seen it."

"No. I . . . I haven't. Sorry."

"All right. You take care now, okay?"

The agent closed the door with a half smile and was gone.

18

After Agent Stayton's departure, Nora reentered her living room, sat on the edge of her couch and vowed to sit there until her head stopped swimming. She gave up after ten minutes. After a half hour she realized that neither the tequila nor the depression was causing the sensation, but rather the realization that her life had just whirled around a most precipitous corner.

Her parents had been perennial victims, she realized, and so would have lacked the strength to assert themselves before such a crisis. She, however, would deal with life differently. She would do everything they hadn't. She had vowed this since the day she'd stood over her mother's grave and felt the tears suddenly dry up within her.

Had Stayton merely spoken to her, or had he also given her a hard, entirely helpful slap beside the head? She could hardly say. But while she set about cleaning up the litter of her self-pity, she felt as though her thoughts had been rearranged. For the better.

She stood and exhaled once, loudly. Leaning over, with an exaggerated unclenching of her fingers, she let the tequila bottle fall and clang loudly into her trash basket. She poured herself a glass of water and sat on the table's edge drinking, staring.

Her vision began to slow its rotations. Her head started to clear.

She felt the edges of a decision begin to gather form and

sharpen. She would definitely heed Stayton's warnings. But she would not merely go and cower in a hiding place somewhere.

Since the attack, something deep inside herself had told her that she'd been no innocent bystander, no random victim. Now she knew that for certain. Nor did she have any confidence that even the CIA would solve this attack against her—any more than the NYPD had been able to solve her father's clearly organized, clearly professional, abduction.

I'll do it myself, she thought.

In the months following her father's kidnapping, when it had finally become clear that he wouldn't be returning, she'd allowed a schoolgirl fantasy to come back to life. She had imagined herself becoming a one-woman detective force, returning to confound the apathetic cops who had bungled the case and allowed the leads to go cold. She had pictured herself brazenly confronting her father's killers, bringing them to justice, and as a result becoming a hero. And restoring her mother to her normal, cheerful self.

Part of her had always blamed herself for not following that dream. The failure had fed Nora's latent guilt that her family's destruction had been her own fault. If she hadn't insisted on going into Saks for that rabbit coat, her father wouldn't have stood out alone on that sidewalk. Who knows how things might have turned out then?

She would not make the same mistake twice. She would disappear, yes, but not to hide. To solve this thing.

Then she stopped still, her hands submerged in dishwater. What about her studies? She was a dissertation away from earning a hard-won Ivy League doctorate. Was she to put all that off on a whim, a fantasy?

True, she could justify a leave of absence, especially given the recent attack, yet when she returned it would be much harder to resume her studies. She'd worked hard to assemble just the right dissertation committee with her favorite professors, those most amenable to her dissertation topic. Two of them had made special exceptions to serve on her committee, measures which would only last until the end of the year. Another was soon to leave on sabbatical. If she took time off now, she would probably have to stack her committee with the stodgy old reactionary faculty who detested her avant-garde premise to begin with. She could lose years.

Her head started to swim again. Angrily, she walked into her bedroom and started to pull a change of clothes from their hangers.

LESS THAN TWO HOURS after Agent Stayton's departure, a taxi pulled up in front of Nora's house. She jumped into the cab with only an empty backpack. The driver steered her to a nearby shopping district and waited while she withdrew her entire balance—thirty-two hundred dollars. She left the taxi outside a hair salon where she had her shoulder-length hair cut in a boyish style barely an inch long, then bleached blonde. She walked to a neighborhood supermarket and bought forty dollars' worth of energy bars, bottled herb teas, ramen soup packets, and assorted snacks capable of holding her appetite at bay with minimal effort.

Stuffing as much of her purchase as she could into the backpack and grasping plastic bags in both hands, she walked four blocks to a seedy car-rental lot. There she rented a twelve-year-old Oldsmobile Ciera and drove back to her home neighborhood. She parked three addresses down from her own, looked up and down the street for strange vehicles or loiterers. Seeing none, she left the car and returned to her house. It took her less than five minutes to return with a sleeping bag, pillow, and a few changes of clothes stuffed into a pillowcase.

By the time she walked across the hallowed front steps of Widener Library, she looked and behaved like any other punk-style undergrad. In fact, those who did know her in passing would have hardly recognized the Nora McPheran of old. And the change felt more than cosmetic. She felt radiant. She was a free woman, feeling unleashed for the first time in years. Her mother would have blanched and nearly keeled over at the dangers of such impulsiveness. But her old life was a thing of the past. Every inch of her body tingled with the thrill of her new resolve, of her self-appointed quest. The danger involved only added to the thrill. Her life was under threat, and because of that it suddenly seemed more precious than ever before. She answered to no one in the world. No one to tell her she could not follow this strange mission to its end. No one to spill the secret, to mock her, to try to stop her. Forget class, and forget the degree, if it came to that. What she was doing now was real, it was personal, and it mattered.

She didn't pause to look back across Harvard Yard, the famous square marked by its huge old trees, surrounded by ancient brick buildings and a spired chapel. Instead, she strode inside Widener and climbed to the second floor to her graduate carrel.

She opened the door to her enclosed cubicle, one of fifty identical compartments, dropped her backpack softly to the floor and looked about her. The entire hall around her stood silent, as she had assumed it would this early in the morning. Most of the small wooden spaces remained empty until either late at night or, during dissertation review season, around the clock. Today was too early for either of these.

Over the next two hours she moved in her food, the sleeping bag and pillow. She appropriated four sheets of computer paper from a friend's outdated dot-matrix printer and scribbled a message with a thick marker: *Dissertation in progress. Do not disturb on pain of death.* She taped the message to the outside of the carrel door as a warning. Certainly no one would dare to knock on the door or begin to question the long hours she remained here, overheard snoring, or unusual quantities of food.

Her move-in complete, she looked around her and sighed. In an odd way, this was one of the most remote and coziest hideouts a person like herself could contrive in short order. The carrel room was locked at all times, located on the forgotten upper floor of a library regularly patrolled by security. A place no one frequented unless they had to.

The place also served her very specific purpose, which was not only to get lost but to study. She hadn't slept nor entertained an idle thought since Agent Stayton's visit.

The one thing Stayton had said that Nora could believe was his last warning. She instinctively knew he'd been telling her the truth then, and at his own personal risk.

She was still in danger.

The only lie she had told him was her parting statement—that she had no recollection of the amulet he had shown her. The symbol on the necklace. She had no idea what had provoked either the certainty or the accompanying vision of her father, but she knew that shape, the delicate arch flanked by a solid oval which matched the arch's interior. She had interpreted it immediately as an open door, with the arch its open frame, and its oval the door standing ajar. Perhaps she was the only one who would see it that way.

Open door, she scribbled on a legal pad after sketching her best recreation of the strange design. The phrase meant nothing overt to her. Why would it lead to her being attacked? Stayton had certainly acquired it from her rescuer's effects at the hospital. Clearly the symbol was benign to her, a representation of something which meant her good. Still, she could not place it.

She pictured the necklace as clearly as she could. Some attribute of the piece had evaded her. *Yes, it's ancient,* she realized. The patina of the metal, the pattern of tiny scratches on its surfaces made it clear it was several centuries old. Nora left the carrel and ventured downstairs to the History section. After lurking behind the stacks to make sure no menacing or unusually inquisitive people were about, she moved forward to ask a tall, gangly young assistant for help in locating historical symbols.

"What period?" he asked.

"I don't know. All periods . . . within a thousand years."

With a weary sigh the young man led her several rows away, then turned in. He gestured up at her shoulder level. "Religious symbols?" he said.

"Well, I'm trying to track a particular shape and I'm not sure of its meaning. Sure, let's start with religious."

"Good." He reached up to the oversized volumes and pulled several tomes off the shelf.

"Do you want me to get a cart?" she asked him.

"No. I think we can just carry 'em."

He handed her a stack of books, and she immediately slumped forward from the weight. Wincing from the load, she made her way back to the carrel, her burdened assistant close behind.

She spent the day leaning back against the carrel wall, half-wrapped in her sleeping bag, sipping bottled mocha drinks and leafing through books. She enjoyed the fugitive role, except for the increasing degree of alarm she felt every time the hall doors clicked open or shut. Her nerves tingled on the edge of panic until either another carrel door opened or it became clear the footsteps were not approaching her row.

It turned out, however, that the books offered her little help. None of the religious symbols she found bore any resemblance to the odd shape she sought to match. For a while she thought Eastern religions with their varied icons might give her the answer, but then something told her that wandering this far afield was not the solution. Perhaps the truth lay much closer to home. And yet Western, Judeo-Christian symbology offered no help, either.

It took her two hours to thumb carefully through the thickest of the books. The other two took half that time. By then it was two in the morning and her brain seemed permanently imprinted with the myriad images and varieties of crosses and menorahs.

She closed the cover of the last book and drew a long, disgusted sigh.

Okay. Time to get real, she told herself. She thought of how she often found lost household items in her apartment. Often she had known where the missing item lay all along; it had simply been a matter of clearing away the preliminary cobwebs and giving her first impulse its due. Usually the quiet premise she had followed or simply ignored would prove absolutely correct.

So what was my first impulse on this mysterious attack?

Me. My family. My past . . .

19

Mont St. Michel

THE SOLITARY FIGURE stood on the abbey's rooftop and savored the glow of the full moon, the endless view, the cool breeze blowing across the sands, the smell of distant seawater.

Father Thierry sat on a stone bench facing him and tried not to stare. But it was like watching a ghost—to look at this face from his youth and see it now utterly unchanged, with the same faint lines on that high forehead, same dark hair, same strong nose and square chin and light brown skin unmarked by the ensuing decades. Yet if he focused, if he stopped and really looked as Thierry did now, he noticed something different. An aloofness. A gaze haunted not by depression, but by a sadness far more powerful and elemental. Years ago Father Gosdich, Thierry's mentor in the priesthood, had said that the man seemed surrounded by a thousand ghosts. Thierry now saw the truth in that comment.

They remained silent for several minutes, peering out toward England and allowing the offshore breeze to assault their expressionless faces.

Finally Thierry reached down to his feet and held up a half-full bottle of red wine, poured the liquid into an empty glass and offered it to his companion. "Here. Drink," he said.

Thierry poured some wine for himself and they both drank deeply as they returned their eyes to the moonlit horizon.

"Talk to me. Tell me how it feels to come back each time."

The man remained still for a long moment, then acquiesced, leaning back to look up at the stars. He spoke with the bitterness still lingering in his voice. "I wish I could explain it to you, Thierry."

"Please try. Please."

"After every one of the imprisonments, the sweetest thing is rediscovering each taste, each sensation, each sight. Like being a child again. Only with memory to inform you." He rested against the stone railing and closed his eyes. "I remembered this just a few hours ago. The morning after the Order broke me out of Torquemada's prison after ten years, I walked down a merchant lane in Seville just as a baker brought out the morning's loaves. I stopped in the street, closed my eyes and smelled the grain and the yeast, and I began to weep. I couldn't stop; I felt like a fool standing there sobbing, yet I was powerless. The baker turned toward me, took his thickest loaf in both hands, and held it out to me. I had no money in my pockets, but he did not want any. It was a gift. I did not tell him, of course, that I do not require nourishment. So I tore off a hunk and put it in my mouth. And just then, for that one second, I thought to myself that ten years of captivity had been worth it. For that one smell, that one taste."

The man fell silent for a minute.

"I have always loved reconnecting with this world. But things have changed. The killing you have told me about, the wars, the machines of death. . . . I don't know if this is a world I want to reenter."

Thierry did not answer for a long time.

"I drove my men nearly mad," the priest said at last, "always searching. But I knew that if you had escaped from the Nazis we would have heard."

"Of course. I would have contacted the Order. I always have."

"I know. And if the Lord had called you home, finally . . ."

"You would have been told somehow, I'm sure of it."

"Yes."

They drifted into a long silence again, like two old friends. A gust of wind blew fiercely for a brief time and then spent itself. As much to revive the conversation as anything else, Thierry decided to indulge his curiosity.

"If I may ask, how do you survive? Your mind? Your spirit?"

"The first hours are usually the worst. But this time they were a relief. You see, I spent the last four days before my entombment in the company of SS Colonel Gebhardt."

Thierry looked away.

"You have heard of him?"

"Yes. One of the Auschwitz butchers," Thierry answered. "One of Mengele's henchmen."

"Yes. That's him." He let out a long breath and looked up at the moon. "He was the most cruel host my enemy has ever chosen. In all the centuries he and I have battled, none was more debased. Thierry, I will only say this once, and only to you. But those four days in that laboratory . . . well, if I had died and gone to hell, I am not sure I could have suffered worse. His inability to kill me only emboldened him, enraged him."

"You do not have to say any more."

The man shook his head as if to scatter the thoughts from his mind. "At such times I would give anything to be mortal. To have a limit, a threshold beyond which I could not suffer, and simply die."

"I know. Nearly every new member of the Order has at some time or other exclaimed to me how wonderful it must feel to be indestructible, immortal. How powerful to be impervious to death. I always tell them in the sternest manner possible that exactly the opposite is true. That you are in many ways more vulnerable to pain and suffering than any person alive."

"Yes, it is true. And yet even during the worst of suffering there are comforts. I receive visitors. From the spirit realm."

"Ah," Thierry said. "Angels come to you?"

"Yes. They comfort me, speak to me, share memories, sing. At times I've had as many as six in the chamber with me."

Thierry wanted badly to ask about the visitors, inquire about their appearance, their speech, their music. But then he reminded himself that there was no end to what he could ask this man if he abandoned self-restraint.

"As for the rest of the time, I sleep. Not sleeping as you would know it, but a state of deep stillness. And I revisit my past. Jerusalem, Ireland, France. I swim in my memories. I revisit Claere again."

"If only I could have known her."

The man winced as though Thierry's words had brought his loss fresh to his mind. He stood and walked slowly toward a pool of moonlight. Thierry came alongside, and the two men strolled quietly, the breeze caressing their faces.

"I have searched for you for so long," Thierry began, "I have neglected my relations with Rome."

"I do not need Rome. What I need are friends like you. Do you know how few true friends I have had, in all this time?"

"Yes, but you have no idea how complicated the world has become. Not many people will be glad to hear of your return."

"I have never wished to announce my presence."

"I understand, but today it will become known. Everything does. The conflicts, the alliances, the conspiracies—it is too much for an old man to keep up with. There are no secrets in today's world."

"Oh, I'm sure there are."

"None as incredible as you. The news of your discovery will travel halfway across the globe within hours. There are still legends of you circulating through parts of the Church. They never die. I take a risk even housing you here, despite the security. I do not know what the future holds for us. I—" The old man's voice broke.

The man turned to Thierry and placed an arm around his friend's shoulders. "Do you remember the first swim we took together, out on the Cote Basque?" Thierry nodded through his tears. "It was '27, I think. You were just out of seminary."

"Seeing the Mediterranean for the first time."

"Yes. The Order would not issue us swimsuits, and you were convinced that the act of jumping from a cliff unclothed would send you to hell."

"I was a young man, and you looked exactly—"

"Yes, I looked as silly as you did, diving naked into the water. I swear to you, I did not know the convent would be out on excursion that afternoon."

"Do you remember the look on their faces?"

Their laughter rang out across the barren roof and drifted into the night air.

"To this day," Thierry said, "every time I see a nun smile at me, I cannot help wondering."

"Even after all this time?"

"My friend, some stories never die."

20

Boston

NORA HAD ALWAYS loved driving through Boston in the middle of the night, for it was one of the few times when the act of navigating through the city's crazed streets did not seem like an act of suicide. She could unclench her fists from around the steering wheel, straighten her back, and relax like a normal human being.

This night proved exactly the opposite. It was a clear evening, affording her a large milky moon that not only silhouetted the distant skyline but shimmered thickly on the waters alongside her. With her hands firmly on the wheel, she tried to reassure herself with the fact that the hour gave her a far more distinct look at anyone attempting to follow her. The beams of other headlights came rarely enough as it was, so anyone following her would stand out immediately. She then realized that this dynamic worked both ways: she was doubly conspicuous to anyone on the lookout for her.

She headed toward Newton, driving more erratically as time went on. "Settle down," she muttered to herself. To calm her growing panic, she turned her mind to its familiar, morose paths.

Her family had never been one for full disclosure, something she'd learned to recognize early in life. It had seemed like peeling an enormous onion just to get to the bottom of anything, especially as it concerned her father. Paradoxically, God had given him a gift for gab and storytelling yet withheld from him the ability to make his family feel like an integral part of his life. There were deeply held secrets in the family. Drawers and boxes marked *Do not open*. Conversations that ended with her entrance into a room, no matter how old she'd become. Relatives who called frequently and yet could not, for reasons unknown to her, drive the hundred miles or so to visit—ever.

More than that were the stories that ended abruptly, in silences and furtive glances from her mother warning against pursuing certain topics. Nora had discovered early in school that most of her classmates had far more extensive grasps of their family histories than she did.

"*Someday*," her father had always said, raising his right hand like the pope. "*Someday you will understand. I promise*."

Arriving at her destination, Nora realized just how crazy she was to be out here at this hour. Even without the threat of a terrorist attack—a threat relayed by, of all sources, the CIA, for pete's sake—most young women would never dream of frequenting such a place, let alone at night. The row of storage lockers lay in a dingy industrial section of Newton, tucked in the shadow of a nearby power plant's steam-belching towers. She had almost forgotten the address. For years it had been a place she mailed a check every month, but no more.

A light rain struck her hand when she reached out the car's window to punch in the code. Clutched in her steering-wheel hand was a yellowed paper bearing the scribbled numbers. She drove into the complex, which clung to a shallow hill long ago smothered by pavement. Today the aging surface offered an obstacle course of furrows, potholes, and yawning cracks.

It was almost midnight when she yanked up on the storage unit's door handle and just about shredded her hand in the futile effort. The last time she'd touched the place was three months after her mother's funeral. There had been no reason to return since.

Waving her hand in pain, she walked back to her car and found a thick towel left in the backseat after a swim. Returning, she wrapped the towel around the stubborn door handle while at the same time cocking her foot under the metal lever. She pulled her leg up, hard. With a groan that sounded as though the metal were rending apart, the door raised a foot. She gritted in determination and reached down to pull it up the rest of the way. In screeching one-foot increments, the door yielded. Finally it stood at chest height, enough for her to dart inside.

Luckily she knew just where to go. She'd been wise enough to sell off most of her family's old furniture. Most of what remained here were personal effects and records of sentimental value. Someday, Nora had vowed, when she had a house and a family and the time to do so, she would take it all home and sort it out properly.

She wove through stacks of boxes to the one containing her father's most secret archives. Even with him dead, she'd never seen fit to violate his reticence, so the stack of boxes remained sealed as he'd left them. The top box towered over her head. Carefully she edged it forward with her fingertips until it slid heavily into her arms.

A noise outside wrenched her head around and plunged her into terror. Again the folly of the time and location struck her. A car approached. What was she doing here, so vulnerable like this? The gloom turned into blackness, and she began to feel like a frightened child.

She heard the sound of tires rolling across pavement, slowly. She felt the hairs rise on her forearms and the back of her neck.

And then the sound faded away.

She closed her eyes in relief and vowed to leave this place immediately. She stacked three boxes into her car's backseat and trunk, relocked the storage unit, and drove away fast through the downpour. It was nearly two in the morning when she made it back to Harvard, and by that time she'd slipped into a state of punchy euphoria, not unlike her all-night cram sessions. Unloading in the rain while the whole world slept, she felt once again on a mission. And of course she was—her mission a legitimate quest for answers. Many people up at this hour were either trying to weave home drunk or up to some nefarious purpose.

She was saving her own life.

Nora appropriated a dolly from the library loading dock and quickly hauled the boxes up to her carrel. Then she crawled into her sleeping bag and, despite her intention of staying up to read her father's papers, fell into a deep slumber.

21

NORA AWOKE FEELING grungy but rested. She had no idea how long she'd slept, for the hall's only lighting came from the carrels themselves. After getting cleaned up in the rest room down the hall, she returned to her carrel, tore into a bagel, opened a bottle of mineral water, and steeled herself for her task.

She positioned the first box at her feet and took out her keys to slice the tape that wrapped it. Amazing how even after this many years since his disappearance, she still felt like a disobedient little girl, desecrating Daddy's private realm.

With a tiny snarl of determination, she ripped at the tape and raised the lid.

And immediately, miraculously, she saw it there.

It lay in the corner of the box, alongside his dog tags, class ring, and a plaster imprint of a child's right hand. A necklace and amulet. Its charm: the small silver shape of a half oval next to a solid one. *The open door.*

With a gasp, she reached for it.

Holding it in her hand, she told herself she'd known it all along. From way back in her memories of early childhood she understood that the symbol meant something important. He had worn it before she was old enough to ask questions. She could swear she'd reached for it, a toddler's curiosity, fingered the odd shape with stubby fingers.

She realized that the shape was within her, a part of her, conveyed by some direct contact in her past. She turned over the amulet looking for an inscribed clue. Nothing.

As she began sifting through the documents, a yellowed letter caught her eye which bore the letterhead of the Secretary of the Army. She opened it and read.

Dear Mrs. McPheran,

It is with deep regret and a nation's gratitude that we inform you of your husband's death in battle. Joseph McPheran was mortally wounded in Amiens, France, during a lengthy engagement between Hun and Allied troops. We hope your grief can be lessened by the knowledge that your husband fought bravely for a just cause.

Grieving with you,
Major George Patton

A postscript followed.

We understand that a discharge order was sent to Mr. McPheran's unit on October 23. It appears your husband declined to leave his platoon and continued fighting for another three weeks. Mrs. McPheran, he was truly a brave and dedicated soldier.

Nora raised an eyebrow. Why had a discharge order been given for her grandfather? She had never heard of this before.

She dug deeper, rummaging through a pile of deeds and birth records, even coming across a genealogical chart going back as far as three hundred years. Then she spotted a thick brown envelope, addressed in a flowing hand, with a letter inside that read:

My dear grandson,

I am so sorry that your father's disappearance, among so many other things, prevented him from sharing with you what all McPheran fathers tell their boys at a certain age.

Because so much time and distance separate us, I will attempt to tell you this now.

As you may have noticed, we do not belong to the most ordinary of families. We are both cursed and blessed. Constant tragedy and undeserved blessing seem to flow upon us from the same even hand. We are a family of widows and fatherless children. Yet we are also an inexplicably prosperous and well-positioned family. Neither one do we understand. Certainly through the years many of our number have arrived at various guesses and theories as to why our men have been taken from us so randomly yet so predictably, and why also some benevolent force seems to be on our side, intervening on our behalf. My dear boy, I do not think you should put too much stock in any of the stories. Our plight is a mystery, and sometimes mysteries are best left at rest.

I love you very much, and I wish I could spare you from the dangers of our lot. But I cannot. I can only urge you to love God with all your heart and enjoy the good times ahead. The more fortunate half of our mystery will make sure you get plenty of those. You may be the one to break the cycle. I would love nothing better than to know you as the one who ended so many years of grief.

I hope to see you soon. Perhaps my sciatica will allow me to tolerate a train trip out to Michigan soon. Please be careful. And remember, my dear son Walter loved you like no other father has ever loved a son. I know you will see him again someday.

Love,

Grandma Myra

Nora read the letter through twice, then leaned back in her chair and took a long, deep breath.

Obviously her father hadn't been spared the fate described in her great-grandmother's letter. She wondered if his desire to escape a violent death had been the reason for all the moves, the wandering from place to place. Her thoughts darted about from one conclusion to another. He'd been abducted just after selling a manuscript and finally emerging from anonymity. Could he have known the risk such a thing would expose him to? Perhaps this explained his reluctance to market his work, his antipathy toward success and possible fame.

She had never once considered that his mediocrity could have been a survival tactic.

Feeling flushed, sweat appearing on her brow, she bent down to resume her search. Beneath the letter was a stack of photographs. She picked up the pictures and started shuffling through them. The first few showed her father with several men she did not recognize, yet whose similar features revealed them to be relatives she'd never met. They seemed to care for one another, standing with arms around each other's shoulders in a series of wooded, pastoral settings. The photographs then turned to black-and-white, followed by sepia, their figures strangers to her. . . .

Wait! She quickly flipped back through the photographs. The very last color one showed a young man wearing a necklace. Yes!

It was her open-door symbol.

She flipped back again, further in time, and pulled out a brownish photo of a stout young man with a walrus mustache and pinstripe suit. Hanging just over his thickly starched collar lay the exact same necklace and symbol.

Flipping more, she came across another photo of two men dressed in priests' habits, standing on a gleaming black rock above the seashore. The dull gray sunlight had outlined the silver thread around their necks, as well as the small, barely discernible round shapes that hung from them. She could not make out the shape for certain, though she would have staked her life on the magnified view.

Priests.

She walked down to the library floor and asked a clerk for anything on the secrets of Catholicism and was handed three equally weighty volumes. This time she could hardly feel them in her arms, so anxious was she to return to her nook and crack them open.

The books became her furniture, her workout equipment, even her pillows for the next two days. Wired on cups of coffee she acquired on quick jaunts to the campus cafeteria, she pored over every page. Even if she didn't know precisely what it was she was seeking—her family name, strange protectors, the necklace—she felt in an odd way that the answer to the mystery would come to her, that she would somehow find it.

In the early afternoon of the second day, just as post-lunch fatigue began to assault her senses, she turned a page and felt a strange thrill run through her even as she held the sheet in her hand and beheld a grainy picture of a necklace posed on a velvet case.

She held her father's amulet beside the image. They were one and the same.

The legend read, *Symbol of the Lazarian Order, 1681.*

Below this was a paragraph with the header THE ORDER OF THE ST. LAZARE. *An obscure, possibly even fictitious monastic order reputed to have been consecrated in 1323 by Pope John XXII and based in the north of France. Its original charter is clouded in mystery and conjecture, almost certainly enlivened by the imaginations of simple-minded French peasants and devotees of the Templar legends. All published references to the Order cease early in the twentieth century.*

Langley, Virginia

"AGENT STAYTON, PLEASE."

"Speaking."

"Mr. Stayton, this is Nora McPheran. Listen, I've heeded your advice and am keeping a low profile."

"Glad to hear it. By the way, call me Mike."

"Fine. The reason I'm calling you, Mike, is that I've been doing some research on that necklace you showed me. I presume you took it from the man who rescued me."

"I can't say, Nora. Sorry. But go ahead."

"Well, I found something. Check out an obscure Catholic priesthood called the Order of St. Lazare. They've been involved with my family somehow for years, and your necklace is their emblem."

"Really."

"Just thought you should know. Gotta run now. I've got to figure out the rest of this thing, and I've finally got a little momentum going."

"Thanks, Nora."

His phone went dead.

Stayton swiveled around in his chair to face a colleague, who was busy poring over a list of overnight dispatches.

"Hey, noodlehead, you still got that number for our Vatican contact?"

Without raising his curly head from his reading, the analyst reached one hand into a tray of contact cards, glanced over while his fingers rifled through them, jerked a single card away, and waved the card behind him.

Stayton wheeled his chair back and snatched it from the man's hand in a practiced motion. "Thank you, sir. I will never call you *noodlehead* again."

"Right," the man replied. "At least not until noon."

But Stayton was already on the phone, listening to the international tones run through their tinny symphony.

"Hello, Monsignor Signorile? This is Michael Stayton at Consolidated Institutes of America. Is the weather clear? Good. Do you have time to talk?"

Vatican City

AGENT MICHAEL STAYTON'S single, early morning telephone call to Bishop Pablo Signorile, the CIA's midlevel contact and quasi-official liaison within the Vatican, appeared to yield little tangible fruit. Signorile claimed only a faint knowledge of the Order Nora had spoken of, yet he assured Stayton he would check into it and return him a brief within the week.

Then, red-faced and shaking, the bishop plunged his finger onto the telephone hook and redialed furiously.

Within minutes, a dozen offices honeycombed deep throughout the sprawling Vatican office complex buzzed with sudden, unwelcome activity. An additional two hundred phone calls were placed in the ensuing five minutes to successive Vatican directorates, each of which had also heard the news within approximately the same time span.

Many of the departments and priests manning these telephone lines were entirely unknown to those beyond their walls. Even to Vatican regulars.

"IS ALL THIS NECESSARY?" he asked sharply in Italian. His words echoed tinnily across ancient stones.

The police officer, not a Swiss Guard but a member of the Vatican's modern *Vigilanza* police force, looked back at him and shrugged good-naturedly. The man walked only three steps ahead, yet the stairs rose so steeply that the questioner's shoulders stood level with the backs of the officer's knees.

"The Keeper insisted on it for your own safety and confidentiality, Your Holiness."

Pope Peter II shrugged and resumed his climb into flickering torchlight, feeling like a doomed character in some medieval tragedy. The Vigilanza's presence, and the absence of Swiss Guards, told him a great deal about this abrupt summons—it was no trifling or ceremonial matter.

He thought back three years before, to his first official papal tour of the secret archives. He'd been led by a large procession across the *Cortile del Belvedere* and through a nondescript door just beside the entrance to the Vatican library. Although the foyer resembled a hotel lobby, the ordinariness had ended there. The Archive Keeper had brought him into a small elevator, and together they descended to the same concrete corridor today's procession had just left.

Peter had glanced down its bare expanse and remembered the

old American television serial some of his less abstemious brothers had grown enamored of in seminary. *Get Smart*. An opening sequence of endlessly opening doors, leading into deeper and deeper secret depths.

They entered a salon bordered on every side by small library carts, each one containing ancient documents with leather covers and faded seals. Hundreds upon hundreds of gray steel shelves, all of them filled with neat stacks—a staggering amount of paper.

And the whole time, the Keeper's monotone litany had droned on beside him, describing incredible things. Momentous holdings of the Church. Repositories of staggering information. They had entered the Parchment Room, a large chamber lined with waist-high wooden display cases. "*Armadio*," the Keeper had called them, which was where the most ancient archives were kept.

The Keeper's list had gone on and on, so long that Peter had wondered when the man would stop for a breath.

Accounts of ancient conflicts, combatants like Martin Luther, John Calvin, Napoleon Bonaparte, Vladimir Lenin. The handwritten records of Galileo's trial. The letters of Joan of Arc. Top secret Vatican communiqués about most of the world's leaders, including Britain's reigning monarch. The President of the United States, the one who proclaimed himself a Catholic.

The Keeper had walked him into a special vault and his voice adopted a reverent tone. He pointed to a drawer that contained Pope Paul IV's final letter from Catholic Queen Mary Tudor, written just minutes before her beheading. Another that held the love letters between King Henry VIII and Anne Boleyn. Ancient parchments dating back to the twelfth century—letters between emperors and popes, documents related to the Crusades, official texts from 1854 about the Immaculate Conception. A letter in Chinese from the Empress Helena to Pope Innocent X. A vellum scroll inscribed in Greek from the Byzantine emperor himself.

Peter had walked out ten minutes later, pale and light-headed. Since then, he could not see the Archives Keeper without feeling a queasiness in the stomach. He felt it today, years now after that initial visit.

They were climbing stairs, leading upward. Whether they were aboveground yet was uncertain. He looked about him and ventured a guess. *Torre del Venti*, Tower of the Winds.

Good thing this isn't one of my predecessors, he thought. *They would have needed an ambulance by now.*

At age forty-nine he was the youngest pope in half a century. A vigorous, highly conservative bishop from the Ukraine when the call had come, he prided himself on the youthful and capable image he portrayed, especially after his beloved predecessor had lasted so far into near infirmity.

Finally they reached the top. His main clue to that fact was a bottleneck of guards before a turret door, glancing outside menacingly. With their guns pointed straight into the air, they nodded at him to turn.

He shook his head in disbelief and stepped forward into the torch-lit passageway. He had never seen such secrecy, even during the morass of rituals and security details that had accompanied his election three years earlier.

Through the gloom ahead an open door radiated light. The Meridian Room. Yes, this was indeed the Tower of the Winds, as the endless climb had begun to confirm. Pope Peter thought back to his frequent history lectures. The building had been commissioned in 1576 by Pope Gregory XIII for astronomical observations. From this tower in the 1620s, Galileo tried to prove why the modern view of the universe should not be dismissed out of hand.

He stepped into the Meridian Room itself, a massive chamber covered with Circignani murals. It was in this very room that the world's calendar had been recalculated after sixteen centuries, when it was discovered that Sosigene's calendar was off by eleven minutes and fourteen seconds a year, an interval that by then had grown to ten full days.

Standing inside this room was like stepping back in time. He remembered from his initial tour that the place had remained virtually untouched since the sixteenth century. High up on the walls a large mural depicted cherubim holding garlands of roses, Paul's shipwreck at Malta, Christ calming the seas. At the room's center stretched a large, blue open dome consisting of six concentric circles of gold and, at its apex, a small hole through which the sun shined on clear days.

A Swiss Guard stood by the opening and beckoned the pope inside.

At the far end of the room sat Bishop Montsegur, a lean, hawk-nosed bureaucrat ideally matched to his position of Keeper of the Vatican Archives—holder of that which was deemed dearest and most secret in Rome.

"Your Holiness, thank you for submitting to these necessary measures. I trust your walk was not too disconcerting."

"Not at all. This must be an unusually secretive matter."

"It is, Your Holiness. I thought the Tower would be most immune to any sort of modern eavesdropping. In fact, this is a matter so confidential that only I am allowed to know the full details unless such a time as this arises."

"You mean even a pope is kept ignorant of this?"

"I am afraid so, Your Holiness. Would you like to take a seat?"

With a nod he grasped a nearby velvet chair by its back and sat down. The cushion, though surely centuries old, gave way most comfortably.

"In fact, sir, what I am about to tell you is the deepest and oldest secret in Christendom. For good reasons, it has been withheld even from the pope unless absolutely necessary. But today a startling new development has rendered its disclosure necessary."

The man inhaled deeply, nodded his head, and continued in a slightly quavering voice, "Sir, Saint Lazarus, the Lazarus of the Bible, friend of Jesus and risen from the grave . . . never died."

"*What?*"

"That's right, Your Holiness. This is not a matter of conjecture. It is fact. Lazarus has lived for over two thousand years, maintaining intermittent contact with the Church, living a hidden existence under a variety of disguises."

"How could such a thing happen? It smells of the occult."

"We have not been told precisely how. However, it's almost certainly something related to the power of God's raising him from the dead. Many have hearkened back to the verse, 'As it is appointed unto men *once* to die. . . .'"

"Incredible," whispered Peter. He felt a light swoon wash over his senses. He shook his head as if to dispel the words he thought he'd just heard.

"After rebel fighting intensified around Jerusalem," said the Archives Keeper, "Lazarus moved with many of the early Christians to Caesarea. A few years later—no one knows why—he was abducted in the middle of the night and placed in a boat, one without a rudder or sail, along with his sisters. They drifted across the Mediterranean and grounded ashore near present-day Marseilles, on the French shore of Provence. Lazarus began preaching the Gospel and became the first bishop of Marseilles.

"It soon became apparent that he was not aging normally. Over time his sisters died, and the issue of his agelessness became too great a factor to ignore. So he left Marseilles and embarked on a series of long voyages too intricate to describe. He wandered through Europe for centuries, becoming an expert in evasion, disguises, and every type of covert survival. He lived as a Jew for many of those years, in the exile communities of Italy and then central Europe—all the while living a few years here and there and then leaving when his inability to age became evident.

"He eventually left the Jewish communities when he realized he would never be able to worship as he wished. He engaged himself as a priest and explored the wilds of northern Europe—Germany, Normandy, the British Isles.

"One day he was mistaken for a heretic and run through with the sword of a Knight Templar. The knight watched him die, and was still rummaging through his things when Lazarus came back to consciousness a few minutes later. Lazarus had no choice but to tell his story. This Templar eagerly passed the information on to his superiors.

"The Templar Order made Lazarus's existence its deepest and innermost secret, a thing to be whispered about only to kings and popes as a means of gaining power and leverage. The Templar taught him great things in return, regarding history and literature and also finance, ways of gaining and multiplying money over time. Soon he began to acquire enormous wealth.

"But the Templars' unwillingness to divulge their famous secret gave rise to all sorts of wild speculations. And the financial leverage they used against kings led to their downfall. As you know, the Knights Templar were violently purged in 1307, their leaders executed and their untold riches supposedly scattered to the winds.

"Soon afterward, Pope John XXII, who had reluctantly acquiesced to their massacre, determined that he would replace the Templar Order with a priestly retinue to protect and serve Lazarus. And so in 1328 a small group came to be consecrated as the Order of St. Lazare."

The pope interrupted. "He truly is incapable of death?"

"It appears that he suffers mortal wounds but then revives soon after, as if rejected by heaven and sent back to finish his work. It's also important to remember that, despite his being immune to death, he still faces grave dangers. There are worse things than dying, Your Holiness. He can suffer an otherwise mortal wound and endure agony most of us could never survive. He can be tortured endlessly and with no reprieve. He can be imprisoned in ghastly places for decades, and frequently has been, in impregnable or undiscoverable locations. He's been bricked into castle walls. Dropped into deep caves. Chained in built-over dungeons. In short, he has as much to fear from his enemies as we do from ours."

"And what is this work of his?"

"He claims to be the earthly emissary of catacon, the Restrainer of destruction spoken of in the Epistles, the one who will be taken away just before the end of time. He is a master exorcist and has literally been engaged in a cat-and-mouse game with the archdemon called destroyer for centuries. The Brothers claim that five times he has come close enough to the demon's human host to start consigning it to hell forever, but each time was prevented from finishing the exorcism. Yet if he ever succeeds, a key fomenter of destruction might be expelled from the earth. If, however, the destroyer's minions succeed in capturing Lazarus and hiding him in a secure enough stronghold, he could be lost to the world indefinitely, perhaps ushering in a new Dark Ages."

"Incredible. And how do we know how to identify him? I mean, after all these years, all his wandering . . . ?"

"The Brothers of St. Lazare claim there is an identifying mark, Your Holiness. Besides, as his appearance has not changed in two thousand years, they claim to have his likeness well recorded. There is much the Holy See does not know, which the Brothers have kept to themselves. We have tried for years to gain possession of his diaries, which reportedly contain many of his secrets. But the Brothers jealously guard all copies."

"I don't understand. Are there *more* secrets about him?"

"Yes, several remaining mysteries. They concern matters like the workings of the destroyer, ancient prayers of exorcism allegedly dictated by angelic beings. And other, more personal enigmas. For one, reports suggest that Lazarus is a very afflicted and tormented man. No one knows exactly why. There are many hypotheses, of course. It appears the diaries would supply the answers."

"Why are you telling me this great secret now?"

"It seems the matter of this man and his identity has come to the attention of world authorities. More specifically, the Western intelligence community. It goes without saying that should this attention continue, the consequences could be explosive."

THE STEPS FELL AWAY beneath long strides as Pope Peter bounded down the ancient stairs it had taken him so long to climb. In the distance behind him sounded the clattering feet of the Vigilanza and the new contingent of Swiss Guards coming from the Meridian Room doorway, all scrambling to catch up with him.

Yet the pope's mind was running even faster than his feet.

Montsegur had served him well. Indeed, the worldwide leak of this crucial information might possibly mean a grave threat against the good name of the Catholic Church. He could imagine the backlash and ridicule over the fact that the Vatican would even entertain such a notion as an immortal man. In some of the seminaries in which Peter had been compelled to study, the very idea would have been met by men of the cloth with a thunderous laugh. A good number of them didn't actually believe in the supernatural, Peter reminded himself.

Furthermore, he thought as he reached St. Peter's main floor and found himself on familiar ground, this man Lazarus could represent a threat to the papacy itself. If the masses came to believe in such a man's identity, his appeal and power could easily come to eclipse that of the pope himself.

Somehow that part didn't frighten Peter. It did not, first of all, because if this man was who he was purported to be, he would not want to assume worldly power. Had the opposite been true, he would have shown his colors long ago. In fact, Montsegur's story suggested that the man was highly secretive and wished to avoid disclosure at all costs.

Hidden in all the dire potentials, Peter's shrewd mind also spied great opportunity. If he grasped the scenario correctly, Lazarus's unique identity was proof of the existence and divinity of Jesus of Nazareth. His unveiling to the world may well be seen as one of the most stunning revelations in Church history. Certainly, bitter debate and perhaps even a measure of international reprisal would be the result. And it would definitely provide much fodder for the world's atheists. Yet if this man's identity could be proven, what could anyone say? Millions of skeptics and agnostics might return to faith and the forces of orthodoxy gain back the ground lost to science and nihilism over the years.

And there was more.

Ever since his induction by a razor-thin majority, Peter had become aware of a quiet war being waged within the Vatican. Slowly, weeks after becoming pope, he had learned of a malevolent creed undermining the Church, led by people hoping to undermine the very fabric of Christendom. This implacable enemy consisted of far more than isolated enclaves of liberal or even atheistic thought. No, atheism was nothing compared to this.

Peter had come to find out that satanic adepts occupied positions within the Vatican bureaucracy, the Curia. Certain members of his loyal staff had had their suspicions, but so far the only verifiable signs were discovered remnants of foul rituals within the complex, as well as warnings from a few of the Church's more spiritually perceptive prayer champions—his lookouts on the ramparts of the spirit world.

Robes billowing in the swiftness of his steps, he stormed into his quarters high atop the Apostolic Palace. He immediately snatched up a private phone and summoned Archbishop Michel

Lorenzo, his chief of staff and most trusted advisor. Then he sat in his favorite armchair to think and pray.

Before he knew it, Lorenzo was there, standing silently in a corner. Peter noticed him with a start.

"I did not wish to interrupt your contemplation, Your Holiness," said the impeccably coiffed, handsome fifty-year-old Milanese.

"No. Please. Have you heard?"

"Bits and pieces, sir. Certainly the most salient aspects."

"Good. I want this Father Thierry brought to me for a full report. And I want our security force ready to assist him in the search for this . . . this . . . I can hardly bring myself to say it."

"I understand, sir. Lazarus."

"Exactly. He will be found soon, and I want us to be the ones who find him."

A MERE THREE HUNDRED YARDS away, in the spacious suite of the Directorate of Comparative Religious Studies, Bishop Eccles picked up the phone on the first ring with an impulsive jerk of his hand.

"So what's this I hear about a discovery?"

A voice on the other line answered in a near whisper.

"The whole world knows about it. The CIA called this morning."

"Send Jamail back to find him. If we don't take him soon, we've lost."

Boston

NORA DROVE TO A LOCAL copy center where she had a photograph made of her new punk-rocker appearance. She then drove the two miles to the MIT campus. Her mission: to track down a pair of notorious grad-student hackers and desktop counterfeiters she had heard of among the student underground. After several discreet questions on the campus intranet, she found a mail drop in a run-down apartment building less than a block from campus. She dropped an envelope containing five hundred dollars and the photo down the chute, left and returned four hours later. She walked back to her car holding a fresh United States passport with a new name, and a matching Massachusetts driver's license.

She found a small travel agency tucked away on a south-side boulevard and bought a single ticket, coach, open return. *Paris.* The word hardly seemed real, even printed on the ticket's flimsy paper. Paris—a city where people go to pursue romance and high fashion, not research their way out of life and death.

From there she drove to within a mile of Logan, left her car in a supermarket parking lot, and took a taxi to the airport. She carried a floppy half satchel, half suitcase on her back, stuffed with an extra pair of jeans, a few shirts, and basic hygiene items. She'd be winning no Best Dressed awards in the City of Lights.

She was a bit surprised to find that as she walked across the Logan concourses the depression of only a week ago had now given way to exhilaration and a sense of adventure. The stifling fearfulness of her family upbringing lay behind her now, tossed somewhere in her grim apartment like a withered cocoon.

It was only the second plane trip of her life and her first overseas.

I've got to be nuts, she said to herself with an inner giddiness while making her way through the aircraft toward her seat. Boarding a plane with no hotel reservations, no foreign currency, no idea of what exactly she would do once she arrived at her destination.

She lowered herself to the seat with a sigh, feeling as though she'd just leaped off a cliff. Just a month ago the prospect would have crammed her mind with endless logistical calculations. But this was too important. As impromptu as the trip was, it was no lark. This was serious, she reassured herself, and leaned her head back against the seat pillow. It was all part of her immersion into the adventure, the mystery that had begun with her attack two weeks before. That fact freed her somehow. Her mind calmed with the knowledge that she would simply muddle through.

Fortunately what she'd discovered from her father's effects had cemented her resolve. The attack was no isolated incident. It was *her* mystery. No one else's. To save her own life, she had to solve it. All the clues had seemed to point to this St. Lazare sect, and because her research had finally reached a dead-end at Harvard, she knew there was only one place to resume her search. France's *Bibliothèque Nationale*—its national library.

Paris, Left Bank—Twelve Hours Later

EXHAUSTED, NORA CLIMBED UP toward a wide swath of sunlight from the underground steps of St. Michel station. *Where was Paris?* Where was the beauty, the charm? Since leaving the airport, all she had seen from her train window was mile after mile of grim industrial wasteland, rusted smokestacks, power plants, and bewildering expanses of railroad switching yard. Finally the train had gone underground and shown her nothing but sporadically lit track and amber-tinged passenger terminals. Now, having reached the stop she had chosen from her travel book, she saw nothing but stairs—stairs which appeared to wind endlessly upward.

Then it loomed ahead. A slash of brightness against the steps, the noise of rushing cars. She emerged into the daylight and there it suddenly came to life before her.

The Seine River, lapping at a quayside, presided over by nineteenth-century buildings. Within yards of her, people sat at a sidewalk café, idly chatting, oblivious to her presence nearby—

the American gawking tourist. In the warm breeze she caught a whiff of coffee, a tang of yeast bread, a trace of diesel fumes.

With what felt like the last of her strength, she walked a block and sat on the stone lip of a fountain surrounded by a throng of pedestrians. A fine spray kissed the back of her neck. The cool evening air rang with the whine of high-pitched car engines, the beeping of Vespas, and flapping as a flock of pigeons took wing. Across the street and beyond a low wall, the Seine's surface curled along the bow of a passing tourist boat. Above the curved slate rooftops she saw the Gothic towers of Notre Dame.

She could hardly believe she was here. She caught herself on the edge of hyperventilation. To be in Paris on her own, no tour guide, no itinerary, here with only the clothes on her back and a small suitcase.

She walked another block and checked in to a modest, bohemian hotel she'd read about on the flight over, just two doors down from the famous Shakespeare & Company English Bookstore, a favorite haunt of notable expatriate writers. Most of all, it was the closest hotel to the grand facade of Notre Dame.

The Bibliothèque could wait, she told herself as the essence of the Left Bank washed over her like an urbane, sooty balm.

She could stay here forever.

FRANCE

24

Bibliothèque Nationale, Paris—One Day Later

NORA RESISTED THE URGE to glance up tourist-like at the soaring eighteenth-century ceiling of the Richelieu Library, while the clerk walked toward her.

"Bonjour, mademoiselle," the man said.

"Bonjour. Do you speak English?"

A slight scowl, then, "Yes, miss."

"Well, I would appreciate your help with finding information on a semi-monastic Catholic order based in northern France."

There was a pause, and he seemed to choose his next words carefully. "I am correct in assuming you are American?"

"That's right," said Nora.

"And do you have your reader's card?"

"My what?"

The man closed his eyes again, slowly, affecting the most condescending form of patience. "This is a research library," he explained. "You must possess a pass card or reader's card. Do you wish to consult our documents only one time? For a period of two days or less?"

"I don't know. Maybe. If I'm lucky."

"If you intend to be *lucky*, then a pass card is enough."

"Okay. And what will I need for this pass card?"

"Ah. You will need an identity card, two photographs, and a letter of justification for your research. Of course, your access with a pass card is limited."

"What if I'm not lucky and need to take longer, or get better access?"

"Then you would need the reader's card."

She breathed deeply and, realizing how loudly she'd done so, forced her features into an amiable smile. "What would I need for that?"

"I'm sorry. You must be a graduate student or scholar to receive the reader's card."

"As it happens I *am* a graduate student." She began fumbling in her leather pouch, took out her ID and said, "Look. Harvard University. Surely you've heard of it, yes?"

He rolled his eyes. "Yes, mademoiselle. I have heard of it."

"So what else do I need?"

"An identity card, a graduate student card like that one, and a letter of justification for your research."

Nora was beginning to feel anxious. "So, this might actually happen, right? Working it out so I'm allowed inside?"

"Perhaps, mademoiselle."

"Because I flew all the way over here just to consult your library."

"Without making arrangements?"

Her face fell. "Yes," she said.

Feeling overwhelmed, Nora exited the building and walked south past the Palais Royal to the columned Rue de Rivoli where she promptly hunted down a stationery shop. Here she bought a pad of writing paper. She spent the afternoon at an outdoor café, writing an elaborate justification for her needing to consult the Bibliothèque's archives in order to—and here she decided the truth to be far too bizarre—support the points of her master's thesis in History.

She proudly marched the document back to the library building, waited in line for twenty minutes to speak with the clerk from before, then calmly presented him the document. "My letter of justification," she said.

"You wrote this just now?" he asked with a bemused look.

"Yes, but that doesn't mean it's not true. I just forgot to bring one from the States."

"There is only one problem, mademoiselle. This is the Republic of France, and our national language is a sweet little dialect we call *Français*, or French. You may have heard of it," he said with a sparkle in his eye, evoking her former comment about Harvard. "And this"—he handed her letter back to her—"is written in something, I believe, called English."

All the patience and goodwill drained from her in a single flush. Her face showed it, too. She saw as much in the clerk's sudden beam of triumph. He reached behind and took out a printed sheet of paper.

"Here, mademoiselle. A list of translation services on the Right Bank. They are very reasonable, I think."

She snatched it from him and started to walk away.

"Oh, and something else, mademoiselle."

She turned back. "Yes, what is that?"

"Your documents cannot be presented to me. Reader's cards are issued by the Information and Card Issue Service."

Without flinching, she asked, "And where is that located?"

He whipped out another sheet, a map. "Thirteenth arrondissement, the main Bibliothèque location. Take the Metro to Chatelet, the St. Remy line to Notre Dame station, then on to the Dourdan line. Exit at the Austerlitz station."

"Sure," she responded, picturing the man burning at the stake. "No problem."

WHEN SHE EMERGED from the Richelieu building into a light rain, the purpose of her quest had hardened into a steely-eyed obsession. She *would* get in. She would reach the inner sanctum of that library if she had to don a ski mask and climb in through one of its pretentious stained-glass windows.

She spent the next few hours wandering the Right Bank while a nearby office translated her document. She found an English bookstore where she purchased a British edition of *Leaves of Grass* and spent the afternoon in a small bistro near the Madeleine Cathedral, alternating between reading and watching the chic passersby. Her translation was ready by midafternoon. By the time she had figured out the Metro system enough to follow the clerk's directions, her frustration had begun to soften. It turned out this pursuit of a library card was forcing her to have to tour beautiful Paris more than she might have otherwise.

Finally she approached the central offices of the National Library, a massive complex of five large office buildings not far from the Seine. Having given up on trying to avoid embarrassing herself, she found the Information and Card Issue Service by mangling the words in attempted French and weaving her way to a small glass-enclosed office.

A sober-looking, elderly woman read over her document and looked out at her through the bottom half of her bifocal lenses.

"Mademoiselle, you are American?"

"Yes."

"Is this an official letter from your university?"

"No. This is an informal letter."

"I am sorry. We need to see an official letter from someone of your faculty."

"I have none."

"Again, I am sorry. I cannot help you."

Nora felt her strength leave her. She nodded blearily and turned to leave. A mixture of disbelief, resignation, and self-loathing washed over her as she approached the door. Her bold initiative, her grand adventure, would end up as nothing more than an aborted, expensive wild-goose chase. Halted before it began by the most trifling of bureaucratic obstacles.

Something slammed shut within her. She felt her teeth clench, her fists tighten. Spinning around, she walked back to the counter and waited stiffly for the lady to return.

"Yes?"

"Please, ma'am," she said in a trembling voice. "I may have made a mistake, but I spent nearly all the money I have to fly over here to research something, something which is *so* important to me. In ways I can't even tell you. This is my life at stake. I am not exaggerating. Will you please make an exception?"

The woman stared at her for what seemed like a very long time. Finally she said, "Do you have phone numbers of faculty who would . . . what is the word, *attest* to this statement?"

Think fast, Nora told herself. She nodded quickly and scribbled down Harvard's main telephone number, then invented two names. Bruce Feinberg, Lois Greenaway. College of History.

The woman scrutinized the names, and her face softened. She reached below her, pulled out a small cardboard booklet and began stamping it with the ferocity of a spurned lover.

THE NEXT MORNING Nora reappeared at the Richelieu counter with the triumphal expression of Napoleon on his return to Paris. The clerk approached her. She slapped down the pass and papers, one after the other. "Here. Reader's pass. Identification. Letter of justification."

His lips widened into a rueful smile. She smiled even wider, her victory luminous upon her face. He turned toward the library's interior. "Come with me, mademoiselle."

He led her through a large doorway into one of the most ornate library halls she'd ever seen. Towering domes mirrored each other in a graceful array of vaulted curves. The topmost dome let in sunshine through a huge skylight.

He turned to Nora with an expectant look.

"As I mentioned to you yesterday," she said, "I would appreciate your help in finding information on a Catholic order in northern France."

"By northern France, do you mean Normandy?"

"That sounds like a logical place to start."

"Good, because there are many, many monasteries in France, and Normandy is a smaller, uh, point to begin."

He brought her three hardbound books, each one looking to be older than the next. She took them and walked back through a twelve-foot-high doorway to a long table where she sat down and began trying to recall her high-school French.

It didn't matter much, though, for she was primarily seeking a single untranslatable phrase. *St. Lazare.* She went straight for the index.

It took two tries. In the second book she found an index entry titled *Saint Lazare, l'Ordre de.* She flipped to the correct page and found a small paragraph under the name. One phrase stood out, a phrase that her eye and her vocabulary recognized.

Le Mont St. Michel.

THREE HUNDRED YARDS away, a concealed telephoto lens nearly a foot long issued a loud click. Then a whir. Then a succession of the sounds in rapid-fire.

The image of a pretty young woman holding a book bearing the words *L'Histoire Religieuse de la Normandie* was instantly frozen in electronic code. With a whine, the digital camera conveyed the data into a series of invisible digits and then into scrambled electronic chatter through a coiled wire to a tourist's backpack from which a short plastic antenna protruded.

Miles above them, hidden by distance and the glare of day,

the bristling form of a United States intelligence satellite performed an imperceptible series of inner stirrings. An invisible beam shot out of its belly and down to earth, toward a city on the North American continent known as Langley, Virginia. More specifically, a bank of dish-shaped antennae beside a sprawling office complex.

Back at the source of the beam, on a Paris rooftop, a dark-clothed, extremely fit man lay prone on the edge of a sharp drop-off. His camera shifted slightly. Its lens focused now on the face of a man sitting on a bench just outside the library doors. A dark-complected, well-dressed young man who had appeared at the spot within two minutes of Nora's return to the building.

Whir. The images flew out to space and back down again in mere seconds. Only yards from the satellite dishes, the second image also flashed, almost instantaneously, on the computer monitor of Agent Michael Stayton of the European desk of the Directorate of Intelligence of the CIA.

Stayton pressed a button on his keyboard, and behind the face dozens of similar portraits began flashing by in an ever-accelerating flicker. Finally, with a beeping sound, a box reading *Match Acquired* flashed. And a name, written in both Arabic and English.

"Great," Stayton muttered. "She's got some serious company."

In twenty years, if Stayton properly recalled the legend, no quarry of the terrorist Jamail had ever survived. If this monster didn't mind killing children, not to mention their tourist parents, he would have no qualm about inflicting on this beautiful and blameless young woman a truly horrific death. And he would not wait long to strike.

25

Avranches, France

NORA FIRST GLIMPSED its outline as a distant gray cone poking through shafts of wheat against an afternoon sky. A winsome little triangle, topped off with a perfect spire that reminded her of a wedding cake. Just to see it like this, still fifteen miles away yet beckoning with a razor-sharp silhouette, filled her with a churning sense of culmination. This was it. She could go no farther without driving into the ocean. This was where her journey would succeed or stall out altogether; she felt sure of it.

She had driven all day from Paris, choosing to take the wanderer's route through Normandy rather than one of the *auto-route* tourist buses. It had proven an exhilarating drive, a winding journey through several villages nearly identical in their antique charm of old walls and jutting spires. The terrain had proven enchantingly varied. Wheat fields surrounding Paris had given way to old oak forests, then to rolling, cow-dotted pastures, then coastal pines, and finally to the flat, cultivated plains of the St. Michel estuary. Driving along the curving landscape, she had come to appreciate the nimble steering of the tiny Renault she'd rented, finding it all very entertaining. The country roads offered a different and interesting view with every turn—often the villages lay less than a mile apart.

Even sheltered in her automotive cocoon, Nora felt a sense of history seep into her bones. She had stopped for lunch in a hamlet with a particularly charming main street. She now knew that *boulangerie* meant a bakery where she could buy a fresh half baguette, and the nearby *epicerie* probably meant a place where she could buy cheese, some sort of salad, maybe even part of a rotisserie chicken. A perfect, inexpensive lunch.

She had done just that, then eaten under a solitary oak tree in the village square, near a monument to the village's fallen soldiers. Sitting in a welcoming curve of the tree trunk's shape, smelling the bakery's yeasty aroma and feeling a cool breeze against her face, it seemed she'd never been a member of a bustling metropolis. She'd always been this gypsy, wandering through a magical countryside.

What a relief it was to forget for a little while the foreboding that had afflicted her last week.

As for the villagers around her, who may have thought their watching inconspicuous, it was obvious that the young traveler had brought company. A car with Paris plates had pulled into town three minutes after she settled herself for lunch. The driver had chosen a side lane in which to park, even though the main street had four spaces left open. Two men in suits had stepped out and looked about altogether too carefully.

Four minutes after that, two other men had entered the village square from what seemed like out of nowhere. Not even the villagers appeared to have noticed. Rather than photographing the quaint twelfth-century church, these men were lensing the previous pair as both focused their gazes on Nora eating her chicken beneath the oak tree.

Abbey of St. Michel, Mont St. Michel

"PLEASE, ANDRÉ." Father Thierry called him by his pseudonym, a careful habit and one he never relinquished even in secure places like this gloomy monastic chamber. "Now is the time to take the initiative. The church is dwindling. Unbelief and heresy are running rampant. By coming forward you could erase all of that with one stroke."

"No, I wouldn't," said his companion. "A heart bent on following its own way will always find justification for its rebellion, no matter the evidence. Besides, that is not why I was kept on this earth."

"I beg you. At least see the Holy Father. I've practically been ordered to bring you to Rome. You don't know what good that would do for the Order."

"Forgive me, Thierry. But what will I tell him? That I was charged by Christ himself with holding the forces of destruction at bay, and that I've obviously failed miserably? That I spent the Middle Ages in a haze of grief and rage, practically ignoring my calling? That I failed to prevent the corruption of Marxism or the ascent of its perverted form, failed to anticipate or prevent the twentieth century's world wars? Some portfolio."

"With all respect, it is not your accomplishments which command the most amazement, though they are considerable. It is your very identity."

"And what do I do to prove that? An interview? Let somebody run me through with a sword and watch me survive?"

Old Thierry stared at the ground, silent.

The man called André reached up from his bed and took the man's hand. "My friend, I am so sorry. I know I have been a keen disappointment to the Order and to the Catholic Church. I've never been the figure you and your predecessors had hoped."

Thierry shook his head, and his jowls shook in the fervency of the motion. "No, do not say that. We took an oath, and we have fulfilled it gladly."

"I know you have. And without you, I don't know how I could have survived. You men have been my only friends. My only source of support."

26

Father Stephen had been warned to stay away from the tourist areas, but Mont St. Michel's Abbey Gardens had always been his downfall. Tucked in a stone pocket just beneath the vast three-story wall known for centuries as *La Merveille*, The Miracle, they offered an oasis of greenery to the dungeon-like surroundings the priests had occupied since their return.

He emerged from a small side door into the gold and turquoise light of a dying sun and kept his eyes averted from the half-dozen or so tourists ambling through the grounds.

Tonight was an unusually sublime evening to be here, for it was full moon, and St. Michel devotees knew that full moons provoked the most spectacular tides to sweep across the sands and swiftly turn the Mont into a true island. Ever since the French government had spent millions to tear down an old causeway and restore the normal tidal flow, visitors had been able to witness the water's real and frightening power—and experience the true feeling of being surrounded by the sea on a mystical isle.

He looked into the darkening sky and found the moon already casting a buttery light onto the scene. He walked to the wall and found a small space between two groups of tourists holding up powerful binoculars and speaking to each other in rapid German. He looked out.

Almost twenty miles away, the English Channel, which

usually stayed confined to a blue strip at the horizon's edge, was already encroaching on the tan of the sand flats. From this distance the invasion seemed static and motionless. But the water was actually racing toward them at thirty miles per hour. It would be here soon.

He turned back to the serenity of the trees and grasses.

One piercing set of eyes sought his. He looked up, away, and then sought to picture again the image he had seen in that instant.

Dark, luscious eyes, short blond hair, an athletic figure hardly concealed beneath loose-fitting pants and T-shirt.

A beautiful woman, looking him over. A tightly knotted spin cycle started up in his stomach. Attractive women were his most consistent stumbling block. It seemed God had removed his carnal urges until two seconds after he had taken his vows. Since then, his primary protection had been the constant male companionship of his brethren, and the solitary pursuits their mission had assigned them.

He tried to focus his gaze casually on the blue of the English Channel beyond the wall, but an obstruction in his side vision told him she was approaching. Now she stood before him. It was impossible to look away. He met her gaze, swallowed hard, and smiled evasively. He looked away, as though his smile had been merely the most cursory of acknowledgments.

She had hesitated. Yet, if his peripheral vision was correct, she'd moved a step closer to him. He kept his eyes fixed straight ahead, willed his eyelids not to flicker in anticipation.

"*Bonjour, monsieur,*" she said in a bad French accent. American, he knew at once.

He looked at her, once again taking in her feminine charm, and smiled indulgently. Her eyes followed his intensely. The girl wanted to talk.

"*Parlez vous Anglais?*" Do you speak English?

Finally a way out. He looked at her again and shook his head.

She did not budge. This girl was obstinate. She leaned in, flashed a smile at him.

"Not even a little bit?" she asked.

He shook his head once more to indicate no, then caught himself. She had not missed the gaffe.

"Ah! But you understood what I just said!"

He smiled and made the motion between two fingers for *a little bit*. If he didn't extricate himself soon, this was going to set his priestly resolve back a year or more.

"Thank God!" she said, her tone one of relief and joy. She reached out and touched his shoulder.

Did I recoil, or did I just think I did?

Then the young woman fell perfectly still. Her eyes focused on him, somewhere below his face, and grew wide.

She was staring at his necklace.

"Are you of the Order of St. Lazare?"

He remembered her at that moment. A photograph handed to him in Boston, at the briefing before their search began. The girl. Different hair color and length, yet definitely the one Lazarus had gone to protect.

His mouth stammered some sort of incoherent protestation. He told himself to stop, to gain control of himself. He edged back toward the monastery door and thrust in the key. Blackness greeted him. An escape.

But she would not relent. She was there beside him, brushed up against him.

"Please. I've come all the way from the States to find him." She peered at him and continued, "He's here, isn't he? He's inside. Look, I have to talk to him. My life depends on it."

Father Stephen shook his head violently.

"I'm not going to leave, you know." Her voice became sharp and tinged with anger. "I'm going to stay here and knock on every door and pester every priest in this place until I see one of you. I'm not joking."

He paused, let out a deep breath, and dropped the pretense. "Just . . . just wait here in the garden. I'll go speak to someone and be back."

He left her, stepped inside, and plunged into the shadowy maze of ancient passageways. Although Stephen had learned all of the abbey's secrets during his early training, it still took him a full ten minutes. He was forced to trace long detours around the occupied tourist zone, run up a short flight of steps and through a door where Father Thierry and Lazarus—André, he kept forgetting to use the name—were meeting.

LAZARUS AND HIS OLD FRIEND had just launched into a spirited discussion about the Reformation, Thierry as always taking the traditional view of Catholic infallibility, when young Stephen burst in—an unheard-of breach of decorum. Father Thierry rose from his seat, his face quivering with outrage.

"Stephen, what is the meaning of this?"

"Nora, Miss McPheran, your, your . . . she's here! She's at the garden doors and insisting that I let her in."

Lazarus felt the blood flee from his face, taking all coherent thought along with it. "How did she know?"

"She saw my necklace. She knows the symbol."

Thierry shook his head adamantly. "No. We cannot allow a breach. Not now, not when we have no idea who is searching for us."

"She will not leave. I promise you, she is determined to see you."

It may as well begin now, Lazarus told himself. What a resourceful girl. He hadn't glimpsed much of her character in Boston beyond screams and victimhood. He almost felt relieved that she had worked hard enough to find him, although her success would complicate things, to be sure. He made his decision and smiled at the pair. "Send her in. Her motives will be pure."

"Does she know?" Thierry asked.

"I don't think so," Lazarus replied. "But it seems she is an intelligent girl. She did, of course, find us here. I suppose we should be ready for anything."

Thierry gave Stephen a quick, rueful nod of the head. *Fetch her.*

27

IT HAD GROWN COMPLETELY DARK in the Abbey Gardens. Nora's legs were growing numb, having been sorely tried on her initial march up the *Grande Rue*. She was actively contemplating the potential injuries from trying to break down the door herself. Perhaps a good kick such as the one she'd been taught in rape prevention class.

No, she needed her ankles for the trip down. Better wait awhile longer.

Finally the door opened with a wooden howl and the young priest stepped out. He looked at her sheepishly, with the same sidelong glance he had given at their first words together. He gave a beckoning wave.

"You may come inside, Miss McPheran."

She sidled past him into a sudden and musty gloom. On her way past, she muttered, "Oh, so you know my name, huh?"

The young man looked down, red racing across his cheeks.

Once inside, the priest took the lead again and led her through a passage that twisted first to her right, then down five steps and through a mangled door, then along for several minutes—after another pair of turns she began to lose track altogether. Long minutes passed with only his back before her, the impact of her feet on hard stone and the growing weariness in her legs. It felt like walking back into the Middle Ages. Finally they entered a round room she took for a turret, one with three narrow windows. In the foreground stood a withered old priest. Beside the priest, in an antique chair, sat *him*.

The man she had been tracking. The man whose appearance in her life had turned everything upside down for her.

He looked thinner than when she had seen him in the ambulance. Of course, lucidity gave quite a change to his appearance. How strange to see him now in control of his senses, when the sight she'd played over and over in her mind was that of a man in unfathomable agony. He looked now to be an ordinary yet handsome, dark-complexioned man in late middle age. The extraordinary part were his eyes, which now gleamed with unusual intelligence and a hint of wariness.

"Hello," she said in a hushed voice, unable to tear her eyes away from him. The old priest's hand stood outstretched toward hers. She finally noticed and shook it while her gaze remained fixed on the man in the chair.

Breathe, she told herself. *You deserve to be here*.

She looked different to him, and so self-possessed. A beautiful girl, even with shorter, lighter hair and faded denims. Her face was made all the more striking by the intensity blazing in her green eyes. The old stone chamber seemed invaded by her very presence, the coltish femininity embodied in her lithe form, her vaguely petulant expression and faintly exuded perfume.

"Hello, Miss McPheran," he said. "Welcome to Mont Saint Michel."

She chuckled. "It seems everyone here knows my name." When no one answered, she said, "And I know no one's."

"Excuse me," said Lazarus. "This is Father Stephen." He motioned to her guide. He then pointed to the old priest. "And this is Father Thierry."

Both men dipped their heads in recognition.

"And who are *you*?" she asked.

No, she cannot know. Not yet. He shook his head slightly. No reply.

"Listen," she said, her voice rising. "Both of our lives are in danger until you level with me. You and I both know what happened back in Boston. I've been briefed by the CIA—"

"You've been *what*?" Thierry blurted.

"That's right, sir. I've been briefed and I know everything."

"Then why are you asking my name?"

She caught herself short. She had overplayed her hand. "Okay. I know as much as the government knows. Which is that you're a very mysterious and inscrutable figure, and no one knows how you recovered from your wounds. Besides that, there's a lot you need to tell me."

"I'm afraid telling you would only increase the danger you're in."

"You don't know that. You're only looking for an excuse to shut me out."

He took a weary breath and aimed a level gaze at her. "Nora, you are not ready to know."

"Ready? For what? When will I be ready? When we're both dead?"

"I appreciate your situation. I understand it must have taken an incredible effort for you to track me here."

"You have no idea."

"Oh, I do. I tracked *you* down, remember?"

"Yes, and why?"

He shook his head. The time wasn't right.

A sudden thunder shredded the abbey's silence. Long, rattling peals. There came another sound—sharp, fleeting pings.

Lazarus's eyebrows furrowed. He had seen no clouds just a little while ago.

The door burst open with a bone-jarring clatter. Father Justin nearly fell into the room, the breath tearing from his large frame in heaving gasps. "We're being attacked!" he panted. He froze at the sight of Nora, until panic overwhelmed him and he raised his voice again. "The garden door has been forced open, and there's automatic fire inside the abbey!"

"It was me," Nora admitted. "I must have led your enemies here. Me and my bungling, mile-wide trail I left. I thought I lost them, but obviously I didn't."

"There's no time for that," Lazarus said. His hand clenched her upper arm and yanked her upward.

"Are you sure they're inside?" Thierry said.

"Yes!" Justin said. "Father Moll's been hit!"

"I never should have removed this thing," Thierry muttered. The old man reached down at his feet, held up a thin headpiece and threaded it around his face. Then he threw himself to the ground and raked his arm under the chair. He straightened, held up three machine guns by their straps and a large pistol in the other hand. He tossed one to Father Justin, who caught it and quickly disappeared through the door into the abbey's interior.

Lazarus whirled around to Thierry, who stood clutching the weapons while adjusting his habit. "The Wheel Route!" Lazarus said. "Everybody to the Wheel Route!"

"No," the old priest protested. "You take her there alone. We'll take the Chemin des Monteux and make a diversion."

"No!" Lazarus shouted.

Another deafening round of what he now recognized as gunfire roared again. It seemed bullets were ricocheting just outside their walls.

"Go!" the old man shouted with more force than Lazarus thought possible. "It's our mission. Go and take the convent stairs; they're most secure! Father Justin and I will cover you!"

Lazarus lurched through the door with Nora in tow. Only twenty yards away to their left, Justin peered around a corner with his gun thrust forward. He jumped into the open and shook from his blast of cover fire.

Lazarus's fist tightened around Nora's and pulled her away in the opposite direction. Still linked, they sprinted away from the fighting.

A stairway beckoned them downward. They tried to descend side by side, but the narrow space bunched them in. Somehow, with stumbling and stomping on each other's feet, they made their way down the steps.

Another machine-gun burst assaulted their eardrums from above. A man's scream accompanied the echo down the ancient stones. They paused briefly. It sounded like Father Justin. His face constricted with fear and sadness, Lazarus turned away.

"Let's get out of here."

The passageways that followed blurred in Nora's mind. She was possessed by the thought of assassins at their heels. Light and darkness, stairs and cavernous chambers washed over her senses in a blur of speeding shadow and furious motion.

They descended for what felt to Nora like an hour, an eternity during which she lost any clue of how they managed to move so quickly through such utterly dark spaces. The man leading her seemed to flow like silent water down a river of blackness. At times her only sensation was his tight grip on her hand. An ageless gloom held captive every unoccupied space.

Before she knew it, the mystery man was leading them outward, into a wide hall whose stone floors shined beneath the half-light of glowing lanterns. They threaded their way through silhouettes of tall stone columns that rose up and met a vaulted ceiling.

A round of gunfire erupted close, too close, and suddenly their quiet room echoed with footsteps—boots scraping the floor. She saw a brief flash of three men running, their forms bristling with weapons. Then a close-up of stone as her companion jerked her behind a column.

Another round ripped through the air. As soon as it ended, the man beside her made his move. He ran across the stone floor, fell and rolled under another deafening volley, and reached a staircase wall just as he ran out of momentum.

He stood, clutched at the wall, and then she saw what he had intended. The room filled with light in a blinding flood. She heard moans and turned to see the three gunmen claw at long, narrow protrusions from their heads. Night-vision goggles.

Before the men could wrestle the devices from around their necks, a blur of motion flew against them. In an arcing swath of legs and kicks, her protector knocked their feet out from under them. Three bodies struck the floor in an instant, and within another second their attacker flung himself upon them, wrestling a gun away and swinging it by the barrel. The gunstock struck two heads in the first motion, and they fell to the floor with sharp thuds. The third man tried to regain his feet but was knocked out by a vicious kick under the chin.

Her eyes grew even wider. Who was this man who could survive the Boston bloodbath and live to fight like this?

He stood, gathered up their rifles and heaved them clattering loudly down a stairwell. He then turned, spotted her, and gestured for her to come to him.

Relieved to be back in motion, she ran to him. They sprinted down a hallway and halted before the sight of a gigantic oddity: a wooden wheel three times their height, mounted beside a vertical slit. Through the aperture the light of the full-moon sky cast a bluish wedge of evening light onto their faces. She recognized the contraption from her guidebook diagrams. It was an intact medieval hoist, laboriously turned by the monks of old to lift supplies up a long stone ramp along the monastery's side.

Her companion did not hesitate but jumped to the beam

holding up the wheel and began unraveling a long section of rope. He looked at her with a fierce glint in his eye.

"The Wheel Route."

She stepped over to the gap in the wall. A cold sea wind blew across her face. She dared not look down; yet her looking straight ahead only gave her a more terrifying perspective of their great height. Shining in the moonlight through the opening, the flat estuary lands stretched for miles beneath her.

"Nora, I'm going to jump out. When I get to my feet, you have to pull back on this rope, keeping just enough tension to keep me upright. When I reach to the bottom and yank twice, you'll have to hold on tight and slide down yourself. It's the only way." He looked at her wistfully. "I'm sorry."

He gripped the wall to either side as hard as he could and glanced down.

The ramp descended three hundred feet from the wheel's opening down the side of the monastery, as close to vertical as one could get and still register the faintest of inclines. In the night she could hardly see its bottom, shrouded in a commotion of bushes and stone wall.

Another volley rocked the abbey, louder than ever. Nora quickly handed him the end of the rope. He tied a knot around his waist and backed up twenty feet.

"Oh, and another thing!" he called out. "I don't know if you noticed, but the ramp is crossed by a trench every ten feet. So you'll be running and jumping. Just keep your eyes open and you'll do fine."

The worried squint around his eyes told her his true confidence level. He took the deepest of breaths and thought about the first time he had done this, three hundred years before. The only way to carry this off was with total recklessness and lack of hesitation.

He gulped a lungful of air, started off at a slow lope, and launched himself into the void.

28

LAZARUS'S BODY REGISTERED the sensations before his mind did—stars wheeled above him, chill air cradled him for an endless, weightless moment, the night tilted on its infernal axis. Spotlights reeled below, stone behind, gunfire above, with only emptiness soaring agonizingly on every side.

He wondered if he would ever land; if he might instead stay suspended at this awful height. He willed himself to keep his feet pumping and his fists churning just as if he were approaching a finish line, until his feet made purchase with the stone.

Finally he struck with a painful jolt and continued downward.

For a sickening instant it seemed his catapult down the ramp would be unfettered by anything but a limb-shattering conclusion. But then a pull jarred him around the waist. Nora had begun to pull. The tugging yanked him off his feet and he fell hard to the stone, knees first. This girl was strong, he told himself with a grit of his teeth. He felt blood on his leg and stood with a wobble. In the distance he saw flashes light up the abbey. The gunfire was not subsiding. Hopefully the terrorists wouldn't think to glance out across the wheel slot's impossible chasm.

He yanked at the rope to let Nora know that he'd landed, then leaned forward and started slowly down the stone runway. There it was, the first horizontal cut. He leaped across it easily. The distance proved only about four feet across. He ran the length of the second span, feeling his confidence rise. He met the next gap with a bit of momentum and cleared it without incident.

No time to stop now.

He switched his mind to autopilot and allowed his limbs to take over. A rhythm of four, five strides, jump. Soon he was at the bottom. Nora misjudged the end of his flight and failed to stop the rope.

A chaos of furious motion—the world somersaulting in his eyes, a whipping across his knees and elbows, the scratching attack of tree limbs.

He stood, leaned back against a wall, and pulled the rope as taut as he could. He noticed a small oak tree behind him. In a rush he threw the rope's end around the tree and tied a knot. Looking up, he saw Nora's shadowy figure moving ever so cautiously from her sheltered perch, starting her way down below the wheel, lurching desperately along the rope's path in defiance of gravity. He held his breath, or rather his breath held him, for an eternal moment while she teetered on her rope hold.

Just then a hoarse shout rang out from the terrace two floors above. Lazarus glanced up and saw the protrusion of two assault rifles against the brightened night sky. He sank back into the bushes. Thankfully Nora had heard them, too. She had pulled the rope off to one side and hid behind the ramp's six-foot elevation.

Gunfire shattered the quiet. Lazarus sighed in relief; the gunmen's casual aim seemed to indicate they were just taking shots for good measure. For several seconds he listened to the whine of bullets ricocheting off the stone parapets.

The silhouettes finally disappeared. He stood and waved frantically for Nora to continue. The young woman tried to jump over the ramp's lip but couldn't gather the required momentum. A second leap, and still she was unable to force her right leg far enough over the stone ledge. A third attempt. He heard a grunt as she launched herself. This time her toes made it over the side, and she scrambled back onto the ramp.

She ran the rest of the way, her hands grasping the rope, her feet dancing across the rock. At last she reached bottom.

"Good work," Stephen whispered. "We're just above a way out now."

They made their way down to a steeply sloping lane. After surveying the area, they set off toward the bottom. The street led to a small courtyard surrounded by a semicircular building. Lazarus didn't pause, but took them around the side of its eastern wing. He fumbled in his pocket, pulled out a passkey and opened the door. They gratefully stepped inside.

The musty odor of an old warehouse greeted their nostrils. Slivers of moonlight shone through a nearby window onto a large pile of boxes. Lazarus moved through a narrow walkway between them and turned into a blackened staircase. His hand found hers and grasped it.

The stair's steps were short and steep, obviously designed for people of smaller stature. History greeted a person constantly in this place.

They reached the next floor and there, a few paces ahead, yawned the bright square of an open ramp leading down to the bay's sands.

Lazarus approached the exit first and looked about, long and carefully. He smiled and waved to her with a nod of the head.

"Stay close to the wall."

Nora stepped out into the night air and looked down. The Mont's walls were encircled by a tumble of small rocks, which, despite their size, had to be navigated carefully in the half-light. It was no easy task to hop from one sharp angle to another, all while maintaining total silence and still huddling as close to the wall as possible.

Her companion's hand jerked up in warning. Slowly, he pointed.

Ahead of them, just beside the road on which Nora had reached the Mont, stood two men who were partially concealing gun barrels in their coats.

Nora winced. Of course they would have left men to guard the only reasonable escape.

He turned back to her, his voice almost inaudible. "We'll have to sneak around them."

Chaos blasted again—the night lit up with a staccato roar. The stones around them began to sing and send chips into the air.

Nora took off running along the wall. It suddenly occurred to her that she was in the lead now. *Good thing the wall's circular*, she told herself. *Won't take long to get out of sight.*

Continuing her flight, she glanced back in time to see her protector following her.

Isolated shots rang out. Shouts echoed across the abbey. Somewhere in the distance, Nora even thought she could hear the distinct sound of a French siren.

She ran until her lungs were desperate for air and her chest heaved so furiously that she despaired of ever regaining her breath again. She stopped in the shadow of a rock outcropping. Hands on her knees, she looked behind her and spied a small stone chapel, its spire appearing to pierce the disc of a full moon.

He caught up with her, panting as well. "You're in good shape," he said between breaths.

She only nodded.

He pointed up. "That's the chapel of Saint Aubert. I know it well. There's a small crypt below the sacristy where we could hide you."

"Me?" she said indignantly. "Why me?"

"Because they're not really after you, Nora. They're after me. There's no use getting you killed in the crossfire."

Her determination flared up, and she shook her head violently. "I'm *not* leaving you. Someone tried to kill me over this, and I'm not through with you until I get my answers."

"Are you sure?" he asked.

"Yes," she snapped. "So where do we go now?"

The now-familiar burst of white light and deafening explosions bellowed again, this time ahead of them.

The island had become a deathtrap.

They both nodded in the same direction at nearly the same moment. *The flats!* They ran together away from the island, down to the wet sand. For a time she could not measure she felt nothing but fear flood her senses, the moist sand beneath her feet, the labored breathing of the man beside her, the firing that continued from behind.

His hand gripped her elbow. She stopped. She thought he needed a break, but he stood ramrod straight, his eyes on the horizon. "Do you hear it?" he said.

She heard another noise, a liquid, rushing sound. A briny smell filled her nostrils, and wet breeze swept through her hair. *Water.*

The tides! She had forgotten. The full moon and its flow notorious for engulfing people. Then the thought struck her just as she had noted the broken lights back in Cambridge. *They had planned it this way*. Attack on the night of the rushing tide, when escape was most difficult.

She squinted into the night before them. There, at the not-so-distant edge of her vision, churned a glowing, wavy line. The English Channel was moving toward them as inexorably as the coming of day.

She turned and pointed. "Let's run to shore. I parked my car over there, in the trees along the bank."

They set off again into the night.

The firing resumed. Suddenly the sand came alive around

them. With the whine of oncoming rounds, small plumes began to shoot up on every side.

"They've spotted us!" he yelled. "Let's go!"

They stumbled into as fast a sprint as their legs could muster, plodding broad, desperate zigzags across the sand.

She allowed herself a quick glance back to see how close their attackers were. Thankfully the waters had already surrounded the island at their backs. The terrorists could not give chase. They might be sitting ducks, but at least the waters kept the shooters at a distance.

The shore was slowly growing closer.

And then her legs locked up under her, and she fell heavily to the ground. She tried to kick free, but her feet were suddenly stuck. *What?*

"Quicksand!" she heard him shout.

Her heart plummeted within her. No way! Not now. Somewhere in the panicked recesses of her mind she recalled reading in her guidebook about the famous quicksands of the St. Michel estuary.

Nora became incensed and terrified at the same time. Her feet disappeared, followed by her ankles. Now her knees began to sink into the stuff. Her body was sinking as though pulled down by an intentional hand. She tried to roll, but her legs were being held in a vice. Panic now gripped every part of her. She started to gulp in loud, hoarse gasps.

More gunshots. The sand began to pop around them with approaching impacts. She moaned, cried for help.

"Don't worry! I'll get you out!" His voice came from somewhere above her.

"No!" she found herself shouting back. "Go! If it's you they're after, then get out of here!"

"I'm staying."

A machine gun round punctured the quicksand with a dull

thud just three yards away. Their aim was improving.

"Go!" she screamed.

This time he simply ignored her. He knelt forward, grabbed her hands and pulled. His face constricted in a tight rictus. She began to feel movement. Faintly recalling the instructions she had once heard, she tried to keep herself as level to the ground as possible. But the quicksand now had her by the upper thighs.

The pulling grew stronger, then stronger still. She felt her shoes sucked off of her feet. She was rolling free, and then . . .

BAM!

A volley rang out. Her mind saw it in slow motion: hands wrenched from hers, the man reeling backward, arms thrown wide, a spray of blood in the night sky.

She screamed and wriggled toward him. He fell against the sand as bullets shot past him.

A scream of defiance ripped from her lungs. No matter what, she would not let this situation do her in. She had no idea such ferocity to survive existed in her. She pulled the man up, tucked her head under his torso, and began to half carry him. Her knees buckled and her neck felt as though it were on the verge of snapping. Her breath became an irregular shredding in her chest.

But she kept moving forward.

One step at a time, she recited to herself. She took several and then found that she could almost steer the momentum of falling into a stuttering half run, as long as she kept her wobbly feet roughly beneath her.

She could hear the sound of water lapping somewhere behind her. She did not care, and this time she resisted looking back. Just another step forward was all she cared about. Let the gunmen take aim all they wanted. She would continue to heave one foot in front of the other. Her eyes seemed to glaze over. She felt she was slipping into another existence—a shrouded realm of denied pain and grim endurance, where her surroundings were mere glimpses through a thin veil, and the thundering commands of her body sounded like the beating of a drum. *Walk! Walk! Walk!*

And then they arrived. A stand of trees in the middle of a thick clump of grass. They climbed awkwardly from the sand. The man clawed at the air in front of him.

"There it is," Nora groaned. The Renault sat waiting in a public parking space, alone. She stumbled and pulled her keys from the front pocket of her jeans.

She deposited him in the front seat, climbed in on the driver's side, started the engine and took off. No telling where the terrorists were.

Besides, the man next to her was dying.

29

WITH THE TWO FIGURES now vanished against the shoreline and Mont St. Michel cut off from the mainland, the gunmen turned away from the outer ramparts and began to climb. The ancient lane stood deserted. The Mont's inhabitants cowered inside their second-story apartments as the dark shapes ran silently toward the abbey.

Not a single resident saw the liquid pools of darkness reach the top and the abbey's doors. But a hundred pairs of eyes trained themselves upward when flashes of light and whines and whistles of silenced gunfire began to carve the island's summit.

For the next fifteen minutes, strobelike swaths of light cut across the abbey's darkened spaces. But the monks were gone. They had vanished as though absorbed like wraiths into the abbey's stone walls.

A dark, floating shape and the staccato *thump-thump* of a helicopter's blades arrived over the Mont. A hundred mouths breathed sighs of relief. *Ah, la police. Les gendarmes.*

Yet those who peered out into the night saw no police markings on the aircraft, only a dangling rope and the quicksilver shapes of dark-clad men shimmying up the rope.

Five minutes later, the chopper, the attackers, and the whole crisis, had disappeared.

NORA'S PASSENGER DID NOT die as quickly as she expected. In fact, he did not die at all that night, but simply sat slumped against the passenger's door, his shoulder still oozing blood.

"I should get you to a doctor," Nora said.

"No. No doctors," he roused himself to insist.

"Why?"

"No doctors."

She drove for hours while he grunted faint directions. Soon her own fatigue caught up with her. She rolled down the windows to keep herself awake and stopped several times to buy water and soft drinks.

At one o'clock in the morning, an ordinary Citroën drove across the Porte de St. Cloud into the brightly lit basin that contained the heart of Paris.

A half hour later, that same car crossed the Pont Louis-Philippe over the Seine a mere four hundred yards from the northern apex of Notre Dame. It then pulled onto the Isle de Saint Louis, Paris's most peaceful and reclusive enclave.

Had any of the island's wealthy inhabitants seen the young woman support the faltering figure of a man through the door of one of its oldest domiciles, they would have legitimately concluded this was simply the bad end of a good night out. But no one saw them pass through the portal. Furthermore, no one cared.

After all, this was Paris.

Paris, Isle de St. Louis

IT WAS THE SLOWEST awakening she would ever experience. She felt she was drifting leisurely from the depths of a vast body of water up to a shimmering reflection of the sun. She lay bathed in warmth, her eyes shut against the onset of morning.

She finally awoke. All was silent.

The texture of this silence immediately sounded an alarm in the deepest regions of her mind. Here reigned a soundlessness deeper than any she was accustomed to, the muffled silence of a closed-in chamber, a space designed to eliminate noise. It caused her to feel that she occupied the farthest reaches of a cave—the most inviting and comfortable cave she had ever known.

She focused her eyes. Before her floated a shape somehow familiar to her. *Oh yes*, she thought. Freshman year, Art History. A *fleur-de-lys*. The French royal symbol. Fashioned of gold. Glowing just a couple of feet from her eyes, suspended in midair.

Her senses sprang to life. Of course the pattern was not floating in space; it was mounted on a dark velvet drape, a damask so rich and authentic that in the dim light of the room it seemed to fade into invisibility.

The light *was* faint in here, she observed. She turned her head and saw daylight streaming in through a window.

She blinked twice, looked again. The open window was roughly fifty yards away. She bolted upright and a heavy quilt fell from her.

Her drowsy eyes hadn't deceived her. She had in fact fallen asleep on a large divan at one end of a room half the length of a football field. She focused her gaze on all that lay between her and the distant window—on the walls and arranged around the floor.

It was then the thought struck her. She had awakened in a museum.

Or maybe not a museum exhibition itself but a back storeroom hidden from public view, where a diversity of artistic pieces lay awaiting display, all of them positioned indiscriminately across the floor.

She smelled age, dust and old wood, items kept shut for so long that their uses had become lost to common knowledge.

She willed her eyes to inventory all that lay before her. A row of shining vertical forms—suits of armor, ten in all, stood against the far wall. Each one bore a white tunic embroidered with a crimson cross. Two of them continued the reddish theme in bloodstains rusted over across mangled breastplates.

Every available foot of the wall space was devoted to paintings. Looking at them struck Nora with the same impression of mastery that she had experienced several days earlier on her brief and bewildering trip to the Louvre. With only two hours to spare, she had told herself that she would take in only the museum's highlights—the *Mona Lisa*, *Winged Victory*, *Venus de Milo*, David's *Coronation of Napoleon*, *The Code of Hammurabi*—but instead found herself staring dizzily at row after row of stunning masterpieces. The sheer volume of ageless artistry had left her feeling lost and small. What an insignificant cipher she represented, against the lurid backdrop of history.

Now she focused on one of the nearest paintings and recognized the dark contrasts of El Greco. The next one she did not recognize, and the piece after that was actually a Grecian mosaic. Next hung a piece depicting two men in sixteenth century leggings, walking briskly down a city street. Immediately she noted the ruddy facial expressiveness and characteristic *chiaroscuro* of a Rembrandt.

Where am I?

Her eyes began to dance across oval battle shields leaned against one another, a large stack of silver dinnerware, bulging leather trunks faded with age, stacks of thick, olive-colored military uniforms, elegant suits, frilly white shirts, bulky woolen coats. The entire space lay studded with the jutting shapes of tables and desks. And instruments: she spotted a mandolin lying against a stack of books, a pair of lyres on a tabletop, a dulcimer whose broken strings curled into the dusty air.

She stood and her knees buckled under her. Her ankles ached, and her knees and shins were scraped and bloody, caked with mud.

Only then did she recall with a shiver the night before: the escape from Mont St. Michel, the nightmarish flight through gunfire across treacherous sands, her stepping into quicksand, *him* falling backward from the impact of a bullet across his chest, and the harrowing five-hour drive through the dregs of a moon-drenched night.

But where did he go? He'd brought her here, mumbling directions through the gurgling of blood in his throat. Strange. For although he had entered the car in desperate need of medical attention, he seemed to regain strength by the journey's end. He had revived even during their walk upstairs. She remembered now that he had escorted her unaided to this room, retreated alone, and disappeared.

She walked the length of the room in search of a door, past the baffling array of antiques. Her side vision alerted her to something strange: they had not been polished or cleaned the way one usually saw antiques displayed in a store. The lack of artifice only intensified the feeling of having been trapped in the junky old attic of Father Time.

She reached a door standing open between two tall, weathered armoires, walked through it and into another jam-packed room. The very presence of so many artifacts, each one exuding so much palpable history, began to crowd in on her with a surge of claustrophobia. She closed her eyes and breathed deeply.

This room was lined with dark wooden bookcases from floor to ceiling, every inch filled with books of all shapes and sizes. This was no tidy library with rows of well-matched, indentical volumes. It was an authentic collection.

She stepped through to a set of French doors. Opening them, she found herself facing a wall that forced her to choose a left- or right-hand turn into a narrow hall, its walls covered with framed sketches, documents, and paintings.

She chose right, only because she assumed that going this way would lead her to the far end of the room where she had awakened. But she was wrong. She wandered through four more rooms, two of them less crowded with artifacts yet richly appointed in an antique style.

The first was a dining room, furnished with a table one would have found in the great hall of a castle. It was nearly thirty feet long. At one end, a large window looked out over the Seine and the West Bank. The dining room led into a sprawling butlery with a large-mouthed oven and a multitude of hanging kitchen implements. Third was what appeared to Nora a personal office, complete with a Louis XIV desk and, at its far end, floor-to-ceiling bookcases groaning with an impressive number of volumes.

It was then that she heard music. Low and rich, quivering with vibrato. One stroke, a chord. A cello, perhaps.

She followed another chord and a slow, minor-keyed lament into the fourth room. And there she found her man.

He sat stiff-backed on an ottoman, next to a large canopied bed. Before him a cello shone its roan hues in solemn half-light. Beyond the instrument's neck she saw that he wore a flimsy T-shirt which bore a large, red-soaked hole.

He faced the far window, away from her, his attention appearing fixed on its view of rooftops and clouds. He did not see her, nor did he stop playing. In fact, his cadence grew more rapid and purposeful.

Then a chill cascaded down her back. She felt a strange presence, as though a highly curious and watchful gaze had materialized over her left shoulder. It was not his presence; she knew that instinctively. Turning slowly around, her body shook in anticipation of being attacked. But she saw no one.

She had the feeling she was violating something sacred. The notion struck her that she needed to leave right away, leave him to his playing and return to the safety of the first room.

She silently backed out of the room with her mind awash in contingencies. Was it safe to stay here with no protection whatsoever? Was she being a fool for not letting someone know where she was? Should she check in with Agent Stayton, as she had promised, and ask for his help?

She didn't know if it was common sense or simply a stubborn love of adventure that caused her to answer no to these questions. Surely the bizarre events at Massachusetts General had given her little reason to think this was an ordinary person. And the CIA hadn't done much for her lately. Or at least she didn't think they had.

No, it was up to her, Nora McPheran. And her first order of business, she decided, was to complete her original mission and find out the truth about this man.

She traced her steps back to the room with the home's closest resemblance to organization—the office. She sat down on an ornate chair and took a long look around her, then came to focus on the back wall of books. She squinted to read their weathered spines. Many were printed in languages she didn't recognize, let alone understand.

On the desk she noticed a thick, leather-bound volume lying open. A gold-inlaid fountain pen lay beside it, open as well.

Feeling guilty almost immediately, she flipped back many pages and began to read.

30

Paris—January 1

So another new year has arrived. It appears you've once more chosen to spare your errant children from the consequences of their technological arrogance. You graciously decided not to punish them, unlike at Babel so long ago, and I suppose I should feel grateful for that.

But, dear God, you know my foul mood these last few months, so I will spare you any insincere attempt at enthusiasm.

I am beyond feeling any optimism for the future of the human race. How "smart" this world is, and how full of its own creations! And yet how infantile. I feel sometimes like I have been released into a romper room full of two-year-olds who somehow killed their parents and now sit among their decaying corpses, wondering what game to play next.

The sheer futility and violence of this human chain we call history is too repetitive and predictable to bear.

Only you can know how thrilled I was at the advent of what we now call the Renaissance. This is it, I told myself. Without losing my faith, I could celebrate all that was beautiful in the arts and the world at large. Humanity would ascend to a new level of wisdom and love for you. But the same old cycles of hatred and murder returned soon enough. And now look what they've done. The most potent uses humanity seems to have found for its cleverness consist of better ways to amass wealth or more efficient ways to kill large numbers of their fellowmen. I thought the death camps were the epitome of evil ingenuity, that is, until I heard of neutron bombs, nerve gas, and biological weaponry.

No, dear Lord, I will never become caught up again in all the age-old hope for a new world here on earth, or any such universal improvement in things. Certainly, life becomes a little easier with every decade. Yet the former human tendencies have remained the same—blasphemy and greed.

I suppose I should learn the lesson that every generation faces the same opportunity for good or evil. That the same spiritual battle is fought in every man's and woman's heart, no matter the era. I suppose such an admission makes this life bearable for those who are bound by its ordinary cycles of life and death. But forgive me, Lord, for it all has become tedium for me. This unending chase after my demonic foe has come to resemble an absurd carousel ride, with no conclusion in sight and no end to his bloodshed.

How do you suffer it all?

I feel I have only the will for one more direct confrontation with my enemy. I know where he will attack me first. I will engage him there and take this fight to the end. With your help, I intend to consign him to hell forever.

Then, Lord, will you at last take me home?

31

BY THE TIME Nora finished reading the diary entry, her heart had sunk. She was certain of two things. First, the man who at the moment was sitting in the next room playing a cello, who had saved her life twice now, was the author of this strange document. Secondly, judging from the various delusions it contained, that he was somehow deranged.

What was all this about the Renaissance? Or his being apart from those bound by the ordinary cycle of life and death?

She began to feel a tide of despair flood over her. Had this whole adventure—this runaway train which had commandeered her life—hinged on the imaginings of a madman? Had her role been that of a randomly selected stranger, someone caught up by chance in another's demented illusions?

Closing the book, she noticed something. Standing upright at the edge of the desk were several such volumes. On the floor beside her lay a stack of at least a dozen more, every one with an identical leather cover. She leaned over and picked up a volume from the middle, then flipped to a page at the center.

Mainz—the year 912

I have not seen my enemy in 45 years, nor witnessed his work at large. I have ascribed this good fortune to the chaotic state of the world right now. It appears the entire realm has shattered into a latticework of tiny, warring fiefdoms, with no one in control of any save their own manors, none in charge of vast quarters as in times of old. As the destroyer prefers to avoid the hard work of coalescing power gradually and favors the seduction of world conquerors with dominions already underfoot, he therefore finds himself now hard-pressed to select the right despot to possess.

This state of affairs suits me well enough. I have used the reprieve to formulate a new strategy: I will let him come to me. Sooner or later he will tire of this standoff and send his forces after his ancient nemesis. A little blood is better than none; it has always been his credo.

In the meantime, I have settled quite amiably into the life of a small-town banker in the Jewish quarter here. The people have taken me in, so to speak. I am their banker, the solitary widower, as I have allowed myself to be known. No children or spouse.

Four times in the last annum have I been approached with this or that match to a girl who happened to be fetching. But I am loath to be rid of my secret to anyone. And I will never betray my beloved Claere or forget her, even to this day. Although I may be cursed with this inability to perish, I still remain faithful to her.

So I concoct excuses about my being content with solitude, and suffer the friendly scoldings which inevitably follow. The women are right, of course. It is not natural to live out the course of one's days without a mate beside you.

Then again, as you well know, Lord, there is nothing natural about my remaining in existence. As well as I have settled into this town—and I have lived 125 different rounds of these hollow charades—I know that no more than a decade or two from now I will be forced to desist from its comforts and be on my way.

For now, it is not a bad life. I occupy a pleasant house in keeping with the neighborhood and secretly maintain a cottage deep in the forest where I can keep my past possessions and find peace during the Sabbath.

I suppose my first danger, besides that of being found out and labeled a sort of monster, is the persecutions which often assail these poor folk. My enemy has made it a priority to stir up hatred for your chosen people, causing the more twisted denizens of this quarter to strike out against their Jewish neighbors. This has not yet happened during my current sojourn, yet I feel that should such a horror occur here, I would be compelled to take up the sword in their defense. That is not the right way, I know. I would probably start a small war and be forced at some point, under threat of torture, to reveal that I am a follower of Christ as well as a Jew.

At this point in my existence I far prefer the life of a smaller town to that of the capitals, plagued as they are by rank conspiracies, betrayals, and outright massacres. Often I have found the lords and so-called nobility far less to be respected and enjoyed than simple people of faith. From time to time I am summoned by the angels to attend to this or that court on the business you have assigned me. Always I cannot wait to return.

I wonder, will this present state of disunity, the constant wars, and the dire poverty go on forever? Will Christian people be eternally confined to performing rituals which they neither fully understand nor care about?

Yet I remain hopeful, Lord, and await your intervention with the bated breath of a young bridegroom, longing for you to come and breathe new life into this stale world.

Either that, or for you to take me home.

Still, I wait.

Shaking her head, Nora flipped several hundred pages ahead.

Antwerp—January 5, 1000

I can scarce believe it, but I am over one thousand years old. Am I truly, as the children speak of in frightened voices, a ghost? A walking spirit? It seems not, for I have corporeal existence. I sleep and eat though I have no need of these. I experience all the sensations of a living person. Furthermore, I touch and am touched, with no doubt of my solidity. My appearance does not seem in any way less human or pleasing than that of any other citizen, except of course for the fact that I neither age nor die.

And yet the doubt assails me still. It is true that I prefer my own company, that I tend to spend my time alone, often wandering through the darkened rooms of an empty home. Is that what they mean by haunted? *I know I sometimes feel that way—haunted by memories of a life too long lived, of people I have loved and lost to the cruelty of time.*

I consume the relish of everyday life far more fiercely than an ordinary man, not because I am a wiser person, but because I need distraction to fix my mind away from memory. But Lord, I do tire of being such a melancholic man. Perhaps this is why I rejoice at trifling amusements, why I seek out whatever human company or public performance or piece of writing I can lay my hands on.

These days I frequent Antwerp, filled as it is with a variety of such enticements. And for the refuge the place offers me from the excessive scrutiny which has pursued me from village to village and for so long. Antwerp suits me admirably, with its large contingent of Jewish descendants and its unmatched trade markets in which my fortunes have multiplied. I suppose the games of money amuse me as well as any other, although the satisfactions of greed have long since paled.

As for my recent and closest brush with the destroyer, my fingers still tingle at the feel of his host's neck writhing in my grip. I will never forget the wondrous sight of the ethereal beast reeling from his place above the man's head, eyes bulging with terror as I spoke the Exorcismus Maximus. I believe I came close to ejecting the demon from him, and perhaps from earth, forever, for his body trembled violently. In fact, it was the sudden pitching of his upper torso that sent me tumbling from my horse and into a humbling reunion with earth. I heard his evil laugh drift back on the wind as he rode away.

It was my closest encounter with victory since cornering the Prince of Saxony in that dungeon several centuries ago.

In recent days my amusement has arisen from a different source—from the terrified antics of the faithful in anticipation of the millennium. The populace has become convinced that you would choose this thousandth interval to return in power, and as a result the churches have been packed beyond capacity with thousands of weeping, penitent worshipers crowding every Mass. I suppose that, taken as a whole, such sentiment is salutary. Yet I could not join the belief that you, Lord, would choose an accident of chronology as the time to effect your return. And indeed, you did not.

In spite of the many diversions I have gathered unto myself, there remain those odd moments, the times when walking alone or falling to sleep. At such occasions I am consumed by a profound sadness. Sometimes I will observe a father pick up his child, or two lovers steal a glance at each other, and remember so many others, now scattered to the winds. And also my own lack of such affections.

Indeed, it pains with an almost bodily ache to watch the ordained cycle of life proceed without me. To know and love others intimately, only to watch them grow old and become resentful of my immunity. Then to watch them die and be consigned to the earth with their absence all the more cold and unalterable because I have no idea when I will join them again. Or to return to a territory I might have inhabited centuries before, and recognize traces of a world I once contended with. To see a church or home now crumbling and ancient, moldering in the infamy of decrepitude, then returning inwardly to the day when it was erected with great energy and passion for a better tomorrow. To remember the young lads who toiled at securing its most laborious heights, the older men who sat on the lawn savoring the shade in the midday heat with wine bottles in hand, calling up instructions, with the young ladies passing by trying not to note the straining male forms upon the girders or giggle at the handsomest among them.

And then, in the present day, to walk through the village cemetery and know that those you just recalled, so living and vital in your thoughts, now rot in the very soil before you.

I find such subtle arrogance in being enamored of the present day. One presumes that the world of today is as good and sagacious as it has ever been and that the inhabitants of the past, by virtue of their being dead and gone, must have been somehow lesser persons, with slighter concerns and vexations, possessed of shallower minds and contemptible affectations. We open their memoirs, regard their fashions and expired political debates, and laugh inwardly, never thinking that someday others will view our own memorabilia with similar derision.

For myself to have known so many such generations and seen each one stacked upon the other, my own youth forgotten and replaced by another, then another, all eventually consigned to antiquity, its vitality stolen by the merciless length of history, well, what can I do but to try and forget?

Nora closed the second book and began to massage her temples. What was all this? The man clearly seemed to suffer from the delusion that he was immortal. But none of it made sense. Certainly a person this deranged would spend most of his life in and out of institutions and would hardly possess the wherewithal to gather such evidence for his claim.

Perhaps it was the priests. Maybe this man's lunacy was so convincing and winsome that a group of naïve and disaffected clerics had somehow flocked to his side. Could the priests have spent years, decades, and untold millions of dollars hoarding the priceless objects she saw around her?

No, that was too much. It wasn't possible that any group smaller than the staff of the Metropolitan itself—and with any less funding than the budget of a good-sized African nation—could have acquired such an impressive collection.

Maybe the diaries didn't actually belong to this man. Perhaps they were something he had acquired during his travels.

She returned to the last page of the final, unfinished volume lying on the desk.

Tomorrow it's off to look in on young Nora. I so look forward to seeing her with my own eyes and witnessing her life firsthand. I know my enemy is watching her, too, knowing that her life and well-being would be a natural focus point for reengagement.

I am ready. I have reacquainted myself with the old prayers. I have prayed more unceasingly than I have for decades. My spirit is fortified.

I also look forward to sampling modern conveniences like a mere six-hour flight across the Atlantic. Amazing to me. I am told today's jet airplanes are so much more quiet and luxurious than the propeller planes of old. I am still becoming conversant with modernities like today's automobiles, the layout of modern Paris, the profusion of electronic devices like the compact disc player or the personal computer. There is, as Thierry warned me, so much new to learn in today's world.

I will go alone. This is quite possibly a logistical mistake but one I make willingly and with a clear conscience. I will see Nora and probably the destroyer as well. If so, I will let the enormity of his cowardice fuel my rage, my disregard for pain, and my willingness to end this contest forever.

32

NORA GROANED. It would not be so simple. The man in the other room was either what he claimed to be, or he was a madman on the order of the homeless schizophrenics who waved yo-yos above their heads in Harvard Square.

She stood, walked numbly through the hallway and two rooms until she found the one she had slept in. She climbed back on the divan and closed her eyes. At the moment she didn't feel capable of processing such staggering information.

She opened her eyes briefly to reassess her surroundings. The light from the distant window had now grown low and dimmer. The day was already slipping away.

This suite felt so empty. Though the man on the other side of the building possessed a strong and singular presence, something about his current infirmity, the vastness of this apartment and its sheer agelessness caused Nora to feel disoriented, confused and alone.

Her stomach knotted. She was famished. She would gain no rest here, so she walked back into the butlery and opened a refrigerator that contained nothing but a little pâté, a remnant of unwrapped Brie, and a clump of grapes. Cradling these against her stomach, she moved into the dining room and, after placing them on the table's end, went over to two tall windows. She struggled to pull the locks free and lift open the sashes.

Cool evening air and the noise of automobile traffic washed over her. She looked above the rooftops and noted that the old Edith Piaf song was true: this city did indeed sport a rose-colored sky on the right evenings. *La Vie en Rose*—standing at the window of an old apartment above the Seine, Nora felt she had lived a rose-colored life for all of her days.

That is, were it not for the outlandish mysteries lying in wait behind her.

She turned away from the window, sat at the table's end and ate quietly. By the time she'd finished, lights were blinking on and the pink glow had faded to a sunset feast of orange and turquoise. The City of Lights was beginning to earn its title. Returning to the window, she leaned against its frame and thought of her ex-boyfriend, the one she'd broken up with six months before, and what a trip this would have been were she with a proper companion.

She dragged a parlor chair from the wall to the window's edge and sat here until the chill crept up her feet and legs. Then she walked back into the first room, dug out one of the flannel coats, returned and draped it over herself. She fell fast asleep.

LIQUID AS MERCURY, invisible to the human eye, the thin beam shot through the gaping apartment window forty-five feet over the Left Bank street and over a bristling sea of Paris rooftops. It flew above the Seine's gleaming waters, a lapping quayside and sleepy street, then the dining room mirror of the apartment at 47 Rue de la Saint Louis—all in just a fraction of a second.

Like a tiny cyclone dancing over a single glassy point, the laser quivered on the window's imperfections until suddenly it fell still.

And listened.

Back across the river, the gunlike aperture that had emitted the beam trailed a single black wire, which drooped in the room's unlit gloom to feed a microphone snugly hidden within a sweaty ear.

The listener cursed once, low. *No one moving.* Next came a faint sound murmuring in his ear. The sound of regular breathing, a light snore.

He sat hunched forward into the eyepiece of a high-powered spotting scope almost the size of a highway construction cone. Seen in his right eye, lightly shaking from the gentle blowing of an evening breeze, was the image of an antique mirror. Before it, almost lost in the detail of window railing and furniture, was the upturned face of a young woman.

The man spoke in Arabic into the tiny mouthpiece that snaked around his cheek to within an inch of his lips. As he confirmed the status of their prey, three fashionably dressed men scattered across the Isle de Saint Louis nodded almost invisibly.

The man in the apartment window stood up. Though the morning was warming quickly, he wrapped his arms around himself and shivered in the grip of a chill deep inside.

Inside him a ravenous hate seethed and smoldered. An imprisoned consciousness fairly roared in its craving for mayhem, for murder. For blood like water in a desert. Death like air to a drowning man.

Give me their bodies, broken like twigs, and then I will give you peace.

SPRAWLED ACROSS the ancient divan, Nora read on, this time her features grimacing, her head seeming to turn away reflexively from the words. Her reading was becoming too vivid, too graphic to readily dismiss.

The Convent at Mantes-la-Jolie—1789

Heads—bodiless and shorn, cut free from one set of shoulders after the other by crimson-streaked shanks of steel, the wooden report of each fresh felling and each new howl deafening upon the ear. Twisted, crazed faces with screams halted in mid-cry, falling as melons into gory baskets.

Such are the visions which afflict both my daytime reality and my anguished dreams.

Paris is aflame. The demon of destruction has attacked once again. With each rising of Dr. Guillotin's infernal blade comes the wail of another soul torn away before its time, its loss accountable to myself.

I write these words by the light of a dying candle flame inside a cell of the Mantes convent, where the Brothers have smuggled me. S., the Order's spy within the Committee of Public Safety, reported that charges were pending before the Revolutionary Tribunal and that I was to be arrested on a fraudulent letter within the half week. Of course, it had grown high time, and I should have anticipated this day's coming. Every other nobleman or wealthy citizen of Paris is already dead or rotting in his cell. Even men whose boldness and courage against the monarchy made the Revolution possible in the first place.

Doubtless my enemies within the Jacobins have dreamed up some accusation against me, disregarding my efforts at undermining the monarchy and the petty fops at court, my support of the Declaration of the Rights of Man and of the Citizen, or my role with the Girondist revolutionaries. My wealth is too great, my visibility too high. Robespierre's rampage has ceased to envisage lofty or even political overtones and now rides the sole vestry of bloodlust.

I summoned the house staff, paid them for the month, and sent them all away except for a strapping threesome whom I put to work at packing and concealing my furnishings upon wagons. Their first trip had scarcely left the gate for our safe house at Rosny before the sans-culottes *approached the front door knocking it with timbers, their eyes glittering hatefully in the torchlight.*

The Brothers led me along the back way into the escape dungeon. We hurried down the dank passages with heads bowed while the stomping of wooden shoes rang above our heads and the shouting of angry voices called out my current pseudonym.

When the rains break and the night falls we shall make for the Normandy coast, from whence so many noblemen have lately departed France forever. I will lose the home and a fair sum to this debacle, but it is of no import. What matters most is the innocent blood being shed. I shall live in one of the homes in Wales or Ireland, where I will enjoy a season of peace, a respite from the last few years of scheming counterplots.

I leave no friends to speak of in France, save my trusted servants. A thousand or more acquaintances to be sure, citizens who at least until now would have known me by face and reputation, and saluted me upon the boulevards. But no one I will miss.

It is madness, this time. My enemy's greatest triumph since the time of the Black Death. Paris scarcely darkens at night but for the burning of churches and grand estates, the towering flames and torches of roving mobs. The Church is decimated. My faithful Brothers of St. Lazare, once the most forlorn and unbeknownst of priests, are probably today the safest, owing to their skill at evasion, their well-chosen disguises and escape routes.

A guillotine stands in the square right outside my door. Yesterday from my attic window I watched a priest at his beheading. I remember his portly carriage from a year before, when I had business at court. The lowly curé had been randomly sent for the exigent task of baptizing the niece of a courtier. Hardly a lofty duty, though the glory of it hung about the poor fool's countenance like a halo. In fact, the tittering sycophant became somewhat of a favorite at Versailles masses after that. Probably for the amusement he unwittingly provided the snickering nobles. And yesterday he paid for his ascent with his life. The man brayed when they put the locks about his neck and soiled himself just as the blade came down. The crowd roared.

Only a year ago Robespierre would have wept and lofted an impassioned oratory about the death of the meanest peasant child. Today he dispatches whole families to the scaffold with nary a flicker of his eyelid, merely on pretext of another's malicious whisper. Last night as I huddled in the back of the hayswain on my way out of the city, I saw the mobs crowding about Place de la Concorde and thought sadly that of all the tyrants the French people could have pulled down upon themselves, the milksop Louis pales in comparison to the murderer they replaced him with. Oh, the hours I have spent pleading elementaries of morality with these madmen, while candles dwindled in the breezes of this or that public hall. Seeing the jowls of so-called great men blush red with the venting of stored-up hatreds. Never have I exhausted the learning of fifteen hundred years in such furious and futile debates. I hurled Socrates at them, Plato, Augustine, assorted Psalms, even some of the saner pronouncements of their own beloved Rousseau. All on behalf of simple restraint, or mere Christian grace. But logic is wasted on these power mongers. Truly, no one is less merciful and more bloodthirsty than a godless man bent on the revision of society.

I could actually glimpse the claw marks of destroyer's demons about these men's backs and shoulders. In fact, this last period has marked perhaps the most furious cycle of pursuit in all my years. I have both sensed and seen destroyer and several of his archdemons peer at me in the distance as I spoke with Robespierre and his fellow conspirators. Once I actually broke off discourse in the middle of a sentence to run after one unusually bold advance in my direction. I never caught him.

The destroyer is having a feast these days, and his foul appetite is being fed by the perversion of philosophies. Just last night, through the crowd at the nightly beheading, I saw destroyer himself whispering into Robespierre's ear and shaking with delight at the separation of each head from its shoulders.

I have failed. God save us.

33

HER IMAGINATION REELING, Nora wandered from artifact to artifact with a growing sense of awe. She counted three El Grecos, two Rembrandts, five da Vincis, as well as a dozen assorted impressionistic and postimpressionistic works. Since she was neither an art collector nor an aesthete, the exact rarity of these pieces remained a mystery to her. Even so, she examined everything in the large room and became convinced she was standing amidst the finest collection in the world.

Some time later, she heard a loud clatter from the direction of the butlery. She raced through the intervening doors and into the kitchen.

There he stood, steadying himself against the center island, surrounded by a mess of scattered implements. He turned at her approach and smiled sheepishly.

"Hello," he said, wincing as though the word itself pained him. He wore a robe that hung open at the chest. A thick, purple mass of dried blood lay caked across his solar plexus. He saw her astonished look and quickly pulled the robe tight. "Welcome to my home. I am sorry to be such a poor host."

"Nonsense," she said. "You saved my life."

"By the way, I appreciate your not driving me to the nearest hospital. That might have been somewhat of a disaster."

"Why?"

"Because I am not ready for a repeat performance of Massachusetts General."

"And why is that?"

"Actually, I apologize. I am still not sure you're ready to know."

"I've been reading your diaries." Her voice sounded harsh and accusing, but she wanted him to know.

His gaze washed over hers and took in her expression, but his other features remained neutral, impassive. Yet a glint in his eye showed he was also poised for conflict.

He spoke at last. "Yes, I noticed that you found the diaries. I am very grateful to the priests for having gathered and translated them during my absence. The bindings are rather nice, don't you think?"

She shook her head, dismissing the surface point of his question. She knew what he was really inquiring about. "I have no idea what to think. At all. You obviously seem to think that you're . . . you're . . . I can't even bring myself to say it, it's so absurd."

"Immortal."

"Yes. That. And of course there's no such thing as immortality."

"Oh, well of course," he said with a smile. He cocked his head back, the grin still present. "I suppose, too, there is no such thing as an invisible force which tugs us earthward and is called gravity. There is no such thing as small beasts tinier than the naked eye can see, yet which actually comprise our bodies, or even smaller ones that make up the fabric of living matter. Nor is there any such thing as invisible waves filling the air so thickly that we can convey entire symphonies and motion pictures through the ether. No such thing as planets also invisible to the naked eye. Blasphemy, for all of these things had the authorities of their day believing that to even speak of them was sacrilege and nonsense.

Why? Because they couldn't be seen. They had never been observed."

Nora took a deep breath. He did not appear hostile over the disagreement, only pleasantly engaged. Yet he now awaited her response; the flat calm of his gaze made that much clear to her. She glanced around her, nodding her head. "You have a point, certainly."

"We do not have to settle this now," he interrupted vigorously, with a nearly palpable look of relief. "More than likely it will take me several days to fully recover from my injury. We will have time then to debate the matter. In the meantime, this immortal is incredibly weak and would appreciate a shoulder to help him back to his bed. Would you oblige me?"

She adopted the now-familiar pose beneath his arm and began supporting his walk.

"I apologize for the disarray in here," he said breathlessly. "No one except the priests have been up here in many years."

"Don't be silly," she replied, grinning inwardly at the thought of anyone wading through such a mass of antiquity as though it were an afternoon's cleanup.

They reached his bedroom and she deposited him gently onto his bed. He grimaced as he settled in, groaning deeply. Looking up at Nora, he gave her a brave smile, pointed to his mangled chest, and said, "This is partial proof, you know."

She said nothing.

"By the looks of it, keeping in mind the range from which they were firing, I would say my heart took a direct hit from an AK-47 round. I should have died within seconds."

"I'm sorry," she said sincerely. "It's just that I'm a rational person."

"Yes, you are," he agreed, "and you're surrounded by irrational things. Looking at an impossible specimen of humanity. You've already forgotten the irrational event which took place the night you were attacked."

"No, that's where you're wrong. I've forgotten nothing."

He leaned back in his pillow at that, smiling paternally. "I understand, Nora. I'm being hard on you. I need to sleep now, but I do have an unfortunate request to make of you."

"Name it."

"I'm afraid I will need a helper for the next few days, until I regain my strength. I was almost recovered from the last incident when this . . . this thing happened."

"I'll be glad to do that. Finding you was the reason I came to France anyway. I'm not going anywhere."

He closed his eyes. "Yes. The answers you've received have been a bit disconcerting, haven't they?"

"To say the least."

"Don't worry, Nora. I'll be stronger in the morning, and we can talk."

Brzezinka, Poland

THEY BEGAN GATHERING at dawn. Father Tsackiewski had heard the first snub-nosed Trabant pull up with a diesel whine, then cough a white cloud into the humid morning air. It parked mere yards from the chapel's front door. He had been expecting no one. Several minutes later a caravan of small automobiles lurched onto the grass and traced a rough beeline in his direction.

When he saw the last vehicle—a white van bearing a satellite dish on its top and the large numeral of a Warsaw television station on its side—he knew he was in trouble.

The young people who streamed out of these vehicles spent the first few minutes in quiet, silently bent over banners and placards. Then one long slogan pierced the mist, and a shout went up. The other banners followed within seconds.

Once an accomplice, always an accomplice!
Anti-Semite Catholics out!
Keep your cross off our graves!
Cross and swastika are brothers!
Respect for Jewish monuments!

Glancing out a side window from the semidarkness of his nave, Father Tsackiewski observed with irony that most of the signs were written in English, the language of neither combatant in this dispute. But the cameras were turned on, and English was, among other things, the international language of the world media. Journalists were multiplying outside his door even more quickly than the incendiary banners.

A chant began, at first low and uncertain, then soon ringing with singsong rhythm and the adamancy of youth.

"Pope, pope, go away! How many graves have you dug today?"

He winced, picked up a cordless telephone to call for help. As he was punching in the number, the first rock shattered his new stained-glass window with a sharp tinkling sound.

"Hello, police?"

Paris, Isle de St. Louis

SHE FOUND IT by accident in the middle of the following morning while searching for a misplaced volume of the diaries. Implausible or not, Nora had been forced to admit to herself that the documents did form quite a tale, one which had captivated her imagination. She'd been busy searching for the leather binder containing a section of the early Renaissance when she found this other, lying on top of an ancient Bible inside the desk drawer.

A simple scrapbook, she'd thought at first.

She turned the first page and discovered a photograph mounted there. A sepia-tinged, black-and-white picture of a man posing with a smile, alone, on the deck of a large ship. Gray mist swirled behind him, obscuring sea and sky. He wore a silk foulard, puffed out from the tightly tailored lines of a dark pinstriped suit. A bowler hat was clenched in one hand, resting against his side. It was the typical prosperous immigrant photograph, which half the families in America held in their own family scrapbooks.

Her eyes seemed to recognize him before her mind did. Her brain simply seized up like an oil-starved engine, poised on the brink yet unable to move forward.

It was him. Lassalle, or whatever his name was. The 1880's gentleman in the picture was him—not a younger version, not a handsomer or unwrinkled version, but *him*. Exactly. As though the photo had been taken yesterday.

She turned the page.

The next spread was composed of smaller photographs of nineteenth-century leisure: a mixed-gender group of friends posing on what resembled the Deauville boardwalk, atop the Eiffel Tower, then on the terrace before the Sacré-Coeur Basilica.

He was in every one of them, barely a haircut removed from the man who lay in a bed not thirty yards from her.

She began flipping frantically through the scrapbook. There was a page of tickets: an autographed theatre pass proclaiming in a beaux-arts style the name of Sarah Bernhardt, a boarding ticket for the HMS *Ramsport*, admitting one on an amusement excursion to the Faeroe Islands. Another page displayed a framed commendation from the Préfecture de Police de Paris. The recipient's name was Jean-Jacques Bouquet. Below it, another photo showed him shaking the hand of a walrus-mustached man in a stiff-looking uniform. The document was dated 1893.

Nora slammed the book shut with an emphatic flip of the wrist and stared into the apartment's gloom, trying to make her mind slow down.

Could it be true? Had she suddenly leaped from a world where things made sense according to an established order, an order she'd mastered with great effort at one of the world's great universities, to find herself now in a strange hall of mirrors, a no-man's land of mythical apparitions and fairy tales come to life?

At the back of her mind lurked another disturbing thought. The painting she had seen in the Great Room—the name she'd invented to describe the cavernous hall in which she slept. Almost reluctantly, she rose, entered the chamber, and walked over to the spot. She placed her hand on her hips like an ordinary museum-goer, as if the casualness of the pose could quell the throb of her heartbeat.

The painting in question did not appear to be that of a master, although it featured all the period affectations and accomplished skill of a Gainsborough or other eighteenth-century portrait painter. On first inspection she had glanced right over the subject, not wanting to admit to herself that her host could have posed for a clearly centuries-old portrait with a wiry greyhound at his feet, and an oak-shrouded hunting castle hovering in the background mist. Lord of the Manor. His features kept slack and impassive in keeping with the patrician expression of the period. Without a doubt, it was him.

She would later describe it as the feeling of a dam bursting inside of her. The accumulated evidence of this place, the unanswered questions she'd been grappling with, the psychological strain of being stalked—all of this overwhelmed her defenses and swept her into a maelstrom of colliding ideas and beliefs. She felt dizzy and faintly sick in her stomach. She had difficulty walking through the various doorways and into his bedroom.

There he dozed, his breakfast dishes lying next to him. He looked untroubled and innocent.

His eyes fluttered open at her approach, and an unpracticed smile crossed his face. "Good morning again."

Nora only nodded at him in response. She looked down at the

weathered quilt covering his bed, and sat down lightly on the edge. She tried to speak but found she could only shake her head.

"What's the matter?"

She inhaled deeply, willing herself not to cry. She breathed in again and forced herself to frame the simple question, "Is it true?"

"Yes." The reply was softly, quietly emphatic.

"I feel like a child who's learned that Santa doesn't exist," she said with a half-laughing sob of relief. "Or maybe one who's learned that he *does* exist. My point is—having to rearrange things. Having to reorganize my whole view of how the world works."

"I know," he said, and then a long silence stretched between them.

"So, are you going to tell me who you are?"

He sighed. "I am not in the habit of giving people that information."

"Well, I'm not just anyone. I'm someone whose life you've saved twice, and who's traveled across the Atlantic to hunt you down. Besides, I'm not leaving you until you tell me."

He chuckled at her persistence, then faced her with a half smile. "Tell me, Nora, do you believe in God?"

She took an exasperated breath. She hadn't wanted such an extraordinary journey to lead back into territory as familiar and unsavory as religion.

"I ask because if things are being 'reorganized' for you," he continued, "then you should know this. You will not make sense of anything without understanding the things of the Spirit."

"I believe in spiritual things. Just not in the traditional church way. More in a general, sort of non-codified kind of way. Do you know what I mean?"

He smiled indulgently. "I think so." Straightening himself in the bed, he looked at her intensely. "You understand: if you don't believe in the afterlife, and in other spiritual realms, and in the existence of a personal Creator God, none of this is going to make sense to you."

"Well, nothing makes sense to me right now, anyway. So I might as well listen with an open mind. But first, please, just level with me. Bottom line. Who are you?"

"I am a man, first of all. Just a man. A man whose story was recorded in the most famous book of all time."

"What?" *The Bible?*

"I am a man who suffered a terrible illness—a form of scarlet fever, I have since guessed. I died. I entered the afterlife. I was denied entrance to the gate that is now commonly referred to as the Great Light. I was turned away not because I was damned, but because I was being sent back. I opened my eyes and there he stood in front of me, barely visible in the half-light of my grave, with his hand still on my forehead."

"You mean . . . *him*."

"That's right. Jesus. And ever since that day I have been unable to age or die. When I have suffered a mortal injury, I've been taken to the brink of eternity, then returned every time."

"So what is your name?"

"You don't read your New Testament very much, do you?"

"No."

"I am Lazarus of Bethany."

34

Brussels, Belgium—Same Morning

BAM!

The impact of the man's fist on the clear Lucite podium reverberated through a bank of speakers suspended above the huge hall, as well as through five hundred earphones covering the auditory canals of most of the European Union Security Council. All over the auditorium, hands suddenly clutched ears in a single, swift motion.

"The attack on the Birkenau chapel by Jewish demonstrators is an outrage against civilized Europe! It is a coldly calculated affront to the national sovereignty of my country! Much as we condemn the Holocaust of the past, we cannot allow Zionist hooligans to attack legitimately ordained Catholic churches!"

Thunderous applause.

"We cannot allow Israel to interfere in the internal affairs of a European nation!"

Several dozen flashbulbs erupted at that last sentence. Polish ambassador Janelski had counted on that sound bite to lead the European news that evening.

"This body must vocally condemn the rioting at Auschwitz this morning as an act of aggression against the territorial sovereignty of Europe. And it must strongly warn any outside nation against meddling in what is an internal security matter!"

This time, amidst even louder applause, a scattering of

delegates stood with their clapping hands held high.

"The Polish government is fully confident that the Vatican is more than able to settle an internal matter to everyone's satisfaction. Let us allow them to put their own house in order. Then let us put this crisis behind us, and return to the planning of a prosperous and unified future for all of Europe!"

He descended from the podium in a roar of applause, the frown still frozen on his face.

Langley, Virginia—Later That Morning

STAYTON THOUGHT SCHORIE looked like an angry bear, shuffling into the meeting late with a swift gait. He made eye contact with no one—another bad sign. His boss merely yanked his chair back with a nimble move of his ankle that Stayton had often witnessed but never duplicated, then sat and slammed a stack of folders down onto the table.

He looked up. "Folks, we have a guest from Operations Directorate here with us this morning. So let's give a hearty Intelligence welcome to Kent Netelman."

A few gave faint nods of greeting.

To those who knew the intricacies of the man's vocal repertoire, it seemed Schorie's voice fairly dripped with sarcasm. Not knowing him, however, Netelman might have been forgiven for actually taking the welcome seriously, although a sincerely warm greeting would have been unusual within the CIA. The twin directorates—Operations, the actual cloak-and-dagger spook division, and Intelligence, which gathered data from all around the world—competed with and disliked each other more intensely than even some branches of the military. Intelligence, to which Schorie and Stayton belonged, regarded Operations as an arrogant bunch of loose cannons and lawbreakers, while Operations regarded Intelligence as an effete lot of ideologically suspect paper pushers.

In short, Stayton knew that Netelman's presence in the meeting today was an obvious sign of defeat for Schorie, an indicator that his boss had failed to contain the situation within his own spheres of influence. Still, as Stayton thought to himself, it was hardly a surprise, given the rapid escalation of the crisis.

"Okay, Stayton. What's with the girl?"

"We think she's in Paris, but we don't know where. I've got three men looking for her. Echelon's satellite caught a car leaving the attack scene and entering Paris five hours later."

"What's the report on that attack?"

"The operation on St. Michel seems to be professionally run, possibly terrorist. The perps escaped in a stealth helo, one of the modified Alouette III's our French friends had the nerve to sell to Iran last year. They think we don't know, except since, every Islamic extremist in the book has been seen racing around in Alouettes like teenagers in new Camaros. Our birds lost the helo in the cloud cover over the Channel. It could have landed on any one of fifteen seaborne vessels with pads or even the tip of the British coast. They're gone. But they were shooting AKs and reports say they're Arab."

"This Lassalle escaped?"

"With the girl, yes. The priests immediately disappeared also. No sign."

The Operations guy suddenly came to life, pulling a thin stack of photos from his briefcase. "Okay, this is Level Ten stuff, folks."

Backs around the table stiffened, and gazes became fixed on the pictures being flung deftly to each of them. A darkened bar, an Arab man in a stylish black suit looking past the face of an older, European gentleman.

"This, I probably don't need to tell any of you, is Jamail. It's the other man's identity that will surprise you. Put a clerical collar, or maybe even a bishop's miter, on this man talking to Jamail and you have one Bishop Johan Eccles of Rome, central liaison to Vatican Special Projects."

He let out a snort of disgust.

"This is a mess. We've got Vatican bishops sponsoring Hamas terrorist hits on other priests who themselves are suspect in desecration of Jewish Holocaust relics. We got Mossad climbing all over Polish authorities, Poland snarling at Jewish authorities; we got half of Europe foaming at the mouth against Israel, fomenting a good old-fashioned anti-Semitic pogrom. Did anyone see this coming?"

The rebuke drew only angry silence from around the table.

"Maybe if our men in the field had given us photos like this earlier," Schorie growled, "we could have anticipated this *very predictable* alliance."

The sarcasm was out in the open now.

"Okay." Schorie's take-charge voice had returned. "Let's prioritize. What's our greatest threat?"

Stayton said, "That Israel will make such a fuss over this, that the European Union will break off relations. Maybe even war."

"War? Ken, any likelihood of that?" Schorie turned to Ken Allen, their most senior analyst.

"Actually, pandering to both Catholic and anti-Semitic elements in Europe is a pretty slick move right now. I'd say a good politician might jump at the chance."

"Even at the risk of war."

"With religion and the Middle East involved, anything's possible."

"Great." Schorie exhaled theatrically and glanced down, as if the consequences were his alone to bear. "And what's the bottom line on this man they supposedly dug up?"

"It's a muddle, sir. The guy's half legend, half of him thick-cover identities. And the French aren't helping."

"What a surprise. Something tells me the whole desecration angle is pure smoke screen," said Schorie. "I think if you find out the truth about this man, you'll find the real scoop behind this mess."

Netelman put his fingers to his lips, comically telegraphing his concentration. Finally, he relaxed and turned to Schorie. "I think we can pull a couple dozen men out of London and help sniff this guy out. He's gotta come up for air sometime."

Paris, Isle de St. Louis

LAZARUS'S FINGERS gripped the pages eagerly and propped up the large volume on the sheet, against his upturned knees in the bed. He read with the thirst of a man regaining his own life, his own lost memory. With every word countless images flooded his mind, along with the reassurance that he had lost none of it after all.

St. André de l'Eure—1438

This world has become the antechamber of death. Within the two leagues I voyaged in this fortnight now live only a small number of souls, out of a half-dozen towns which once harbored five thousand. My guardian priest and I trod wearily through one deserted village after another, stepping over bodies lying like piles of rags. I grow sick of the odor of rot, the cawing of crowes, the scurrying of rats about their cruel business, eerie silences on the wind.

In Ivry we did not encounter a single living person. The stench of the town assaulted us at La Chaussee, before even our first sight of its steeple. We proceeded anxiously, seeking a nurse or nun such as commonly remain as the last brave souls in these accursed places. All medicants of lesser fortitude have long since fled. But no such figure appeared. We crossed a small bridge over rancid waters and felt our knees give out at the sight before us. The lane was choked with carrion. Dark lumps lay atop one another in a thick sprawl. A raven perched atop a swollen belly turned to us, its beak stained crimson from a shred of flesh choking its maw. It watched us through a single eye for a moment, then reared back to gulp its meal and bent down to its repast.

This Black Death has felled more people than I ever imagined possible. And as no respecter of persons, for prince and highborn alike have fallen to its fevers and ghastly effusions of blood. I fear for the survival of the human race itself.

Four of the Order's seven have fallen. I dispatched the remnant to safety but for my faithful Didier, who impetuously threatened to cast himself upon a nearby corpse if I left him behind.

How the destroyer is gorging himself right now, on the suffering and death of souls beyond number! Perhaps my only consolation on this grim journey has been catching the hundreds of demonkind perched greedily over the bodies of the dying. Most of them do not know of me, and many who do are so satiated and filled with bloodlust that their reflexes are sluggish. I hurry over and administer last rites, then quickly consign the spirit to hell forever. There are too many of them to count, of course, yet it is a small solace.

For what seems an eternity, I have sought to lessen the suffering of the wretched ones. I gather the dying into my arms and hear their confessions, speak words of hope into their ears, and seek to calm their final tremors with a firm embrace.

Sometimes I am rewarded with a tiny glimpse of heaven as a pious one rends through his suffering and shouts forth visions of awaiting angels and the glory ahead. I am touched with pangs of envy, too. Their earthly agony consumes itself soon enough, and then many of them are carried away to a place I know. A place I once visited for too brief a time. Some days I wish I could join them. I would gladly suffer their bodily travails if only to see Paradise again.

Oh, the piteous scenes I have witnessed in these last nine years! In Amiens I helped deliver a pestilent baby even as its mother shuddered her final gasps. I will never forget the tiny girl in Alsace, whose begrimed face appeared one cold dawn atop a teetering pile of corpses. I could not discern at first whether she was a person or some species of rodent until her eyes betrayed her as a child in apparent search of her parents. I called out to her through a rush of tears but the wretched thing peered at me quickly, her tiny features contorted with fear, and she disappeared. I sought her for two hours through the abandoned village but to no avail.

This world seems such a foul place to me now. As for those who survive this disease, many are afflicted with a hateful madness. In Paris I witnessed a mob of peasants set upon a family of Jews, screaming the familiar jeremiads about the Hebrew race being responsible for the Black Death due to some alleged ritual. The crowd kicked an old woman to unconsciousness and a younger man whom I took for her son had his head split open for his troubles defending her. His wife and four children ran away in shrieks. This is how I know my enemy is behind this. The enemy has engineered his old foe the Jewish people as the most unlikely of scapegoats. Everywhere Jews are being killed and hounded out of their homes because of the Death.

My good health is now the brand of my separateness, my loneliness, and so I have been forced to move about even more ceaselessly than usual to avoid suspicion.

Late yesterday afternoon Didier and I reached my Normandy manor with a great sense of relief. A late afternoon sun had broken through the rain clouds and bathed the low valley in a sparsely lit yet piercing shade of green. I am always refreshed by the walk about the secluded glades that surround the manor house. Finally on safe ground, we walked slowly, feeling free and more relaxed. The rivulet which issues from the manor pond's spring has become quite a stream. The rains have certainly done their share in the past month.

The central quarters, having been well sealed by the priests since my last visit, seem untouched so far by the rats which infest the land. Upon arrival I urged Didier to stay in the guest quarters as an honored visitor would, not as a servant. He obliged, disappearing until morning with naught but a bottle of red wine. There being no food in the house I also retired to my chambers and spent a long stretch of time in my bedclothes before the fireplace, drinking tea.

Just before dawn I awoke from a horrific dream, the sort of dream that causes one to wonder if it was the idle wandering of the soul or actual prophecy. I was the last man left on earth. I had inherited a world littered with death and decay, and yet I was its sole master. I could not suppress a sense of pride in my sovereignty. I strode through scenes of carnage, each more revolting than the last. All at once I heaved backwards and spewed forth a large volume of blood, and knew that I was not special after all. I was merely the last to die.

It was then I awoke, with the echo of my screams still bouncing about the rafters.

And still, despite the dream, unable to expire.

35

Paris, Isle de St. Louis—The Following Morning

BY THE FOURTH DAY Nora had come to feel that she'd been locked away in a large and ornate prison cell. Father Thierry and five of the Order had arrived the night before, bearing fresh groceries and news of their narrow escape from the Hamas hit squad at Mont St. Michel. Father Moll wore his injured arm in a sling. Father Justin still lay critically wounded in a Normandy convent hospital.

The priests disappeared into another part of the building later that evening. So Nora woke up this morning as alone as ever.

She stood before the dining room window, looking out over the Left Bank's sea of mansard roofs in the morning light, when she heard a faint rustling behind her.

She turned and screamed—and saw that it was her host, walking slowly toward her. Startled, he halted and raised his hands reassuringly.

"Just me."

"I am so sorry," she replied. "I've grown accustomed to being the only ambulatory person in this place. Are you sure you're up to walking?"

He nodded. "I feel much better."

"Good, because I'm going to get out of here for a while. Maybe you'd like to walk with me."

He paused a second, then shook his head. "No, I'm afraid that will be impossible for either of us. It's too dangerous. There are too many people looking for us."

"Fine. You stay then. But I'm dying of cabin fever."

He frowned. "Cabin fever? An illness?"

"No, an expression. It refers to growing tired of being cooped up someplace. I have it bad and I'm going for a walk, no matter what you say."

He placed his hands on his hips and appeared to study the floor. Finally he looked up at her with a wisp of a smile. "I'll just be a few minutes."

When he emerged again from his bedroom twenty minutes later, he was a different man. An elderly tourist with graying hair, silver beard, and jowls hanging from his cheeks. He wore a white T-shirt bearing an imprint of the Statue of Liberty, long khaki shorts, and bright white athletic shoes. A small knapsack hung around his shoulder. She hardly recognized him.

"I've had many years to learn disguises," he said with a grin. "Let us spend the day outside."

He pulled out a cellular phone and pressed a button. "Thierry, Nora and I are going to leave the premises for the day. I know. I know. She insisted. It's all right—I am in full regalia. And I really don't think they'd strike so soon. Besides, we're taking one of my little-known routes. Would you check the exits? . . . Thank you. We'll take the back route."

He hung up and nodded sideways. "This way."

They descended more flights of stairs than Nora could remember. At what she perceived as the bottom, a window looked out over a vestibule and an outside view of a bustling street. But Lazarus—she'd now come to think of him by this name—instead led her to a side door which he opened with a key. Inside, a dark, unfinished tunnel led away into darkness. He flipped on a switch, and they walked a hundred yards or so in the light of a series of bare light bulbs. At the last one, he stopped and pulled out the cell phone again. He punched a button and muttered a few affirmative grunts, then switched it off. Turning to his left, he pushed open a door and they walked into brilliant sunshine.

They emerged from an inconspicuous side door onto an expanse of bench-lined gravel beneath a canopy of trees. The roar of auto traffic immediately filled her ears. A humid breeze roiled up against her, bringing with it the smells of diesel fumes and a fishy whiff of river. The early morning light Nora had seen from the window survived only in a salmon-tinged glow against a high bank of clouds.

They loped across the street toward the edge of the Seine. Nora pulled alongside him and took a long, deep breath. "It's not Mother Nature, but it's an interesting smell anyway," she said.

He turned to her with a bright look. "Would you like a little Mother Nature? Paris can oblige, you know."

"Okay."

"It's one of my favorite walks."

They turned around and an arched row of flying buttresses came into view, soaring above the treetops. Nora stopped short and said, "I didn't realize we were so close to Notre Dame."

"Yes. We're on the Isle de St. Louis. It's another island just to the east of Paris's original island, La Cité."

"I never knew."

They headed for the opposite shore.

"How long have you lived here?" she asked.

"How long in Paris, or on this island?"

"Let's start with the island."

"Well, let's see. I was one of the first people to buy land when the canons of Notre Dame finally let the king build here. Before that we'd all known the place as the 'Isle des Vaches.' The island of cows. It was empty pastureland. So I probably had my hotel built in the 1640s."

"Hotel? You—"

"Not a lodging establishment. *Hotel* back then was just the name for an elegant building."

"Oh." For the first time in years, she felt small and uneducated.

"It's been my home base for about three hundred and fifty years." Even he seemed stunned by the calculation.

"You know, I'm still having a hard time with all this," Nora said.

His hand grasped her shoulder lightly. "So am I. I have a very long habit of not talking about my life. Instead I am an expert at the kind of everyday conversation people routinely share with mere acquaintances."

"Small talk," she offered.

"Yes," he said, smiling at the expression. "A good American idiom, I presume. I have made centuries of small talk. Avoiding any intrusive questions, any inquiries into my background or my place of origin."

"That sounds very lonely."

He said nothing for a long time. "Yes. I suppose it is. But I've grown accustomed to it."

They walked for a half hour in peaceful silence, punctuated by Lazarus's occasional pausing to share another anecdote. They crossed another bridge, and he launched into another.

"Centuries ago these bridges were lined with houses and buildings three, four stories high. So high that the street level was in shadow most of the day," he said, his manner suddenly cheerful and marked by energetic sweeps of the arms. He looked as if he'd never been injured. "And filled with the most bustling marketplaces you could imagine! Medicine shows, harlequin clowns, money changers, prostitutes, goldsmiths, orating philosophers, bookstalls, pastries and breads of all kinds, freshly butchered meat hanging everywhere. They had a saying about Pont Neuf, that you could hardly cross it without seeing a monk, a harlot, and a white horse. It was a sight to see."

Nora smiled and glanced at the pavement around her, imagining herself surrounded by medieval houses and a crowd of merchants.

"It was even worse during the Feast of St. Denis, Paris's patron saint. People came from all over the world. I even remember meeting Syrian merchants come to sell spices and incense. Sometimes the churches would be so crowded that worshipers were crushed to death, and the priests had to climb out through the back windows."

Satisfied for the moment, he fell quiet. They walked on for several minutes while Nora began to feel that she was walking through crowds of long-dead predecessors. Jostling the ghosts of the past.

36

THEY CROSSED THE RIVER, climbed a flight of steps, went through a large doorway and entered a vast botanical garden. Nora gasped in delight. Within seconds of stepping within the leafy canopy, Paris's street noise abated, and they were surrounded by greenery dense enough to rival the thickest greenhouse.

They strolled through the garden for a half hour. Nora's pace began to relax, and her smile became more unguarded. She started to believe, if nothing else, that this man had truly sheltered himself from human contact for a long while. His tales grew more animated and fascinating by the minute.

They emerged from the end of the Jardin des Plantes and crossed a wide boulevard. "I'm going to take you to the most charming street market in Paris," he shouted over the roar of traffic.

But when they'd reached the other side, he paused before a stand of shrubbery leading into a kind of park. He turned to her, his face suddenly ashen.

"Let me show you something first," he said.

They proceeded up a sandy walkway. Up ahead, Nora saw a large curve of weathered stone. As they grew nearer she recognized the remains of an amphitheater—circular tiers of eroded rock. Tall houses rose behind the structure. Four small boys kicked a soccer ball across its dusty stage, their shouts echoing in the late morning light.

Lazarus's gaze lay sullenly glued on the sight. "This is one of the oldest structures in Paris. I first came here on my way back from Ireland. This was Lutetia then, a Roman garrison. And standing right over there"—he turned and pointed to a sloping mound of grass to his right—"I witnessed a family of Christians being disemboweled by gladiators."

Nora groaned.

Still fixed straight ahead, his face contorted into a grimace. "There were, oh, five thousand people here. Of course, the stands were twice as tall then. Everyone dressed up in their finest clothes. I'll never forget the face of this little boy. He was maybe four years old. He walked out and just looked around, not knowing whether to let go of his mother's hand and go play or just stand there and cry. Then, incredibly, he looked up at all the people seated before him, raised his hand and gave a tentative little wave. A roar of laughter swept across the audience. Not a sympathetic laughter, but one of superior derision. Several of the golden-robed people closest to him actually waved back to the boy, smiling leering grins at him and mocking him. Then a pair of gladiators in full armor stepped away from the wall and walked over to where he stood. The boy started to cry when the men were still a hundred paces away from his family. The crowd was on their feet cheering before the broadsword had even been pulled out of that boy's stomach. . . ."

Lazarus choked and turned away.

She followed him back down the walkway. Neither of them looked back.

He now seemed lost in a trance of sorts, captive to wild thoughts. "Strong emotions leave a residue," he said, "an invisible film that almost anyone with sensitivity can feel. Step onto the stage of an old theater and you'll feel it instantly. It's another reason why I cannot stay long in a place like that. Besides the memories themselves."

"It looks to me like all of Paris is that way."

"Absolutely. People have been arguing and fighting here for thousands of years." He sighed. "You would not believe how much death I've seen," he muttered. "In Britain we would come upon villages where whole families had been impaled on stakes. And they weren't even prisoners. Just pagan rituals. The Druids would predict the future by stabbing someone in the back and watching how the blood poured out. I once saw a Druid escort forty-five men, women, and children into this enormous basket, close it up and throw a torch on it. The whole thing went up in a flash. The only thing louder than the people screaming was the Druid's chanting, which he did at the top of his voice, laughing and dancing."

"That's enough," Nora said. "I think I get the picture." She looked up at him and broke out in laughter. "You really are uplifting company, you know that?"

His features softened, and he laughed as well. "You're right. Look, here's Rue Mouffetard, the marketplace. Let's buy something to eat and forget all of these sad thoughts."

He led her across another street to a narrow, winding lane jammed with rickety, wooden market stalls. Aromas that Nora had never smelled before—warm with spicy marinades, exotic meats—wafted over her while she walked. She strolled past rows of produce, hams, fresh poultry, baskets, relish salads, their prices scribbled on tiny staked chalkboards. An aged woman wearing a bright red scarf shouted at her through broken teeth, breathing out a rich aroma of red wine and pâté. Lingering just behind her and conversing in fluent French, Lazarus began buying the makings of a picnic lunch.

After purchasing a bagful of food, they walked to a nearby Metro station.

"I have another surprise for you," he said as they headed down the steps into the ozone-scented air of the subway. They entered a white-tiled tunnel featuring posters for American movies and emerged onto a station platform just as a green subway car rattled in. They climbed aboard and exited three stops later. Nora found herself in a quiet, genteel neighborhood.

After crossing the street, Lazarus turned to her and said, "I may not have told you this, but I have been imprisoned for the last sixty years. Don't ask how; I'll tell you later. My point is that it is such a joy to be here after more than a half century and still recognize so much of the city around me. In times past I would be rescued and be rejoined to a world I knew nothing of."

The pair came to a veritable forest crowded behind tall metal fencing. A sign fastened to the fence bore the name *Jardin de Luxembourg*. They walked through an open gate, then the forest, and stepped back out onto a sun-drenched manicured lawn. Continuing their walk, they passed through another stand of trees adjacent to lanes of well-tended sand. In the distance Nora saw a cluster of men stooped over the ground. One of them launched into the air a metal ball which caught a ray of sun before dropping heavily and rolling into a dozen others. She remembered the game's name—*boules*. She'd heard of the French pastime.

Lazarus led her to a nearby bench where they sat down. He pointed to her right. Towering in the sun stood a perfect replica of the Statue of Liberty, hardly thirty feet tall.

"One of Bartholdi's working models," he said. "I thought it might fend off homesickness."

She laughed at the whimsical thoughtfulness of it. What a perfect place in which to enjoy their picnic.

They ate slowly as Nora continued to drink in Lazarus's fascinating stories. It seemed as if an endless line of grandfatherly personas were channeling through a single voice, releasing a gush of tales that spanned the ages. He spoke of studying Latin in the Middle Ages. Of seeing scholars bound in chains and tossed into the Seine to drown for the amusement of an evil queen. He told of one such professor notorious for claiming that a donkey placed halfway between two equal stacks of hay would starve before choosing which to eat. The man was saved from drowning by students who'd floated a barge made of hay below the window of his execution. He told of one winter after the crops had failed when wolves roamed the city gnawing on the living and the dead alike. He described the dank, cramped space of the sewer worker's chamber below the streets of the Rue Gay Lussac just a few blocks away. The same place that had housed Resistance headquarters during the early Nazi occupation.

After finishing lunch they wound their way homeward through the Latin Quarter, while he told her of the stench which had reigned over Paris before Baron Haussmann modernized the sewer system. He described for her the fighting of the 1848 revolt and the whistle of artillery shells flying over his head while he stood on a barricade in the Place de la Concorde.

At a small street-side restaurant she asked him about the liberation of Paris. "Wasn't some of the worst fighting along Boulevard St. Michel, just a block from here?"

Lowering his wineglass, he shook his head. "I have no idea, Nora. I was imprisoned from 1942 until just weeks ago."

"By the Germans?"

"I guess you could say so. More specifically, by my enemy."

"How is it you could be locked up for sixty years, in this day and age?"

"What do you do with a captured opponent who cannot be killed? Think about it. You lock him away—in a place so remote that he may never be found. That's all you can do. That's what my enemy has been trying to do with me for centuries."

"Who is this enemy?" Nora asked.

"He goes by several names. The destroyer, the strong man, Satan's evil spirit of destruction, war, and bloodshed. He and I have been dueling ever since I became aware of my special condition."

"I don't understand. How do you duel with a spirit?"

"A good question. It's far different than a physical battle. Spiritual conflict is waged in the hearts of individual people. Sometimes an entire war or massacre may hinge on the prayer or choice made by a single person—not always a famous ruler, either. Sometimes it's one pivotal individual, perhaps anonymous even, whose behavior will either ignite or avert a catastrophe. If I can be directed to that one person and influence him or her toward the right choice, I can have a profound effect on history. Often I have failed, and mayhem has ensued. If I could somehow get close to the destroyer's human host to speak the Exorcist's Prayer, I could exile him to hell forever. That is my highest goal right now."

"And how do you get to this destroyer?"

He looked at her directly, with an inscrutable gaze that caused a shiver to ripple down her spine. Finally he broke the scrutiny with a tiny shift in his features. "I can see him. I see his spiritual body."

"You mean from continents away?"

"No. I mean when I am within sight of the host. I'm guided to his general vicinity by other combatants, beings who work by my side. Spiritual intelligence operatives, you might say." He coughed, clearly ill at ease, and looked into his wineglass.

"You might call them angels."

IN A DIMLY LIT room on the floor just beneath the level inhabited by one André Lassalle, seven men in cassocks stood in various poses of disbelief before a small television.

On the screen, a man in priestly robes stood before a bank of microphones, speaking in Italian-accented English.

"Furthermore, the Holy Father wishes to express his deep sorrow to the Jewish people over the apparent desecration of a Holocaust site. However, he and the Vatican wish it to be known that no legitimate arm of the Catholic Church had anything to do with this regrettable act. It appears that a renegade group of men who have usurped the name of a long-expired monastic order may have been involved. But we repeat that, despite published reports, legitimate Catholic clergy have not had anything to do with this outrage. Thank you."

An anchorman returned, glancing down at a sheaf of papers in his hand. He disappeared, silenced by a swift click of the remote from Father Thierry.

"I begged him to go to Rome with me," the old man said with a sigh. "If he had, none of this would have happened."

"Have we been disavowed by the Church?"

"No," Thierry said sadly. "This is just a shot across our bow. A warning. But we tried. We have never been able to control him, least of all the Church. One reading of the diaries proves that in an instant."

37

Strasbourg—1522

At long last, I have met with Martin Luther. My heart still beats at a stallion's gallop, even after having quit him some three odd hours ago.

Finally a fresh ray of hope for Christendom. How long have I despaired of the Church recapturing her purity. But I rush ahead of today's events.

The meeting proved delicate to arrange. My faithful Brothers, loyal to my person though they may be, are in the first place good Catholic monks. And the movement which this Luther has birthed is commonly envisaged as a heretic aberration of exceedingly high order. I too thought so at first. Then I was given reading of Luther's tenets and felt tears rush to my eyes.

Still, it has gone at a snail's pace with the Brothers. Having taken oaths to the Mother Church and the Holy Father, most fail to believe that Luther's reforms could purify and redeem the body rather than pollute it further. Brother Phillippe has given me hope that he perhaps understands my view. In the past he and I have spent hours speaking of our distaste for the various clerical excesses, the huckstering of indulgences, the greed of so many priests, the taking of concubines, the ownership of entire serf families. I often wish my friend Jesus of Nazareth could stand beside me to see what is being done in the name of his person. Doubtless he would be revolted as well. And of course I know he is here in spirit, and just as keenly dismayed.

Phillippe insisted that contact with Luther be made in secret, under cloak of night.

Therefore, I met the man on the cusp of sunset in an oak grove just inside the Roman border. He fairly bounded from the shelter of a large trunk—a thick, solid man of high spirits. I found him to be bursting with vigor and vehemence. He was of course keen to learn the reason for my need for secrecy, a truth which I chose to politely withhold from Herr Luther for the moment.

I greeted him under my current name of Simon-of-Evreux, an identity made true by my possession of a sizable forest manor in Normandy but one day's carriage ride from Paris.

We spoke at length of his future. He claims a wish to remain within the Church, a desire upon which he cannot place great support. Yet I gladden at his desire for reform and conciliation rather than outright hostility.

I gave him a tidy sum for the furtherance of his movement and assured him that, should he continue to pursue his present course, I would prove a most persistent and generous benefactor. He shook my hand and bid me farewell. The encounter left me hopeful and even ebullient.

I thank God for my Brothers and companions, the monks of St. Lazare. It is true that I conduct many of my affairs beyond their company. Nevertheless, I am forever indebted to them for their help and succor. Surely my life's vagabondage, this incessant wandering from city to city, land to land, only pausing occasionally to establish a domicile on the flimsiest of pretexts, grows more wearisome by the year. Often I simply find a suitable manor house deep within hospitable cover or ancestral forest, purchase it, and burrow in for a decade or two with my monks as sole lifeline.

In such periods I maintain my religious observances by having a private mass said in a room of the abode by one of the Brothers, who are most kind in allowing me the favor.

Most soothing to me is the time I spend remembering and writing of my times with the Nazarene. The repeated thinking of it has worn smooth the edges of my recollection, so I focus instead on details. The gleam in his eyes, the warm timbre of his voice, the familiar drape of his robe. Small things. And the way others like my sisters gazed upon him, full of longing and affection. And of course, the staggering power he revealed to me after I had slipped away into the realms of light, the force that drew me back to this world.

As for my last sight of him, I am content not to summon that into my thoughts. It is enough that the Church adopted the cross as its symbol. At times I have recoiled at the sight of a crucifix, especially the statues imitating the way I did indeed see him hang, so horrifically broken in comparison to my old and hardy friend. I wish I had summoned sufficient courage to try to see him during the days they say he appeared following his resurrection. I know the man, I saw his death, but I am not an eyewitness to his risen state, though I do not doubt it.

Perhaps if this Martin Luther succeeds in restoring the Church to a true love of Christ and his freedom, I shall find it acceptable to venture forth more often into common places of worship. I will bend all my powers towards his success, I know that. Yet I cannot guarantee the outcome. I still remember the savagery of so-called Christian armies against the Cathars of Accitane. I walked through Beziers, past the dead bodies of men, women, and children, Catholic and heretic alike.

Remembering that, I can only hope.

THE NEXT MORNING Lazarus had risen early while Nora slept on. He sat before an artist's easel with the warm light flooding in from an eighteen-foot-high window to his left. In the window's view, the long neck of the Eiffel Tower rose up from a tangle of curved roofs and rust-tinted treetops. He picked up a paintbrush, then a wig, for instead of a canvas, this easel held a mirror. This morning he almost relished the tedium of making himself up in the pony-tailed wig and sixty-something wrinkles which the day's disguise would require.

He smiled to himself, not in appraisal but for joy, realizing he hadn't felt this way in years. He had to admit, Nora's presence had been like the proverbial breath of fresh air—not only in his stuffy apartment, but in his life. Her brave outlook on the world, her innocent questions, her naiveté about matters that weighed on him like invisible anvils, all left him captivated and eager for each new encounter.

He heard footsteps and sensed her feminine presence drawing near, like a pleasant scent that preceded her through the door. He almost laughed with pleasure at the unkempt sight of her. Even the bleary self-absorption of her morning state amused him.

He turned her way and smiled at her. She responded in a way he hadn't anticipated; grimaced with surprise, recoiled as one frightened and peered at him intensely.

"Is that you?"

"Of course, my dear. Who else would it be? This *is* my home."

"Good one. I feel like I'm talking to Gauguin."

He stood and bowed ostentatiously. "Unfortunately this is not Tahiti. However, we have the Left Bank. Would you care to accompany me there?"

She accepted his offer. Before long they were crossing the Latin Quarter on their way for a breakfast of stuffed crepes from a sidewalk vendor in the tree-shaded square of St. André des Arts. Afterward they boarded the Metro for a destination Lazarus would not disclose. The artist in paint-stained overalls and the young blond-haired woman switched trains at the Montparnasse station and rode until the bell rang for a stop several minutes later.

Lazarus stood, looked back at her and smiled faintly. "This should give you a small clue, Nora. It's the Denfert-Rochereau exit. Loosely translated, *Of Hell in the Rock*."

They emerged into daylight and walked two blocks to what resembled a Metro entrance, except for a sign which read, *Ossuaire Général des Cimetières de Paris*.

"Can you translate that?" asked Lazarus, pointing.

Nora squinted and mumbled an attempt.

"Ossuary of the Paris Cemeteries," he said. "The catacombs."

She turned to him with an incredulous expression. "All the great sights in Paris and you choose this! You're a very morbid man, you know that?"

He shrugged as they descended the stairs. "It's humbling, don't you think, to remember those who have passed on? At this point in time, the dead so greatly outnumber the living." After he paid for their tickets at a small wooden counter, they walked through. "This place actually comforts me," he continued. "I like to see real proof that all these people existed. We can leave if you'd like, but I think you will find it educational."

She followed. Soon they found themselves trailing a crowd of guided tourists into a darkened room. Dim lights turned on.

Nora gasped. Prior to their arriving here, she'd visualized the scene as one of human skeletons lying in neat rows, yet the actual sight sucked the air from her lungs. A wall of skulls stared back at her, causing the hairs of her forearms to stand on end. Each pair of black sockets felt like a set of living eyes boring into her with a morose curiosity, a reproach at her living state. She felt trivial, insignificant, a flyspeck on a huge mural.

"These were moved here from the Paris Cemetery over two hundred years ago," Lazarus said. "You should have seen it then. So many tombs had been built on top of each other that the cemetery's ground level came to be four, five feet above the earth. Every time it rained, this foul, rust-colored liquid would pour onto the sidewalks. Dogs would run around with partially decomposed rib cages in their teeth. The resulting diseases were awful."

"You're so nostalgic," she said, smiling wanly.

Leaning in close, he whispered, "Yes, but these are people who really lived. They walked in the sun and worked hard and raised children and tried to improve their lot and never thought about death, as most of us do not. I walked these streets with nearly all of them."

He turned and they walked past an array of femurs and rib cages and assorted human bones. Nora tried to imagine the flesh that had once surrounded them, the variety of clothes which had adorned their limbs.

"If you get a sense of futility from seeing this," he said, "imagine what I feel. I endured every one of these generations."

"Endured? Has it been that bad?"

He kept his eyes trained on the bones. "Sometimes, yes. I envy these people."

"I don't," said Nora. "Anyway, they've become anonymous. Swallowed up by history. You—you've beaten anonymity. You're probably the most intriguing man who ever lived."

"You don't understand. Many of these people are in heaven right now. Their suffering and pain are over. They endured their share, and then the burden was lifted from them."

Nora looked at him with a bemused smile. "Your view of life is pretty confusing, you know that? One minute it's the richest, most amazing tapestry a person could imagine, the next it's the bleakest, most depressing picture possible."

"I know. But I think that's what life *is*. Alternating previews of heaven and hell. Isn't that as it should be?"

"I suppose. It's just I always imagined immortality would be . . . bliss."

"It can be. But it can also be unending torment. I face dangers and threats you could never know."

She moved on in silence. Heaven and hell were subjects she preferred to avoid. If forced, Nora would have said she believed in a kind of fuzzy, sublime place where souls spent eternity following death. As for the traditional religious interpretations, she'd decided years ago she had little use for them.

This man, she realized, was supposed to have been raised from the dead.

He is saying he was there.

It was then that it hit her. Accepting his story meant also accepting the whole litany of traditional dogma. All of it, from the Good Book to heaven and hell and the unlikely pronouncements of every nun and priest and preacher she had at one time or another taken the pleasure in reviling. She did not want to be one of those people—the credulous, the easily swayed. It wasn't like her to buy in to such a hoary old myth. It was too much. Too much, and yet . . .

She turned to face him, her mouth suddenly, absurdly, slack with shock. In that moment it struck her that, as astonishing as it was, she *did* believe him. All of it. Every outlandish, sensational iota of his story. The full weight of the evidence fell upon her with a crushing weight.

She felt reserve and skepticism flush from her with a cold shiver, replaced by a simple belief. Then she was struck with the realization that walking beside her was the greatest enigma in the human race, one of the most fascinating persons in all of history. And, invisibly, also one of the most influential.

She fought to regain her breath. Frantic for a next move to make, she grabbed his hand and nearly pulled him from the tunnel. They stepped out into a cloudy day and found a bench on which to sit.

"You went there?" she asked. "To heaven?"

"Of course." He looked at her with a tinge of exasperation, as though the idea should have been at the forefront of her mind all along.

"Well?"

She suddenly *had* to hear his description, needed it like she needed oxygen.

"I don't think I've ever told anyone the full story," he said in a barely audible voice. "Not even the Order. Except maybe for—"

"Who?"

"No one. Forget it."

"Please tell me."

He stiffened, inhaled loudly. His face instantly reddened, and his eyes, wet now, began to shine. His shoulders seemed to collapse inward, his features to melt from what was happening inside him.

"I'm not sure I can," he said in the voice of a very old man fighting for breath. "It was so . . . so unbelievable." His lips trembled and he bowed his head.

She watched his chest rise up and down, then reached out for his hand and grasped it tightly while an oversized tourist bus passed by in a cloud of fumes.

He straightened back up and began to speak.

"It's never quite the same every time. But usually I hear the deepest and most peaceful silence. It's like somebody suddenly turned off the volume on the world. Everything goes dark—you'd have to call it dark because it contains no light, yet it seems filled up with something. Then I feel this light pop in my chest, like a thin cord has been broken, and I feel lighter than a feather. I'm pure soul."

He took a deep breath, his countenance strengthening with the momentum of his words.

"It's often at this point that I begin to float over the earth. I see it all: the continents, the weather, cities. I see lightning in a thunderstorm. The northern lights. I feel like singing, or like I've become song. It's hard to frame the experience in earthly terms, because these are spiritual things. It's easier to talk in emotional terms or in metaphors. It feels like I've come home—to my *true* home—after a long absence. Like my earthly self is a sort of heavy scab that I'm shedding as a chrysalis. It just peels away, with all its stains and wounds and flaws, and blows off in the current of this wind that isn't composed of air, but of love. Yes, that's it. Love shooting out like a gale-force wind.

"Then I turn and face the source of that love. That's something I could describe forever. I'll just say the sight is the most beautiful and desirable thing you've ever set eyes on. And when you move into it, instantly all longing is satisfied and in every way."

He faced her.

"I'm not doing such a good job, am I? Like I said, I haven't described it for centuries, and then only once and more vaguely. It's always just hovered in my memory as a wonderful ball of images. I've never tried to reduce it into words before."

Nora shook her head. "You're wrong," she said. "I'm getting the picture."

"There's something else. I suppose I haven't wanted to think of it most of the time. Granted, it's an enormous comfort to know that the afterlife and heaven actually do exist, but when you're confined to this world as long as I have been, it all begins to turn cruel. A taunting image of something I cannot have."

"I think I understand."

"But the story goes on, you see, because I spent three days there. What I've shared was just the approach. How do I describe heaven to you? First of all, it's a real place. It's not a state of mind or a private fantasy. It's a physical location—though not one I can point out to you in the sky or through a telescope. It's in another realm—the spiritual dimension—which is in a way just another universe, like our own physical dimension is a universe. Only this dimension operates under entirely different laws. There's no gravity, obviously. Energy is expressed in terms of what we would call emotion. Love has the weight and force of pure fire, although I don't mean fire in the sense of something burning. No, I mean fire in the sense of that which is raw power, which purifies. Does this make any sense?"

She didn't decide that it did until she replied. "Yes, all the sense in the world."

"Of course, love has one specific source," he continued. "One being. As you move forward, deeper and deeper into heaven, you're seeing these beautiful sights. A vast city that seems to glow from the inside from all the emotion that surrounds it. Everywhere around you, souls are reuniting. Mothers and fathers and grandparents and friends are all greeting you and pouring this wonderful stream of love into you. The experience feels like standing under a waterfall. Even while that's happening, you become aware of the fact that you're approaching something more solemn and momentous than anything you've ever imagined. There's this throbbing under your feet as if signaling a coming earthquake, like the sky itself is about to split open. Even so, you keep going because at the same time you know that this destination is the culmination of all you've ever wanted. And, finally, you catch a glimpse."

His head jerked back and he uttered a startled sob, almost like a hiccup. His voice immediately became breathy, wistful, and high in pitch.

"And how do I describe *God?*"

He made small gestures with his hands, those of a potter attempting to shape an invisible lump of clay into something tangible.

"Coming home, maybe? Think of your most beloved ancestral homestead. A place generations of your family have cherished. The place on earth you know you belong, where you are most at peace and where all your memories seem to roll into one. Multiply such a feeling times infinity.

"Or like yourself as a child again—a baby cradled in your mother's arms, against her breast for the very first time—only much stronger, of course.

"I'd like to tell you how I saw him, how he appeared, but I'm not sure how to express it. In the spiritual realm, personhood and life are expressed in a purer state, beyond the physical. You don't look for features or a visual appearance. Yet I know that I *saw* him. I know he exists as a sovereign, distinct being."

Nora finally spoke. "I always thought God was more of a force. That we all make up God, every one with our energies put together."

Instead of replying, he stood and they began to walk together. She knew instinctively that he would make no move to hurry on to the Metro or draw a straight line for home. They were walking for the sake of motion only.

"Think of it this way. The sun. The sun is definitely a separate heavenly body. We know the specific spot it occupies in the sky because if we look up at that part of it, our eyes burn. Its energy radiates through every living thing on earth. I heard it said once that if the sun were to stop shining, life on this planet would last no more than thirty minutes. Even the cells of our bodies are shot through with the sun's power. So it is very much in us and part of us. Yet we are not *part* of the sun; if we were, we would be incinerated in an instant. We know where the sun is, even how far away from us in terms of miles. But no one confuses themselves with the sun, with the source of that energy. It's the same with God. Yes, he's a force. Yes, his being radiates through every part of the created realm. At the same time, he is also a distinct and real being. With very specific emotions."

"He showed them to you?"

"When you're close to him, you sense his feelings like the temperature of the air. Like changes in the weather. He delights in seeing us approach him, similar to how an earthly parent delights in seeing his child walk for the first time, hold out those little arms and say, 'Daddy! Daddy!' It's very much a father's love. And a mother's love, too. Both qualities together."

He sighed deeply, waved his arms as though releasing a long-held tension, and looked around at the afternoon sky stretching gray across the tops of the apartment buildings.

"Suffice it to say that I spent a long time in heaven, a time which I learned after my return to earth had actually lasted only three days. Returning was the most disappointing, dismal experience I have ever lived through. My earthly body and the physical world wrapping around me again felt heavy, laden with all sorts of ominous residues. Suddenly I had an awareness of others' spiritual states. Not strong, yet still a discernible picture of what a person looked like in the spirit world. Some people caused me to shiver, and I knew that not only were they shriveled and wasted, but they were being consumed by foul spirits—wicked beings hanging on to their backs. When I am spiritually attuned I catch a glimpse, like a partially exposed negative."

He paused. They walked on in silence and soon found themselves on Boulevard St. Michel, the Left Bank's central thoroughfare.

"You asked," he said, turning to her with a broad smile.

"Yes, I did," Nora said, feeling light-headed with a sort of fever.

39

Paris, Left Bank

SHE HAD NOTHING ELSE to say, or to ask. A great mystery had just been answered for her. She wanted nothing more than to curl up and sleep for a while, to digest what she'd heard. St. Michel's trees and bohemian bookstores seemed pale to her all of a sudden. Washed over with a pale film.

She saw chairs nearby, and a table, and almost lunged for them. Anything to restore her balance. He followed her calmly and raised his index finger to a waiter. They'd chosen the outdoor seating area of a sidewalk café.

"*Pernod pour moi, carafe d'eau pour la mademoiselle, s'il vous plait*," Lazarus said. Pernod for me, ice water for the lady, please.

She noticed that he spoke the same rapid, Parisian French as the people around them and that his speech aroused no reaction in the waiter—unlike her own halting attempts. She gripped the small round table. "I'm sorry," she said, and laughed. "I guess it finally sank in."

"No need to be embarrassed, Nora."

The water came, and she gulped down the cool liquid, drawing a stare from the departing waiter. She took a deep, calming breath. "So," she said, "what would you call yourself? Jewish, Christian? Catholic, Protestant?"

"I'm not really sure. All four, I suppose. Though I doubt any of them would take me." He stared into his glass for a long moment. "Call me a God-fearing man, that's all."

"Do you ever go to church?"

"Seldom. Every once in a while I'll slip into the back of a congregation I've heard good things about and try hard not to be distracted. It's rare but sometimes I do find a church that has kept the true spirit of our Lord and his teachings. It usually has little to do with the sign in the front lawn."

"Do you have any friends?"

He leaned back in his chair and considered the sky. "I have had friends, yes. Several of the Order's priests. A few men through the years. Those I never told the whole truth to, so I suppose the . . . the closeness was rather limited."

"What about Israel? Do you go back there often?"

"No." He thrust his hands deep into his pockets and shook his head. "No, I have not been back since . . . well, not in a very long time."

"Not even once? Even since it became a nation again?"

No response.

"Because," Nora continued, "if I were Jewish and I heard the news of their becoming a nation, I'd travel there in a heartbeat."

"Jerusalem is not the place of my fondest memories," said Lazarus. "Someday I will go back. When I feel strong enough to face it."

"Another secret?"

"It's not so secret, not if you'd do your homework."

At that, she turned quiet.

A man and woman in their twenties strolled by arm in arm. She watched the man lean over and awkwardly kiss his companion as they walked. Still following the couple with her eyes, Nora spoke in a tone, which, to her surprise, came out far deeper and breathier than was intended.

"Lazarus," she said, "have you ever been in love, in Paris? Surely after all these years . . ."

His eyes clouded over, and he answered, "I was in love with *life* once. I fell in love with literature here. With art. With music. Even in love with God, though that's a use of words you may not understand."

She beamed at him. "You know that's not what I meant."

He laughed. Instantly she felt she was on a first date back in America. Playing get-to-know-me. The coy smiles, the knowing laughs. The verbal repartee.

"I think I've told you a lot today," he finally replied. "Maybe there's a little mystery I ought to keep about myself."

"That's all right. I like a man of mystery," she said, and immediately regretted her choice of words. His face fell and she saw she'd played the charade too far. She wasn't on a date. Yet now, filled to bursting with the force of his personality, she asked herself why not. The man was fascinating to be around, and handsome in a sad-eyed, dark-complexioned sort of way.

He stood and pushed in his chair. The direction of the conversation had put him off, she could tell. His eyes were fixed too strongly on the palm of his hand as he counted out the change.

She fell in alongside him. A thought then thrust itself into her mind, a question both inevitable and urgent.

"Why me?" she asked him. "Why did you come visit me? What's my part in all of this?"

He inhaled sharply, shook his head and said, "Believe it or not, Nora, I have not reached the end of my secrets, and I don't feel ready quite yet to divulge that one."

"Please. It's why I came here."

He turned to her again, his eyes ablaze, and his words came out clipped and sharp. "Is that all you want? A piece of information? After hearing the secrets of a two-thousand-year life, what you really wanted was a bit of data?" His voice rose as he spoke.

"No. I'm sorry, but please understand. You've shown me this incredible truth, except I still don't understand how I fit into the picture. I know I do, just not *how* or *why*. It's very disconcerting."

He seemed placated by this. He nodded slowly, and his features softened. "I understand. And yet I'm asking you to wait, only a day or two, until I reconcile it all."

She shrugged. "All right. But you have to let me in sometime."

He paused, then whispered, "I know."

"And now I have to tell *you* something." Even as she formed the words, she knew she would not let him know of her growing attraction. There was something else just as palpable to share. "You are the saddest person I've ever known," she said. "You have so much to live with, live for. Yet I've never seen such regret in a person. I don't know where it comes from, but I wish you'd tell me what about your life could cause this grief I see in you."

"Maybe someday," he said, moving his indrawn gaze to a small dog lunging toward them from its master's leash.

"Another one of your secrets?" she ventured.

"I guess you could say that."

After walking for what seemed like forever, she started to recognize the sights of the Latin Quarter. She immediately felt, in the easy silence that had descended over them, the deepening intimacy of a friend, the kind with whom talking is not required. They ambled through the Sorbonne district and northward toward the river. When the riverbank came within a block, they turned right onto a cobblestone lane filled with a string of ethnic restaurants and small produce markets.

They followed the lane to where it ended at a modest old church beside a park that flanked the Seine and, just beyond it, Notre Dame in all its glory.

"I helped build this church," he said, nodding to the small edifice nearest them. "It's the oldest in Paris. I have some old friends in there."

Nora wrinkled her eyebrows. Did he mean friends *buried* in the church? Did he mean to use the past tense of *have* and just forgot? She set the incongruity aside and followed him toward the cathedral.

She smelled it first—an acrid scent that stung her eyes and made them water, sent her into a violent cough. The bitter scent caused her to look around questioningly. Lazarus eyed her, a puzzled look on his face. Then he too started to cough. Suddenly all those around them were hacking loudly, holding handkerchiefs to their mouths and running.

The stone railing over the Seine lay just ahead, across a street. Surely it would offer clearer air and a fresh breeze. She turned to Lazarus, whose whole body was now heaving.

"Let's run to the river!" he shouted.

Nora nodded her agreement, and they took off across the street, past the opposite sidewalk to the river's wall.

But the bitter assault only grew worse. Her eyes now flowed with tears; her breathing stuttered through gasps. She doubled over as it became clear that she could be choking to death. Lazarus stayed standing, staring.

Nora raised herself to see what he was looking at. His arm extended across the river, toward Notre Dame. The blood rushed from her face.

Among the trees facing the cathedral, a thick gray smoke billowed, obscuring all other landmarks. She became aware of a noise—raucous shouts, angry chants—and caught glimpses of movement through the tears streaming unprovoked down her face: human figures writhing and running, arms jerking forward and releasing projectiles. Then, on the receiving end of the hurled objects, a black wall. Men in uniforms and helmets. The smoke cleared further and a banner came into view. She squinted to make it out.

It was a portrait of the pope, a swastika superimposed over his face.

Lazarus turned to a coughing bystander. "*Qu'est ce qui ce passe?*" he yelled. What's going on?

A scowl on his face, the man unleashed an angry torrent of French. Lazarus turned to Nora, his expression now frantic.

"It's because of the Order!" he told her. "It's because of *me*!" He turned his back to her and began to run.

She followed as best she could, holding the bottom of her shirt over her mouth and nose.

Tear gas, her mind finally conveyed to her.

A good afternoon riot, the French national pastime. Only this one seemed to have disturbed Lazarus profoundly. What did he mean "*because of me*," she asked herself as she pursued his fleeing form down a sidewalk and onto a strangely vacant street.

When she caught up with him, the wisps of smoke had vanished and her throat was beginning to allow lungfuls of air again. He stood at a news kiosk and reached into his pocket for change. A heavyset man with a cigarette dangling from his lips sat inside and held out a paper with a disinterested look.

Lazarus turned around. His eyes were fastened on the paper's front page.

"What?" she said, still catching her breath.

He slapped the paper with a hand and looked to the sky.

"What?" she repeated.

He shut his eyes and said, "I should have been more vigilant. The enemy has been at work already. He's turned my burial place into an international scandal. Those people"—he stabbed his finger at the far side of the river—"they're rioting against the Church for rescuing me. Don't you see? The enemy's trying to capture me while at the same time turning my release into a pretext for war."

Grimacing with anger, he quickly led her back across the park. They entered the small church he'd spoken of earlier. She blinked her eyes, for the musty sanctuary was dark, lit only by a row of narrow windows set far above the floor.

"What are we doing here?" Nora asked.

He gave her a stern look. "Gathering intelligence."

They sat in wooden chairs at the back of the empty church. She turned to speak with him but saw from the quick, furtive darting of his eyes, and the smile drifting in and out of his expression, that he was not idle. It soon dawned on her that, in the alertness in his features, he appeared to be offering greetings in various directions. She saw that his lips were moving, speaking almost inaudibly. She leaned in closer to hear what he was saying.

"Hello, my friend," he whispered. "It's been a long time."

He seemed to listen to the air before them, then, a few seconds later, smile as if a response had been given.

"Who are you talking to?" Nora asked in a loud whisper.

"My friends." He neither turned his head nor altered his expression. "The ones I mentioned earlier."

"And they would be . . . ?"

He turned to her and said, "I wish we had the time for me to teach you to see them. They're everywhere."

She had just begun to accept the ramifications of this man's identity. And now came another element, straight out of a children's book. Her mind rebelled at first, until she reminded herself of all she had already embraced that day.

Then she felt it: the same sensation of a watching presence which had overcome her in his apartment. Now it came from everywhere.

"Angels?" she said.

He nodded, motioning with a twist of his neck. "There are nearly a hundred in this sanctuary at the moment. Some I've known since the Middle Ages. They're standing in the aisles, lined across that window ledge. In front of the transept. They surround the altar."

"Are they just here, in the churches?"

"No, they're outside, too. But in smaller numbers. Out there, they're usually engaged in battle. There's a war going on, you know. It's been raging since the very beginning of time. Even though we're a part of it, most people only see the tiniest moments of the conflict. A skirmish, through the corner of an eye. A second of clarity. We don't even realize the role we play."

"You can see the whole thing?"

"I do, but only because I've trained myself over a long while. It isn't something you want to see unless you have to. I try not to engage my spiritual sight unless I'm in battle myself. You'd be horrified at how badly demonic beings have infested most places. Their warfare with the angels goes on all through night and day. The sight of it is repulsive."

"This war—you play a greater role than most of us."

"I suppose. You could call me a kind of sniper, only in the spiritual realm. I've been assigned to exterminate the same enemy for two thousand years now."

He touched her arm, his attention drawn to some invisible spot in front of him. He nodded as though receiving a long batch of information.

"Thank you," he mouthed. He stood quickly, pulling Nora up by her arm. "It's time to go."

They stepped outside and the smell of tear gas struck them, stronger this time. He turned into it.

"I consult with angelic scouts sometimes when I'm worried about approaching my home. The church is a good place to lose any demonic pursuers, because they won't come inside. The defenders turn them away."

"So what did they tell you?"

"It's too late. There's a full-scale contingent about to attack. I have to go back and warn the priests, gather some things. I guess it would be futile for me to ask you to wait here."

"That's right."

At that he turned and made for his street with the severe look of a man late for his own execution. They were within half a block of the apartment building when a figure approached them, moving briskly. It took Nora a few seconds to recognize Stephen, the priest she'd first encountered at St. Michel. The priest was wrapped in a designer jacket and resembled a typical island resident.

He failed to make eye contact with Lazarus, whose sudden grip on Nora's elbow warned her not to initiate any interaction, either.

They passed each other, and Stephen merely nodded like a polite passerby, imperceptibly shook his head. Lazarus led her past the apartment door as if it didn't exist. She realized then what had occurred. They'd been shaken off, warned away from their destination.

Lazarus took an abrupt left at the next street and strode by several doors, glancing at each as they walked. Finally he turned down a driveway leading through a gap in the building. The gate, unlike all the others they had encountered, stood open. It faced a courtyard lined with well-tended bushes and several trees. *So this is what all these driveways lead to*, Nora noted. Most of the residential buildings in Paris featured such entrances, but she had yet to see inside one.

Together they crossed the courtyard, approached a side door and he rang the bell. Waiting, he turned back to face the drive with a nervous look. The door swung open and a fiftyish woman in stylish clothes stood in the doorway.

Lazarus turned to the woman. "*Oui, madame. J'habite Rue de St. Louis, et j'ai besoin de prendre votre petite oubliette. J'ai une petite amie, vous savez.*"

The woman looked Nora over with disdain and then turned back to Lazarus with a hint of a smile. She nodded.

"*Alors, allez vous,*" she said.

He reached to take Nora's hand and rushed inside. The

woman pointed and shouted a phrase in hurried French. A series of wood-paneled hallways flowed past Nora, each growing narrower and narrower.

"What did you tell her?" Nora asked.

"I told her you were my girlfriend and that I needed to use what islanders call the little dungeons. It's an intricate network of passageways that servants, deliverymen, and philandering husbands use. It loosely connects all of the buildings here. The island's buildings have been around so long that they've all gotten burrowed into one another."

The hall took them through a door and into a tiny alleyway open to the sky. They entered a cold, tiled passageway, then down three steps to a metal door where he produced a key. Pulling the door open, they ran into the glassed-in lobby Nora had left earlier that day.

"Quick! They can probably hear us!" Lazarus whispered.

Through the lobby they tiptoed, on their way to the elevator. Once inside, the door shut and the old motor starting its ascent, Nora collapsed against his shoulder.

"Whew! That's a little too much excitement for one day!"

"It's not the end of it, either."

They reached his floor and emerged into the main hallway. He warned in a whisper not to turn on any lights, make any loud noises or turn on any appliances, then disappeared into his bedroom.

Nora retreated to her divan in the great art-crammed room, hoping the hundreds of objects would keep her company and give her a sense of being surrounded by friends. They did—for a while at least. But soon the shadows lengthened and the room grew dark. And she began to hear noises. Whispered fragments so faint she could not distinguish whether they were Lazarus's voice or not.

She rose hesitantly and, appalled at her own fearfulness, tiptoed toward the door where she had left him.

AS SWIFT AND DARK as the onset of night, the four black-clad forms sprinted silently through the shadows of the great buildings. They flattened as one and dissolved into the cover of a darkened wall as a teenager zipped by on a noisy moped. Then waited while a black Mercedes sedan drove past in a flash of headlights. Their forms materialized again and gained speed, legs churning in a silent lope.

They reached the front of Lazarus's building and the long shapes of assault rifles emerged from their coats. They disappeared inside, swallowed up in stone.

McLean, Virginia

JAMES SCHORIE SAT stalled in Saturday traffic on the Dolly Madison Expressway, his thirteen-year-old daughter fuming beside him over their tardiness for a soccer team bus trip—when his phone rang.

He first flipped open his domestic cellular to dead air before realizing which phone still beeped impatiently, hidden in his windbreaker. His company phone. The one double-protected with both old-fashioned electronic signal scrambling and software-based encryption. The one that rarely rang. Most of his associates avoided the mind-numbing tedium of initializing the devices by calling on normal lines and using coded jargon.

He dug frantically in the pocket, raised the unit to his ear and winced, remembering that he had to wait for the flat tone of a clear signal before the caller would be heard.

"Hey, Schorie?"

It was Netelman, shouting and windblown as though calling from the deck of some yacht on the Chesapeake.

"Netelman. What's up? I'm in the middle of a family thing."

"No, you're in the middle of a career thing. Listen, man, it's crunch time. You know that surveillance you requested on your girl in Paris? The Hamas target?"

"Yeah . . ."

"Well, we just spotted Jamail himself along with three of his men in full op regalia approaching her location. This is a courtesy call, Schorie, to tell you Intel folks that we're going to intercept."

"Have you notified the French?"

A guffaw sounded clearly on the line. "Are you kidding? They wouldn't let us play footsie with the guy. If we let them handle it, they'd probably negotiate. Jamail would fly home on the Concorde, for cryin' out loud!"

"What are you going to do with Lassalle after you intervene?"

"Nothing. Hopefully he'll never even know we were involved. You want us to take him?"

"I don't think you could if you tried."

"Right. Well, word from on high is to forget about Lassalle for now. Catching Jamail is our top priority. If his capture is the only thing this wild goose chase of yours produces, it will be a success. Don't worry."

"Yeah, but there's a lot more to consider, the ramifications of—"

"Look, I gotta run. I'll have somebody keep you posted."

"Have them watch the crossfire!"

"What does it matter? Isn't your guy impervious to bullets?" Another guffaw. "See ya."

The droning secure dial tone returned. Schorie slammed the phone on the dash and cursed. Then, remembering his daughter beside him, he shut his eyes in disgust.

Isle de St. Louis Apartment

NORA FOUND HIM in a small room off of the bedroom closet, surrounded by electronics. One of the priests stood beside him. Four small video monitors sat stacked, one showing different black-and-white views of the building's pulse points—front door, delivery entrance, elevator, and stairs. Headphones covered his ears and a mouthpiece curved around to his mouth. His hands swiftly recharged a black handgun clip with gray-tipped bullets.

"Stephen, have the plane ready at Bourget, all right?"

A low, raspy crackle responded.

He turned to her, his features taut with exertion and the strain of planning.

"They're inside the building, Nora. I hope you're ready to move."

Just then the lights flickered out and plunged them into a smothering darkness. The monitors wavered for a moment but remained on, casting an unearthly glow into the space surrounding them. A loud splintering sound crunched somewhere in the apartment.

"They're in," Lazarus whispered into his mike.

She felt his hands grasp her by the shoulders, light yet insistent. His mouth came close to her ear and he whispered, "The escape route is on the other side of the apartment. Hold my hand and don't make a noise."

She nodded, suddenly so flooded with fear that even the tiny crack of her kneecaps threatened to unhinge her. Ahead of them, the doorway to the rest of the suite stood framed in black, a yawning entrance into everything dangerous and terrifying. They walked slowly out into the hall and Lazarus glanced to either side.

A strobelike light flashed quickly throughout the apartment, accompanied by a whooshing sound like a violent sucking of air. Then the thud of a heavy impact against the floor.

Lazarus whirled around to her, his round eyes unable to mask the shock. He touched his mouthpiece and whispered again. "Stephen, have you engaged?"

"We're on our way."

"They launched a stun grenade, and someone's been shot with a silencer."

"Wasn't us."

A shadow leaped before them, brandishing a rifle. Nora screamed just as the rifle butt struck Lazarus's face and sent him with a loud smack into the wall. Two paintings slid onto his slumping head. The attacker yanked Lazarus upward in apparent preparation for a head-butt.

Rage like that of a lioness protecting her cub exploded within Nora, and her muscles tightened with superhuman strength. Without thinking, she lunged at the man. She felt the rubbery surface of his black outfit against her hands and pushed with every ounce of pent-up, panicked force she could muster.

An odd sound came from the man, the combination of a grunt and a question. He tumbled back into the juncture between the hall and two galleries. A squat machine gun clattered to the floor beside her.

He began to clamber to his feet, groaning now. She threw herself on the weapon, clutched at its trigger guard and turned to face the attacker.

Lightning shot forth.

A blinding chaos shredded the small hallway and slammed into the man. His body jerked and writhed. A sickening whine oozed from his lungs and he fell to the floor.

She looked down at her hand, and only then remembered the flexing of her finger, the tension of the cold trigger giving way, the explosion leaving her fist. Her hand felt like it had burst—and smelled as though it had been singed.

She struggled to wrap her mind around the idea tugging at her stomach with a terrible weight. *She had just killed a man.* Ended a life by her own volition, with the mere twitch of her index finger.

Lazarus raised himself up and almost threw Nora against the wall for safety. She fought to still her breathing as she sensed footfalls approaching them from the room on the right. First the silhouette of a head appeared, then, lower, the tapered barrel of a machine gun. A man stepped through and faced them. He raised his hand.

"CIA. Here to help," were his only words. The man bent over the body to yank a ski mask and night-vision goggles from its head.

A smaller flash and whining sound told Nora the CIA man had just taken a Polaroid of the dead man's face.

The gunman whirled to one side and unleashed another burst of gunfire down the hallway. She turned away from the blinding flash. Then he turned to them and motioned his head toward the room from which he had come.

They stepped out of the hall and into the far end of the vast room where Nora had slept. His gun ready before him, the man walked slowly forward. She felt the potential violence of every passing second like a tightly coiled spring, primed to snap and fill the next instant with another rage of blood and death. The tension in the air clamped Nora's limbs and breath in a vice. But she held the gun before her and tiptoed ahead.

There was a commotion several yards ahead: a darting shape followed by a loud burst of gunfire from the CIA man. They were running ahead in what looked like a pursuit. The American turned to the right and disappeared through a doorway.

Just then a roar blasted through the room, illuminating the forest of antique objects in a hundred dazzles of fire. She hurled herself to the floor, felt the hard rebuke of hardwood against her knees and elbows and an arm around her waist. It was Lazarus again, pulling her sharply into the thicket of artifacts. She could feel his body beside hers and glimpsed him at the far end of her vision crawling forward in the flickering of gunfire. Turning back, she saw with terror the bullet impacts follow them up the floor. She could see as well as hear paintings getting split open behind her, a suit of armor ripped apart, porcelain fly in pieces through the air. She winced in a frantic effort to burrow as far into the mass as possible.

A bullet whizzed past her ankle—she felt the displaced air and stifled a scream. She crawled even more furiously across the floor. Then came a clawing on her shoulder; it was Lazarus's fingers, clutching for her. The next thing she knew, she was clasped tightly in his left arm while his free hand pulled something dark and heavy over them. She gazed upward and saw a thick slab of steel—an ancient shield—slide up to block out the gunfire.

Their two bodies pressed together under the sheltering metal curve while several sharp pings rang above them. The medieval implement was doing its duty. And the destruction was working in their favor, as shattered and torn objects fell together in a pile around them, further sheltering them from discovery.

Then a hoarse shout seemed to divide the air like a tearing of canvas, and the firing stopped.

Nora tried to assess their predicament. Either the gunmen had run out of ammunition, or they had realized the futility of their shooting and were preparing to change tactics—perhaps sift through the broken pieces for her and Lazarus. With a chilling rush she realized the latter made the most sense. She then heard kicking and the sound of things being thrown around with loud shouts and single gun blasts. Their ability to see in the dark would make short work of their search.

Lazarus gripped her arm, pushed the shield away and tensed his body. His head motioned the opposite direction. "On three," he whispered, nodding to the gun in his hand, then the one in hers.

She winced, for she hadn't wanted to use the thing again. Yet she nodded grudgingly. He mouthed *one, two, three*, raised his revolver over the shield, aimed it through a gap and pulled the trigger. Thunderous fire lit up the darkness. Nora willed herself to rise and shoot. In the chaos they both clambered to their feet and began to shoulder their way toward the far wall, reaching backward to shoot on their way.

Turning back every few seconds to unleash torrents of lead, she pursued his lunging form under a fallen armoire, through the shards of an enormous mirror, over the antique ruins and to the end of the room. A fleeing shadow told her the attackers had run from the room, a fact which gave her no solace. Even a second's pause in cover fire and they would surely be back, she knew. Lazarus launched himself against the far wall and pushed hard on the wood panel. A tall square flipped open sideways, revealing darkness. He stepped inside and beckoned her in with an outstretched arm.

She quickly obeyed and disappeared into a closet-like space. Pressed close in front of her, Lazarus reached back and struck the panel, which swung shut. A small penlight came on at his wrist and illuminated a large, wall-mounted pipe just a few feet beyond a hole in the floor.

He turned to her, his face grim. "We slide down here. I'll go first and catch you if there's any problem. Here, take my gloves."

Pulling thick leather over her fingers, she watched Lazarus grasp the pipe and then, with a screech of skin against metal, descend out of view.

This was no time to think about falling or her fear of the unknown, she realized. She willed her legs to step forward, take hold of the pipe and wrap herself around it. Then, relaxing her grip, she slid slowly into darkness. Great wood beams, horizontal slats and rats' nests flew past as she dropped lower. She peered downward to see where Lazarus was. The dizzying perspective showed the glow of his penlight and the top of his head already fifty or so feet below her, descending quickly.

Nora grimaced and concentrated on maintaining her grip. Still, it felt comforting to know she was already two floors away from the scene of so much sudden, capricious death. A place where a second's inattention was the only margin between surviving and winding up a punctured heap of flesh upon the floor. The cruelty of gunplay still left her breathless.

A moment later she felt an obstacle against her feet. She glanced down and saw Lazarus's hands reach up to help guide her to the bottom, a hard floor. Planting her feet, she let go of the pipe, thankful for the gloves Lazarus had given her.

She took a couple of deep breaths and followed him into what revealed itself, under the roving beam of his lamp, to be an old brick-lined Parisian sewer line. A stream of refuse trickled at the base of a conical passageway. With the aid of Lazarus's tiny beam, they proceeded through a series of twisting turns along a narrow concrete walkway. Every so often, another passageway would intersect with theirs, and his flashlight would reveal an otherwise ordinary, blue Parisian street sign. They turned left once, then again.

Finally a light shined ahead, a half-moon shape of lesser darkness and, through metal bars, the sight of moonlight rippling on water. They walked to the edge of the opening and looked out.

They stood mere yards above the Seine. About three hundred yards away, a large tourist boat lumbered toward them, its decks lined with blinding spotlights. Lazarus recoiled.

Seconds later, another sound emerged—this one more high-pitched and approaching fast. Nora leaned forward and recognized the onrushing shape of a Kodiak boat. Lazarus turned to her with the first expression of relief he had shown all evening. She understood. The roaring engine was their salvation.

The boat pulled below them, piloted by a middle-aged man with very short hair. Lazarus wedged his hands beneath a metal bar and pushed hard. Seconds passed, marked only by his flat grunts of exertion. Finally, with a rusty squeak, the barred door swung upward and out of sight into a hidden groove. Without a pause Lazarus leaped down and into the Kodiak. Summoning her courage once again, Nora jumped behind him. A soft bounce of rubber gave way beneath her feet, and she felt the instability of water under her. A cool breeze immediately touched her skin, soon to be replaced by a bracing wind as the boat's motor throttled up and the river began to hurtle before her.

The two boats, the sewer opening, the island itself—a site of much fascination, discovery, and terror—receded quickly into the warm late night.

41

Paris, Isle de St. Louis

"THEY'RE OUT. Repeat, they're out."

The voice whispering in Father Moll's earpiece conveyed the relief he himself felt at the news. Lazarus had reached the escape site at the apartment's northwest corner. Unless he had been seen and followed, he and the young woman were already far away. Their primary task was accomplished.

Yet the drumbeat of his heart told him the terror was not yet over. Intruders still lurked in the building, and, worse still, there were two sets of them—one friendly, the other not, each indistinguishable from the other.

"What now?" Moll whispered back.

"Get into the darkest corner you can find and wait there," came Father Stephen's reply. "Shoot at anything wearing black. The CIA men are in street clothes."

Easy enough. The whole place was one giant black hole. He backed around Lazarus's desk, eased his barrel over the top and tried to still his breathing. He never felt more out of place and less like a priest than at times like these—when grasping a gun. He knew, of course, the rationale for such a necessity. Protecting this friend required the option of deadly force. He had been trained on the matter for years and had settled it in his mind. Nevertheless, the knowledge did not dull the strange feeling of holding a loaded gun in his hands, getting ready to pull the trigger and possibly end someone's life.

He blanched—a figure moved before him, tiptoeing in the hallway beyond the office door. The blood rushed from Father Moll's head. Whoever it was had already finished reconnoitering his room before he had even noticed. The figure probably hadn't seen him surrounded by a pile of books.

Father Moll squinted, trying to discern friend from foe. It was a flat shape carved out of darkness; he could not discern whether it wore black clothing or the street clothes he had been warned about. For a moment he pondered the irony of the Catholic bishop warring against the Cathars, who had slaughtered heretic and innocent alike and uttered the fateful phrase, "*Kill them all and let God sort them out*."

Actually, he realized with a surge of frustration that he would have to be just as indiscriminate now in order to act quickly. He did feel almost like shooting regardless—these CIA goons had not been invited. They were making things impossible. Moll's fingers trembled and tightened against the trigger, the gunstock. *Who are you?*

Gunfire rocked the hallway and the figure before him jerked backward in a horrific rhythm then collapsed, one arm falling into a pool of light. A sweatshirt. The CIA men were being picked off!

Then a new voice rasped in his earpiece. A voice with a Middle Eastern accent.

"Surrender now. We have a gun to the old priest. If all are not surrendered in three minutes, he will get a bullet."

IRELAND

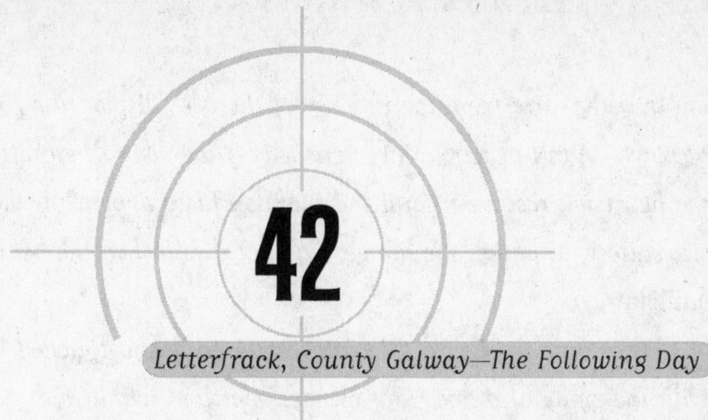

42

Letterfrack, County Galway—The Following Day

HE SAT IN A THICK armchair with the diary open at his knees, reading again. Every few seconds he lifted his head, closed his eyes and sighed heavily, as if fighting to keep control of his lungs. Then he looked down again and resumed reading with shallow, panting breaths.

Western Isle of Irlandia—May 3, 641

Today I met the loveliest woman I have ever set eyes upon. She appeared almost as a nymph straight from the thickest forest we have yet traversed, reddish-black hair falling down below her waist. Her green eyes glittered in a flood of sunlight which seemed to follow her every step.

I am certain my heart ceased to beat in my chest, for I began to have difficulty in respiration, and my fellow travelers regarded me most vexedly. But the sight of her climbing forth from the thicket was the most stunning vision my eyes have drunk since leaving Palestine. I felt as one struck by lightning.

She was traveling overland with a small band of relatives of which her father and mother made number. The two proved a somber pair of farmers who greeted us with warmth and yet a prudent reserve as well. Father Lydius, who is fluent in their Gaelic tongue, informed me that they are from the interior of the isle, displaced by marauding Saxons. Many of her family perished by the sword before they made the heartsick resolve to quit their lands. They appear on the verge of starvation, although the hunger has not diminished the beauty of their daughter.

Her name is Claere. She spoke the word and touched her breast with the smile of a doe, and my heart melted within me.

I know not whether God willed it that I should have traveled this many miles merely to encounter her. My brethren, Lydius and Marcus, and I made voyage from our monastery at Clonfert. For days we have trod through a luscious green country of rounded hills and dense forestry, encountering tribesmen along the way whom we promptly befriended and told the message of Christ. Many have heeded our missionary message and become Christians, and we will send priests for them at a later date.

I now thank God I did not take final vows before leaving Clonfert, for I fear my heart is captured forever by this young beauty. I made no pretense in seeking her company this afternoon, when I brought for her and her younger brother a hunk of fresh venison to eat. As she and the boy devoured the meat with delight I smiled at her, and she smiled back with a comeliness which caused me to blush. I felt an ache deep inside me.

I am afraid my brothers regard my sudden turn of heart with some alarm. Though they do not dispute that Claere is a most perfect creation, they rightfully question a commitment to God so easily jolted. I must admit that, while my piety is unshakable, I now realize my priesthood itself is mostly a pretext to travel northward in relative safety.

It is not only her beauty that has rendered me to such a state. It is the sweetness and innocence that pour forth from her enormous green eyes like water from a spring. I feel I could float forever in the purity of her gaze, and perhaps recover a drop of my own youthful hope. Dear God, you know of the many gentlewomen I have encountered in my countless, dreary days. So you alone know what it means that Claere is the most marvelous woman I ever dreamed could exist. I would gladly leave the priestly life for her.

I must hurry and learn this Gaelic, else teach her proper Saxon. For I fear my life is unraveled until I take this young beauty for my own.

EVEN BEFORE HER EYES opened, Nora felt herself awash in three different sensations.

The strongest was the sound of rain, a light yet ceaseless pattering on the slate roof. Something told her she'd been hearing it come down for hours. Still half asleep, she had a sense that this was a distinctly European downpour. Not a storm whipped up by an unruly young continent, but the patient and civilized discharge of an ageless overcast.

Another feeling was a damp, nearly outdoor chill against her cheeks and forehead.

The last, paradoxically, was a dry warmth sheathing the length of her body from the neck down. She had been put to bed in a most sheltered embrace, tucked under an immensely thick down comforter.

She wanted to lie here forever. The temperature contrast between her warm body and cold face reminded her of being a young girl again, lying cozy snug on a winter's night, protected from the severe cold outside by the curl of fabric beneath her chin and the sheer weight of blanket over her body. Yet curiosity tugged at her, so she rose to a sitting position. Where was she? What kind of place was this? And where was Lazarus?

She tried to remember the night before, but only random

images careened through her mind: the boat ride down the Seine; racing along narrow roads through the darkness in a cramped car; struggling to stay awake amid the yawing motion of a small airplane, continually being awakened by the bumping of her head against the window.

Then, with a jolt, the terror—the flash of light and fire spewing from her side. The sickening sight of a human silhouette jerking to the rhythm of her twitching index finger. The almost nauseating solemnity of knowing she'd killed someone, however justifiably. The gravity of what took place felt like a dead weight upon her. She shook off the unwanted thought and shifted her attention to her surroundings.

She noticed she'd been staring upward for some time without registering any sight. She focused her eyes and penumbra sharpened into large wooden beams high overhead, their dark spans giving off a gloom so thick and permanent that the place seemed never to have witnessed electric light. She breathed deeply and recognized the smell of burnt hardwood, the smudgy remnant of ash or perhaps oak. Then came a faint scent that she could not identify, vaguely redolent of herbs and mint.

When she went to heave her legs over the mattress edge and onto the wood floor, she had no idea how much time had passed since she woke up. She stood and faced a dim chamber flanked by high white walls. Immediately a damp chill enveloped her. A single narrow window ushered in, through rain-splattered glass, the pallor of a wet morning. The room's only other furnishings consisted of a large armoire in a corner and a small couch that sat beside a tall door.

Turning to search for her clothes, she saw them folded neatly and lying on an antique chair she hadn't noticed near the bed. She shakily pulled on her cold clothes, then her shoes. She walked to the door and proceeded down a hallway until she was facing a wall that forced her to turn. To the left the hall stretched on into further gloom. To the right she saw faint motions of firelight on the wall. She followed the golden glow to a doorway, the entrance to a large chamber.

Her first view was of a three-foot-high quiver of flames snapping loudly within a roughly hewn frame of stone. The fireplace's chimney rose ponderously to a nearly indiscernible ceiling. The room stood large and rustic, swathed in shadows. Its walls bore four of the same narrow windows through which she could see dripping tree branches and bright green grass. At the center of the room was a thick wood table, strewn with kitchen utensils. And next to the towering fireplace, huddled beneath a tartan blanket in one of a pair of leather chairs, was the man she'd come to know as Lazarus.

He stood and almost dropped a thick volume. "Well, hello," he said, looking genuinely glad for the pause in his study.

"Hi. Uh . . . where are we?" Nora asked.

He smiled warmly and answered, "Claere Wood. Galway. My other favorite place."

She strode across a thick fur carpet toward the nearest window. Through the downward trail of droplets she could make out a thin strip of grass mixed with wild flowers fringed by the onset of forest—a misty, shadowed wall of gigantic oak trunks. "Are we safe here?"

"I believe so. We weren't followed beyond central Paris. We're at the end of a half-mile-long gated drive in a forest so overgrown that no one believes it leads anywhere but the National Park, Connemara, which backs the property. Everyone thinks this parcel is actually a little-used bit of the park itself."

"Wow. True seclusion."

"That's the idea. I've been coming to this area for fifteen hundred years."

Nora shook her head at the odd sound of the statement. Despite her newfound belief, it was still jarring to hear him refer to centuries the way normal people spoke of decades.

She paused to drink in the feeling of isolation. After days in the heart of Paris, this felt strangely wonderful—to be holed up inside a warm cottage in the corner of a forgotten forest.

"Here, Nora, have a chair. And a blanket." He went to her, took her by the hand and steered her to one of the deep chairs. He sat her down on top of a shaggy green blanket, picked up its edges and carefully wrapped them around her. "There. Can I get you some tea? Or hot mulled wine? The priests were here last week and left a pantry full of salted meats, pasta, and half a rack of spirits."

"Tea would be wonderful," she said.

He disappeared behind her, leaving her to the crackling of fire and the dance of warm light against shadow. This place looked as solid as the land, she remarked to herself. Like some organic creation of stone and wood and mortar. She wondered if this was how old places lasted when modern folk left them alone. Truly alone.

A steaming mug descended in front of her, held in his flushed grip.

She received it and took a long drink. It burned going down, immediately igniting an inviting glow within her. A whiff of mint struck her nostrils. She looked up at him and smiled. It was perfect. All of it.

"May I get you some food?" he asked. "You must be starving."

She suddenly realized that the grinding, empty sensation within her was hunger. "Yes, I really am," she said.

He moved back to the table, where the sound of knives and shuffling began.

She stayed seated, basking in feeling warmed and sheltered from a hostile world, in a place that time seemed to have skipped over. She wanted to linger here and let the days and weeks pass in languorous procession, the rain unceasing, the restful rain clouds bathing her in their silver light.

After several minutes of activity at the table behind her, he brought her a wooden board lined with dried meats, hunks of cheese, and crackers. In the other hand he held a pewter cup of cold water. "I'm sorry, but this is all I have for the moment. Maybe later today we can figure out how to light the stove—if it can be lit at all."

"This looks wonderful," she said, truthfully. "Thank you."

She began to eat while he returned to his chair and sank down into the leather, bringing his blanket back over him along with the leather-sheathed volume—another diary.

He flipped the pages, back and forth. She allowed the receding stupor of night and the warmth of her tea to lull her into a delicious trance.

He inhaled once, heavily. She looked up and became aware once again of his gaze upon her.

"Did you find something?" she asked.

"Yes. It is the reason I brought you here. I found it. The *Exorcismus Maximus*. The curse that will send my enemy the destroyer back to hell. It was here in my Irish diaries."

"Our troubles are over, then? So you find him, just walk up and say this to his face?"

He chuckled. "No. It isn't that simple. He knows I have this in my possession. He will make it as painful as possible for me to approach him."

"So what will you do?"

"Approach him anyway."

He frowned at this last foolhardy statement, yet she could tell he was speaking the truth.

"Why do you look so glum?"

"Many reasons. The man who helped us in Paris—CIA, remember? A disaster. I've spent my whole life remaining unknown to world governments. I've taken great pains to stay hidden and anonymous. Now American secret agents are showing up in my house. Oh, and another worry. The priests gave me this"—he held up a sleek-looking cell phone—"to use to contact them. They never fail to answer. Until this morning. I'm very concerned about them. I should have left Paris and come here as soon as I was able to walk."

"But you would have missed our long walks and conversations," she said, feigning glibness.

"Yes. I would have indeed."

He did not smile with his reply.

Again she felt how powerfully attracted she was to him and all he represented. This quiet figure beside her was the most profound of anachronisms: a man of impenetrable religious faith yet endless worldly acumen, of great wisdom and knowledge, of anguish and loneliness beyond anything she'd ever encountered. In that moment she wanted nothing more than to embrace him, to give him what he appeared to have lived without for ages.

Therefore, she was only half surprised when her voice seemed to speak of its own accord. "You know, a girl could fall for the man who gave her all this."

He looked up. "What do you mean?"

"The ambiance here. Picture-postcard Ireland. A rainy evening alone in a manor house . . ."

He smiled weakly, then shook his head and said, "That was not my plan."

"Oh, come on," she said, raising her voice a little, emboldened. "You mean none of this was intended to create a desired effect? You've just spent a week arm in arm with me, showing me *Paris* of all places. You can't tell me that none of this has been calculated to woo unsuspecting women into your lonely clutches." She took a deep breath. She had intended this as a light gibe, but somehow his expression revealed that he was taking her ribbing a bit too seriously.

For a long moment he looked down and said nothing. Finally he spoke, his voice measured and calm. "You're suggesting I bought this house three hundred years ago for the express purpose of setting the stage for *you*."

"No. I'm sure I am not the first."

His features seemed gripped with a mixture of anger and embarrassment, and Nora realized he was being truthful. She *had* been the only one with whom he'd shared his secrets, bared his soul, provoked an attraction that grew more undeniable by the day. *Oh no.* Now she was the one feeling embarrassed and ashamed. And yet, she knew, here was all the more reason he should feel something for her.

The words burned even as she spoke them. "You're saying you feel nothing for me, other than a—"

"It's not a possibility," he interrupted sharply.

"That's not what I asked. I asked if you felt any attraction to me."

"And I'm telling you that we will not be having this discussion."

"You're *ordering* me? This is the twenty-first century, you know. Women do not have to obey men anymore."

"No, I'm not ordering you. I'm simply refusing to discuss it. Please, let us stop this conversation. Let us enjoy the day and the safety of being here."

But she felt anger now, rising in her chest. "Well, that's just fine," she said. "In the meantime, forgive me for feeling manipulated. I mean, you couldn't have orchestrated this whole . . . whole adventure any more cunningly."

He looked up, his face red. "I orchestrated nothing, nor did I set out to deceive anyone. You came to me, remember? Refusing to leave without answers. How flippant of you to act like what we've been through is just some lark contrived for romantic amusement."

She sensed that dreaded twinge of sarcasm enter her voice. "No. How beyond you to have a romantic bone in your body—you the stoic, longsuffering servant of the Lord, the immortal one who sees women as nothing, as nothing but—"

She felt a vice grip now upon her upper left arm. She looked over to see his hand on her. The real surprise came when she looked into his eyes. Rather than the anger she had anticipated, she saw tears flowing freely, a face twisted in anguish.

"Come with me," he said.

He led her to an outside door—one she hadn't noticed when entering the place—and yanked a dark green rain slicker off a peg on the wall beside the door. "Here," he mumbled, and then reached to open the door.

43

STILL NUMBED WITH surprise by his reaction, Nora did not think of disobeying him. Instead, she threw on the raincoat, which of course was several sizes too large for her, and followed him out into a pelting downpour suddenly loud and angry in her ears. She turned to pull the door shut, then swung back around to see Lazarus walking already fifty paces ahead through the rain, toward a narrow path in the trees.

"Wait!" she shouted. "You have nothing over you!"

Without looking back, he waved her on and kept moving at a manic pace. She started to run, for he seemed in no mood to stop and guide her to his destination. The onslaught of exertion and falling water and guilty bewilderment caused her to feel that she was running through a cascade of tears. She was no longer sure whether her heaving breaths came from the running or a great sob welling up inside her. She just kept running. The muddy ground slipped beneath her feet, and a small branch that proved hardier than she had anticipated whipped her in the face.

She followed his figure up a long, gradual hill and past a cluster of trees, where he finally paused, his hands on his hips, looking downward. His clothes clung to him, soaked.

A moment later she stood next to him. Looking around breathless, Nora observed that in clement weather this place would offer a magnificent view. A shrouded sheet of blue betrayed the ocean far below them, and she could hear waves crashing on an unseen beach. Toward the horizon she saw a wide green hill that sloped down to the shore, dotted with cottages and small fishing boats at anchor.

His eyes remained fixed on the ground around his feet. His cheeks twitched; he blinked hard through tears as his chest rose and fell. Nora's eyes followed his index finger, which was jabbing emphatically at a large square stone embedded in the soil below them. Something had been engraved into the stone's surface.

"She's there," he said. "Claere. She's lain there since the latter part of the first millennium. I've cried an ocean of tears on this spot." He turned to Nora and fought another sob in an attempt to continue. "Claere was the most beautiful, gentle soul I have ever known. She converted soon after we met. A green-eyed girl with black hair to her waist. She thought every word I spoke was pure gold. She was the first one I entrusted with my secret. I told her everything. The only one . . . until you."

Nora reached out for his arm. How cruel she had been, she now saw, to say that he didn't esteem women or somehow used them.

"This was our favorite place," he said, "where I first told her I loved her. And where Father Denis married us. Yes, I was married. But I failed. I failed. . . ."

He fell to his knees with the abruptness of someone who had just spent his final ounce of strength.

"What do you mean?" Nora asked.

"I had sworn no one would touch her. But they took her from me, and I couldn't protect her. I didn't protect her."

"Who?"

"My enemy—by employing some men in his service, those who hated Jews. They came and took me away to a dungeon, and because they couldn't kill me, they took their rage out on Claere. The things they did . . ." He stopped and swiped at his eyes. Looking up again, he said, "When I finally escaped, she'd been dead for decades and my son was a grown man who knew nothing of me. All I could do was find her body, bring it to be buried here."

"I understand," Nora whispered. "I'm so sorry."

"No, you don't. You don't understand any of it."

"Tell me, then."

He shook his head as though the effort would be too great, the pain too excruciating. She thought she saw exasperation in his features, and suddenly she felt like the dumbest person on earth not to have captured his meaning.

"Please," she said weakly.

He turned back to the stone, pointed again, and spoke in an angry growl. "This is the grave of your grandmother twenty-four times removed." Then in a much louder voice, "Your ancestor! Claere is your ancestor! *I* am your ancestor!"

Nora found herself staring. Raindrops began to strike her open mouth.

"You're my offspring, don't you see? My descendant. I can't! I CAN'T!"

Nora now sank to her own knees. Facts collided in her mind like a slow crashing of icebergs. The reason he had followed her back in Cambridge, why she had been a target in the first place. And deeper mysteries still . . . her family's shroud of secrets, her father's mysterious disappearance, the Lazare amulet.

She felt his hands about her shoulders, bearing her up.

"Please . . . let us go," he said. "Let us rest."

They walked slowly back down the hill. Through wisps of cloud the manor house drifted into view, and she saw that its complex of squat, stone buildings, though large, was still dwarfed by the surrounding forest. She only caught brief glimpses—in the rainy distance beyond the treetops—of an end to greenery and the highway beyond, and beyond that the dim resumption of fields.

As they descended, her view was swallowed up by the

towering embrace of old forest. She glanced down to keep her feet from sliding in the mud and slick grass, and spotted a thick growth of mushrooms.

He followed her glance, walked over swiftly and picked them with a practiced sweep of the hand. Bringing the bunch to his nose, he breathed deeply and smiled. "They're safe. Irish wood ear. Perhaps I'll put them in a soup later on."

"Come on," she urged. "Let's get out of this rain."

Soon they reached the manor and entered the great room. Lazarus disappeared into the hallway to change his clothes, but Nora was drawn back to the fire and the inviting chairs. Her head still swam from all she'd just learned.

She sat and felt her thoughts careen within her. She felt like a schoolgirl again, tossed about by events beyond her control. Another thought then struck her. He truly did love her, though in a far different way than she'd considered. His reserved way of expressing that love was indication of how profoundly alienated and lonely he was. It had been ages since he'd enjoyed the company of a confidante.

She noticed the familiar shape of a diary volume, sitting open beside Lazarus's chair. She saw a date and realized that it corresponded to the time and place of his account. He had been reading of Claere even before their conversation. Glancing toward the hallway, she picked it up and began to read.

Glendalough, Galway, Irlandia—October 17, 685

I will write of this only once.

It may perhaps seem needless for me to write this down one time, for I keep a diary in order to remember, and these matters I am certain never to forget. In this case I might desperately wish to forget. Of all but for Claere herself, whose memory I would gladly blazon across my chest forever.

We were married on the same hillock overlooking the sea where I first told Claere in faltering Gaelic of my love for her. The vows were administered by my old friend Denis, with her family in attendance. I received many queries as to the absence of my own relatives, and replied that they lived across the sea and so were unable to make the passage.

Claere had never appeared so fair as on that morning. I remember that a pine-scented breeze blew through her hair, and I fought the urge to stop the vow-making and run my fingers through her curls.

After the wedding, the two of us made voyage to a nearby island by means of a small currach, *which despite worrying us with its shallow draught, took the waters well. I had been told of a clean fishermen's shack which could be used for brief habitations. We spent ten days upon the island's shores, walking hand in hand along the beaches. I remember marveling that she truly loved me. How could someone I loved so completely love me in return? What heavenly coincidence.*

From hereafter I referred to this blessed place as Claere's Isle. Afterward we returned to Irlandia and made domicile in the small village where her mother and father had settled, in the foothills of the Twelve Ben.

How shall I speak of our year together? Shall I besmirch Paradise and claim that it could not compare? I know I am sorely tempted to venture such a thing. I will say that of all my days in this world, none have compared in joy to the blessing of sharing every day with Claere. I assumed the occupation of a weaver and took great pride in bringing home wool to spin into blankets and outer garments. We worked together in our modest stone cottage and I found myself stopping my work periodically with the goal of gazing at her beauty, or of partaking once more of the wondrous act which had delighted us since the wedding night.

I never felt more at peace than during that year, more at home in the company of men. I felt as a vagabond returned home, only to a home I had never known existed. I told her of my strange predicament, and after recovering from her surprise, she only loved me the more for it. She told me she had always known I was an otherworldly man, a force of nature. My relief was beyond measure. For the first time, I took joy in small things. The turn of winter into spring and then summer. The growth of small flora outside our door. The companionship of Claere's family. The tiniest changes in her as she turned from a blushing maiden into a loving wife.

On a warm afternoon in late summer she approached me with a special light in her eyes. She sat me in the open threshold, as we often did to watch the sun set over the sea, then grasped my hand and told me in a soft whisper that she believed herself with child.

That moment was perhaps the happiest I was ever given, happier than I ever expect to feel again.

On a moonless night months later, her belly only begun to swell, the vassals of my lifelong enemy attacked. The men were giants, clad in chain mail, wielding huge sword axes, swearing at the top of their lungs in foul, unknown tongues. They burst into our home with shouts and grunts, waking us from our slumber. Claere awoke screaming and received an iron-gloved slap across the face which sent her crashing to the floor. Seeing her struck turned me into a wild man; I launched myself against the men shouting exorcists' prayers. This was to no avail, however. These men worked in service of the demon but were not possessed by him.

They laughed, grasped me by the arms and legs and dragged me from the house into the night air. I screamed Claere's name and heard her scream mine in return, for a time. I cannot describe the horror of being separated from her in such a manner.

The men threw me onto the back of a horse and took me to a faraway castle where they beat me and tortured me for two days. They then dragged me to a building site and threw me into the center of a half-bricked wall. They began to lay mortar and soon had me bricked into the surface of the rampart itself.

And there I remained. God dispensed his usual mercies upon me, snatching me up into realms of the spirit and places I might marvel about and weep for—things I knew I would not soon partake of due to my special state of being. I dwelt in a dream for what must have been years, my eyes shut against the blackness of my prison and the stifling confinement about me.

Finally, realizing no one was going to find me in this cunningly hidden place, I began to claw with my fingers against the stone before me. One might think such a gesture futile, but with a decade or more of imprisonment, I knew I had the time to scratch my way out, one fingernail at a time. It is amazing how even the stoutest rock will give under years of constant labor.

I knew not how many seasons it took, but one day I reached a thickness which allowed me to hear voices on the outside. At times when such clamors reached their peak, which I supposed to be feast or high holy days, I began to shout from my prison as forcibly as my weakened lungs would give me aid. And one day, after many such attempts, a voice replied. It was a high-pitched rant, that of a young man who had not yet reached full maturity. I remember how it grew nearer and nearer until a thumping commenced right against my face. I continued to shout that I was trapped inside and needed rescue. Before long, the thumping became a thunder of hands assailing the wall.

Lord knows how I appeared when the first breach pushed two stones inward and showered daylight upon my face. I could not even reach up to shield my eyes, such was the closeness of my confinement, and so I uttered a loud cry of mixed astonishment, shock and joy.

I could hardly see to judge the consternation which came over my rescuers' faces, as near as they loomed. Had I but seen, I might have taken the chance to offer some small thanks, to have them see me as a normal human being, frightened yet grateful. But as it was, while they continued to tear down the stone surrounding me a gasp of horror swept through the assembled crowd. By the time I stepped free, their number had begun retreating from the sight of me as though I were a fiend.

I stumbled forward, my hair having grown down below my waist so that I resembled a wolf, grunting and making strangled attempts at speech, and heard cries of "Monster!" *rise from the crowd's midst. How could they have thought otherwise, after seeing that I had survived being a part of that wall for the long years the edifice had stood?*

It did not take long for my saviors to become bloodthirsty accusers, for in a moment's time stones began to hurl my way and I was forced, despite my weakness, to flee from them. Fortunately the village was surrounded by the thickest of woods. Following several minutes of anxious pursuit, I escaped into a deep glade of oak and bramble with a sucking mire of bog beneath my feet.

There I stomped about in a daze for hours, until the evening brought a relief of darkness to my eyes. Covered with mud, I curled up on the outer fringe of dry land and went to sleep.

The next morning I was most thunderously awakened by the baying of hounds and the pounding of horses' hooves. I opened my eyes to the sight of warriors arrayed for battle, come for me. I stood and cowered. I tried not to make myself appear as a beast, yet command of my limbs had not fully returned, and without practice, my ability for speech had decayed. Instead, I sought to make myself look fearful to my attackers as the hounds advanced and the men growled to each other commands on how best to dispatch me into hell.

Suddenly a clarity of mind and tongue descended on me with a rushing like the wind. I straightened myself and spoke in a loud voice, "Men, do not be afraid of me for having shown you a wonder in the castle wall. I am neither a foul spirit nor a practitioner of witchcraft, but a servant of Jesus Christ. It is he, through his great mercy, who has seen fit to spare me from death!"

There fell the most profound silence. The soldiers had not a priest among them or else the controversy would have ended. No, these were men of brute strength who brought with them death, not unlike those who had placed me in the wall in the first instance. The tallest of them stepped forward and shouted, "Show yourself to be a true Christian, if you not be a fiend!"

I replied, "I shall do so at once, for it is written that the devil's minions cannot confess the Lord with their tongue. I tell you now that I follow Jesus of Nazareth, son of the living God, who died on the cross and resurrected on the third day. Does that sound to you the utterance of a demon?"

The men did not reply but conferred among themselves, even as I stood shivering in the forest chill. Seeing the dismay I had spoken into their number, I told them, "I will leave this place and not return, for I have caused you to be troubled, and that is neither my nor God's will. If you will equip me with a horse, clothes, and a bowl of soup, I promise I will be on my way, with a blessing for the lot of you upon my lips."

They readily complied, and within the hour I had been bathed and shorn and was speeding atop a worthy stallion toward the home where I had left Claere, Lord knows how many years ago.

My heart sank when I approached the cottage. Its caved-in roof lay barely visible through a thick wall of bramble and vines; its walls stood blackened with soot. Through the open windows and doors I saw heaps of stone and plaster several feet thick. I let out a loud cry as I walked forward. I stepped across the same threshold where I had first learned I would be a father and waded into the rubble of my once joyful life.

As I found no sign of Claere within, I left the place and began searching the cemeteries of nearby towns. In the third one I found a headstone that was marked, Claere Conleagh, n. 613, d. 647, widow of Brian and mother of Ian. *Brian being my name at the time. An aged woman passed behind me and I asked her what year it was. She gave me a puzzled look and said in a crackling voice, "It is 685, lad. What, are you so daft that ye have forgotten?"*

I began to sob. I collapsed to the ground and lay there, hating myself, and wept until the tears no longer came. I never felt more alone than in this moment, to know that nothing remained of my dear companion, nothing but a scattering of precious bones in the earth. I remained prostrate and allowed the torturous minutes to wash over me.

The moon hung high upon the night when I finally gathered myself and quit the yard. I steered myself to the nearest drinking house and asked at the door whether anyone around knew of the Claere Conleagh buried in the yard.

A man two benches away turned to me with a frown on his face. "Why do you want to know?" he asked.

I swallowed hard and considered my answer. "Because I knew her for a time, many years ago." The voice that came from my mouth seemed not my own.

"Well, she was my mother," the man said, staring into his mug. He then turned around and faced me. "And any friend of my mother's is a friend of mine."

So this is how I met Ian, my son, in appearance a good ten years older than myself. I found out that night that he did not know of his father. His mother had returned to her family after being tortured and raped by my abductors. She had given birth and lived a quiet and melancholy life as the widow of a man presumed dead.

In the early hours of the morning, drunken from spirits and the far more intoxicating power of my grief, I entered the church cemetery with a spade and carefully dug out the pine coffin which contained my Claere's remains. After loading the box onto a wagon borrowed from a farmer, I drove her six miles to our favorite spot in the forest. The place where we were married. I buried her there while the sun rose above the far hills and the never-ending sound of the ocean rang in my ears. I wept so long and hard that I feared I might never stop.

The following day I made my way here, to the monastery of Glendalough, and reentered the novitiate.

The time passes quietly, here in the vale of the two lakes. Let this accursed world wallow in its bloodlust and hatred forever. For now I am pleased to rest in the company of gentle, God-fearing men and devote myself to prayer, the presence of God, and the copying of scripture. I find that the tales of Palestine return me to brighter, more carefree days.

I am given to sitting here, in the solitude between two eternal pools of water, with nothing but distracted moments before me. I sit in the half-light of the scriptorium with quill in hand and transcribe thousands of words from countless stories. And not a single one of these words have to do with the awful fate of my Claere, or the destiny of my beleaguered descendants.

SHE SAT STILL FOR A long moment and tried hard to return to the twenty-first century. It was beginning to feel like a time warp to navigate this man's orbit, to imbibe his long life in these incremental doses. Between the sense of distant past and unrelieved sadness, she felt herself in danger of losing her bearings. She took a deep breath, looked up into the dancing firelight on the ceiling, and waited for the present to return.

After several interminable minutes Lazarus appeared, his hair combed back, wearing a dry sweater and a pair of new pants. Only his reddened cheeks betrayed the onset of a coming cold. She walked up and embraced him in a deep, long clasp.

They broke and he sat beside her, looking at her with a weary smile. "I am sorry, Nora. I did not plan on telling you that way."

"It's all right. I provoked you."

He sighed as though trying to gather something to say but still overwhelmed by the day's events.

"It's one of the things I do," he finally said. "I watch over my descendants. I track them down and try to help them, if I can. Over the years they've turned into thousands, so I made the choice centuries ago to concentrate on the firstborn of the line. And that's you. You're the only one left."

Nora stared into the fire. "The family curse—is it because of you?"

"I believe it is. The destroyer uses your family as both revenge and bait. That's why your father was taken. And his father before him. But after I was freed, my enemy's warriors knew that I would not be able to resist seeing the last of my line. They used you as a way to acquire contact."

"Have you ever revealed yourself to one of your descendants before?"

"Never. I've never had to. None of them was ever brave enough and determined enough to find me before." He began to shake his head as though he knew his words would sound pathetic even before he uttered them. "Sometimes I would take another identity and befriend the descendant. I would become a long-lost uncle, an old friend of a family member. I always knew enough about the family to be convincing in my claims. Sometimes I was a priest who would befriend the person during a tough time."

Nora nodded. She could almost feel the puzzle pieces fall into place within her. *The family photos*. Once again, the sadness of the man's existence washed over in a wave of melancholy. She pictured him lurking in the background of countless people's lives year after year, too reticent to make himself known yet desperately needing the sense of belonging their existence offered.

"Your story becomes sadder by the moment," she said. "Is Claere the major reason why you're so miserable? The memory of her? And the dumb, really dumb, idea that her death was in any way your fault?"

His gaze turned downward. "No. It's only a small part of it, Nora," he said.

"Then what's the rest of it? What's the reason you've been moping around like this through the centuries?" After a brief moment, she said, "I'm sorry. I didn't mean to phrase it that way."

"It's all right," he replied. He stood up and walked to a corner of the room. He walked back over to her and placed a book on her lap.

She looked down. *Holy Bible*, the cover read.

"I will let you read it yourself," he said casually. With that, he turned and walked out of the room.

Outside Paris—Later That Night

A BLINDING LIGHT seared Father Thierry's eyes. Another gun butt crashed into his cheekbone. This time he heard as well as felt the cataclysmic pain of bone shattering and blood starting to flow down his chin.

The face again, looming large. A Palestinian face that reared back and disappeared. Another one filled his vision. A well-groomed European, maybe in his early fifties.

"Father Thierry, you are a man of God, so I will be merciful. You see, I am a brother of the cloth, a fellow cleric of the Church. A bishop, for that matter. Oh, does that surprise you? Do you find that hard to believe?"

The man reached down and pulled out a wallet. "Here. Here is my Holy See passport. My Vatican pass. See? That's my picture. Bishop Johan Eccles. And here's me with the pope. A casual chat, I assure you. I may be a bureaucrat to you, a petty deskbound paper-pusher, but in the Vatican hierarchy I outrank you. Yes, we are colleagues, you and I. I've waited to meet you for a long time."

"No wonder I could never stand Rome," Thierry muttered through clenched teeth.

"Yes, I am sure you wouldn't," Eccles said airily, as though engaging in British parlor talk. "So much . . . ideological impurity, lack of belief. Questionable doctrine, wouldn't you say? Even so, Rome is where your Order got its start, and its support. I read, you know."

Eccles held up one of the bound diary copies, flopping heavily in his left hand. "Fascinating little scribbles of self-pity, wouldn't you say? I believe I read something about Rome and your very own Order. Ah, here it is."

Drawing closer to Thierry, he started reading aloud.

"The Vatican—1323

"Sleep evades me in this grand mausoleum. Bereft of clocks to mark the hours, I have resorted to watching the progress of a blade of moonlight from its curtained slit upon the far wall to its resting place astride a nearby pillar. My bed, the height and heft of a royal berth, stands nearly twenty feet below a cage of gold-trimmed beams and trailing velvet damask.

"This Vatican is too grand a place for a follower of Christ. Jesus himself often slept on my bare floor with but a single robe curled up beneath his chin. And he never spoke a word of it being beneath his station. I think back on the lowly foxholes his disciples used to sleep upon, and they the patron fathers of the faith, and it causes me to shudder at what he would say at seeing his vicar living in such splendor.

"I suppose, given the reason for my presence here, that I should cease such petulant thoughts. Mere hours ago I suffered my identity to be certified by the Church and a new Order of priests sanctified for my very own protection, assistance, and succor. The Order of Saint Lazare. Seven men whom the Holy Father bade me choose from my own travels. Among them Peter of Nantes, my good friend Laurence, Xavier the Tuscan, and of course the meek Didier, who in countenance resembles my Lord more than any other man I have met in many years past.

"I did not ask for this cognizance, but the travails of history appear to demand it. The story begins several hundred years ago when the Order of the Templars became aware of my existence

through some foreign, arcane source, before they were even properly constituted. I was once told on good authority that it may have been one of the Carolingian documents in the library at Alexandria. In any event, the ambitious Soldiers of Christ used the secret of my existence to their highest benefit, and lowest. Ere a decade passed, nearly half the Christian world knew that the Templars possessed a secret of high order. And, being ill to part with it, they allowed all sorts of rumors to arise.

"What fools the so-called scholars are. Much of the confusion has come due to a dim-witted confusion of Marys. While Bernard of Clairvaux caused each Templar to be clearly sworn to the loyalty of Mary and the House of Bethany, many have overlooked the latter and assumed this surnamed Mary to be the mother of Christ, or even Mary Magdalene. The fact that my sister was also named Mary is record enough in the gospels.

"Whether God himself caused this ignorant assumption to spawn the Templars' demise, I dare not guess. Yet it must be stated that both the secret and the Order's haughty mishandling of it gave rise to that which hastened their extermination.

"I remember the first time I revealed myself to Templar leader Jacques DeMolay at court in Madrid. He pulled me aside as though I were an accomplice. While clearly taken aback by my appearance, he could not shake his customary demeanor as king of all he surveyed. He offered me what he said he had never offered to any person—to multiply my monies through the labyrinth of borrowers and lenders which constituted the core of Templar wealth. Banking, he called it. Of course I would be remiss to overlook the fact that I did entrust the Templars with a substantial sum, which they promptly multiplied to my great amazement.

"Yet I kept silent with all due caution as I stood amidst the crowd outside Notre Dame when DeMolay was put to the torch and, as the

flames began to kiss his feet, shouted his famous challenge to the pope and king to meet him in heaven within the year—a challenge which was met as both men died within months. I recall that in front of me, a tall, large-nosed peasant woman, still wearing her bloodstained apron, leaned down and murmured to her adolescent son that the man before them was being executed for worshiping the devil.

"It was common knowledge that the pope only grudgingly assented to the annihilation of the Templars, bullied into it by his lack of power to quench the vengeful mien of the Frankish king Phillippe LeBel. And so it must have been a penance of sorts for him to summon me for this present gesture of ill-conceived atonement.

"I was taken through a side passage in a lesser chapel, down an endless series of stone stairways. The guard nearest me kept a constant hold of my arm. Later, as we entered the first of many unlit tunnels, I understood this to be merely assistance. Finally we arrived at the chamber.

"He is not the first pope I have met, of course, but he was the first to meet me with a knowledge of my identity. I noted right off that the man, a small leathery Italian with the restless mien customary to those of precarious station, could not meet my eye. He was apparently ill at ease with the unsettling meaning of my presence and what my life represents. And how disconcerting must it be, for one accustomed to being treated as having no equal on earth, to meet an actual friend of Christ?

"A small table lined with scowling clergy stood behind him. For the next three hours I was assaulted by angry questions ranging from details of the Nazarene's life to the nature of my own bohemian existence. I found myself willing for the first time to part with the secrets of my life. I told them of my identities, my various incarnations as a priest or monk or even bishop of this or that municipality. I saw eyes grow wide with astonishment, although something about my confidence

and boldness prevented them from giving vent to their tempers.

"It all concluded with a look of resignation and disappointment from the Bishop Grand Inquisitor, who did nothing more than wave his arm desultorily, thus ending the inquiry. He seemed almost disappointed to have nothing with which to accuse me.

"So it is done. I am no longer a purely solitary person. I suppose my dealings with this group bearing my name will define my life from here on. While I do not intend to live in their direct company, I will doubtless return to their midst from time to time. And they may well assist me in the assignment God has entrusted to me."

Eccles finished reading, tossed the book onto a nearby table, and faced Thierry with a fey smile.

"I love reading other people's diaries, don't you? Such a window into their soul. It reveals qualities the author never intended to tell—like in this case, self-pity, disaffection, and such overwhelming cowardice."

"Cowardice," Thierry responded curtly. "You and your master have specialized in cowardice for centuries. Preying on the weak. You people wouldn't know courage if it struck you in the face."

"This spoken by the so-called friend of a man who abandoned him to die. Anyway, what 'people' would you be referring to?"

"Followers of Satan."

Eccles kneeled beside the man's chair and leaned in close. Just inches away from the old priest's nose, Eccles's inner tormentor sprang to the surface. He flexed his cheeks and growled, issuing a slobbering sound through his teeth. "You are right!" said the demon's voice. "And do you know what followers of Satan do to sickening, lily-pale followers of the Nazarene? As we are already condemned, our only pleasure is sending as many of you home to your daddy-God as quickly and painfully as possible!"

Turning his back to Thierry, Eccles then faced the table. The old man heard paper tearing and containers being popped open.

"Now, if you will tell us where this man—this coward who betrayed you and your friends—can be found, then I promise to kill you quickly. You can go to your God along with the others."

Father Thierry knew the human monstrosity before him was not joking. He had heard the screams of one St. Lazare priest after another in the adjacent rooms. He'd recognized each voice, each dying groan.

Thank God Stephen had left to escort Lazarus to Ireland. He would be their only survivor. Their last hope.

He looked about him. So this is where it would end, he told himself in a grim assessment. Not on that stone bench beside the trout stream in Auvergne, as he had often dreamed of, but in a squalid back room with peeling wallpaper and rat droppings scattered across the floor. Some nondescript dump in one of Paris's industrial suburbs.

Fine, he thought. *Just let me go be with my Brothers, and my Creator.*

What were they doing? He focused his eyes on the shape crowding his vision. Something tapered and long. *Ah, yes.* A *needle.*

"I've been saving my one vial for you, old man," Eccles snarled. "I was told to save our little stash of tongue loosener for the oldest and weakest of the lot. And that's you."

Despite himself, Thierry grinned widely, and chuckled. He wondered if any of his now-deceased Brothers would have ever designated him as the weakest among them. Probably not, he pondered. They probably would have wished he were, he thought with a rueful shake of the head. He should have treated them better. All these years, working them like dogs, only to stir up this hornet's nest at the end of it all. What a bitter finale.

Well, he knew it would all be for a good cause. A worthy victory would soon emerge from all this insanity. He felt sure of it. He had staked his whole existence on it.

The needle went in. A brief pain in his arm was followed by a cool sensation spreading outward from the bicep. Its plunger inched its way to empty. And then an endless pause enveloped them. Finally, the bishop spoke again.

"So, Father Thierry, where will I find your friend André Lassalle, or Lazarus, as we both know him to be?"

From the numb remove of his own conscience and will, Thierry amazedly witnessed his lips beginning to move, the air forcing itself from his lungs. And his voice began the betrayal.

"County Galway, in Ireland, along N59 just east of Letterfrack. . . ."

45

Isle de la Cité, Paris

ACROSS FROM THE PALAIS DE JUSTICE, France's Justice Department, lay the Rue de Lutece's vast square—a broad, cobblestone expanse facing the Palais's gold-tipped fence and imposing facade. The space rarely stood empty, even at the early hours of the morning. But then again, it had been a misting, rainy night, the tail end of a damp weather system that extended north into the British Isles. So the Parisians who frequented the well-known square, site of France's raucous 1998 World Cup celebration, forgave themselves for not spotting the sight until the pale light of morning.

The first to see it was a commuting judge who emerged from the Isle de la Cité Metro tunnel, looked up and gasped. His mouth contorted as he rushed to a nearby bush, bent over, and vomited.

By the time he straightened out, a scream let out across the square. Two secretaries had walked up from behind him and seen it also. The scene had gone from long-undiscovered to the object of horrified scrutiny in less than five minutes.

Soon a gendarme ran out into the square from the Palais de Justice guardhouse and allowed his gaze to follow the outstretched arms.

Slowly swaying from a thick cable strung between streetlights hung the dark shapes of six bodies. Just below their clerical collars, sheets of paper had been knifed into each torso, each bearing an identical slogan underscored in a trailing stain of blood.

Death to Catholic desecrators!

Claere Wood, Ireland

NORA AWOKE TO AN even colder, damper house and a white sheet of fog pressed against the windows. She rose from her bed and dressed herself in the woolens Lazarus had given her the day before, then padded into the Great Room.

It was empty. A dying fire smoldered in the fireplace. She looked about her, feeling a tide of apprehension sweep over her.

There on the end table sat a letter.

Dear Nora,

I have left. Please do not think ill of me or, worst of all, label me a coward. I brought you to the safest place I know. I have left you ten thousand dollars in cash in an envelope by the front door and the car to drive to the airport. Just leave it in the parking lot. A map on the front seat will show you the directions to Shannon.

So you see, I did not just run away without having thought of you. In fact, I think of you every moment. How did I let my human faculties atrophy to such a point that I would be so stricken by your arrival in my life? I have surprised even myself, and that is a hard thing to do. Yet the time I have spent with you, our walks and conversations, as you put it, have brought me more joy than any human contact I have had since my time with Claere. You have been a fresh breeze in a stale, old existence. You are a wonderful, enchanting girl, Nora, even if your skepticism about spiritual matters puts us on opposite ends of the age-old debate. I love you dearly.

Please do not try to pursue me again, for I will take every step to remain hidden. Believe me, after centuries of doing this, I know how to disappear. Any effort on your part will only bring you into danger's path again, and I am sure you've had enough of that for one lifetime.

I am giving up this quest to defeat the destroyer—even though no less than God and his angels have been my allies in the pursuit. I have failed them all. To tell you the truth, I now despair of knowing his inscrutable mind on this whole conflict. Sometimes humanity's lust for destruction seems stronger than even the Almighty's grace and love. I know better, of course, yet at times the impression can seem overpowering. Maybe he simply declines to intervene. Perhaps he is allowing his children to drink of their own deadly brew in order to teach them. Or maybe he is waiting for some ripeness of time before stepping in and ending it all. In any case, I no longer possess the strength to wait.

I know that having seen heaven with my own eyes I should have greater hope than any man. And when I dare to recall those days spent in the afterlife, my hope does revive. But it is usually too painful to contemplate for very long. The endless travails of my earthly life loom so bleakly in comparison that dwelling on the splendors of glory amounts to something like torture. I must admit that surviving in the company of men has been laborious enough to dull even the most blissful of memories.

Meanwhile, your generation believes itself at peace, while continuing to ignore the genocides going on all over the world. How do my heavenly allies and I compete with such apathy? How do we confront hundreds of towering missiles, each of them capable of blasting humanity back into the Dark Ages—a time which I remember so well? How do we staunch the half-dozen or so madmen around the globe who are hatching super viruses and new Black Deaths?

I am but one man. Even with God and all his armies beside me, how do I effect a lasting change in the face of a species-wide death wish? I no longer have the will to try. Maybe the fact that humanity has not yet destroyed itself is victory in itself. But that flimsy construct gives me no comfort. I know that Jesus' death and resurrection is the guarantee of ultimate triumph. Yet, like any other man, or perhaps more than any other man, I am lured by the oppression of living to take my eyes off the Cross. I forget, and so lose heart.

Nora, I must be honest. It is largely my own failure that I am running from. It is due to my weakness that things have reached this point. I was left here to be a potent salt and light, to help the forces of light restrain the destroyer, and I have miserably failed. The problem is that meeting you has reminded me of what I have missed all these years. It has brought me face to face with the pathetic nature of my nomadic, furtive existence.

You asked me why I have never gone to see Jerusalem. It is a valid question, for like every other Jew in history I have longed to make a pilgrimage back to my holy city. For years and years I celebrated Passover and sadly spoke the words, "Next year in Jerusalem."

Maybe someday I will return. Right now, however, it is too difficult. Please read that Bible I gave you and figure out for yourself why Jerusalem is in fact the place of my greatest shame. I have memories of Jerusalem which will not leave me in peace, even a thousand miles and two thousand years removed. I cannot stand the thought of being confronted by them again, despite my longing to see my homeland.

Nora, you've uncovered many deep secrets. This secret is not so hard to discern. When you figure it out, I'm sure you'll think me a coward. I probably deserve your scorn. Please, I beg of you, go on with your life. I will miss you tremendously. Your absence will leave a huge, new hole in my life. But I can only bring you danger and unhappiness. Forget this tragic saga, go and live a happy and productive life. Get married, have children, and love them inordinately.

I am gone into the world, and will be so well concealed that I may as well be dead. For that is what I wait for now—nothing but the end of this whole human mess. When I can finally go home and see my Lord and friend again.

—L.

Nora lowered the letter as a surprising feeling of sadness descended upon her. She hadn't expected to feel so much pain for this man. Her questions had been answered. Her quest had produced enough adventure and intrigue for a lifetime. She ought to have felt satisfied and prepared herself to return home. Instead, it felt as if she'd triggered the final defeat of a very close and very old friend.

She raised a trembling hand to her forehead and glanced around for the means to pack up and leave, when a brief shadow crossed the far window.

She whirled around, and screamed.

West Ireland Highway

HAD THE FOG not smothered its lanes in a gray shroud that morning, the N59 Highway might have offered the kind of scenery tourists travel from all over the world to admire: the Twelve Ben peaks receding into misty oblivion, presiding over a succession of small Irish towns and plunging seascapes. Even the glimpses of wild white ponies galloping across the hillsides.

A single car braved that morning's fog at highway speeds, racing along the straightaway and recklessly hugging the curves as though its driver knew the road better than the lines on his own face.

Which he did.

Usually Lazarus enjoyed the drives to and from Claere Wood, but not today. Now this pea soup was obscuring the green peaks he'd always loved watching from vehicles beginning with wagon seats, then carriage windows, then Model T windshields. And finally this—a Renault sedan with more power than all the vehicles he had steered in his life combined.

On his journeys through long-remembered territory, he typically allowed the faces and sights of times past to swim over the present like the ghosted remnants of some partially erased movie. The pictures of olden times would superimpose themselves as though faint layers upon a thin gauze veil. He saw log-hewn settlements on top of a bustling town square, an isolated farmhouse and hayfield over a line of tall brick buildings, the gallows over an elementary school playground.

He saw Claere on nearly every inch of this country—turning

to smile at him from a familiar streamside, laundry in hand, or running toward him through a break in the trees.

That was not the full extent of the oddities he saw. His time in heaven had left him a sort of spiritual freak, he had concluded. He was always seeing shapes and transparent afterimages trailing people, not unlike the double vision that afflicts those who have been struck on the head. Sometimes a handsome man would trail the spectral visage of a corpse or a raging madman. Sometimes the stooped form of an old woman would precede a blurred version of herself gnarled with hatred and disfiguring grudges. Or sometimes, like a rainbow-streaked bubble shimmering away from a child's wand, he would glimpse the opposite—the pale cheeks of a radiant young teenager.

Once in a while he caught a glimpse of a similar being standing unattached to any human form. These often smiled at him, occasionally raised a hand in peace, both instantly aware of and amused by his ability to see them.

Lazarus knew them well, for they were all his friends. Those beings who had visited and comforted him during his many imprisonments.

There was one such angel he knew better than the others, the one who visited him the most often. He knew this angel more from the distinct sensation that surrounded him whenever it drew near—for he rarely saw any of these creatures up close for very long. Often the very glow of their presence would force him to close his eyes and instead rely on the Spirit to assess the visitation.

For centuries this one angel, who refused to name himself, had come to give Lazarus knowledge and instruction. It was this same being who had first whispered to him, on a spring night only a hundred years after leaving Israel, the task assigned him as the catacon.

He broke away from these thoughts and told himself that

perhaps fog was best for this day. He was being consumed by dark and tortured thoughts and did not wish to contend with anything like beauty.

Or love. He could not think of love, could not afford—on pain of watching his carefully maintained reserve melt away—to examine too closely how he felt about Nora. He had to forget the diffuse warmth that ignited his chest when she came close to him, as though the centuries had faded to oblivion and nothing mattered but those few seconds of allowing himself to look into her inquisitive eyes and intelligent face.

Forget all categories, he told himself. *Carnal*, *paternal*, *romantic*, *platonic*—all he knew was that he cared for her as he had for no human being in centuries. The intensity of it all weakened his every defense, each careful habit he'd cultivated for dealing with women he found attractive. He usually dealt with this kind of desire through a mental journey back to Claere—the way she had appeared stepping forth from that Irish glade with the morning sun highlighting her cheeks.

Nora threatened it all. To think he had allowed himself to care like this. How amateurish. How foolhardy!

Worse yet, the fact that she had burrowed into his life had somehow stirred up all his latent pessimisms and recriminations about the world at large. At that moment he felt like anything but the earthly emissary of the Creator himself. Rather, he felt adrift in a world of infinite coldness and mechanistic cruelty.

He truly was a failure, he reminded himself for the eleventh time that morning, tightening his grip on the steering wheel. As long as he stayed away from excessively close relationships, he had been able to ignore the fact. But Nora's friendship had caused him to see that he'd accomplished little in all these years except perfect methods of evasion and disguise. He had indulged small entertainments, diversions, and petty joys with the care and attention some people devote to bonsai gardens. They were his salvation, his means of passing the thousands of days without losing his mind. But Nora had sent the spinning plates off to shatter, dashed the china in all directions.

He would have phoned Father Thierry and indulged in a two-hour conversation with that satellite phone of his, but he couldn't risk raising the suspicions of any of the Order members—and they weren't answering the phone anyway. Another nagging bit of foreboding.

Ahhh! He pounded the steering wheel in frustration. Why had he relented? Why had he allowed this girl into his tightly guarded routine? Had he forgotten how well and how long the paradigm had served him? Had that last imprisonment finally worn down his self-discipline and resolve? Whatever the cause, he now felt like an idiotic schoolboy, racked by feelings and thoughts beyond his control.

Let this death-addicted world follow its madness into perdition, he thought. He was past caring. He could not remember all the genocides and ethnic cleansings Thierry had tried to brief him on; the numbers piled up in his head—a grisly pile. No, this world did not need him, did not want him. It certainly wanted nothing of the God who had sent him.

He drove by the lakeside castle of Kylemore Abbey and left the Connemara region behind. The fog began to lift, revealing a sky of wan turquoise. The country now began to rise again into the embrace of another mountain chain, the Partrys.

An odd clarity came over him, seemingly from nowhere but the suddenly revealed landscape. *What am I doing?* Abandoning the person who meant more to him than anyone? Running off to hide from a task given him by the Creator of the universe?

How absurd.

Most of all, how cowardly. He had spent enough years wrestling with that self-imposed attribute to now hate it with all his being. And yet he had to confess that cowardice was exactly what this flight embodied.

Furthermore, he realized, had he ever been expected to extinguish every single fire raging around the globe? Of course not. His had always been a carefully targeted contest against a specific, demonic nemesis and its human servants.

And over the years he had enjoyed many victories. In fact, he'd come agonizingly close to succeeding at the supreme task of sending the destroyer back to hell.

He could do it. He had found the Exorcismus Maximus. He knew the destroyer was on his trail, risking exposure and contact in the process. Most of all, he knew that he was on the winning side. He served the omnipotent Maker of all.

At that precise moment, rounding a curve toward a vast highland valley, he felt the loving presence again. In the seat beside him. Yes, in an automobile. He turned quickly in hopes of catching a glimpse but only gained an overpowering sense of a nearby luminescence, a gathering glow.

And a whispering voice in his ear. *You're very close to finishing the race, Lazarus. Turn around and go back.*

Still his fingers gripped the wheel and his foot pressed down on the accelerator. If he had indeed lasted until the end of things, then let that end come without him. He deserved to seclude himself from the world's madness and watch the final resolution from some isolated perch. He had failed, that was clear, though on the other hand he had endured. He had continued to assert himself against a pitiless existence. He had earned this desertion.

The presence and the voice returned. *Nora needs you.*

The Renault executed a perfect braking turn with screeching tires and an abrupt turnabout on the empty highway. He retraced his route at nearly half again the speed, aided by the lifting of fog and the brightening daylight. He marveled at the open sky behind him; it was as if he'd parted the fog with the nose of the car, leaving a tentative dawn in his wake.

He arrived back at Claere Wood less than a half hour later. He drove up the lane beneath the interlaced treetops, hoping that Nora had overslept and he would not have to explain the embarrassing note.

But as soon as the manor house came into view, he sensed trouble. Then he saw it. The front door stood open, torn from its top hinge. A shining pile of broken glass lay at the foot of one window. He ran from the car to the stone house and peered inside. He entered warily. It was dark inside, and silent except for his footsteps. The dining table was overturned, food and silverware scattered across the floor.

A foul residue assaulted his senses. His enemy had been here.

"Nora . . . ? NORA!" he yelled. His voice echoed throughout the house. He was standing amidst the disarray when a chirping sound emitted from his shirt pocket. He startled, then remembered. The cell phone. He reached in and flipped it open.

"Hello, sir. Stephen here."

"Yes, Stephen. Please—stay by the plane. Have it ready and fueled, and file a flight plan back to the Bourget."

"Actually, sir, I was calling to give you news."

"Oh. What is it?"

There was a pause on the other end. Lazarus could hear a faint static buzz and an electronic hum.

"What, Stephen?"

"They're dead, sir. The Order was wiped out. Their bodies were discovered this morning across from the Palace of Justice. It's all over the world media. I'm sure it's Hamas, but if it is, they were awfully cunning, sir. There were hateful anti-Christian slogans knifed into their bodies, and today the European Union is severing all ties with Israel and calling for reprisals."

The phone dropped to the floor and skidded off the side of an overturned water jug. The manor echoed with a scream—from his own lungs—of mixed anguish and fury.

Never had he felt so alone. Not even nineteen centuries earlier, when his sisters had died and he'd found himself bereft in an unknown land thousands of miles from home. Nora, who had just brought a bright light into his life, was gone. The Order, his only semblance of companionship for centuries, his only lifeline to Rome, was decimated.

It struck him with the force of a thunderclap that there were no more excuses. No more distractions. It was up to him now. The sense of defeat that had overwhelmed him earlier simply disappeared, replaced by an avenging vigor. His limbs screamed to move, to act. His fists clenched, ready to strike something, anything. And he did; he punched the wall with all the rage he could muster. The hand throbbed with pain but the sensation soothed him somehow. The fire shooting through his hand matched his emotions perfectly.

Lazarus stalked from the house and nearly launched himself into the Renault. His resolve was back to stay. His enemy would pay forever for what he had done.

BLACKNESS—AS DEEP as the earth's center. A thin mattress beneath Nora's side. Warm blankets around her shivering shoulders. The rumble of a ship's engine vibrating through her body. Be grateful for small things, she told herself.

Her grasp of time had become elastic. She was certain she'd been here forever, floating in this netherworld. Everything else, her whole life before now, faded behind her like a hazy prelude.

After finding Nora at Claere Wood, the men had harassed her and grilled her mercilessly, asking of Lazarus's whereabouts. Finally she remembered the note in her pocket, showed it to them, and they believed her. After much angry shouting they had injected her with a substance that left her weak and sleepy. Then they had stuffed her into the trunk of a car.

The lights had gone out for her, for a very long period punctuated only by moments of terrifying clarity. From time to time she would briefly return to consciousness only to find herself tied hand and foot, trussed like a Thanksgiving turkey, bumping along in the luggage compartment of what both sounded and felt like an airplane.

Certain saving graces had made the time bearable. First, the drugs, which they gave her at regular intervals. The injections had caused her to sleep through most of the ordeal, and when she was jolted back to an awareness of her surroundings, they had dulled the terror considerably. Second, her captors seemed to consider her a hostage, no longer a primary subject to be interrogated or tortured. She was clearly being kept for a purpose. Until that purpose was fulfilled, it appeared they weren't going to treat her any worse than they already had.

Only one shred of what had come before still lingered in her mind like a tattered remnant—Lazarus. The man who had abandoned her to this. Left her with a note as though they'd been tawdry lovers and then failed to intervene when these thugs had arrived. Her emotions vacillated wildly between unending fascination and resentment.

At least trying to decipher the man had given her mind something to chew on for this eternity in which she now found herself. For what seemed like weeks she pondered his unfathomable anguish, his peculiar despair. After a while his precise appearance began to fade, along with his exact words. All that remained of him in her memory was his sadness.

Next came the anger, slowly rising up within her. It simmered for a time, then erupted into outright resentment. At that moment she'd decided this man was responsible for untold misery in her family and her own life. The premature deaths, the pall of grief over generations, the constant danger—it was all because of him. His personal battles and agendas had brought undeserved heartache to herself, her parents, and their extended family. And now he had the gall to run off into his private pain and leave her to a captivity intended for him!

With her eyes closed, her limbs coiled in a fetal ball, she began to picture her impending death. A fiery moment of agony, no doubt, and then what? Rather than venture into the unknown she preferred to imagine her corpse. Motionless, cooling to the touch, grown pale and gruesome with its inevitable bullet hole somewhere on a vital spot.

Nora began to seethe. What a coward he had been, leaving

her to this! What a sorry, self-indulgent . . .

Then she felt someone.

She recoiled in her tight resting place, but no door had opened, and no physical cue whatsoever indicated the entry of another person. It didn't feel like the approach of her tormentor, the one who had visited her a half-dozen times since her being locked up in here. And yet it seemed as palpable as a hand on her arm. A very specific sense of another human being, just above her right shoulder. A male presence, strong yet also tender. Compassionate. How she could ascertain these qualities she could not say; they simply emanated like a fragrance. She shook her head in disbelief, but the feeling did not diminish.

A face began to materialize in the gloom. Or the outline of a face, characterized not by form but by a frame of negative space, its edges not illuminated by light but by a lesser depth of blackness. Farther out she glimpsed a pair of broad shoulders. The face altered, and she saw a smile ripple across the dim features.

"Who are you?" she whispered.

"A friend," said a voice, though she was unable to tell if it was audible or spoken into her mind.

"Do not give in to the hate," the voice said. Again, whether this came from his moving lips, she couldn't say for certain. "It is a lie. Here now, close your eyes."

She closed her eyes and felt peace come over her, like a warm oil trickling down from her forehead erasing not only discomfort but every form of distress. The relief was so acute and different from her recent discomfort that she suddenly fought the urge to weep.

"Where would you most want to be right now?" the voice asked.

She thought about the claustrophobic compartment that had surrounded her for hours now, and replied, "The Rockies. Near a tiny stream feeding a very still lake."

She heard the gurgle first—the soft, liquid trickling making its way through a forest. The sun then appeared, and with it a mountain breeze that caressed her cheek. A speckled green trout jumped from the stream's surface. Up ahead a crystalline lake shimmered in the midday sun, reflecting a stony peak and an impossibly blue sky.

"Oh, thank you," she heard herself say.

Her eyes still closed, herself still sitting beside the mountain stream, she reached out for the newcomer. She groped forward blindly, but the man was gone. Then she remembered. Lazarus had told her of spiritual beings giving him companionship in the blackness of his dungeons. She had come to believe a great deal since meeting her mysterious ancestor. Somehow now, this latest visit did not come as such a shock.

Whatever it turned out to be, she told herself, it was wonderful. And she felt grateful.

Nora spent the next four hours of her captivity lounging in the alpine meadow, as blissful as a child.

ROME

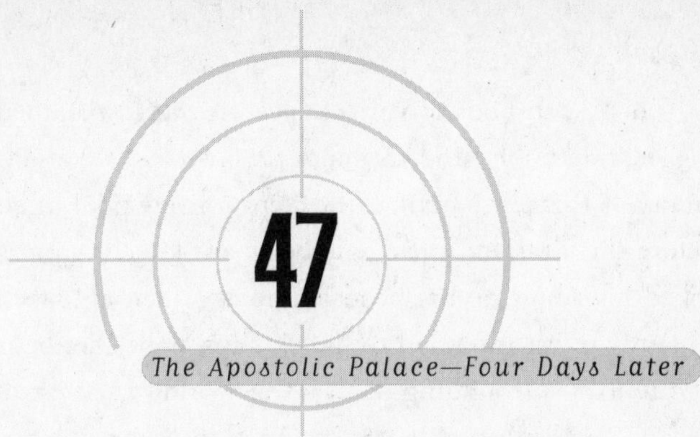

47

The Apostolic Palace—Four Days Later

DAWN BLUSHED AGAINST a low veil of clouds and kissed the curve of St. Peter's as it had every morning for centuries. As it had on that spring day in 1626 when the dome had stood shorn of its scaffold filigree for the first time in nearly a hundred years—and nearly 140,000 dawns since then. As it had on several hundred mornings not so long ago when German tanks had lurked in gray columns just outside the Vatican walls. As it had on that morning a half millennium before, long before the dome's intrusion on the Roman sky, when the dawn had slowly brightened over a square thick with the tents and soldiers of the invading Emperor Charles V and piles of corpses and the moans of dying and defiled nuns.

The very spot where, on another morning further in time still, a small knot of Christians had clung to the shadows and scurried away from the secret vault hiding the remains of their venerated spiritual leader, Peter, skirting the once marshy farmland of *Vaticanus*, circus of Caligula, former garden of his royal mother, Agrippina, towered over by his Egyptian obelisk that would one day mark the very center of Piazza San Pietro.

Today, nuzzled beside the gigantic dome, sat the four-storied Apostolic Palace, a squat little box of an edifice by comparison. Yet inside its walls lay the seat of Vatican power, the day-to-day haunt of the pope—Bishop of Rome, heir to St. Peter, Vicar of Christ.

The fourth-floor private chapel with its low stained-glass ceiling, marble floors, and intimate proportions, stood darkened and empty at this early hour. All except for one pool of electric light before the altar and the single occupant kneeling in its glow. The robed man bowing his head before a golden crucifix was in fact the only priest intended to use this space, besides being the ruler of the 108 surrounding acres—the world's smallest autonomous nation—and spiritual leader of one-fifth of the human race.

At the chapel's rear doors stood Pope Peter III's two private secretaries, his secretary of state, and two Swiss Guards, waiting in a state of anxious irritation. The stop here had been unscheduled, prompted by an early morning news bulletin reporting that tensions between western Europe, Israel, and the world's Arab nations were growing more and more vehement. The pope was supposed to be taking breakfast in his private quarters at this moment, two floors above where they currently waited.

The secretary of state, a stout middle-aged Italian, bridled especially at this sort of diversion. This new pope was always falling to his knees during every crisis, instead of taking action like a vigorous pope ought—calling world leaders, issuing eloquently drafted encyclicals and worldwide press releases. There were practical measures to be taken, rather than running to God with every new geopolitical contingency. But such was the nature of this pope; a notoriously pious man, with a greater trust of the spiritual than the material world.

There was a commotion, a new arrival. A parish-level priest appeared out of nowhere, showing papers to the guards. The senior guard glanced from the documents over to the secretary of state with a look the prelate had never seen him adopt before; a mixture of surprise and innate mistrust. The secretary stepped forward, taking in the priest's demeanor as he walked. The man carried an unusual bearing for a street-level priest; his eyes harbored a weary yet highly intelligent cast. He was neither agitated nor angry, yet a palpable intensity seemed to radiate from his face.

The secretary scanned the proffered papers. The top sheet was a form even he had rarely seen, a personal invitation from the pope himself. Not the pro forma audience invitations celebrities brandished upon their arrival to the Palace, but a personal appearance request. It was written in Latin, signed and dated in real ink over three weeks before. He shuffled the papers. All the usual Vatican passes and visitor clearances had been issued.

The visitor bowed his head and removed a necklace which he slowly lowered onto the secretary's open palm. The older man glanced down at its design: two overlapping circles, one solid, the other hollow. Intriguing.

"Would you give this to His Holiness when he rises from prayer?" the visitor asked in a faintly French accent.

"I'm sorry, but that is entirely impossible," started the secretary's typical reply.

"Please, sir, just show him the necklace, and he'll know what to do," the man insisted.

"What is the problem?" came a voice from behind them. The guards parted, and the figure of the pope emerged, his private moment finally over.

The secretary noticed that the visitor hardly bowed as he handed the pope the necklace and the invitation. The pontiff held up the necklace and immediately stiffened. He coughed, then dropped the papers to the floor. The man did not react but tore open his clerical collar and began unbuttoning his shirt. The pope froze and stood watching intently as though he had known what was coming.

The man-priest exposed his bare chest. There a small tattooed version of the necklace symbol lay just below the hollow of his throat.

"I need your help," the newcomer said in a strangled voice.

The unthinkable happened next. The pope began to sink to

his knees. A small cry rose in unison from the lips of the private secretaries gathered around, but Peter waved them away distractedly, his eyes still fixed on the visitor. The younger of the Swiss Guards reached for the nine-millimeter pistol hidden in his tunic while his partner took a threatening step toward the stranger.

The pope's knees touched the floor. He removed his cap with one hand and took the visitor's hand with the other. Then he kissed it.

"Sir," protested the secretary of state, "this is most unseemly."

The pope turned to him and said, "Do you know who this is? Do you, archbishop?"

"No, Your Holiness."

"Then be quiet! You know not of what you speak!"

Now it was the priest's turn to act; he grasped the pontiff by the forearms and helped him back to his feet. "Please," he said, "there is no need. I am just a man. A man who was altered."

Once standing again, the pope looked around frantically. To his staff he asked, "Did anyone besides you see him enter?"

"No one outside the Curia saw me come in," the stranger said.

"Then let us go to my apartments right away." The pope turned to the oldest of his secretaries. "Mario, cancel my schedule today. And not for health reasons, as you can attest."

They walked together in silence down the wide marble hall to the pope's private elevator. A guard inserted the key and the door slid open. The pope motioned for his visitor to step inside, then turned to the others and held up a hand in a gesture of warning.

"Do not follow us. Genevieve can enter with coffee and wine and a few biscuits. That is all."

And the door shut over the pair.

Once inside, Peter turned to Lazarus and grasped his wrist. "I am so sorry to learn of what happened to the Order. I know how much they meant to you."

"Thank you," he responded with a sudden quaver of emotion in his voice. "Father Thierry always spoke highly of you, sir."

"I have waited anxiously to meet you ever since learning of your . . . your existence. What should I call you? Your true name? A pseudonym?"

Lazarus smiled. "I have not been accustomed to being addressed by my true name in a very, very long time. But perhaps now is a good time to start again. Lazarus." He seemed to taste, to relish the feel of it in his mouth. "Lazarus."

"Lazarus it is. There's no reason why you of all people should not be allowed to call me Peter."

Lazarus nodded. He already liked this man. "Thank you. You know, I'm beginning to think that if all the popes and priests I'd known had been like you, I'd still be a Catholic in good standing."

The pope smiled and walked through a narrow hallway into an expansive, lushly furnished suite. He sat in an armchair and motioned for Lazarus to do likewise.

"Yes, I was told that you have long since taken up with Martin Luther and his upstart little movement." He chuckled, touching his chin with two fingers. "You may not know this, but in fact we've been holding conciliation talks with many Protestant leaders for years. The time has long passed since we considered Protestants to be vile heretics."

"I assumed as much," Lazarus replied. "For myself, I'm no more a Protestant than I am a Catholic. I am but a wayfarer, a follower of the one true God. That is all."

"Well stated," said the pope.

"If you had witnessed the outrages and disgraces I've seen carried out in the name of the Church," Lazarus continued, "I have little doubt you would have abandoned Catholicism as well."

After pausing a moment to evaluate this statement, Peter said, "Ah. You mean in centuries past. The Middle Ages and such."

Lazarus nodded.

"You must forgive me. I've not yet become accustomed to the idea of speaking to someone who has lived for . . . so long."

"Of course. I'm speaking of priests who owned serfs and treated them like slaves, who kept mistresses, who demanded bribes to perform spiritual functions. Surely you know the history."

"Yes," said Peter, his expression lost in a somber fog.

"What I'm trying to say is that my defection from the Church was in no way a repudiation of my faith. I simply quit a corrupt bureaucracy in favor of its idealistic reformers. And, in time, many of those reformers themselves fell prey to the same lust for power and control. I have had a hard time interacting with the faithful, especially as I have lived through so many of the events in question. It's been hard to watch the most incredible events of my life become watered down. Domesticated. Commercialized."

"I think I understand," Peter said. "I truly do. So how can I help you?"

USS Anaconda, Atlantic Ocean

NORA OPENED HER EYES again to pitching shadows, to the smell of her own dried vomit and urine-soaked clothes. The tiny bunk room was dark, its tiny porthole revealing only night and raindrops which mirrored a light on deck. Her eyes sluggishly reported an alarming sight. He was near. The man who had paid her three or four visits since her arrival. He must have seen her eyes sag open, for he leaned in and spoke in a voice saturated with menace and a childish, animalistic relish.

"I see you're awake. Just in time for us to make port. What a moment. What a glorious moment you're sharing in. History making, really."

He shifted his weight and leaned in closer to her.

"Did I tell you I am a bishop? A spiritual leader, as they say." He said the words as if each one gave him a shiver of pleasure. "Well, I wouldn't be the first man of the cloth to go astray when alone with the female form."

With a vicious slash he tore at her shirt, leaving her half-exposed. She screamed, quickly pulled the tatters together and glared at him.

"Do you know how ridiculous the whole vow of chastity thing is? Of all the torments I've had to endure in this masquerade of priesthood, that is the worst. And do you know the cruelest twist of all?" His eyes ignited with a vengeful look. "The way they decorate the blessed Vatican, gathering place of grudging virgins, global shrine to self-denial? With statues of nude women!" He was shouting now. "That's right! Statue after statue of women, exquisitely rendered! That's what we see all day long as we sit around mortifying the flesh and plotting the perpetuation of morality around the world. Do you smell the irony? Do you feel it caress you?" His head shook with some private indignation; his lips contorted in a grimace.

Nora pulled her knees up against herself. Instead of striking her, as he'd done several times in his early visits, he looked away, his interest distracted by something. He began speaking quietly toward the porthole.

"Believe me, if I wanted to take you, or allow you to be taken, it would have happened a long time ago. But Master says no. Master says the woman is to stay as enticing a bait as we can keep her. Keep her sleeping, clean her up at the end. But don't be fooled, little girl. You're going to die in less than a week's time. It might be a bullet, or maybe a blade to your throat. But it's going to happen soon."

A curious sensation began to wash over Nora, similar to the tingling on the back of her neck that had come to signal the arrival of her strange, ethereal companions. Yet it was different as well.

It was peace. Peace now flooded her innermost being. She was reconciled with the thought of dying. At peace with the prospect of leaving this realm of suffering and struggle, to rejoin her family. Thrilled even at the thought of spending eternity in the company of the ones who had come to give her such comfort in the last few days.

He broke the silence, seemingly irritated at her lack of interest.

"Would you like to know what will happen to your friend?"

She only smiled, still floating in a sea of contentment.

"Huh? Aren't you curious what Master has in store for your immortal ancestor?"

Her gaze finally focused into his, and her smile of ambivalence grew more direct.

"Well, I'll tell you! Your beloved friend will rot until the end of time, locked away in a nuclear waste container twelve thousand feet under the sands of Nevada! Let's see the priests find him there!"

At that he began to laugh, loudly.

"Your Master is lying to you," Nora said with a thick rasp in her voice. "He doesn't want me unharmed so I can look presentable. He wants me unharmed because he knows if you touch a hair on my head, Lazarus will track him down to the ends of the earth if need be and consign his spirit to hell forever, and he will probably have to kill you for his troubles."

"Stop!" he shouted. "You were better off staying quiet." He had said this in the most normal, human voice she'd heard him speak yet. " 'Cause I may just like the sound of that. Death can be a mercy, you know. Shall I tell you of your father's death? How Master tortured him for days with little more than a pocketknife and a pair of tweezers? Death certainly came as a mercy to him, I tell you. Oh yes, and it wasn't even necessary. Your ancestor was already under control. Master had no need to lure him. He did it for nothing more than revenge."

A dull chill throbbed across her chest, and it had nothing to do with the gruesome words. No, it was the realization that the man speaking these words hadn't been the one who carried out the acts he spoke of. Only then did the knowledge drench her like a sheet of ice water: *So demons do exist.* She'd come to believe in angels these last few days, but had given little thought to their spiritual counterparts: disembodied spirits who invade and occupy willing human bodies. A pitiful human specimen like the one before her. She squinted and tried to get a better look, to picture what the man might have been like before becoming possessed.

A thought came to her, and with it returned the sweet wave of serenity. All of her family members had been visited by these good angels before they died. None of them had passed away in terror or fear. All had been given previews of eternity similar to those she had swam in for the past several days. She felt the burden leave her—a lifting of the weight of her self-imposed quest for answers, for resolution and justice. It was all moot. Important only from the puniest of earthbound, myopic perspectives. She felt as if she were looking down on her life, her world, even this place of confinement, from a great height of calm understanding.

Nora found herself speaking again, fueled by a blissful ferocity. "There's no comparison between my father's death and yours. He's in heaven right now, in eternal bliss, whereas you are on your way to hell. Not much in common there."

A grunt of protest. The man shook his head wildly several times as though trying to shake her words from his mind. Then a needle glinted in the faint light. A familiar pinprick stung her arm, and her world went mercifully black.

48

The Vatican

THE DOORS OF THE PAPAL apartments remained shut all day, and the lights burned late that night. Outside, a cordon of personal secretaries and assorted handlers milled anxiously about. The two men spoke far into the morning hours, discussing everything from the real goings-on at the Council of Trent to the bloody fate of the Albigensians. Most of all, Peter urged Lazarus to make himself known to the world, to make himself the greatest evangelist who ever lived. "Millions would come to God once your identity was proven," Peter argued.

At that Lazarus only shook his head. "I regretfully disagree. Through the years all kinds of supposed proofs and irrefutable arguments have surfaced to defend the faith. Yet someone steeled against God will find any reason to deny even a seemingly airtight case. They will dodge the inevitable. All that would happen would be my becoming a circus sideshow."

In spite of Lazarus's opinion, Peter proved persistent, amiably pressing him again and again to consider going public. Each time Lazarus patiently declined.

Finally, after having given up his quest around three in the morning, Peter took a deep breath and fixed his guest with an intense look. Both men had long since stretched out on the apartment's antique divans.

"I have to ask you," he began in a hushed voice. "Any pope,

indeed any Christian, would be a fool not to ask you." His voice then grew even more breathy as he whispered, "What was he like? Jesus, I mean. What was it like to speak to him? To spend time with him?"

Lazarus smiled, stared up at the gold-inlaid molding that adorned the ceiling. He started suddenly, with a wry smile. "He could be maddening, you know. During unguarded, ordinary times of the day, he could seem amazingly distant. Not because he was unfriendly or haughty, of course, but distant in the truest sense of the word. He often appeared wrapped up in something beyond us, some thought or controversy or spiritual pondering we hadn't quite grasped.

"When I addressed him during those times, he'd turn back at me with a look so intense I thought it would burn my skin. Sometimes I wondered if he was angry with me—that is, until he began speaking to me like a mother might speak to her child.

"He hardly ever answered a question straight, either. I think the apostles captured that beautifully. And just when people had decided he was brain-addled, he would say something so insightful, so perfectly suited to our deepest need, we knew he was not of this world.

"There were certain times when I thought I'd go crazy trying to figure him out. But I never lost the overwhelming impression that I was in the presence of someone truly divine, especially when the miracles began.

"You see, at first he was seen as just one of a thousand wandering mystics who stood on every street corner in my day. One afternoon my sisters, being always in search of meaning, brought him home as the latest of a long series of fascinating guests. Some people collected pottery or jewelry—my sisters collected religious crackpots. And I considered him no more than that when I first met him. Something unusual happened, however. Over time, instead of growing disillusioned and tired of him, my sisters grew closer and closer to him. I began to suspect he was manipulating them, though I had no evidence other than the time they spent together. I suppose I was jealous, too. My sisters were the two most vibrant, funny women I had ever known, and the three of us were closer than most siblings. And this man seemed to be coming between those bonds. So I resented him.

"Then I started listening to what he was saying. I realized he wasn't twisting complicated wrinkles in the Torah, or coming up with the usual farfetched interpretations of prophecy. He was speaking simple truths. Besides that, he wasn't self-centered or an egomaniac.

"And that is how he grew to be my best friend. He would even confide in me from time to time, tell me of what weighed heavily on his mind and heart. We began to spend time together as other than teacher and student. Sometimes I think my anger all these years has arisen from my feeling betrayed by my best friend."

THE NIGHT-BLACKENED SHAPE of a bishop stood in the shadows of St. Peter's Square, as still as one of Bernini's columns arrayed in their stunning row before him. The motionless head of this living statue remained focused on a location above the colonnade: the hulk of the Apostolic Palace above, facing the yellow glow of lights shining from its top row. The papal apartments.

Bishop Eccles's body suddenly shivered to life. *He's here*, whispered an eager voice inside him. *The man we seek has come. Summon your men and make your attack. Now.*

THE TWO MEN SIPPED COFFEE eagerly, like those who knew all too well that their conversation had sapped their bodies' capacity to stay awake.

"This present crisis," Lazarus explained, "is the direct result of the destroyer's work. He seized on every aspect of my release. The exhumation at Auschwitz, my desire to protect my kin, even the geopolitical implications of my identity. He brought Hamas into this for maximum disruption. And I believe the destroyer is going to escalate things very soon." He paused and took a sip.

"How will he do that?"

"By way of a provocative act. Perhaps something to do with the kidnapping of my descendant, Nora. I fear he's planning a horrible public death for her, something the whole world will see, just as he did with the Order. Or as with the First World War, when he exploited the world's political and religious alliances to drag us all into battle following a single assassination."

"Is that why you're here?"

Lazarus looked away, his eyes glazing over. "Yes, partly. The other part of it was just to find refuge, to be back where someone knows who I am. You don't know how terrifying it is, after all these years with the Order's help and protection, to suddenly realize I have so little support base left. And virtually no one in the world who will believe my story. I used to have these nightmares where I would become trapped and be unable to prove myself, or to contact the Order, or to access the various safe houses and money caches I have stashed away for my protection."

"Well, you have a friend here, Lazarus. I promise. And I will do anything to stop this."

Lazarus fixed his host with a brooding gaze. "You do know the other reason I do these things. Did they tell you of my mission?"

"No. I don't think so."

"I had a dream, shortly after becoming aware of how I was blessed—or cursed, as the case may be—with unending earthly life. In it an angel appeared to me and charged me with acting as the Restrainer as long as I remained here. The catacon of Second Thessalonians, the one who holds back the hand of destruction until the end of time."

"I see." Peter stared hard into his coffee mug. "Does this mean that if you one day disappear, the end of the world is upon us?"

"If I truly die, it is most likely. I have disappeared many times, imprisoned by the destroyer's minions. Sometimes I have even chosen to make myself vanish for years at a time, when I become weary of the world. I go to my cherished places and burrow in for a while. But if you discover that I have died, then be prepared for anything." He suddenly leaned forward, enthusiasm peering once more through the fatigue in his eyes. "Here is the role you can play. Defuse it."

"What?" Peter said.

"Defuse it. Take the religious heartstrings you hold in your hands, which are being used to play the world like a puppet, and cut them. Make a gesture of conciliation. If the world's Catholics are being manipulated against Israel, or Hamas, then forgive them. As publicly as you can. Anything but anger or confrontation. Forgive. Deflect. Take some personal risk and embrace the high road."

Peter nodded and a weary smile grew wider across his face.

Menwith Hill Intelligence Base, England

JAMES SCHORIE STORMED into the Quonset hut's spare briefing room as briskly and unceremoniously as if he'd just been summoned from down the hall, rather than having been awakened in the middle of the night, driven to a private airstrip and flown for the past seven hours across the Atlantic in a government jet. Netelman entered behind him. The two men had barely spoken during the long flight over, their already tenuous relationship now genuinely hostile after the disastrous results of Operation's intervention in Paris.

Agent Stayton sat just beside the head of the table. Across from him, his hands loosely clasped on the tabletop, a young man in a clerical collar sat and studied the grain of the wood. Two dark-suited men sat beside him wearing clearly possessive scowls. Schorie steered himself to the head of the table and took the top seat, forcing Netelman to sit next to Stayton.

"Okay," Schorie began, "my first question is, what in the world are we doing here in an NSA facility?"

A wave of exasperated sighs circled the table. It was common knowledge in the intelligence community that Menwith Hill was the National Security Agency's headquarters for Echelon, the massive, international eavesdropping project. In fact, Echelon had recently grown so large and so effective that word of it had leaked to the European press, and citizens afraid for their civil liberties had begun to regularly picket its gates. Even the European Union had decided to investigate. So much for high-level secrecy.

"It wasn't my doing," Stayton responded. "Father Stephen here seemed to have made that happen himself."

The nearest dark-suited man spoke up in a Cockney accent. "We intercepted a call from only half a mile away." He punched the Play button on a small handheld tape recorder in front of him.

Father's Stephen's voice came on, muffled with static. "Look, I know you can hear me. I have no wish to kill the queen, but I need to speak with the CIA right away. I have information about the true nature of the Auschwitz desecration, as well as the recent terrorist attack on American soil. And Hamas has just conducted another operation, now on Irish soil. You know where I am. Please come get me."

"A rather cheeky thing to do," the intel man continued, "but effective. The words 'kill the queen' immediately triggered an emergency trace and a full recording of his words. We forwarded the call to Langley, who tagged it as 'likely authentic.' But until you blokes decide what to do with him, we have to keep him here."

Schorie turned to the young priest with the look of a principal addressing a most wayward student. "So. What have you got to tell us?"

"You'd like me to repeat what I told Agent Stayton?" asked Stephen.

"Yes. I'd like you to repeat it in full."

"In general, I'm offering you my services. I know everything about what is actually taking place. Secondly, I want you to know that Hamas has captured an American citizen on Irish soil."

"And what order do you belong to?"

"The Order of the Brotherhood of St. Lazare."

"Who is the person you people have been smuggling all over the place?"

Stephen paused and examined his fingertips as if to underscore that such information was not routinely produced.

"Come on, enough with the games, Father," Schorie said. "I flew all through the night to hear your story in person. The one you wanted to tell, remember?"

"Lazarus, sir. Lazarus of Bethany, of the Bible."

"This Lazarus, is he somehow alive and walking around? Is he the same man you guys dug up, the one we've been looking for all over Europe?"

"That's absolutely right, sir."

Whoah. Schorie squeezed his brow line between a thumb and index finger.

"There's more," Stephen said. "The whole anti-Semitic angle to this thing. It's being manipulated. Stirred up on purpose. The forces behind it all are hoping to foment a war out of this situation, and they'll stop at nothing. But no one in the Catholic Church was trying to slight the memory of what occurred with the Holocaust. We were outside camp walls. In fact, we were digging with permission."

Schorie let out a loud breath and glanced at Netelman. The

Operations man was staring sullenly ahead, probably stewing over his having lost his usual seat. *Tough.* Schorie was in no coddling mood. "What do I do with you," Schorie said, "and with what you've told me? Run off and join a monastery? Fall on my knees and repent?" As soon as the words left his mouth he knew he'd overreacted, said too much too quickly. This young priest hadn't said anything to provoke such an outburst. Schorie blew out another long breath in an attempt to give his overheated mouth a reprieve.

No way would he ever admit to these men how powerfully this case had shaken him—the sleepless nights, the late-night sessions reading his family Bible, even his first conversation with a priest in twenty years. He was a man of objective data, and the data in this matter was leading him in directions he could not process. Realms no intelligence man had ever, to his knowledge, been forced to invade.

"I'm not trying to proselytize you, sir," the young priest said. "I'm only telling you the truth. As for what to do with me, I want to help, to get involved. You see, I'm the only one who has half a chance of finding Lazarus. He's the biggest expert on concealment history has ever known, and I'm the only person in the world he trusts. Except for maybe his descendant, who just happens to be the Hamas hostage. Sir, give me some of your best men, some broadly trained black Ops guys, and let me find him. If he sniffs the CIA, you'll never find him again. Not in a hundred years. He'll disappear."

Schorie snorted, nodded Netelman's way and said, "That's out of my league, Father. Ask him—he's Operations. The one responsible for the capture of your colleagues, by the way."

Netelman scowled at Schorie, then turned and looked Stephen full in the face. "Okay," Netelman agreed, "I'll assign you some of my men. But you answer to them, not the other way around."

49

The Apostolic Palace

AS PETER AND LAZARUS talked in the papal apartments and a faint glow appeared in the eastern sky, five uniformed men began to deploy across the broad squares and esplanades of Vatican City. Approaching St. Peter's Square, the men walked confidently into the small guard office of the *Carabinieri*, the Italian regular police who kept guard over the square. The newcomers wore police garb, and when the lone watchman turned from his video monitors to greet them, the nearest visitor whipped around his arm and blew a hole through the man's forehead with an automatic pistol in his fist. Another calmly withdrew a rocket launcher from a black nylon bag, and the group walked out toward the Apostolic Palace.

Minutes later, in the utter darkness of a narrow, ninth-century stone corridor, one gunman wearing an infrared mask crept along the cobblestone floor of the *Passetto*, the medieval escape route hidden in a fortress wall stretching from the Apostolic Palace to the ancient fortress of the Sant'Angelo a mile away. He took up a station twenty yards from the corridor entrance, aimed his machine gun into the gloom, and whispered an Arabic word into a mouthpiece.

At that moment, two men wearing the traditionally baggy red, blue, and yellow uniform of the Swiss Guard walked swiftly through Bernini's famous Bronze Doors, the official entrance to the Apostolic Palace, and up to the papal apartments without being accosted. They carried more than the standard issue Stig 7.5 millimeter pistols; their coats were stuffed with hand grenades and ten clips apiece for the machine pistols hid under their armpits.

It was early, and few Vatican staff were about. The only activity in the area was the start of the pope's early morning Mass.

The pope and his mysterious visitor emerged from the private elevator and greeted the retinue who attended daily the pontiff's five A.M. Mass. Two new Swiss Guards came bounding up the stairs beside them, earning a sour look from the secretary of state. These men were supposed to be at their stations a full fifteen minutes before His Holiness arrived. But then, he thought with a sigh, like most entities in the Vatican, the guards actually answer to their own authorities.

Lazarus saw the men and felt a cold chill come over him. He blinked twice. At first he thought what he saw was the result of too little sleep, but in only a second's time he realized otherwise. There was something desperately wrong about the guards. He blinked several times again and wiped his eyes, but the sight would not go away.

Dark, menacing wisps of what appeared to be smoke curled and roiled around their bodies. The clouds churned with faces: reptilian mouths and hateful canine eyes seething with hunger and rage and agony. The apparitions clung to the guards' bodies like thick stoles of living, swirling fur.

Lazarus followed the pope into the chapel, caught up with him and placed his hand on Peter's shoulder. Peter looked back at him warily. This was an official moment, not the time to break protocol and divulge the extent of their camaraderie. But Lazarus leaned in anyway.

"Your Holiness," he whispered, just in case someone was listening, "we cannot stay. The Swiss Guards are possessed. They're planning something evil."

"Evil surrounds me on every side, friend," Peter whispered back with a heavy-lidded expression of resignation. "That should not surprise you."

"Yes, but this is to be an ambush. An attack, I'm sure of it. I can sense the same powers that have pursued me."

The pope raised up and paused, thinking.

Lazarus turned to look back just as a roar shattered everything about him. The wall behind the altar flew apart in an inferno of fire, smoke and dust, a shower of glass and plaster. Deafening chaos gave way to screams and moans from all around the floor.

Lazarus looked frantically around him, but all he could see was dust and smoke. He felt something against his stomach, although he couldn't recall having fallen. A squirming mass lay beneath him. He rolled aside and saw a robed figure rise to all fours and attempt to stand. He had somehow, unconsciously, thrown himself on Peter. He reached out for support, felt his hand brush the broken base of the altar and realized the altar had sheltered their prone bodies from much of the blast. In a split-second reflex, he had saved Peter's life.

He felt bits of hardness imbedded in him, and blood trickling down his arms and legs. Something told him this was not over. *The guards*. They had not caused this. The explosion had come from behind the chapel, from the Palace's outer wall. No, the guards were the next wave, just outside the door. He and Peter were trapped.

They had no time to lose—now while swirling dust still obscured the chapel interior. Lazarus pulled Peter to his feet and looked about him for anything to use. Instantly an idea jumped in his mind. There glittering on the floor lay the broken end of a large golden crucifix.

Lifting the cross, he thrust it into Peter's hands. "Go!" he yelled. "Just pray, keep this in front of you, and charge the exit!"

Bits of Latin phrases came to him; bits of the Exorcismus Maximus he'd memorized. He steered Peter in the direction of the door, barely visible through the haze, just as the bright shapes of the guards entered the room with guns.

Lazarus shouted at the peak of his volume, then pushed himself and the pope forward. The guards startled and raised their guns just as the cross's heavy beam struck them. The first guard was struck across the face and fell backward, blasting an errant hail of gunfire as he hit the ground. The second man fell behind him and screamed also, adding to the din.

They ran out into the hallway, their feet skidding through a carpet full of debris. Lazarus drew Peter toward him and they began heading toward the stairs.

"The Passetto!" Peter yelled.

Breathless, Lazarus nodded. It was the logical place to go—the ninth-century escape route popes had used to flee the area ever since Clement VII had evaded German mercenaries through its passages in 1527. As he'd told Peter in their conversations, Lazarus knew the Vatican better than most of its current caretakers. He had spent years navigating the Vatican's labyrinths, so he took the lead in their escape.

They rushed down the stairs with footsteps close behind them. A shot rang out, then a flurry of them. Bullets ricocheted down the steps around their feet.

"Hurry!" he shouted when Peter started falling behind.

They had three floors to descend before reaching the Passetto level, and it seemed to take a half hour to bridge the distance. They reached the floor and careened into a wall before regaining their momentum down a marble hallway. Above the pants of his own breathing, Lazarus could hear sirens.

But the gunfire had ended. He no longer even heard footsteps behind them.

The door to the Porta Viridaria and on to the Passetto loomed ahead. Lazarus froze, his feet skidding on the marble floor. Peter caught up with him and bent forward to rest his hands on his knees, trying to catch his breath.

"What's the matter?" he asked.

"It's too easy," Lazarus answered. "Anyone would know about the Passetto. It's a landmark. The rocket attack was a diversion, and now our pursuit has dropped away."

"You think it's a trap?"

"They expect a pope to use the Passetto. Yes, it's an ambush. I'll bet they have a man waiting inside."

"Where do we go, then?"

Suddenly Lazarus remembered. The year Columbus had sailed from Genoa, 1492, he had visited Rome and seen the handiwork of Pope Alexander VI's workmen on the Passetto. They had added a walkway above the encased corridor, on the wall itself.

"Not through it but *on* it," he whispered.

He pointed. Next to the Porta Viridaria doorway stood another, smaller exit door. They ran over and Lazarus tried the handle. It was locked. He grasped Peter's hand and shuffled backward, clear to the other side of the corridor. Then, on a nod from Lazarus, they both surged forward. They crossed the hall in a rush and struck the door with both shoulders at once. Old wood splintered outward with a crunch, and they found themselves sliding through cold air, outside now. A short series of steps led upward, to the top of the wall. They scrambled up the thirty-foot-high palisade as a crisp morning breeze tugged at their clothes. To their left lay St. Peter's Square, the basilica a hulking shape at the edge of their peripheral vision.

They climbed and reached the walkway itself: a narrow span between stone battlements that stretched onward, above the rooftops and streets of the Vatican, then on to the Borgo district surrounding it.

The throb of an engine above drew their gazes to a helicopter hovering ahead. They looked up into the spotlight glare of a police chopper. Its blinding light swerved behind them, and only then did the pair witness the damage done to the Apostolic Palace. The upper floors of the famous facade overlooking St. Peter's bristled outward from a charred, jagged gash. The smoking mouth of the wound was studded with protruding slabs of plaster, flooring, and shreds of carpet—the same carpet they'd sat on when, earlier that morning, the couches had become too stiff against their backs.

Eccles stood stock-still in the intact hallway of the Palace's first floor with his cell phone held tight to his ear. His eyes closed with a flutter as he spoke in a whisper.

"Do it. It's time."

On cue, in a unison made unnoticeable by the hundreds of yards between them, the attackers pressed the weapons' barrels into outstretched mouths. Without pause, seven sets of fingers tightened on seven triggers.

A strangely echoed roar like a distant thunderclap traveled through the decimated building.

Eccles stood alone in the hall, leaned back and cackled in ecstasy. *Seven souls released into the destroyer's gullet!*

No witnesses to tell the cops who was behind the failed assassination attempt.

But one still remained, one who hadn't obeyed.

That one remained in the Passetto, a gun barrel to his temple. His eyes shot upward.

Noise. Footsteps above him. The targets were escaping on the passage roof!

His mission was not over. The men were not yet lost to them. He lowered the gun from his head and instead aimed it at the stone wall stretched above him in the blackness. He pulled the trigger several times, but the stones wouldn't break under the onslaught. Ricochets told him the only target he would strike here was himself.

He scrambled to his feet and began running for the Passetto entrance mere yards away.

50

FROM DOWN BENEATH LAZARUS came an odd sound—the muffled roar of automatic fire, then the high-pitched pings of stray bullets. He whirled around to face Peter. "That's our trap, down below," he said. "He heard us. It's only a minute before he comes topside. Go."

"Are you coming?"

He almost answered yes, but then changed his mind. *No*, he thought. *No more running. I'm tired of fleeing, of always being the one escaping from danger. I'm making a stand.*

"I'm staying behind," Lazarus said. "But, please, you have to get going. Now."

With a reluctant glance back, the pontiff began to run along the narrow path, toward safety.

Lazarus turned back for the Palace, praying he could make it back inside before the terrorist reached the windows. He was a sitting duck out here. He sprinted the length of the remaining span while trying not to notice the hundred-foot drop-off on either side. The Palace wall greeted him like a stolid friend.

As he began his climb toward the window, a metallic reflection blinked from the sill above and a volley of gunfire angrily ripped the morning air. Lazarus ducked, then looked back to see that the bullets were striking far beyond him, just behind where Peter ran. The pope was now a dwindling figure two hundred yards down the stone path, dwarfed by Bernini's colonnade on the right and a row of rooftops on the left. Lazarus took a deep breath. Maybe the terrorist hadn't seen him lurking below the shattered window frame.

On a silent count of three, he launched himself up to the windowsill. What he saw burst upon his mind in angry flashes: upthrust gun, black-clad body twisting away from him, snarling features. The gun came crashing into his head, and he grasped the burning metal for sheer survival.

Then, in a rage, he did the unforeseen, the nearly suicidal. Instead of pushing against his foe, Lazarus took hold of the gun and pulled backward, into the void behind him. The gunman's body flew above his, both men's hands gripping the same gun, both of them tumbling down together.

He felt the rush of wind, then a sharp pain in his back. He struck the stone floor and everything went black for a second. A harsh voice shouted from the police chopper, but his mind was too overcome with anger and determination to translate. He rolled over to gain his bearings. The terrorist was already on his feet again, running toward him.

A foot slammed into his face and sent his body shuddering backward. He fell on his side and flipped over to catch sight of his attacker's black, lunging shape. In a desperate reflex he threw his feet upward, as much to strike the man as to protect himself, and kicked as hard as he could. With a grunt the terrorist was catapulted into the air and landed with a thud several yards away.

On the offensive now, Lazarus threw himself against the man, grabbed him by the shoulders and shoved him into the Palace wall behind them. The man's head bounced off the stone with an audible crunch that seemed to dim the fire in his eyes.

And yet the man, reeling, his head swaying from the blow, somehow regained his balance and swung a right jab at Lazarus's face. The blow connected above the eyebrow and sent Lazarus into an even more ferocious rage. Bellowing, Lazarus charged the man, seized him and wheeled him around over the wall's edge. In brief, swirling flashes of the drop-off, he glimpsed a crowd of tiny upturned faces gathered far below them. Specks on a sea of unforgiving asphalt. A wash of air gusted against his face—rotor wash from the blades of the helicopter that had spun around and moved in closer to the fighting pair.

The two men continued to battle—Lazarus pushing his foe backward, the other flexing every muscle in his body to keep from falling to his death. Suddenly the man brought Lazarus down with him and they both landed hard against the stone walkway. A blinding kick to the stomach had Lazarus rolling away.

Now it was him over the edge, watching more than occupying his body while it slowly, unavoidably, fell over the brink. His legs, then his torso tumbled free. He focused every drop of his energy into the frantic tips of his fingers, searching, fumbling for something to grab. Just as his full weight was about to give in to gravity and commit to the awful plunge, he felt a lip, a row of masonry, and managed to curl his fingers around two bricks. He clung by his fingertips, his feet churning in the air, the faraway sidewalk seeming to tug at him.

A commotion above him: the terrorist had withdrawn his mask and revealed a smiling countenance, beaded with sweat. He brandished a revolver, aimed it down at Lazarus's head.

The helicopter thundered even closer, and a voice rang out in angry Italian. A single shot fired and pinged off the stone by Lazarus's feet. A warning shot? The man grinned even wider as he pointed the gun's barrel back to the head of the one dangling.

Exactly how the doomed man found the strength would occupy spectators' minds for a long time afterward, but the video clearly showed that Lazarus *had* done it—hurled himself upward, so violently and explosively that he seemed catapulted from his precarious spot against the wall and straight into the terrorist's face. His hands grabbed hold of the man's shirt, pulled him over to the edge and hurled the terrorist over just as he himself came up on his stomach against the ledge. He looked down and saw the man fall. Then he heard him—a long wail. Then a harsh crunching sound. Through the deafening rotors he heard a gasp, then a wave of cheers sweep across the square.

The helicopter took off toward the Passetto to follow Lazarus's fellow escapee. It was then that the commentators, aided by the increasingly unsteady view of their zoom lenses, identified the lone runner to breathless audiences worldwide. The solitary one being pursued sprinting across the rooftops of Rome, pursued by gunfire and the gasps of onlookers, was none other than Christ's emissary on earth, Pope Peter III.

USS Anaconda

THE RENEWED DRONE of the ship's engine yanked her back from the sunlit bank of a mountain stream to an inferno of contorted pipes and deep shadows. She opened her eyes slowly and saw with relief that even the gloom of her prison still glimmered with a now-familiar luminescence.

Her friends had not left.

She turned and saw the face where it usually hovered—just off her left side. The face of a good-natured giant in his thirties. The odd sensation always returned when she saw him again—a feeling that the light bathing his features did not shine from some halo or inward glow but was actually the daylight from another sky—that shined upon another, more blissful world. His face reflected that light like the planes of a crystal, and the whole room shimmered with glints of mirrored color.

He smiled and she felt warmth return to her senses. Nora tried to ignore the filmy quality of his torso and those of the two companions behind him. She had learned that trying to scrutinize the oddities of his appearance only removed her from their conversations. And his words were far more important to her right now than his otherworldly appearance.

"You are leaving again," he said in that voice that, while audible, sounded as if it had traveled a thousand miles or more to reach her. "He has failed to capture our friend, so he is putting the last part of his plan into action. It will not take long now."

Nora swallowed hard, and thought of something. "Are you my guardian angel?"

He smiled and said, "I am one of them. My friends behind me are the others."

"Have you been with me all my life?"

He nodded.

Another thought struck her, a far less amiable one. "If you are my guardian angel, then haven't you failed? Look at my predicament. Here I am, kidnapped by terrorists, about to be killed . . ."

"There are so many worse places to be than right here," he answered with another smile. "You don't understand. Your captor thinks he has the upper hand. He thinks he is engineering another world war. But the only trap at work here is the one set for him."

"Are you saying you have a plan?"

"No. The trap is of his own making, although you might help by exploiting his weaknesses. Do you wish to?"

"Of course. Anything."

"Destroyer is not invulnerable, you see. For instance, when one of his followers dies, he will gorge on its soul, no matter what is happening in the physical realm. He is compelled to do so. And while he does this, he is incapable of flight."

"What do you mean?"

"His greatest danger is that Lazarus will approach his human host and banish him to hell using the Exorcist's Prayer. Usually he sees him in time and flees. However, if it happens when he is in the middle of gorging, he may not be able to leave. You can also delay his flight by restraining the host's body. Its limbs usually shake violently during the exit. If those motions are prevented, his departure will take longer."

Another voice interrupted, human and menacing. "Hey! Who are you talking to?"

She turned abruptly and shuddered in combined surprise and fright. It was him—the man who periodically visited her here.

"I said—who are you talking to?"

She pointed behind her. "To them. Can't you see them?"

He squinted into the blackness, and, slowly, Nora began to notice the glints of color materialize on his windbreaker. Then he saw them—his eyes grew wide and he leaped backward. An animalistic snarl twisted his features. His mouth opened with teeth outthrust like those of an enraged wolf.

"You can't harm me!" he hissed at them. "You can't touch me! I am embodied!"

"Yes. But we are watching," the lead angel said. "And Nora is learning more and more all the time."

"She can never know enough to harm me," he barked. "She is not a believer."

"Just wait," the angel said with a confident smile. "You do not have long."

With a growl, Bishop Eccles turned and left, slamming the door shut behind him.

Washington, D.C., White House—The Following Morning

JAMES SCHORIE MADE A pretense of looking down to read over his notes. In fact he was using his peripheral vision to see which faces he recognized in the elegantly subdued illumination of the White House Cabinet Room.

Next to the president's empty chair at the head of the table, he of course recognized the familiar bald pate of National Security Director Romwell, the man who had invited him, along with CIA Director Whiting at his left. He saw a smattering of generals in assorted colors, their stars glittering from their epaulets. He'd never been much of a Pentagon watcher, so he only recognized Chairman of the Joint Chiefs Walters sitting at the table's center. Opposite him sat a young woman who seemed clearly out of place, tired and ill at ease. Then Secretary of State Adams, his posture ramrod straight. Another pinched, self-conscious woman in a plain business outfit, with three other men in suits of fine tailoring, whom Schorie took for White House advisors.

An air-conditioner kicked on with a hum from some invisible alcove and pushed a cool wave over the group. They sat in awkward silence, lulled by the artificial breeze and the half-light radiating from dimmed, gold-plated wall sconces. Two of the generals leaned their heads together and mumbled something to each other about a lost bet on the Army-Navy game. They were sharing a private chuckle when the back door opened and a well-coifed middle-aged man bearing the most recognizable features on the planet strode into the room. The men and women stood in a sudden rustle of fabric.

Schorie had never been this close to the commander in chief before, for in latter years even the most arcane intelligence tidbits had been delegated to only the highest CIA officials for White House briefings. Upon the president's entrance a suffocating air of power seemed to cloud the place like smoke. Schorie marveled at the sheer relaxation global authority conferred on a body. President Maxwell exuded an awareness of his position from every inch of his six-foot frame; the radiance of a superpower chief executive seemed to trail him like a force field. In fact, his most potent aura of control seemed to flow from his lack of excess tension or motion.

The president walked forward briskly, a shiny, light-brown suit quivering smartly about his legs and shoulders. He flashed a quick, preoccupied smile, sat down without so much as a glance around the table, and flipped open a folder before him. National Security Director Romwell began to speak before the chief had even lifted his gaze.

"Hello, Mr. President. I think we have an assessment of the situation following the recent Vatican attack. Sir, this raid on the Vatican, on top of the murder of the priests in Paris and the previous desecrations at Auschwitz, has brought us to the edge of world war. This morning France, Spain, Italy, and a majority of NATO countries are calling for military reprisals against the Palestinian Authority. This has caused Palestinian Chairman Fulani to lose effective control of his Parliament. He's had no choice this morning but to join Islamic radicals in calling for an all-out Arab assault on Western interests. Egypt, Syria, Saudi Arabia, Iran, Yemen, UAE—they've all recalled their representatives from every Western nation. Israel has closed all borders, of course, and declared a state of emergency."

"Any recommendations?" Maxwell asked, still staring down at the document.

"Well, sir, because of the volatility of this situation," Romwell said, "we'd like you to hear from a few of our experts before attempting any recommendations."

The president rolled his eyes and shook his head in exasperation. "All right. Let's hear it."

"Sir, we've flown in Betsy Arens, the head archaeologist from the Auschwitz-Birkenau site. Ms. Arens is an Israeli citizen and a scholar from Yad Vashem in Jerusalem. She has some very provocative things to tell you."

President Maxwell looked up and his eyes suddenly brimmed with apologetic charm. "I'm sorry for the rather brisk tone here, Ms. Arens. I visited Yad Vashem on my first visit to Jerusalem and I . . . I was, well, overwhelmed."

Watching the chief, Schorie nearly gasped as a perfunctory film of tears developed over the president's eyes as if on cue.

"Thank you, sir," Arens said in a low voice. "Sir, my government has authorized me to report to you that we have produced rather baffling results from the site."

"I'm sorry, Betsy," Maxwell interrupted, then turned to Romwell. "Dick, is this absolutely germane to the political crisis before us this morning?"

"We believe so. All of these events stemmed from the excavation at Birkenau and the ensuing protests."

"Okay." The charming smile lit up again, focused back on Arens.

"As I was saying," she continued, "our reports show that a man was indeed interred in a concrete casing on September 18, 1943, by *Sonderkommando* workers under the direction of S.S. Colonel Wilhelm Gebhardt, a protégé of Josef Mengele. The casing was undisturbed for over half a century, until just recently when it was uncovered at a depth of nine feet and breached by a blow from an ordinary pickax."

"Who did the digging?"

"Well, that's a question for your intelligence sources, sir."

"Right. CIA," the president said, his eyes scanning the room for the director's face, finally coming to rest on the man sitting next to Schorie.

CIA Director Whiting's voice rang confidently across the room. "It was a renegade group of Catholic priests, sir, known as the Order of Lazare. A quasi-official group dedicated to the protection of Saint Lazarus."

The president shook his head in a sort of urbane incredulity.

Whiting continued. "We haven't been able to ascertain whether this Order is actually recognized by the Holy See. We do know that dozens of unrecognized, bizarre orders follow their own agendas and make their own trouble all around the world. Despite the pope's power, he exercises very little direct control over the world's Catholics, Mr. President."

"I know that," said Maxwell with a smirk. "I'm a Catholic myself. And I think the pope would sometimes like to give me a kick in the butt."

The room came alive with knowing laughter.

"We have conclusive proof of human habitation within the concrete chamber," Arens cut in, "and no sign whatsoever of human death."

"What?"

"Sir," the national security adviser interrupted, "this is why we wanted you to hear from these experts first. This," he said, turning to the woman in the plain business suit, "is Dr. Marion Byrd of the CDC. Doctor?"

Byrd, a strong, large-framed woman in her middle forties, gazed straight-eyed into the president's face. "Mr. President, several minute samples of human sweat residue were taken from the chamber and analyzed. First I'll tell you that its DNA matched that of the blood recovered from a very strange incident at Massachusetts General Hospital in Boston. Not to digress, sir, but in that instance a man died of massive gunshot wounds to the chest."

"During the attack by Hamas operatives against a Harvard student," the CIA director interjected.

"Yes, thank you," Byrd countered, maintaining her rhythm. "Anyway, after being declared clinically dead, the man stood up off the table and walked out of the hospital. And the DNA and cellular structure in question are . . . well, how do I put it . . . nearly superhuman. The cells, if you can even call them that, show an ability to maintain themselves through unlimited numbers of replications. Normally, cells die off after several hundred cycles. These do not; they radiate some sort of perpetual energy, and show mutations we have never seen before, or even imagined possible. All of them add up to an extraordinary level of hardiness. Practically an inability to die."

"And the chamber bore markings of ancient Hebrew," said Arens. "With linguistic affectations that date back to Roman times."

President Maxwell threw up his arms in exasperation. "All very fascinating, but what am I supposed to make of this? What does it have to do with whether we call DEFCON 4 before lunch?"

Schorie felt his hand rise, palm up. Almost like he was raising his hand in elementary school. "Sir, uh, James Schorie of Eastern Europe Intelligence, CIA." He felt his heart pump fast in his chest and his head grow light. "I . . . I believe the first inference we can draw is that the supposed desecration at Birkenau, which sparked this whole crisis, was not frivolous or malicious in nature. It concerned a human specimen that legitimately interested the different parties."

"Even the Vatican?"

"Well, sir . . . yes. I think the type of human aberration we're speaking of could be of enormous spiritual interest to those of a . . . theological bent. One could even speculate that he would be seen as like a messiah, a kind of deity."

"Great," Maxwell grunted. "Besides World War Three, I've got the Second Coming on my hands. So, Mr. Schorie, what's the second inference?"

"Sir, every scientific result points to the most fantastic conclusion. That is, some sort of super-humanoid was exhumed from that vault at Birkenau."

Maxwell began to laugh derisively. "That's ridiculous," he said.

Several around the table joined the mirth.

Schorie felt his blood boil at the condescension. "If nothing else, sir," continued Schorie, "it may shed some light on the

Vatican's motives. Our information is that the priests of this Order smuggled someone out of Poland and also, following the Boston attack, out of the United States." He paused, drew a deep breath. "And, well, we have a man who appears to be the last surviving monk, who tells me his Order believed this person to be Lazarus, the man raised from the dead by Jesus Christ just prior to the Crucifixion. That he was rendered immortal in the process of being resurrected. The pope himself may share this belief."

"Great," the president muttered under his breath.

Schorie caught a dirty look aimed his way from the director beside him, and all the air shot out of his balloon. "True or not," he said weakly, "the information may at least give us an idea of their agenda."

"I can say that the archaeological data supports this conclusion, however unlikely it may be," Arens added.

Schorie felt his shoulders relax. He had just gained an ally.

Maxwell turned away. "I don't want to deal with any of this pie-in-the-sky mumbo jumbo. I want to focus on the geopolitics, and on solutions. How do we get Gaza to settle down?" With that, he turned to the secretary of state.

The gray-haired, patrician head of Secretary Robert Adams turned toward the president. "Sir, my people tell me things are growing very serious, and quickly. As already mentioned, the western European nations are talking about military reprisals. The Arab world is likely to put its differences aside and counterattack jointly if that occurs. Israel stands in the middle, as usual, actively supported by no one past ourselves. I suggest either a lightning trip out there by myself or an emergency summit."

"Between who?" Maxwell said, now wearing his exasperation like a badge. "Chairman Fulani and the pope?"

"That wouldn't be such a bad idea, sir," Schorie heard himself say.

The room's occupants froze. Maxwell's gaze fastened on

Schorie, who realized that in the following moment his comment would either be laughed at or become the topic of serious consideration.

"Mr. Schorie, the pope is not an individual I can just order around," Maxwell said in a level tone.

Schorie let out a sigh. Outright ridicule had been averted. "No, sir. But he is amenable to suggestions coming from the White House." Schorie could feel himself sinking by the second. "We've . . . always found him to be quite open to Western concerns."

"Everything except the twenty-first century," the president added.

The sycophantic laughter started up again.

Something shifted inside Schorie. His cheeks burned with adamancy and a reckless disregard for his career. He turned again to the president, his caution and solicitousness now gone.

"Sir, permission to speak candidly?" Schorie said.

Maxwell shrugged. "Permission granted."

"I think everyone in this room is in denial. We're playing footsy with the truly decisive issue here. Mr. President, this man Lazarus, if that's who he really is, has taken up the great question of the ages—whether God actually exists—and dropped it on your front doorstep. There's no way to ignore it. So, before you can make a responsible policy decision on this matter, you are in the unprecedented position of weighing all the evidence now, and deciding if the Judeo-Christian canon is indeed based on fact. Then looking at your own capacity for belief. One way or the other, you must choose, and then let the outcome flow from that choice. There's no way for a prudent decision to sidestep the issue."

"I'm not sure I follow you. I have no wish to decide any such thing, Mr. Schorie."

"I'm sure you don't, sir. The subject of whether God is real is a profoundly disturbing dilemma, the great ideological punching bag of the modern age. Nevertheless, this case demands—"

"We all appreciate your philosophizing, Agent Schorie," Romwell interrupted "but I doubt whether this is the best use of the president's time."

"But it's not philosophy!" Schorie shot back. "That's my point—don't you get it? What's happened with this man has turned things like philosophy and theology into hard-nosed, rubber-meets-road national policy imperatives. Sir, before you can act, you must know precisely which forces are at work here, those provoking the situation. And it's entirely possible that, deep below the surface of things, this is all about these powers colliding either to assist or prevent this Lazarus from gaining the world's attention. Here is a man, a loose-cannon rogue, whom every nation in the world wishes dead, from the Palestinian Authority to the Cabinet of the United States."

"Excuse me," the president said. "Speak for yourself."

"Sir, have you read the book of Revelation lately? I mean the part about the world ending, fire and brimstone, the plagues? Do you want all that to take place on your watch, Mr. President? Because this man hasn't even surfaced and look at the global polarization he's already caused. We've got the Middle East about to explode, western Europe about to set off the detonator themselves, and the man has yet to say one word in public, yet to face his first microphone. Are you willing to risk what he'll say when he does step up in front of the cameras for the first time?"

The president sighed. "Okay. I can't believe we're having this discussion in the cabinet room of the White House, but let's make history, folks. Let's discuss religion." He turned to Schorie. "I take it you'd like to continue."

"I'm not a religious man, sir, but this case forced me to face these things. As I said before, it's unprecedented. No matter how heartfelt and real your personal faith, until today it was still faith.

You've heard of Pascal's wager? The old philosopher's belief that those who believe in God lose less if they're wrong than those who remain skeptics? Yet even Pascal had the luxury of not knowing for sure. That said, what do we in the real world do about this? The man in question—his surfacing will lead to chaos and war."

"So, Mr. Schorie, after all this, I trust you have a recommendation for me."

"First of all, Mr. President, I do think a reconciliatory summit would be a good idea. A way to defuse tensions for the whole world to see. As for the man whose emergence started all this, I would consult with a priest or cleric, and make up your own mind about what you believe. Personally, after much reflection, I believe the evidence overwhelmingly leans toward his being genuine—which is the most frightening scenario of all. We ought to do everything in our power to make sure he is either captured by his enemies before we have to deal with him, or pray, no pun intended, that he never makes it anywhere near the world stage."

The White House
1600 Pennsylvania Avenue
Washington, D.C. 20500

Dear Deputy Director Schorie,

In regards to your most extraordinary outburst in last week's planning meeting, I must say that I was both taken aback and quite impressed by your temerity. You showed courage in saying what you said, which I realize could have placed your career in peril. And yet you did so anyway, all in the interest of providing me with the best possible insight.

Thank you. Your boldness will not be forgotten.

As for your position that I must decide the veracity of the Judeo-

Christian canon, I was intending to write and give you my conclusion.

However, an irony of all ironies then occurred. God, and I can only call it that, took the decision out of my hands. You see, I have thought of little else in the busy week since that meeting. Carol can attest to the sleepless nights that afflicted me. She thought me troubled by the world crisis itself. If only she knew. Of course, she would have given me the answer at once. As you have no doubt read, my wife is a woman of great conviction.

So I decided simply to act as though it is all true, as though your mystery man is who so many seem to think he is. Because in my world, appearance is indeed substance, the fact that the pope, my scientific advisers, even the CIA, it would seem, all hold to the same view, will soon make it a reality. And since I am, in Time *magazine's words, "the ultimate pragmatist," de facto truth is to me far better than conjecture.*

I admit, I was poised to prove part of your challenge wrong, to show that it wasn't essential to make up my mind after all. I was going to make your ill-considered proposal come true and invite the old Muslim and the old Catholic to shake hands.

I was extremely reluctant to make this move, for I trust religious leaders even less than I do political ones. I was fearful that it might backfire in the worst of ways.

And then the pope beat me to it. You must have thought, on hearing of his bold invitation in the media, that I asked the pontiff to initiate the gesture. I remember your urging that I do that very thing. Yet I must admit that he alone made this move without any attempt on my part to sway him to do so. In fact, I will not be attending the summit, much to the Secret Service's relief.

Anyway, your speech had a profound impact on my thinking about foreign policy, Mr. Schorie, if not our actual conduct of it, and I thought you deserved an answer.

Sincerely,
David Maxwell
President of the United States

BETSY ARENS RETURNED from Washington to find the excavation site in a state of siege.

Driven in a local police cruiser like some junketing dignitary, she found herself being threaded through a cordon of riot police, dressed in all black, then the melee itself by a burly sergeant who refused to slow either for the field's ruts, which had since deepened into motocross-worthy obstacles, or for the ring of snarling, rock-throwing demonstrators. She felt like a collaborator seeing them: their youthful, idealistic rage, their Zionistic banners. But for a change in employers, she herself might easily have been one of them.

Was she in fact colluding with the desecrators of a Jewish site? she asked herself for the umpteenth time as she stared out the mud-streaked window at a banner proclaiming *The Church Collaborates Again!* It certainly didn't feel like collusion—haggling with the Polish authorities, yelling and bullying everyone from her own archaeological peers to the local diocese to protect the site for proper examination. She had felt guilty abandoning her beleaguered team for her grandstanding flight to Washington, but eventually the team had convinced her to concede that the trip represented her truest task as site director: to lobby the powers that be for their continued support. To keep them abreast of the latest developments and the importance of what they were doing.

The truth was, as she'd learned while at the White House, never in archaeological history had a dig proven more pivotal to current world affairs. Every world-intelligence body she had ever heard of was now looking over her shoulder, either searching for a face-saving escape to this standoff or for a reasonable explanation to a mystery that grew more bizarre by the hour. She thought of the CIA man, Schorie, and his impassioned soliloquy on behalf of the case's spiritual implications. He seemed to have been ignored by a roomful of sober-faced operations types to whom the whole discussion was strictly over their heads. But she knew what he was saying. She understood the true dilemmas of the matter; they stared her in the face every time she contemplated the mystery of that concrete wall.

Finally the car reached the makeshift fence perimeter summarily established around the site one night during a lull in the rioting. Already it sagged as though it had stood here for years. But then, as she had learned, nothing ever stayed new in the former Soviet bloc. A sullen young policeman slowly swung open the gate.

Betsy found that work had come to a near standstill during her absence, something she'd assumed would take place. The weather had turned wet and muggy. The ongoing demonstrations, with round-the-clock slurs hurled their way through megaphones and the occasional, far-flung rock finding its mark, had taken their toll on the team. The vault's bewildering contradictions had entangled the archaeologists into a myriad of controversies, with as many factions as there were mouths around the conference table.

The place had been largely examined, explained the colleague whom Betsy had left in charge. Their work nearly finished. Yes, there *had* been a man inside—the second in command had enumerated on adamantly outstretched fingers—who had somehow lived without adequate oxygen, carved a smattering of ancient

Hebrew into the wall's surface, survived continuously for a period of fifty-seven years (spectrum dating had just ascertained this) before being extricated from the burial chamber by half a dozen middle-aged men, presumably priests who had trudged over from the nearby Catholic chapel, and then disappeared.

"Can we go home now," the colleague whined, "and watch the *X-Files* with the Polish overdubs? 'Cause that's gonna seem tame to me now."

Betsy laughed briefly, then fixed him with a piercing stare. "Melvin, you're sure we're through?"

"I certainly hope so."

"No more layers?"

"We dug six more inches in all directions, took seismic impressions. There's nothing else."

"Okay then," Betsy said. "Let's clean up. The rest will come out in the lab, anyway." It was the archaeological slacker's typical excuse, only in this particular case it happened to be true. No use exposing her team to this much abuse when they had clearly extracted all they could. This wasn't, after all, the Middle East, which often meant replacement teams, midday breaks for the heat, and coolers full of chilled mineral water.

"Oh, and by the way, Betsy, there's a man to see you. Says he's from the BAR."

She frowned and then doubled back on the thought. Biblical Archaeology Review, *my foot. Hmm . . . Let's see which spook bin he'll turn out to be from. The CIA? NSA? MI7?*

Yet when she found the man crouching in the vault itself, peering knowingly at the concrete wall, she had to admit he was the unlikeliest spook she could have imagined. He turned to her and revealed a weary face with clear brown eyes.

An interesting person, she immediately told herself as the man's hand extended to hers in greeting.

"Max Helegeland," he said with a voice in which her

practiced Jewish ear discerned the husky timbre of another good Jew, one accustomed to hour-long chants in the synagogue. "I'm here to write about your extraordinary find."

"Yes," she replied coolly. "For the BAR, I hear."

His eyes shifted as if searching for his reply. The hesitation was all she needed. She turned away from him and began thinking about which tent should come down first.

"That's right," he said. "*Biblical Archaeology Review*. You've heard of us?"

"Oh, please. I'm a Middle East archaeologist. It's our journal of record. And I've never heard of you."

"I'm new on the beat. Freelance, actually," he offered.

"It took you this long to tell me." Feeling a bit disgusted, she shook her head. She'd received several of what she concluded to be bumps, or reminders of "continued support" from various intelligence sources, during her tenure. But this was the baldest, the most poorly disguised.

She turned to him, taking in his interesting features again and regretting the need to be blunt. But she'd regretted the need to be blunt ever since the mantle for all this had fallen on her in the first place.

"What in the world does the BAR want with Birkenau? This has no biblical relevance."

"I heard that it does."

"You were misinformed. Now tell me the truth, or I'll have you kicked off this site. Who are you really? Who are you working for?"

He looked at her blankly.

"You know what? I don't care. All I know is, you're not a journalist, and whatever your agenda is, it's far beyond my patience right now. So get lost."

Watching the man's eyes widen in sudden reassessment of his situation, Betsy surprised herself with the way she was treating him. This post had driven her to it, she thought. With the whole world looking on, she'd be eaten alive if for one minute she let herself revert back to the sweet young grad student she still sometimes imagined herself to be.

The man winced good-naturedly, a reaction which crinkled the crow's-feet around his eyes and made his face all the more interesting. *Shake it off, Betsy.* Lately she'd been increasingly afflicted with these sorts of romantic whimsies. She had to find herself a man, and quick. Hadn't had a liaison to speak of since her Jerusalem days.

"I assure you," he said, "I am no undercover operative. Although why you would think such a thing is another question." The man turned back to the wall and bent low. "I find this scrollwork fascinating. What do you make of the Hebrew inscription here?"

She grimaced and said, "I have direct White House access, you know. You have no reason to be evasive with me. Just identify yourself, and I promise to tell you what you want."

He straightened and laughed. "I promise you, I would. But I'm just a journalist, here to investigate the hottest archaeological story of the decade—or, who knows, maybe the century."

Pausing for a moment, Betsy decided to follow her deeper instincts, which told her the man was indeed no spy. She considered herself close to being a psychic in her ability to read people, and this man had none of the inner hardness the profession demanded. *A soft soul,* she decided of this one. *A broken spirit.*

She finally replied, "In fact, we find the inscriptions most peculiar."

"I would imagine. They bear some linguistic features that have more in common with the Dead Sea Scrolls than modern Hebrew. Here"—with an index finger he pointed to a place on the wall—"look at this spelling. That hasn't been in common usage since Jerusalem fell."

Not bad, she thought. *The man knows his stuff.*

"I've already interviewed some of the locals," he continued. "They spoke of this legend, what they call Judensargen, although the historical record shows no trace of a structure like this."

"There's definitely some unanswered questions here," Betsy added.

Unwilling yet to face the task of briefing the rest of the team and initiating the process of abandoning the place, she gave the man a tour. She spent an hour showing him the vault's most intriguing features: the meandering spiritual writing, the genealogical chart, the residue marks. Then she walked him through the adjoining tents as she checked in with the others.

At the end of the hour, with the tour complete, the one calling himself Max Helegeland leaned in close to Betsy and asked, "So, having heard the rumors before you arrived, what are your conclusions? Do you actually believe some sort of humanoid survived in there that long? And if so, who is he?"

Suddenly the feeling of his eyes upon her face felt to Betsy like twin beams of driving curiosity. Her instincts ignited at once. *This* was what he wanted to know. The rest had been pure formality. He had breezed through the site tour with the expertise of one of the members of her team, as if he'd worked on the site himself. This question was his true mission. Perhaps he was a spy after all.

She decided, however, that sincerity offered no particular risks here. She shook her head at him. "I don't know what to believe. The most obvious conclusions are too fantastic for me to accept. There are a lot of other pieces to this story, which somehow I think you know as well. And together they don't add up. At least to anything I can swallow."

Just then, her phone—the satellite phone given to her by the CIA liaison—rang at her belt. Betsy excused herself and snatched it up. She grunted her identity, listened for a few moments, then gave a cursory good-bye and hung up. The man was still watching her intently and she decided again, inexplicably, to keep him informed.

"That was Washington," she explained. "The pope is about to make a statement. He's going to Jerusalem tomorrow for what they're calling a 'Summit of Reconciliation.' The old Palestinian's going to meet the pope in front of the Western Wall, where they're planning to embrace. Make a gesture for peace and resolution of the crisis."

Helegeland seemed to blanch at that. Except for the smile spreading across his face, she would have believed he was dismayed at the news. He began to nod—slowly, continuously.

"That's a good thing," he said. "A very good thing."

"Anyway," Betsy continued, "since we're closing the site, I'm being recalled to Jerusalem for a briefing. I'm to be on hand for any consultations with Vatican officials."

The man Helegeland stared into the vault with a strange, faraway look—as if the enclosure contained the most cherished treasures of his childhood.

Of course. It all comes down to this.

Pope Peter took my suggestion. He called together the peace summit. The destroyer will try his best to stop it. He will try to capture me beforehand, or maybe even during the event itself. And he will bring Nora with him for bait, and for insurance.

Either way, it's the ultimate showdown.

The culmination.

Lazarus took a big breath and looked up to the sky. "I think I'll go, too," he said, almost to himself. His voice resonated with a thick tone of finality, as though making the gravest decision of his life. "I think I need to see Jerusalem." He suddenly turned to her, smiling oddly. "I mean, see Jerusalem . . . for the summit. It ought to be a historic moment."

"Yes. I would imagine it will be."

He stared for another long moment, then said while looking embarrassed, "I have a chartered plane, a small jet." He waved his hand dismissively. "They needed me here in a hurry. Seemed like your situation was developing quickly. So, uh, would you like to accompany me?"

52

Skies Over Romania

THE JET'S CABIN was strangely void of conversation, quiet except for the droning of engines and the creaking of leather when one of the pair shifted in their captain's chairs.

He had tried to keep up pretenses—the small talk, the friendly smile, the blithely invented cover stories—for the first hour of the flight, before the immensity of their destination had overwhelmed him. Instead, he'd lapsed into a dreamlike fugue state. His lips fell silent while his heart raced wildly in his chest. He tried to calm himself by staring out the window toward eastern Europe as it passed by far below them, but since he was still unaccustomed to the velocity of modern jet travel, the sight of farmland speeding past only reinforced the dwindling time before they arrived.

He turned to the diary volume he had brought for distraction purposes. It was one of the earliest, detailing the first century of his life. This voyage home had put him in mind of those days—of his sisters, his first home, and his parents. He turned to the beginning and began to read with his eyes half closed, almost in a trance.

Marseilles—a.d. 52

Martha died yesterday. I buried her this morning on the hill above the bay. She succumbed to no more than the weaknesses of old age. Both my sisters are gone now.

My life has been spent in the company of these two wonderful women. When I was forced to enter the boat and voyage here many years past, they accompanied me with no fear for themselves. Only of our being separated. Even the occasion of Mary marrying her Gaul fisherman did not diminish our bond, and his times at sea afforded the three of us much time together.

Martha's spirit never healed from the death of Mary, ten years ago now, and I must confess that neither has my own. The scriptures are certainly true about the curse and pain of childbirth, and of its dangers. Even Mary's child did not survive, and her husband was lost at sea soon thereafter. It seemed a dire cloud followed our lives from then on.

Martha spent her days caring for the sick and poor of the city. In the long evenings of summer she loved to sit outside our home in a chair I wove for her of olive branches, and look out over the island which obstructs the bay.

Today both lie on the same hillock, swept by the brisk, dry winds of Provincia, looking out over the crystal blue of the Mediterraneum.

For reasons only God knows, I have not aged a mite since we left our beloved Israel.

We did not speak of it, my sisters and I, although I often caught them in those last years looking at me in the strangest of manners. There were small, laughing banters about my youthful appearance, and the felicitous effects of this dry air and plenteous sun upon my countenance. But my sisters grew frightened of the truth of it, and in the end it proved the only subject we could not address together.

I have tried with great effort to solve the mystery of this and the only answer I can summon is that perhaps it is an odd effect of that which I am famous throughout the empire, my having been raised from the dead. I wonder that somehow the miraculous power of it has rendered my body outside the powers of time. I have cried out to God to release me of it, to allow me the normal cycle, yet my body remains suspended in time since that moment Jesus touched me from beyond the grave.

At one time I might have rejoiced at such a thing. Today, however, I find myself without the two anchors of my life, and even the members of my beloved flock here in Marsellus have begun to eye my appearance with suspicion. They love me, for I am their spiritual father, having brought the faith here to Provincia, but I know they cannot understand why I will not wrinkle and stoop.

I have decided to leave. I know not exactly where I will go. Perhaps as a missionary, or at least the guise of one. All I know is that I cannot remain here for long. My time has passed, my loved ones are gone, and my work of planting the Good News has yielded a stable crop.

I received word last spring of the Body at large. All of his disciples are gone now, except for John, who is reputed to have been exiled to the isle of Patmos. Peter suffered a death too horrific to describe, at the hands of Nero. Most of the others have been killed for their faith. Saul of Tarsus, who I met only days before leaving Palestine, was beheaded. He took the word far into the world so that today I am told thousands, including many Gentiles, embrace the faith.

It is a wondrous and incomprehensible thing that the events of my youth, however astonishing, should have such an effect upon the vast world. Yet I suppose it should be no wonder, for the nature of them, even of my own resurrection, are powerful enough to change mankind forever.

And still, none of these heartening matters bear at all upon the solitude I feel. Perhaps in the undiscovered lands to the north of here I shall find solace, or at least hardy company with whom I might pass my days until God wills that I should go home with him again.

Perhaps an entirely new landscape will allow the days to flow by unhindered, without the constant memory of places where my sisters and I walked and laughed and spent our lives. I will travel, and forget. And if I do not forget, I will travel even farther. Until I reach the end of the world and fall off its edge into eternity.

That, again, would not be such a thing to fear.

"No, it would not," he silently answered himself, looking up from his reading. If only the Lazarus of that day had known what lay ahead. No, it would have been too much. Too overwhelming. He turned to his guest.

Betsy, at first intimidated by the plush interior of the jet, seemed to have accepted the dearth of conversation and had begun to immerse herself in her reports. He eyed her surreptitiously while she shuffled her inch-thick stack of documents and scribbled notes. A splendid woman, he thought. Intelligent. Passionate. Assertive. How many generations of women had he known who possessed these same attributes yet had been forced by the oppressiveness of their times to bottle up their talent, suppress their innate authority? He found the women of today dizzyingly fascinating, with their lack of overt barriers or social reticence.

But even this remarkable woman could not keep his thoughts away from what lay ahead.

Israel.

Jerusalem.

He mouthed the words silently, savored their texture. A melancholy ache rose in his chest every time he thought of them. The land of his birth. For that matter, the land of his death and resurrection. A place which had never once entirely left his thoughts, his emotions, his very identity, for a single minute of his interminable life.

Yet he hadn't returned to Jerusalem in almost two thousand years.

For most of that time it hadn't been possible. Jerusalem had been closed, off-limits to Jews. He had to admit that with his skill in assuming various disguises and languages and his ability to pay the requisite bribes, he could have returned any time he had truly decided to do so. He thought back to the Norman lord who had offered to pay his way to the First Crusade. "*Go and retake God's City*," the man had bellowed over a goblet of half putrid wine in his dungeon. But Lazarus had declined, swiftly and emphatically.

It would be too painful. Over time he'd harkened back to this mantra over and over again, thinking how it would feel to revisit the land of his betrayal, the place of his deepest shame. He had walked the winding streets countless times in his mind, replayed the agony of watching his best friend suffer a horrific death until the internal montage had grown too painful to bear.

After so many years, the thought of Jerusalem had begun to shift in his memory. It came to acquire the luster of fantasy, the haziness of a thought so burnished by the mind that it begins to blur into the realm of the surreal.

Now Jerusalem had blossomed to life again, given shape and weight by the fact that it rested just four hours ahead of them. A mere formality of jet propulsion and a few hundred pounds of fuel.

He glanced at the cabin's galley and realized that he'd been a poor host. He hadn't offered Betsy anything since before takeoff.

"Would you like something to eat?" he asked her, stepping away from his seat and walking over to a small wall-mounted refrigerator. He peered inside. "We have Brie and crackers, some crab salad, a tin of foie gras, and wine."

"Brie and crackers sounds wonderful," she replied. "Thank you."

He returned to his seat with the food. She raised her eyebrows, smiled and said, "Look. I once dated a man who wrote for the *Biblical Archaeology Review*, and I know they're not in the business of lending their journalists private jets, especially for impromptu trips to Israel."

Trying to contain an impish smile, he said, "Really?"

"Really. So, given the fact that I enjoy your company and would rather not write you off as a pathological liar, I'd like you to tell me what you're all about."

Rather than respond, he handed her a napkin piled with a stack of crackers and a thick wedge of Brie. Finally he said, "I'm sorry, but I can't, Betsy. May I call you Betsy?"

"Depends. What's your real name?"

"The name is André."

She offered her hand with a smirk and they shook.

"André, were you already planning this trip to Jerusalem, or did the prospect of my company entice you to go?"

"I assure you, I was not planning this trip." He chose his words carefully. "And your company is an added bonus—that's all."

She smiled and accepted his explanation before taking her first bite of the Brie.

After a moment of enjoying the food, Betsy suddenly turned to him. "What I can't figure out is this. If you're not with the magazine, you're sure one whale of an expert on Jewish archaeology. Don't think for a second that I missed that," she added with a sly grin. "As a matter of fact, my field isn't so big—I ought to know who you are."

"Perhaps you do," he said.

"What university are you from?"

He shook his head with a sympathetic look.

"You're not from a university?"

"Not even a graduate."

She stared at him, hard. "How many years did you spend in Israel?"

He sighed, looked at her and responded, "I have never been to the State of Israel."

"That's impossible."

"You're right. It is. But it's the truth." Betsy crumpled up the napkin and started gathering together her papers. She would do no more work on this flight; she could sense it. "So how in the world do you know so much about the site?"

As soon as the words left her mouth, an expression of mixed embarrassment and bemusement crossed his face, and a slow, fantastic realization began to invade the corners of her mind.

No. It can't be true. Yet I myself argued that it's the only remaining explanation, however bizarre, however insane. I stood up for the theory in the White House, for goodness' sake!

Her mind froze on the threshold of considering the idea. It had been easy enough to argue for a wildly novel conclusion when its inevitable result was not staring her in the face.

"Oh my . . ." she whispered. Another notion hit her. What was she doing on a plane with this person—someone she had just met? The stresses of her situation had obviously dulled her judgment. A *guy shows up at your workplace, you talk to him for an hour, don't learn his real name, then you take off with him on a jet across the ocean? You get what you deserve, woman.*

And then to learn that he may be a freak, a human mutation whose improbabilities had bedeviled her work and threatened her career.

She'd been thrown off her bearings by the steady stream of government types, the ready access to cars and aircraft that had surrounded her trip to Washington. It had all been so official, so trustworthy. Somehow it had seemed to her an unspoken truth that someone with a jet at his disposal must be an upstanding, responsible person. She scolded herself for being swayed once again by the male trappings of power. *Wake up! You could be in danger here.*

"You're him, aren't you?" she said with a sternness to her voice.

He turned away. "Let us talk of other things."

But she would talk of nothing. Her eyes remained wide open, fixed on him. The shock of knowing—and in that instant she knew in her heart that the premonition had been correct—rendered her speechless, motionless.

"Are you angry?" he asked.

She shook her head and answered no. At that moment she discovered her fear had left her, just like that. This man simply wasn't frightening.

"Good," he said. "I apologize for the magazine charade. I think it's the flimsiest disguise I've ever contrived, but I had little time, and I needed to know your conclusions."

Betsy spoke slowly and had to work to keep herself from hyperventilating. "You're . . . you're the man everybody in the world is looking for." A question then occurred to her, and she began to feel a returning twinge of the fear. "What *are* you?" she asked with a voice that sounded more little girl than adult woman.

"I'm a man," he said. "Just a man who experienced a remarkable event."

"Don't tell me. You woke up one day and found out you were amphibian. You didn't need oxygen. No, no, that doesn't work. Or somehow you were born not needing air?"

He laughed at her wide-eyed brand of sarcasm. "Betsy, I don't expect you to understand. You hold a modern, mechanistic view of the world. In your universe, my existence is not only inconvenient, it's impossible."

"Yet you're here," she said.

"Precisely my point. I am a direct refutation of every theory you hold dear."

"Just because you're sitting here in front of me, I'm supposed to toss out every scientific thought I've ever entertained?"

"Not every one, of course. But the choice is up to you, Betsy. Before you decide, may I ask you a favor?"

A pause. Then, "Okay."

"Would you walk with me through Jerusalem? I could use the company. Besides, I've forgotten my directions."

"Where are you going?"

"To see this reconciliation ceremony. At the Western Wall."

He read on. Somewhere outside of his immediate consciousness the sense of his approaching destination grew stronger by the second. He read purely for diversion now, strictly to calm himself, though the subject only served to remind him of the events that had driven him from his homeland so long ago.

Mare Mediterraneum—a.d. 54

We are adrift.

Mary, Martha and I sit cramped together in a small fishing vessel constructed, I would guess from its build, for the temperamental waters of the Galilee. It has been a cold night, and sleepless. But the waters have been strangely calm, for which we are all grateful.

I still do not understand why we of all the believers were chosen for such a fate. Do we present a threat? I know the fact of my being alive disturbs many, for it is living proof of the supernatural power which flowed freely during the days of Jesus' life with us. Yet I am sure no one has since been given cause to fear me. Rather, I am sure to be viewed as a reticent, even cowardly figure in all these great events.

So it came about that, four nights ago, a band of what I can only describe as mercenaries burst in upon our home, armed to the hilt, and dragged us three from our beds. We were bound hand and foot and thrown into a wagon which carried us to the sea. There a man waited for us, a man whose countenance I could not describe to you, so wracked was he by the influence of foul spirits which I glimpsed writhing all about him. He gave us a chance to be run through by the sword. We all declined of course. He then turned to reveal what he had in store for us—this boat with no sail on its mast, no rudder or steering whatsoever.

To this moment I cannot understand what he meant by such an exile. If he meant for us to die, why he did not kill us forthwith. Israel is a place of sudden death and cheap life in these times. If he meant for us merely to be gone someplace else, he could have sold us into slavery or taken a dozen other measures to ensure our departure.

His men did throw us into the vessel and push us off into morning tide. Soon we were borne away on a current, and the shoreline of Israel shrank to a dark haze against an eternity of blue.

We hardly spoke to each other for the first hour, stunned as we were and reeling from the long night of terror. Slowly, as the sun warmed us, we began to thaw and quietly discuss our predicament.

Mary and Martha have resorted to praying, which I will soon resume doing as well. In the two days since our launching we have drifted steadily into the center of the sea. All sight of land has long since abandoned us, so that we have lost all sense of direction. I must say it is an adventure, one which might seem more thrilling if we could only be sure of surviving it. My sisters have resorted to huddling beneath an old scrap of sail to escape the sun. I will attempt to rig a fishing line, for we have become terribly hungry.

Most of all I fear starvation, a slow wasting with no food or water in this accursed boat. I could not bear to see my beloved sisters wither to skin and bones. I would like to think myself brave enough to cast my body overboard and succumb to the currents before such a thing would happen. But I fear I love my life too much, and my faith in God's provision is not yet extinguished.

As I write, I cannot believe it. Up ahead, at the edge of things, I see a dark towering line of land. I have blinked my eyes for several moments, but it is real. We seem headed straight for it. I must quit this scribbling and wake up my sisters with the good news!

JERUSALEM

53

THEY FLEW OVER WATER for what seemed like a full day. Just when he had finally succeeded at calming himself, he glimpsed something through one of the small round windows, at the fringes of his peripheral vision.

A bank of solid color rising up from the horizon.

His heart leaped inside of him, and he wanted to shout like a child. His lungs, his brain, his stomach went into roller-coaster mode, an exhilarating sensation that coursed throughout his body. He peered out the window, feeling himself coming out of his skin.

He had to regain control. Poise and mental alertness had always been his saving grace, and now was no time to lose his grip. He took a few deep breaths and willed his hands to stop shaking.

He looked out again. They were circling a city that might have been Tangiers or Nice; it swam in the same golden Mediterranean sunshine. A grid of modern office buildings flanked a palm-lined beach against which a long strip of foam pounded in slow motion. *How did Israel become so modern?* he wondered. Cars inched their way along narrow boulevards. The scene below added to the thrill somehow: to know that, even in this land he'd dreamed about, people were busy going about their normal business with hardly a thought to the place they inhabited.

A groan beneath them signaled the lowering of the flaps and

caused Betsy to awaken from her slumber. With the relaxed look of sleep, her face appeared even softer, more beautiful.

"Are we there?" she asked.

"We are."

She looked up at him and must have noted the excitement displayed on his features, the fevered intensity of his gaze reflected in the window. "So you are Jewish, after all," she said.

He turned to her, surprised at her question.

"Oh, come on. Only a Jew reacts like this to seeing Israel. You should have seen my parents on their first trip. Matter of fact, they live here now. Come to think of it, it's the most normal thing I've learned about you so far. I mean, I knew you'd written those words in Hebrew, but then when I remembered what you'd lived through, I didn't think you were even human."

"I told you. I am human. I am Jewish, too. At least ethnically."

A sudden lurch and squeal. They had landed. Lazarus jerked back in his seat with a mighty gulp of air as the reverse thrusters roared and the realization struck him that he was on Israel's soil at last.

"You know," he said while they taxied, "I was born in occupied territory. There hasn't been an independent Jewish state in twenty-five hundred years. Do you know what that means? Or how that feels?"

Betsy unbuckled her seat belt, leaned over and grasped him warmly about the shoulders. She pulled back and gave him a smile. "Welcome home, then."

Just then a wedge of sunlight invaded the cabin with the door's opening and with it a wealth of aromas. He breathed in deeply. Orange. Sea air. Kerosene fumes. His ears began to convey sounds to him. The roar of a departing jet. The amorphous rush of background auto traffic. The jarring clang of unseen routines being performed along the jet's underbody.

He lost the wonder briefly in the effort of keeping his head down as he stepped out of the fuselage, then the concentration to keep his footing on the four steps down.

Then his foot met pavement. And the other. He took a step.

Don't look like an overexcited tourist from Brooklyn.

But his knees buckled. His chest began to heave in a wave of powerful contractions. He fell forward. He felt his face meet the pavement; a searing hot crumble kissed his skin. He pursed his lips and kissed it in return.

It may have been an airport runway smelling of tar and creosote, but it was Israel all the same, and he was her child.

Betsy helped him to his feet with an arm around his shoulder, a gesture for which he felt grateful. He straightened up and looked behind them for the luggage the pilot had already unloaded. He turned back, and his eyes took in a sight that sent a shudder running through his already overloaded nerve endings.

Up and down the tarmac, in the shadow of a line of commercial jets, the forms of a hundred or so other pilgrims lay prone across the pavement. He heard weeping, the unsettling echoes of grown men and women piercing the air with loud, keening cries.

Betsy said, "You see, there's no shame. It's a part of life here."

A part of life here.

She led him through immigration check-in, a numbing flow of queues and desks the likes of which he had experienced before—only here they were much longer. It looked like an endless chore until he happened to glance up at the patch on the officer's uniform. A Star of David, blue against white. A badge.

Another chill ran through him. He was under Jewish authority.

Soon he was free, practically washed out with the flood of travelers onto a broad sidewalk, sheltered from the sun by an outthrust canopy. The air throbbed with the slamming of taxi doors and the shouts of tour guides and the clamor of people in every national costume of the world saying their greetings and farewells.

Suddenly Betsy stood beside him, having fallen behind in an adjoining customs line. She took his hand, acting maternal now, and tugged him forward. "Come. Let's get a taxi into Jerusalem."

He felt relieved to sit back and allow the sights to wash over him. The taxi surged forward, and soon the familiarity of an international airport flowed into a modern jumble of curving overpasses and freeway lanes.

The urban scene thinned out and they drove into an open plain of palm trees, low hills, and orange groves. He could hardly bring himself to tear his gaze away from the window and look back at Betsy. He saw an irrigation canal bisect the rows of a sugar beet field and stretch away to a cluster of farm buildings. A swath of water falling from a crescent-shaped pivot. Row upon row of bright green stalks.

"How green they've made it," he whispered.

How odd, also, to see some of the conventions of ancient Palestine—stone huts, Bedouin donkeys, camels—interspersed with such modernities as gas stations, telephone booths, and billboards. And how strange to see it all speed past him like this. It had seemed like such a vast place when he'd last been here.

They drove across the fertile plains for a few minutes before approaching a clump of low hills. *Judea.* His pulse quickened again. He knew what lay ahead . . . or so he thought. For instead, foreign-looking pine trees began to crowd alongside the highway. He frowned.

"I don't remember trees—" he began, and then caught himself.

"They've been planting them steadily since forty-eight," said Betsy. "But I thought you'd never been here."

"I said I'd never been to the *modern* Israel."

"Oh." She snorted in frustration and looked away.

Before long they had entered a thickening urban area crowded with busy intersections and compact European cars. They were weaving rapidly through the crush when Betsy leaned forward and spoke softly into the driver's ear. The man nodded with a blank expression. She leaned back, smiling.

They sped onto a highway, followed it for several minutes, then rounded a corner and nearly collided with the last of six tourist buses parked in a row. The driver cocked his head back and held out a hand. He spat out some words as Betsy shuffled through a stack of bills. She paid the driver and they stepped out onto the pedestrian-choked street.

"Come with me," she said.

She grabbed Lazarus tightly by the hand and led him in the direction all the tourists seemed to be heading. The curve continued its turn, its outer lane walled against a sort of drop-off, and then the thickest crowd of tourists parted for a moment and he saw through.

That was when she appeared to him at last.

He recoiled visibly, as though someone had struck him across the face. His vision seemed to soften and shift somewhat off kilter. He began breathing rapidly, faster than he knew was healthy, yet he could not still himself.

There was Jerusalem. Those familiar curving walls straddling that same hilly horizon. Its jumble of white, sardine-packed buildings roasting beneath a blue Judean sky.

His eyes danced over every detail, his mind desperately searching for images he had formed as a young man, a child even. In the foreground the Kidron Valley sheltered a sloping stretch of grass punctuated by thousands of shining tombs. The simplest details seared into his mind. The Valley appeared shallower than before. It had always seemed like a chasm plunging down to the center of the earth itself. Putrid smoke no longer drifted over the Kidron as it always had from the trash pits of Gehenna. But the pointed tower of Absalom's Tomb still stood cradled in its nest of stone. The Dung Gate stood right there, as before. He could make out the white forms of sheep grazing on the slopes.

But what absences he saw. His eyes ached to see the old Wall in its former glory. Or the stone massif of the Temple soar from its surrounding frame of ramparts, with its courtyards and rows of marble columns. Instead of the Temple, the Dome of the Rock shined golden in the light. Mocking him.

So much was missing. So much had been destroyed.

He gripped the wall for support, leaned forward and closed his eyes. He breathed deeply and the smell of what he inhaled almost overcame him. The scent of Judean dust warmed by the sun blended with a tinge of wafting sheep dung and olive wood. The touch of a dry, warm breeze drifting up from the Kidron. A faint whiff of roses. Somehow the fragrances made the place come more alive than ever.

He squinted to make out the path along the Kidron's flanks, the same one the Romans had taken to escort Jesus to jail on the night that marked the beginning of Lazarus's nightmare. Now a dozen such tracings carved their way through the grass. And yet he knew that down there, within only yards of his stare, was the exact location where the disciples had straggled lamely, wondering what to do, whether to attempt a rescue.

"Thank you for bringing me here," he whispered to Betsy at his side.

"You're welcome. It's the best overall view of the Old City. A tour guide's gambit, you could say. They get the tourists going with a warm-up talk on Jerusalem, then take them around this corner and say something like, 'Now you've come home.' And bam, here she is. There's never a dry eye on the bus."

"A worthy trick."

"Yes. I suppose it is."

He turned to her, his eyes bright and alert. "I want to go to

Bethany. For just a while. Will you go with me?"

With a bewildered expression she nodded her assent and turned to hail another cab.

They drove up and over the Mount of Olives and were in the town within moments. Lazarus thought back to the days when traveling from Bethany to Jerusalem meant several hours' hike over the Mount's well-trod path.

A multi-turreted church appeared beside them. He peered out. "What is that?"

"The Church of Lazarus," Betsy replied.

The Church of Lazarus. He closed his eyes with a wry smile. Yes, of course. He was, after all, a saint.

He squinted again, trying to superimpose the layout of his hometown over the accumulation of modern buildings. The hill, the slope of the land.

"Would you stop and let us out?" he asked the driver.

They exited the cab, paid the fare, and began walking down a crowded street. The familiar line of tour buses signaled their destination. He turned toward a stone wall punctuated by a small tower. A black sign hung at the tower's middle, its message written in Arabic, Hebrew, and English.

The Tomb of Saint Lazarus

Betsy stopped dead in her tracks. "Of course," she muttered.

He darted inside. She quickly followed and found him waiting patiently at the end of a line of tourists snaking down the steps. A smile played lightly on his lips. They waited for fifteen minutes, hardly saying a word.

"I don't believe you," Betsy finally said, sounding weak and scattered. "I'm Jewish. I can't believe you."

He gave her a look tinged with pity, and said, "Then don't, Betsy. Pretend I don't exist. You can leave, too. I'd miss your company, but again, it's your choice."

"Don't patronize me!" she said, and a little too loudly. A matronly tourist ahead of them turned around with a scowl.

"For that matter," he continued, taking the offensive, "why don't you discard all the findings of your research. Just ignore it. It'll avoid quite a few problems back at Yad Vashem, I'm sure of that."

She shoved him in the arm, spun around and stormed back up the steps.

He sighed, affected the smile of a man publicly rebuked by a woman, and continued to wait.

A few minutes more and his turn came. He stooped and entered the burial chamber surrounded by rock. He walked over, sat and shut his eyes. He ran his fingers over the smooth stone. Then slowly, without thinking, he lowered himself onto the unyielding pillow that had once cradled his head.

A fiery dawn courses through his limbs, races through his inward parts like the path of a rapid thaw.

The touch of a hand upon his forehead, at first barely felt, then a solid pressure, and soon the source of immense, welcoming heat that races through his every cell.

He begins to re-inhabit the decaying bundle of flesh lying on the slab to animate the fingers, restart the heart, send blood flowing through collapsed veins.

His eyes flutter open, send faint signals to his optic nerves and his sight strengthens, grows more definite.

His friend Jesus stands over him, his arm extended. The familiar face is streaked with tears.

"Rise, my friend. Rise!"

LAZARUS OPENED HIS EYES to a group of impatient tourists. He smiled indulgently and did not move an inch.

His resurrection seemed to have just happened a moment ago, with the intervening years reduced to, just now, only a dark chasm, an interruption.

Minutes later he emerged back into the sunlight and found Betsy leaning against the wall with her arms crossed, unsmiling.

She moved to him as he walked over, and immediately began speaking.

"You had to know what I knew. Is that it? Is that why you came to the Birkenau site? Everyone knows everything about you—CIA, Mossad, Hamas, you name it. And it doesn't make you any more welcome anywhere in the world. They're all scared of you, do you know that? They don't know your agenda; they're not sure what you're capable of. They only know that you haven't even surfaced yet and already you've brought the world to the brink of another war. Does that sound like a scenario for the red carpet treatment? For being guest of honor at the White House?"

"I'm not running for public office, Betsy. I don't care about that."

"Well, you're likely to catch a bullet from them if they find you close to a world event."

He turned to her with eyes suddenly gone cold.

"I know."

54

AT TEN O'CLOCK the following morning, an Alitalia Airlines 727 carrying Pope Peter III and hundreds of cardinals, bishops, and security agents landed at Ben Gurion Airport to a full military welcome ceremony. Israeli Prime Minister Ladich led the pontiff past rows of Israeli soldiers, then ushered him into an armored limousine for a circuitous ride into Jerusalem. The route, so haphazard as to foil potential attackers, would turn what was normally a half-hour drive into one taking well over an hour.

Ten minutes later a Cadillac Seville flanked by soldier-filled Humvees left the gate of the Palestinian Authority at Gaza and began the long drive northward, through Israel's coastal plains, toward the Holy City. Inside sat the weathered form of Palestinian President Fulani, once a reviled terrorist, today elder statesman and beloved leader of the Palestinian cause.

The moment the Cadillac passed through the Gaza security checkpoint, forty miles away in Jerusalem four young men took their stations in a small third-story apartment facing the Western Wall Plaza—the large esplanade across from the Wailing Wall. Three of the men dragged a table to within four feet of an open window and withdrew from black bags an assortment of spotting scopes, tripods, and sniper rifles.

Without a word, working with precise, swift motions, the men assembled a state-of-the-art reconnaissance post and sniper's nest inside of ten minutes. Then each of the three knelt at their respective scopes and peered out at the ancient site before them.

The fourth man, wearing a priest's cassock, pulled up a chair behind a scope and began his own scrutiny of the Western Wall.

The plaza had been cleared of the usual crowds by Israeli troops hours before the start of the Moment of Reconciliation. Its only occupants now were a smattering of soldiers, priests, and political officials along with four ramps lined with television cameras and reporters. Twelve hundred chairs sat neatly facing the wall in anticipation of the ceremony, a wooden divider through the middle to separate the men from the women.

Father Stephen considered the day's schedule. Between this moment and the respective leaders' arrivals an hour from now, a select group of invited guests would filter into the plaza by way of the high-security checkpoints at either end. He trained his scope on the walls of the Al-Aqsa Mosque and the Temple Mount overlooking the square. Each bristled with Arab onlookers, all of them supposedly screened and their weapons checked.

He shuddered. These Arab onlookers had a perfect vantage point and would soon be looking down on two of the world's most important leaders at one of history's most vulnerable moments.

And the terrorists were present, he knew it. His CIA companions had handed him a grainy photograph only an hour before, showing a dark, swarthy man holding a veiled young woman on a city street. "*Jerusalem,*" he had been told. "*This morning.*"

God only knew what means the CIA possessed in order to acquire such a photograph, a picture of one man out of the world's six billion. But they had found him. *Jamail.* He would be here today, probably already up on those towers right now. Planning mayhem. The madness was that the event had not been canceled. The weapons checks had merely been redoubled; the leaders been given a chance to back out, and neither one had done so.

One other thing Stephen knew for certain: Lazarus would be here. He was sure of it.

The Lions Gate—Five Minutes Later

HAD FATHER STEPHEN been able to aim his scope northwestward, not only seeing through the walls of his small perch but through the stones of several churches and prayer towers and city walls, he might have viewed the tiny form of a man dressed in Christian monk's robes standing beside the Lions Gate.

The monk—Lazarus clad in the robes of the Order—had waited there for nearly an hour when a taxi pulled up and Betsy stepped out. She walked over to him, her eyes downcast, her body stiff with hostility.

"I came to tell you I won't be walking in with you. In fact, it's best if we end this friendship right here."

"I'm sorry to hear that," he said. "Why?"

"You know why. I can't deal with you. Whoever you are, you're an assault on everything I stand for."

"Please, Betsy. Do not judge me. Don't decide right now. Just walk with me awhile."

She stood motionless.

"Please?" he pressed. "Walk with me. I could really use a friend beside me right now."

She remained where she was, yet he could feel her resistance melt by the second. He held out his hand to her. Slowly, she reached out, grasped his hand and turned with him toward the Gate.

They walked silently at first. Lazarus took ten steps through the Gate, stopped and drew a lungful of air. The city's smells wafted his way from narrow alleys and carried him back beyond the crowded memory of the last two millennia—to the time of his youth. He smelled mud coffee, flatbread baking, lamb roasting, falafel, the sweet aroma of the nargileh pipes.

The sounds as well. The shouts of street vendors, children laughing, the low murmur that rose from a few hundred acres jam-packed with as many people per capita as any city on earth.

His mind reeled, as if the whole scene before him were spinning on a wondrous carousel. It was really here, he told himself. It had never stopped; it had remained here all along. The ferocity of his nostalgia all those years had made it feel like his homeland had risen to a place of suspended animation somewhere in the heavens, rather than surviving as a real place of living and dying. But no, every day he'd lived those two thousand years—trod the forests of Normandy and Britain or the medieval byways of central Europe—the City had been right here, waiting. As a fact, he had always known this. Now he felt it in his soul.

Betsy's presence beside him made him think of Mary and Martha and how much they'd loved to stroll the City's lanes and squares on Feast and High Holy Days, days when it seemed the whole population of Israel had descended on Jerusalem all at once. His beloved sisters came alive in his mind more vividly than ever since their deaths: two willowy women with bobbing shocks of black hair, striding in purple and crimson robes along the traders' stalls with that vigorous gait of theirs, laughing so heartily that it would echo across the stones.

He began to recall old, familiar voices calling him from a great distance of years, people he'd once known and loved, speaking and whispering and shouting and singing in the various languages he'd adopted during his wanderings.

He glanced ahead. A single dust-strewn beam of sunlight flooded the lane ahead of them and shined across the beard of an elderly Hasid standing at a fruit stand, lighting the silver protrusion into a translucent, luminous sphere. The sight made his heart stop beating for a moment. A burrowing melancholy began to spread through his chest. It became hard for him to breathe, yet he somehow relished the sweet pain of it. The sensation was familiar, in fact most appropriate for a Jew returning to Jerusalem. The ache spread across his torso and flooded his body with a thick chord of emotion.

Passing, he heard the old man's voice haggling good-naturedly over an orange—rich with deep intonations and the pungent timbre of old Yiddish—and recognized the man. Or at least thought he did. How many hours had he spent listening to similar voices read the Torah, argue the Midrash, say Shiva? How many such elderly, devout men had he known? And how many buried?

Flowing like an ethereal montage over the street scene, his mind began to reveal the faces behind the voices. Faces that had stamped themselves indelibly into his memory and now stood out from the crowd of strangers before him. The faces began to run together until he could only distinguish their most basic features—man, woman, young, old—faces and bodies whose expressions and attire traced the passage of the centuries and the jagged path of his travels. The dead seemed to spring back to life in his mind, each one's will to live seeming to well up inside him as if his mind were its last remaining outlet, the sole validation for its forgotten existence.

He had both feared and anticipated that Jerusalem would do this to him, for the past overwhelmed his senses like a heady wine. The very stones around him felt saturated with the sadness of time, the residue of living.

They rounded a corner and stepped into full sunlight. He shaded his eyes against the glare. His head swam in the immensity of it all. He felt light, unsteady on his feet.

Betsy turned to him and took his hand again. "Are you all right?"

He nodded, incapable of speech.

They entered a square filled with people milling about. Up until now, according to his memory of Jerusalem, not one building inside the Old City had survived. Yet here was a small cistern of water that shimmered just ahead. At once he knew what it was. *The Pool of Bethesda.* A familiar landmark from his younger days. He moved forward and looked around its stone walls and colonnades, into the cloudy, tired-looking water glistening there.

A curious thing took place within him. The hum of voices and cascade of ancient faces disappeared, replaced by a ringing silence that overtook him and stilled his limbs. Suddenly it was as if he'd never left this place, as if the past two thousand years had abruptly dropped away and all of his adventures and endless solitude and eternity of waiting had simply ceased to exist.

He felt like he had come home. The years in between shrank into mere interlude. Only the here and now mattered.

It struck him then. Seeing this place meant he was on the Via Dolorosa. He thought of Christ on that day, the one whom he'd tried so hard and traveled so far to forget.

Jerusalem—a.d. 33

He is gone. And with him the hopes of thousands of Jews. How after the blissful entrance into the City only days ago, the promise of triumph waving through the air with palm fronds, could it end this way? With his broken body hanging like that of the worst of criminals?

I must admit that I both pity and am infuriated with him, for he seemed to embrace his fate, even hasten his own demise through sheer passivity and willingness to be broken. Jerusalem's crowds were such that through most of these last days one word from him would have roused them into a fury and sparked a revolt that would not only have saved his life but quite possibly won our freedom from Rome as well. The people were a tinderbox. They awaited the slightest signal from him. He could have been their Messiah.

But how can I deny his power? I, of all people, whom he raised from death itself? I do not understand it. It is a dark mystery that will haunt me the rest of my days.

I witnessed most of it from a hidden place in the crowd. I followed him from Pilate's Palace and through the streets, as the cross he bore weighed down his shoulders farther and farther and he struggled to walk. Every time he lifted his head I held my breath, waiting for him to speak the word, to summon angels, to rend heaven from earth. At least to call for help.

I have never witnessed such suffering in my life, even from those on the threshold of death. Even the people turned against him at this point. Something about the abject manner in which he accepted the pain seemed to inflame them, to fill them with a rage equal to what they feel against the Romans.

And so he walked, one agonizing step after another, through a throng of his countrymen turned against him, who jeered at him and spit upon him. And this was before he was lifted up.

From a distance I saw the hammer blows. I saw the ghoulish construction lurch against the overcast sky as it was raised and lowered with an awful thud into its hole.

I spent the next two hours glancing up at him and, hardly bearing the sight, looking down just as quickly. I stood as still as a statue, the crowds striking me this way and that. I glimpsed his mother, Mary, and John the apostle, and several others huddled at the foot. I could not bear to walk forward and greet them, so badly did I fear their contempt.

Finally my head remained down, as his suffering reached a state I never imagined possible. The clouds broke open and a cold rain began to whip the place, but still I stood, unable to move. His body lapsed into a stillness that I will never forget, though small parts of him—a toe, an eyelid, a finger—continued to move, to show signs that he had not yet died.

Then he raised his head and, without even opening his eyes, spoke something to the wind, words I did not hear. His head slumped forward.

At that moment something shifted in the universe. I cannot describe it. I know of no other outward sign except that a mighty bolt of lightning split the sky. Yet I felt certain that something mighty and terrible had just taken place. As though the air had been ripped apart, the fabric of time and earth sustained some huge, invisible gash. I half expected the world itself to break open, the fiber of my body to shred asunder.

Afterward I felt relief, I am ashamed to say. It was done with. The agony of waiting and hoping was finished. He had borne his death with a grace and courage that left me weak and shaking like a leper. I walked away.

I am a coward. I allowed my best friend to die when I was intended to share his fate. The chief priests had planned to kill me too, but I went into hiding before they could put me on trial.

I wish I could accept what Mary and Martha have told me in the days since, that he meant for me to live on. His raising me from the dead meant he had work for me here. But the life has gone from my world.

So much hope and love died along with the man. This ending is the cruelest mystery imaginable, yet I will never forget him.

Continuing his walk, Lazarus remembered how, three days after writing that diary entry, he had been sitting on a rock in the hills near his home, nursing his despair, when a teenager he did not know came running up to him, out of breath. The young man was gasping as he fought to form the words.

He had news. *"Jesus is alive! He has risen from the dead!"* It was no rumor. A number of his disciples had seen him, talked with him.

Lazarus began panting as excitedly as the exhausted runner. He could not catch his breath. A combination of shock, wonder, joy and, yes, *dread* instantly numbed his senses.

He had dreamed of this, had fantasized about Jesus pulling on the mantle of the Jewish Messiah—leaping astride a white stallion and riding off to vanquish the Romans with the nation of cheering Jews behind him. Defying imprisonment, capture, even death. Leaving his enemies breathless and utterly defeated.

But when Jesus had died, Lazarus had left Golgotha unsure of what would come next if anything. Of course his best friend had the authority to overcome death, having done as much for him. Lazarus was himself chief witness, evidence of Christ's power over the grave. Only, would he? He had embraced his own execution with such acceptance, such willingness.

It had all been too confusing.

Catching his breath in front of the young messenger, Lazarus had pictured himself approaching Jesus in front of some massed crowd made up of his adoring followers, trying to control his emotions, to contain the outpouring of his shame. Would he fall to his knees weeping and embarrass himself? Would Jesus even receive him? Would he ask Lazarus where he had fled to? Would he speak of his absence at all, or would Lazarus's disgrace wash over the whole scene in a single mortifying wave?

He had so longed to see Jesus again and to ask his forgiveness. Yet he also fought a crushing sense of remorse he knew would overwhelm him the second he laid eyes on him.

After giving the teenager half a loaf of bread, he sent him back alone. *"I will come to see him soon"* was his message to the disciples.

Then he had lingered, still shuddering at the thought of their actual encounter, vacillating between shame and a yearning to see his friend.

When he had finally gathered up the nerve to go see him, he walked over to where he had heard the Master was last seen and found that he was gone. Hundreds of eyewitness reports had him ascending bodily into the skies and disappearing.

Jesus had departed, until the end of time it seemed. Lazarus's grief had then multiplied tenfold. He'd allowed his fear to deny him the chance to say good-bye, to ask forgiveness.

He would later come to understand what most followers saw as the foundation of their faith—that Jesus' death and resurrection had not been tragic but essential and triumphant, that this had actually been the Creator's way of restoring fellowship with his once-estranged children. That knowledge had greatly eased Lazarus's regret. But it never completely eased the burdensome weight of knowing that his own role in history's defining moment had been one of cowardice and evasion.

55

LAZARUS WALKED THROUGH a mist of tears and churning emotions. He began to recognize the path he was tracing. For even though Jerusalem's buildings had changed, the twists and turns and gentle slopes rekindled some of his earliest memories.

He saw corners where he had cowered within the crowd, watching. Now he occupied the lane's center, following Jesus' steps. In his mind he traveled back to the place of his ignominy. He saw Jesus recoil at the impact of a stone thrown against his back—already shredded and bleeding from the whipping he'd received—and his own back quivered. He swung around and winced at the remembered sounds of cursing hurled Jesus' way. He winced at the jolt of a nonexistent cross being dragged across the stones.

"Greater love hath no man than this, that he lay down his life for his friends."

Then Lazarus thought of the real reason he was here, and his thoughts came hurtling back to the present. Another face flashed before him, another source of regret.

Nora, you asked me about the true source of my unhappiness. "Angst," *you called it.*

It is here. What started in Jerusalem so long ago. At the most pivotal moment in the history of the world, I ran. I failed. I gave in to fear and fled from death. I stood by, hiding, while my friend suffered the most gruesome and lonely death ever. In the ultimate irony, my flight from death ended in an agonizing life without end.

That was the beginning of a long string of failures.

For two thousand years I have perfected ways of rationalizing, fleeing and hiding, of lying about my true identity. And every one of those was a way to justify my inability to catch and dispatch the destroyer.

But now, as of today, those days of running and failing are over, done with.

I'm coming to find you. You are my flesh and blood, and my friend. If God wills it, I will find you and then fulfill my lifelong destiny.

Nothing will keep me from it. I will not shrink, or run, or turn away. This time I will face the trial head-on.

He suddenly regained his awareness of Betsy and turned to her. "I'm sorry," he said. "I have been so quiet. There are such emotions going through me right now. Just to be here."

"I understand," said Betsy.

"I fear I have become quite reserved over the years. At first I didn't know what was wrong with me, not being able to age, and so I kept silent about it. After I realized what was happening, I withheld myself out of fear. Fear of being captured and tortured as I have often been. As I was tortured in Auschwitz, before being placed in that hole you've been studying."

"Gebhart, Mengele's man."

"Yes," Lazarus said and walked on. He pointed to the sky and changed the subject. "From here you could once see the center roof of the Temple jutting up from all the other buildings. At sunset it would hold the last bit of sunlight after everything else was in shadow. After the day had gone, it alone gleamed like some enormous jewel. At such times it seemed God was blessing Israel all over again, like a sign of the *Shekinah* itself—the divine presence glowing from inside the walls."

He stopped and nodded toward a street corner where an Arab

vendor was selling falafel pitas and shouting out his specialty with the same quavering fervor of a mufti calling for prayer.

"Right around here is where he looked at me. I had been following in the back of the crowd. I thought he'd seen me throughout his ordeal. But then he paused for a second, turned my way, and saw me. He gave me a look that . . ." Lazarus swallowed, looked down. "I'm sorry. I can't describe it." He resumed walking as tears streamed down his cheeks. Both of them turned silent for a while.

He took out two engraved bits of stiff paper, their gold writing standing out in the sunlight, and examined them. The ceremony invitations. The pope. The Palestinian leader. And a world crisis he had helped to provoke.

It was time for him to end it all. Forever.

The Muslim Quarter, Jerusalem

HOW CONVENIENT THAT *Islamic women are forced to cover their bodies from head to toe*, Nora thought to herself. The veil covering her face amply concealed the duct tape that cruelly bound her mouth, as well as the bruises on her cheekbones and forehead. Her billowing wraps also concealed the gun barrel, which her lead captor had kept pressed painfully into her ribs since they had pulled her out of a car trunk in an alley and begun the long walk over here.

Nora looked down at the large stone plaza filling up with soldiers, and tried to figure out where exactly she was. Beyond the square a mass of white buildings stretched out into the distance. She saw church steeples, an old wall, sheep grazing. She thought of Cairo, Beirut, Athens. Then she was roughly turned away from the landscape, she assumed in order to prevent her from orienting herself. But the sight now before her made her whereabouts quite clear. The blue-and-gold mosque shining in the sun could only mean one place. She knew where she'd seen that plaza before too, only from a much different angle.

Closing her eyes briefly, she concentrated on gathering her thoughts. All had been a blur since she'd been kidnapped at Claere's Wood.

Jerusalem. Not a bad place to die, as places go, she mused. Her parents and ancestors had seen their lives end in far more mundane locations. Strange how this would be the finale of her grand adventure, yet she'd never imagined it would end this way, with her death. She had imagined a new life maybe. A freer one—unleashed from the fetters of her family's fearful legacy. But she had never dreamed that her days on earth were already counting down to their last.

Now, Nora thought, glancing back down at the plaza and soldiers, it appeared the moment of reckoning was fast approaching. The man behind her tightened his grip on her bound hands and shoved the machine gun even harder against her side. Three young men walked alongside them, each wearing loose robes, and for a split second she saw something protrude from the top of the nearest one's tunic. A sharp metallic tip.

A gun, or perhaps the top of a shoulder-fired missile.

She had a sense of something tightening within her, something that felt oddly like eternity. The hourglass neck of her time on earth. She was seized with a desire to give these final minutes dignity, to do something with appropriate gravity. She thought perhaps she ought to pray. Wasn't that what people did when their inability to believe in God had been stripped from them? When their final moment seemed as close to them as their own heartbeat? She wished she could close her eyes for a while, but she feared falling and hastening her end. Narrowing her eyelids, she thought of all the prayers she'd heard. She was supposed to acknowledge her guilt, wasn't she?

God, I don't know how to do this, so please, cut me some slack. I just want you to know— She paused as her arm was yanked to avoid oncoming traffic. *I want you to know I'm sorry and that I believe in you now. I really do. It took a pretty major effort on your part, I can tell. But I believe in you. And now I want to know you better. Forgive me for ignoring you for so long. I just didn't know. Or was it that I wasn't listening? I'm not sure. In any case, I want to walk with you through whatever time I've got left. Can we do that? Uh . . . amen.*

And with that, a calm serenity descended on her.

LAZARUS FELT IT before he saw it grow nearer. His inward being jumped to attention as though assaulted by too much sensation at once, too much overload.

He could feel it stronger with each passing step: a thick cloud of regret and anger and unquenchable sadness swirling ahead of him in waves, as if he'd felt the residue of the past during his entire walk down here.

Then he and Betsy rounded a corner and there it loomed ahead, faded and weathered, studded with the green tendrils of plants shooting up through tiny cracks in the stones. He squinted and saw it as he once had—as one section of the Temple's grand facade, a portion of Jerusalem's once-soaring architectural wonder. And today, the last remnant of the city's former glory. Its sole survivor. The Western Wall.

He was seized by an irresistible desire to touch it, to just lay his hand on its stone and feel, solidly for the first time, a link to his past. To his days of ordinary life, so long ago he could hardly remember them anymore. He noticed that the usual prayer-book tables and benches had been removed. The plaza had been cleared for the platform that now stood at its base.

He didn't care. He would go anyway.

He turned to Betsy, who, as on several occasions during these past two days, held a respectful silence.

"Would you mind if I approached the Wall . . . alone?" he asked. "I'll be back soon."

"Not at all."

With a parting touch of her arm, he left her and started forward. He approached and the spiritual emanations issuing from its surface seemed to intensify. His view of the world dissolved into the familiar vision of its spiritual twin. The Wall now seemed to swim with rainbows of intensity like a coating of oil on water, like the random patterns of an infrared image.

An Israeli soldier appeared before him, blocking Lazarus's way. The young man leaned in close with a faint smile. "I'm sorry, Father, but even our guests are asked to stay away from the Wall. It's a security matter, you understand. Something to do with not enticing the crowd on the other side." With a sneer he glanced up at the Muslim side.

"I see," Lazarus replied. "All I want is a minute or two at the Wall, to touch it."

"I'm sorry. I'm under strict orders."

"You don't understand. I've come many thousands of miles, waited many years to see Jerusalem. All I want is one minute. One touch."

"Then I'm *very* sorry. Besides, the ceremony will begin in less than ten minutes. We must keep the area clear."

"Please." He was begging now.

The young man took off his helmet and fixed Lazarus with a perplexed look. "You're a Catholic priest. I fail to see how this could matter so much to you."

"This is just a garment," Lazarus explained. "In truth I'm Jewish. I'm of Jewish blood, Jewish descent."

"You converted, then. You became Christian," the soldier said with an expression of one having smelled something repugnant.

"But we are all children of God. We all pray to the same Yahweh."

Lazarus could feel his opportunity slip away by the second. He reached out and lightly fingered the Star of David on the young man's sleeve.

"*Ah-nach-nu sh'nay-nu bnay Yisrael,*" he said in a tongue he hadn't used in years.

We are both children of Israel.

The soldier's scowl softened, and he turned abruptly. "Quick," he said. "I'll escort you."

In the apartment perch overlooking the plaza, Father Stephen suddenly jerked up from his spotting scope.

"There! Those are the robes of St. Lazare, on that priest who's walking forward there. It has to be him!"

"You mean the one walking forward to the Wall?" one of the CIA snipers said, still peering into his eyepiece.

"Yes! Yes!"

"I thought the Wall was being kept off-limits," another of them muttered.

"I'm going down there," Stephen said impulsively. "Maintain visual contact. Keep your eyes on anyone approaching in a threatening manner."

He ran from the room.

56

THE FEELINGS BECAME overwhelming as he approached the Wall. With every step he felt an almost palpable sense of thickness in his soul. The air seemed dense with matter and beings he could barely push through. Finally he took the final step and stood right before it, the wrinkles in the stone close enough to count. He knew he had little time, yet the moment warranted a pause.

Reaching out his right hand, he extended his fingertips and grazed the rock ever so lightly. Then he recoiled. A charge leaped into his hand, an intense tingling.

He trembled, fought to keep his balance.

The *Shekinah*. The divine presence. A trace of it did indeed remain here, like a lingering trail of God's breath. His overloaded spiritual circuits nearly burned out at the single stroke.

He felt as if he were experiencing the emotions of God himself. It occurred to him that *wailing* might not only describe the feelings of Jews regarding this place, but also those of the Creator himself at the sad outcome of his most cherished creation. His tears for his children, for all the wayward choices and hateful paths many had taken, the ensuing death and agony, the state of the Holy City and of all humanity.

Then a far more elemental sadness struck him. He tilted his face skyward and shut his eyes against an onslaught of tears. It was the Ancient One's sorrow at Lazarus's own folly, at his stubborn addiction to guilt and regret. And something else he'd hardly even contemplated—his endless self-reliance.

Suddenly he felt as foolish as a child. How many years had passed without his learning so simple a thing? The courage he had lacked, that which he coveted—it did not come from himself. It had never been his to summon in the first place.

No, it came from on high.

The victory had never been his to win.

He realized that the victory he craved would only come when he no longer relied on his own ability, his own strength. Even Jesus himself had not been, in that awesome act on the Cross, attempting heroism or some manly feat. He had emptied himself. He'd surrendered completely. It had been supernatural power magnificently filling him—not any feeble human capacity.

Of course. It came to him again: the victory had never been his to win.

He felt dizzy and shook his head in amazement. *I should have known. I should have been wiser.* But then he remembered all the foolish old ones he'd met in his lifetime, mature bodies perpetually stewing in the most childish of follies and senseless grievances, and he understood that human nature's tendency to resist truth can last forever. How, even after oceans of time, one's thoughts can become mired in the meanest of ruts.

"Time to go," the soldier said.

Lazarus nodded and turned. The sun was now high, and many of the seats were already darkened with occupants. The hour had come.

The soldier's radio crackled at his waist while the figure of a robed man loped across the square, heading in their direction. As the figure neared, Lazarus squinted and looked closer.

"Stephen!"

The young priest rushed to him and clasped his arms around Lazarus. His face was red, and he was panting. "Yes, it's me! I knew you'd be here! I knew you'd come. Your assumption was right. Jamail is here. With Nora."

"Where?" Lazarus said.

A message murmured into Stephen's earpiece. At once his face blanched, his entire body stiffened. He reached out and grabbed the soldier's arm, the arm that held the young man's machine gun. "Quick!" Stephen said. "There's a man coming—he's the Code Blue you were briefed about."

The soldier looked at Lazarus again, feverishly reevaluating him. He snatched up his radio to his mouth and barked a command so fast that Lazarus couldn't decipher it. He waved his arms and let out a shout that echoed across the plaza. Soldiers began to converge on them from out of nowhere.

But not before a man in bishop's robes—Bishop Johan Eccles—ran over to them with an animal scowl raging across his features.

Lazarus discerned reptilian beings crawling all over and around the man's body. He felt his muscles tighten, his lungs breathe in deep.

This is it. This is where it begins.

The man was bearing down on Lazarus when both Stephen and the soldier seized him before he could bridge the last two feet. The man surged forward and snarled like a lunatic; above him Lazarus saw the beings' yellow eyes. Then came a raspy, growling voice, "Go to the Moor's Gate and take a look, you coward. If you lift a finger to intervene, your flesh and blood will die in the same manner as I."

Lazarus opened his mouth to speak, but before he could utter a word the other soldiers leaped on the man, shoving their gun barrels against his head. The bishop smiled devilishly, kept his eyes locked on Lazarus, and grabbed the barrel nearest him. Lazarus began shouting the Exorcist's Prayer when, with both of his hands shaking, Eccles forced the gun barrel forward and took it into his mouth. The smile remained. With his teeth firmly clamped around the barrel, the bishop reached down and clawed at the soldier's hand covering the trigger guard. The soldier resisted, but the madman was determined.

A single shot rang out.

Blood splattered into the air and the bishop's body fell limp. His head thumped on the ground.

A communal scream shook the plaza as hundreds of guests jumped to their feet and their chairs overturned in a loud clatter. Television cameras swiveled as one toward the commotion. Soldiers at the farthest ends of the plaza began to yell, brandishing their guns.

For a few seconds a hush fell over the square while the assembled crowd waited for what would come next.

This is it. I am with you. It is time to make your move.

Lazarus's spiritual instincts told him that Nora was very close now. And the destroyer, who had just fled the bishop's corpse, was probably drawing near her, fled into the body of her bloodthirsty captor.

He felt the decision less in his thoughts than in his muscles, his bones. Every inch of his body shook with resolution and certitude. He raised his arms high in the air, stepped away from the group and started striding across an open area.

Inwardly he formed the words.

Empty me, Almighty One. I want none of myself at work here. I want you. My strength is nothing. It is but dust. Forgive me for depending on my own wavering self all these years. Please fill me with your great might, my Father. Your measureless courage. Flood me with your Spirit until I can scarcely contain it. Because without you I cannot do this.

A rock-solid certainty of will gripped his mind and body. In a single ripping motion he reached down and tore off his outer robes to show the world he was unarmed. Only a flimsy undershirt and gray shorts remained. He started up the ramp toward the Moor's Gate, the portal into the Muslim Quarter. He was breathing heavily, his muscles poised like a prizefighter about to deliver the knockout blow.

With a metallic clang, hundreds of guns ratcheted their rounds and aimed their muzzles at him. He gritted his teeth and continued on.

Fifty feet from the top, he stopped. The crowd of Muslim onlookers parted in unison with a rustling of robes, a shuffling of sandals on stone. Here at the center of a mass of humanity a vicious hand peeled away a woman's veil, ripped the scarf from her head.

"Lazarus!"

It was Nora. Relief washed over him at the sound of her voice.

He recognized Jamail, not only from the man's stranglehold on Nora, but by a sickening apparition perched on his right shoulder: the grotesqueness of twisted features, the warped, leering eyes which marked the destroyer himself. This was the demonic visage Lazarus had pursued for so long. The one which only minutes before had stood atop the bishop's back.

The destroyer isn't fleeing this time. He thinks he's luring me into a trap.

Jamail struck Nora across the face with the back of his hand, and she crumpled to the ground. The crowd gasped at the sight. He then yanked Nora to her feet and stuck a revolver to her forehead.

"Come here!" he growled to Lazarus, in the very same voice the bishop had used. "Come get me! Either way, I win. This event is over. A colossal failure. Security breakdown cancels the summit. The world goes to war."

Lazarus said nothing but instead took another step forward.

Jamail swerved, whipped around his gun and fired.

A crushing impact struck Lazarus in the chest. As though

watching from alongside himself, he saw his torso jerk back and a fine mist of blood spray from his left side. Pain flamed across his chest in a searing wave and he stumbled.

But somehow, a surge of ferocity drenched him in a courage and a resolve that made him want to smile, for he knew beyond a doubt that he would keep pressing forward. He ground his teeth and poured every drop of his will into staying upright, raising the next foot and planting it down again.

The last person he belonged to in this world was standing up there, depending on him to continue opening himself to God's power. Propelled by this flow of vigor from outside himself, he refused to fail her.

Up on the ramparts above, a Hamas soldier scowled at what he saw below him. With a curse he reached inside his robe and pulled out a Stinger shoulder-fired missile rig. Those around him began shouting in an effort to stop him, but others from behind had formed a human shield. In a second's time the man aimed the weapon downward and sighted it on the one walking.

From the Gate, Jamail screamed the signal to fire.

Aaaaiiieeee!

At the sound, two others pulled out Stingers and aimed them swiftly downward.

A roar of thunder shook the air—bodies, arms and legs and heads were sent flying through the stifling air and hundreds of bystanders stampeded across the plaza. Round after round of staccato gunfire raked the ground in deafening waves.

Then suddenly it all stopped.

The dust reared back from a breath of wind and revealed the carnage. Instead of Lazarus or Nora, it was Jamail's men who lay dead along the parapet, their launchers lying unspent on the ground next to them.

Standing at the ramp's bottom, Stephen nodded. The CIA

sharpshooters had found their mark. In the split second given to react, they had done so with pinpoint precision.

Lazarus also stood, rooted to his feet. Ahead of him Jamail alone remained of the terrorists, shielded by Nora's body writhing before him.

Now we know who the real coward is.

Jamail's gun glinted in the sunlight and exploded again, blasting through the swirling dust.

For a second time, agony pounded Lazarus's chest. Another bullet pierced him with liquid fire, nearly knocking him off his feet.

He didn't falter but kept right on walking, whispering "Thank you, Lord" and forcing his legs forward. No bullet could keep him from her.

He reached the Gate's threshold swaying like a drunk, blood trailing on the ground behind him. His world became gray; all color faded, drained into a yawning dark whirlpool. Sound muted itself and a strange peace filled the air around him. Then came a sound, high above everything else. Whether just a distant ringing or a chorus of angels, he could not tell. His limbs seemed hardly attached to him, no longer in his complete control. He felt like the sparks from his brain were trying in vain to move appendages no longer attached to him anymore.

He moved a step at a time, each footfall sending fires of pain raging through his body. Yet, through it all, elation.

I will reach them.

Then he had. He was there, with Nora only a few yards away. Her brown eyes shined beside the gun barrel at her head. Her bound hands clutched against the forearm about her neck.

Why isn't the destroyer fleeing? Surely his plan is ruined.

Lazarus's eyes focused on the grotesque shape astride Jamail's shoulders. The demon's maw was agape as it stuffed down the writhing limbs of a dismembered being.

Of course—the souls of Jamail's henchmen. Their deaths released them, and now he's feasting. He cannot help it, cannot make himself move.

Lazarus had one more step to take.

At that second Nora did something incomprehensible. She spun around and elbowed Jamail in the jaw. Even as he twisted and spat and snarled, she turned toward Lazarus and pleaded with her eyes. *Come! Hurry!*

A great communal gasp rose from the watching crowd at what Lazarus did next. He held up his arms in a wide embrace, stepped forward and grasped the terrorist by the shoulders.

Across the plaza and before television screens around the world, faces scowled and the same confused question emerged. After all that, why was this man giving the terrorist a *bear hug*?

The demon's eyes bulged with fear and it began spitting out pieces of its feast while at the same time reaching down to Jamail's body—apparently trying to wriggle free from an invisible bond.

Jamail could only curse and grunt as Lazarus tightened his grasp. He allowed his head to fall forward onto Jamail's shoulder. A seeming display of affection.

What those gathered around could not see was Lazarus's lips moving, speaking furiously.

Even Lazarus could not see the impact that his words—Latin phrases of the Exorcismus Maximus—were having on the inward parts of Jamail and the foul being tormenting him.

The monstrous demon within recoiled as though acid were being thrown on it. *No, no! Not those words! Not that place, not that eternal pit . . .*

With a roar Jamail reared back and shook wildly as the unseen presence of the destroyer, sworn enemy of peace, architect of war and genocide, was ejected screaming from his open mouth, throwing off Lazarus and Nora both and leaving the terrorist's sides exposed.

Instantly another burst of gunfire erupted and thrashed Jamail's body into a jerking marionette of blood and flesh.

Finally, with the last of his strength spent, Lazarus collapsed to his knees. Inside, however, he was awash in gratitude. *Thank you. Thank you . . .*

He had broken his curse, redeemed that shameful day of myopic self-absorption so very long ago. He'd shown courage and at the crucial moment. More than that, he had rid the world of a foul demonic influence. He could finally let go.

57

THE EXPLOSIONS FADE *all at once, replaced by a deep calm. A peace as thick as honey settles itself around him, soothes his pain with the most exquisite coolness.*

He looks down and sees the plaza fall away below him. He's floating. The whole extraordinary scene recedes like pieces of a chaotic, intricate jigsaw puzzle.

He notices white walls stained red, great numbers of people running, massed together in clots. He sees Nora with her face upturned, cradling a body he recognizes as his own. Her tear-stained eyes are looking his direction as though she could see him escaping gravity's hold. Farther on down the square he sees a frantic Betsy sprinting toward the Gate, sobbing as she runs.

A warm, caressing wind carries him up and over the massed rooftops of the Old City, the steps, the mosque domes, the winding alleyways, the ancient gates, tourist buses, crowded streets, modern buildings, the Judean hills, and the ocean boundaries of his beloved homeland.

Then he raises his eyes and sees a great light awaiting him, and an indescribable hope wells up within, as fresh as the first time.

The Knesset, Jerusalem—Thirty Minutes Later

"THE FORCES OF DESTRUCTION could not stop this moment! They couldn't keep this wonderful gesture of peace from taking place! Here, in a land where so many bear the scars of our last world war, of genocide, we will stop the power of aggression before it can take another single life!"

A roar, this time of cheering voices and applause, filled the Israeli Parliament building, the alternate site chosen just days before in the event of a disruption at the Western Wall. Less photogenic, certainly, yet still enormously significant.

During the applause, at the edges of the platform, two figures emerged, each with his arms extended.

On one side, Chairman Fulani, his familiar military garb having been exchanged for a Bedouin robe. On the other, Pope Peter III, in full regalia.

And from the base of the steps, dressed in a black suit, came Israeli Prime Minister Ladich.

The three men walked forward, reached each other and collapsed into each other's arms. Somehow, enmity and resentment seemed to have disappeared from their midst, as if a stench in the air had been suddenly purged. What remained were forgiveness, relief, and goodwill. Those closest to the platform, along with the focused lenses of television cameras, saw tears cascade from the eyes of each one.

The applause refused to subside. It seemed it never would.

In another place—a place so far above the scene that one could not measure its distance in physical miles—a wandering soul finally crosses the threshold of a luminous, wondrous homeland that Jews for centuries have wistfully called the Bosom of Abraham.

A throng of people materializes before him, composed of dozens and dozens of ethereal bodies. One by one they make their way closer to him. He does not recognize faces but spirits, whom he finds easy to recognize because they are the people he's lost and mourned. A faithful old priest. A loving Irish bride. One sister, then another.

A voice then resonates through Lazarus with the power of what mortals would call "thunder" back on a distant orb he's already beginning to forget.

The voice marks his assignment's end with words he has longed to hear: "Well done . . ."

And at last, welcoming him home.

ACKNOWLEDGMENTS

Before publishing a novel of my own, I was once dubious of authors who thanked a whole host of folks supposedly "essential" to their book's completion. After all, I reasoned, isn't an author an island? Isn't writing novels a basically solitary endeavor? Surely all those acknowledgments are little more than apple-polishing.

Now I know better. The following list consists of people without whom this novel truly would not exist:

First, I thank Stephen Bransford, gifted author in his own right, who let me "run with" a concept of his, one which had never blossomed for him—that of Lazarus being immortal—along with the *Catacon* motif. I appreciate it, Stephen, and you.

Second must come the indefatigable Claudia Cross, my wonderful agent, who has invested so much time and thoughtful strategy into coaxing my career, and this novel, off the ground.

Many thanks also to industry luminary Jan Dennis, who parlayed his enthusiasm for the manuscript into a gracious freewill recommendation on my behalf.

I'm hopelessly indebted to my parents, the Rev. Walther and Rachel Olsen, who have stood behind me with faithfulness and godly encouragement many writers could only dream of.

And I tip my hat to my visionary Bethany House friends—Carol Johnson, who brought me to this publisher with so much support and enthusiasm, and Luke Hinrichs, who has poured heart and soul into making this novel what you read today.

I thank you all from the bottom of my heart.

ABOUT THE AUTHOR

Mark Andrew Olsen is a full-time writer. He grew up in France, the son of missionaries, and is a Professional Writing graduate of Baylor University. He and his wife, Connie, and their three children make their home in the mountains of Colorado.